THE
WHITEFIRE
CROSSING

THE
WHITEFIRE
CROSSING

BOOK I OF THE SHATTERED SIGIL

COURTNEY SCHAFER

NIGHT SHADE BOOKS
SAN FRANCISCO

First Edition

Printed in Canada

ISBN: 978-1-59780-283-3
eISBN: 978-1-59780-352-6

Night Shade Books
Please visit us on the web at
http://www.nightshadebooks.com

To Robert, who knows the landscape of my heart

CHAPTER ONE

(Dev)

I knew right from the moment I opened Bren's back room door this job was going to be trouble. See, here's how it should go: Bren, waiting, alone, with a package on the table and my advance payment in his hand. Simple and no surprises. So when I saw Bren, waiting, not alone, and no package on the table, I got a little twitchy. My first thought was that Bren had crossed someone he shouldn't, and sold me out as well. But the stranger in the room didn't look like a guardsman, or even someone's freelance enforcer. He was young, well-dressed, and nervous, which settled me somewhat as other possibilities became more likely. Maybe a younger son of a wealthy family, hock deep in gambling debts? Bren sometimes worked as a collector. Didn't matter, though. Whatever the stranger was here for, I wanted no part of it.

"I'll come back later." I started to shut the door. Bren caught my eye and motioned me in.

"Dev! Just the young man I was looking for!" His deep voice had the annoyingly cheerful tone he used on highsider customers. He'd even dug out a magelight in place of the battered oil lamp that usually

1

perched in the corner. The brighter, harsher light from the faceted crystal sphere only highlighted the cracks in the adobe walls and the wax stains on the table.

I took a few steps into the room but left the door open at my back. "Who's he, then?" I jerked my head at the stranger, glaring at Bren. I don't like surprises when I'm in the city. They never turn out well.

"Shut the door, and I'll fill you in." Bren ignored my obvious displeasure and waited patiently. The stranger shifted on his feet but didn't say anything. Eventually, as Bren had known it would, my curiosity got the better of me. I shut the door, but didn't come any farther into the room. I still wanted to be near an exit.

Bren's lined brown face creased in a satisfied smile. "Dev, this is Kiran. He's looking for passage over the Whitefire Mountains to Kost. I told him you were the best, most discreet guide I know, and you know the mountains like nobody else. You can take him along on the usual run."

I choked back the first thing that came to mind, which was along the lines of "You've got to be fucking kidding me," but didn't bother to keep my feelings off my face. I hadn't missed his emphasis on the word "discreet."

For several years now, I'd run packages across the mountains and over the Alathian border to the city of Kost for him. The Alathians were strict as hell on magic, piling on all kinds of laws and regulations to try and stop people from using it except in the tame little ways approved by their Council. Human nature being what it is, that makes for a thriving trade in certain specialty items. And since they'd outlawed all the darker, more powerful kinds of magic, it wasn't too hard to get around the poor bastard of an Alathian mage stuck with border inspection duty. Easy money as far as I was concerned, but smuggling a few illegal charms and wards was one thing. Smuggling a person was a whole different story.

One corner of Bren's wide mouth quirked. Yeah, he'd seen what I was thinking.

"I know you're a busy man, Dev, but I promise this will be worth your while. The pay is very generous. Very. And what man couldn't use an extra windfall?"

This time I kept my face blank, although inside I was furious. He knew, then. Gods all damn this city. Nothing stays secret here for long, but I'd hoped for a few days' grace before word spread of the disastrous end to my partnership with Jylla. We'd only split yesterday. That meant Bren must have asked after me special, and he must have known he'd need extra leverage to get someone to take this job. Worse, he had it on a platter, damn his eyes. I needed money, and badly.

"Good point," I said. Bren looked like a kitfox with a mouthful of plump sage hen. To take my mind off my anger, I eyed the human package, Kiran, or whatever his name was. Why in Khalmet's name would some highsider kid want to go to Kost, especially this way? He looked a little old to be running away from his family in some kind of teenage snit. Highsiders played power games with each other same as streetsiders, but I'd never heard of anything like this.

He'd listened to my exchange with Bren in solemn silence. His black hair was long enough in front that it fell forward over his face and shadowed his eyes, making them hard to read. I could tell they were light-colored, probably blue, and that was about it. I'd seen men from the far north with skin pale as his, though never with hair so dark. That might not mean much, since we were all children of immigrants here in Ninavel, highside and streetside alike. No sign of a family or merchant house crest on his clothing, but that only meant he wasn't a complete idiot, assuming he didn't want anyone to know about this meeting.

"What are the specifics?" I asked Bren.

"Same as always. Make sure there are no questions, no records, and get him across the border into Kost, along with my usual package. Ten percent in advance plus expenses, the rest upon return with proof of delivery."

Bren made it sound so easy. It usually was, with a package and enough money for what Bren called "expenses." But I had serious doubts a person would be so easy to hide, no matter how idiotic the Alathian mages were.

"And payment?" Bren had better make this good.

"Triple the usual, plus expenses."

I made a disgusted noise. Bren had me over a barrel, but I had leverage of my own. There probably wasn't anyone else desperate enough to take this job, and he had to know it. "Triple, expenses, and I want ten charm-grade gemstones from Gerran for each item I deliver." Gerran was Bren's partner in Kost, who handled the distribution of the smuggled goods to their buyers. His legal business was the import of gemstones, metals, and mineral ores.

It was Bren's turn to snort. "Gerran would never go for that, and you know it." He studied me, one finger tapping on the table. I kept silent. Eventually he said, "I think I can talk him into five charm-grade stones per item, but only for this run, you understand?"

I was careful to keep my surprise from showing. I'd never thought Bren would actually go for such a wealth of high quality gemstones. I'd figured he'd offer me two or three stones total and nudge my flat fee higher. Huh. This Kiran must be paying him an absolute fortune. Either that, or I was missing something about this job.

"Anything else I should know?"

Bren didn't blink, despite my pointed tone. "It's a simple enough job." The flat finality in his eyes told me I'd get nothing more out of him. I hesitated, weighing the pay against my niggling sense of unease.

"Done," I said at last. Bren's smile widened until it nearly reached his ears.

Kiran had been watching us with a small frown line between his dark brows. "It is arranged, then? When do we leave?" His voice was soft but clear, with the faintest hint of an accent I couldn't place. The accent made me even more curious about him. We get all sorts here in Ninavel, and I'd thought I'd heard just about every possible accent by now.

Bren turned that broad smile on him. "That's right, everything's set. You'll be in good hands with Dev here, I promise. You'll leave when the first trade group of the year to Kost does." He tilted his head toward me.

"Day after tomorrow," I said. "Meet me at the Aran Fountain, near the Whitefire gate, two hours before dawn. You know where that is?" Kiran nodded. "Don't bother bringing anything with you, I'll provide what you need for the trip." I'd bet a thousand kenets he didn't have any clothing capable of standing up to a trip over the mountains. I eyed the smooth, delicate skin of his hands, and sighed. I'd have to make sure and bring gloves. And salve. An awful thought struck me. "You can ride, right?"

"Yes." Some of the nervousness I'd seen in his stance showed itself on his face. "That is—not well, I don't do it often—but I do know how."

"That's fine," I said, relieved. Some highsiders didn't bother riding, thought it was something only servants and streetsiders did, who couldn't afford carriages. Others were horse-mad. You never knew.

Bren made a few more pointlessly glowing comments about me as he ushered Kiran out the door. With a supreme effort, I managed not to roll my eyes. Thankfully, the instant Bren shut the door he lost all the fake cheerfulness.

"Damn, Bren, laying it on like a Sulanian charm dealer, weren't you?"

Bren shrugged. "Fucking rich brats, they all expect it." He splayed his hand on an engraved copper panel set into the smooth adobe of the back wall. The ward tracings flared silver as they recognized him and revealed his strongbox.

"What the hell is this all about, anyway?"

Bren smiled, a much smaller, tighter smile than he'd displayed in front of Kiran. "Want me to make up a nice lie for you?"

I made a face but didn't reply, figuring I'd deserved that. He'd made it clear enough back when I started working for him that he expected a courier to keep his mouth shut and ask no questions.

Bren removed a bundle of tightly wrapped items from the strongbox, laid a banking draft on top, and slid the lot across the table to me. "Once you get him across the border, no matter what he says, take him straight to Gerran's. No delays, and don't let him out of your sight." He leaned forward and held my gaze. "The job's not done until then. And Gerran and I expect discretion on this. Full discretion. Understand?"

Yeah, I understood, all right. Either Kiran was an errand boy for someone who didn't trust him, or Gerran intended to turn an additional profit on Kiran's little trip and didn't want him to know about it. Shit. This job got crazier by the minute. I scowled at Bren.

"A little tricky for such a simple job, don't you think?"

"You agreed to the terms," he said, his tone a warning.

This was my last chance to back out. I eyed Bren's banking draft. Damn Jylla to Shaikar's darkest hell for making this job a necessity.

"Fine." I slipped the draft into a pocket. "This had better be worth it, Bren."

※

Only the highest towers of the city still showed a faint gleam of sunlight warming their pale stone as I hurried away from Bren's place. The high walls and buildings surrounding me blocked my view of the mountains to the west, but I could imagine their snowy serrated ridges deepening toward the blue of twilight and their vast shadows spreading out over the desert valley. Damn, but I couldn't wait to get up there again. I always got a little edgy after a long winter in the city, but this time I had other reasons for wanting out of Ninavel.

My pace slowed as the evening crowds gathered. Ninavel is always liveliest after sunset, when cool night breezes relieve the searing daytime heat. People filled the streets, shopping, drinking, standing around in loose groups laughing and watching street performers. Out of the corner of my eye I caught sight of a kid darting through the crowd, chased by another, both giggling and shrieking. The adults around them didn't look twice, but I noticed the careful pattern of their ducking and dodging, and smiled to myself. Taint thieves, both of them. Not that powerful, or they'd be doing something tougher than crowd work. I tried to spot their minder, but he or she blended with the crowd well enough that it wasn't an easy mark. I checked the protective amulets I wore on both wrists. Their silver shone untarnished, and the stones remained clear. My money and Bren's goods would remain safe, at least from lesser Tainters like those kids.

The crowd noise abruptly hushed. People melted away from the middle of the street like rime ice in noonday sun, clearing a path for a lone, distant figure.

I'm told in other cities, it's kings and lords who cause that kind of upset. Not in Ninavel, so far out in the western territory of

Arkennland that it takes a year's journey to reach the king's city. No, Ninavel is the haunt of mages, of all kinds, and ordinary men learn fast to stay out of their way.

When Lord Sechaveh first came to the Painted Valley and started building Ninavel, people thought he was crazy. Only a moonbrained old fool would try to found a city in a waterless desert, they sneered. But sly Sechaveh sent word to all the mages he could find, saying if they came to his city and helped conjure water, he'd let them do whatever they wanted. No rules, no laws, no taxes—spend time on water duty, and any other magic is fair game, no matter how dark. That promise drew mages like fire ants to peachflower honey, especially the ones who practice magic in ways forbidden elsewhere. Of course, mage talent is rare, strong mage talent more so, and even here in Ninavel you mostly see middling types who can't do much more than make a decent charm. Yet a charm can boil a man's blood, or leave him a mindburned ruin; even a middling mage makes for a terrible enemy when crossed.

From the fearful silence of the crowd, the approaching mage was a lot stronger than middling. I craned my neck around a group of tradesmen in hopes of spying the sigils on the mage's clothing. On occasion I'd seen men whose silken shirts bore the looping golden scrawls signifying sand mages, and once—from a distance—a woman with the eerie, pale spirals of a bone mage patterning her dress, but none more powerful than that.

The tradesmen gasped and shrank back. I sucked in my own breath with a startled hiss, as I glimpsed jagged red and black sigils.

A blood mage! Gods, I'd never thought to see one in the flesh, though I'd heard plenty of spine-freezing stories. Everyone knows mages have to raise power for their spells somehow, but most of them find ways that don't turn grown men pale. Blood mages, on the other hand…they're rare as mist in the desert, but the word is their magic's as powerful as it comes, fueled with pain and death. And the bloodier, nastier, and more lingering the death, the better.

I plastered myself against the wall right alongside the cringing tradesmen, but I couldn't resist sneaking another look. From the stories, you'd think a blood mage should look deformed and evil, but he just looked like a man. A tall man, broad shouldered, with thick wavy chestnut hair coiling past his shoulders, highsider-style. Arrogant as all get out, in that way ordinary highsider men tried so hard to imitate. What would it be like, to know you could do anything you wanted? Anything at all?

I darted a glance at his face, then nearly shit myself when his eyes locked with mine. For a long, frozen interval his cold hazel gaze pinned me in place, like a mudworm pierced by a dagger. At last he smiled—a smile whose predatory, amused malice turned my gut hollow—and strode on.

I slumped against the wall, my heart hammering. Next temple of Khalmet I passed, I'd make an offering. A *big* offering, because clearly I owed the god of luck for saving me from my own stupidity in attracting a blood mage's attention. He'd probably come streetside to claim fresh victims for his spellwork—a fate I shuddered to imagine.

I pulled myself together. I still had a visit to make before preparing for the trip to Kost. I ducked down the next alley and made for the far corner, where the mortar between the great stone blocks had crumbled away. It was all too easy to scramble up the hundred feet to the building roof, using my fingers and the edges of my shoes in the cracks. City climbing's never as fun as climbing in the mountains.

City views aren't bad, though. Colorful magelights gleamed and sparkled in the highside towers like Suliyya's thousand jewels of legend, outshining the stars in the darkening sky and contrasting with the warmer glow of lanternlight radiating up from the streets. Above the soaring outlines of the western city towers, the dark bulk of the Whitefires rose like a great saw-toothed wall, the snow on their peaks pale in the twilight.

My mood eased by the sight, I headed across the roof to a small cupola and a window glowing with warm light through a gauzy curtain. I made quick work of the window lock and pushed my way through the curtain, dropping into the brightly painted room beyond.

"Dev!" Liana beamed a welcome from the long table where she was clearing away the remains of a meal. Toys lay scattered over the floor, and she had to raise her voice over the excited shrieks of the kids playing on the far side of the wide room. "You could use the door, you know. I promise we'd let you in."

"Nah, it's more fun this way," I said. "Besides, I remember how you always liked surprises." The kids tumbled across the room and threw themselves at my legs, giggling and shouting my name.

"Dev, what'd you bring, what'd you bring?" the littlest one yelled. I picked him up, tickling him gently, and tossed him into the air. Where he stayed, floating. I did an exaggerated double take.

"No! This can't be Tamin. Tamin can only lift himself a body length!" I said loudly, and reached for him, ready to tickle. He darted backward in the air, out of my grasp.

"I am so Tamin! Look what I can do, Dev! Liana says next month I'm old enough to go out on jobs with everyone else!"

The other kids clamored for attention. I handed out the candies I'd been saving for the occasion and made sure to marvel as they showed me their prowess, making the candies float and dance and have mock battles in the air. My eyes roved over the group. Jek, Porry, Alsa, Kuril, Ness, Jeran, Melly...I frowned. "Where's Tobet?"

I'd asked Liana, but it was eleven-year-old Melly who answered me. "He Changed and couldn't lift no more, so Red Dal sent him to his new family." She raised her chin, her amber eyes sparkling. "Red Dal says I'm boss Tainter now, Dev. I call the ward tricks tonight and the littlies have to do what I say."

Only long practice kept my voice light. "'Bout time, huh, kid? Taint like yours, you'll make a fine boss."

My eyes met Liana's as I spoke, and we shared a moment of bitter memory. The Change is a terrible thing, for a Taint thief. One day you're happy, and cared for, and can fly and lift and kip and do all kinds of fun tricks. Then puberty hits and the power dwindles away, never to return. You're useless to your handler then, so he sells you off to whoever will take you. New family for Tobet, yeah, right. Just another pretty lie from Red Dal to make sure his Tainters stayed complacent, backed up by his follow-me charms. And if I tried to say different, I'd be dead before dawn, and the kids with me. The city ganglords won't risk Tainted kids turning on them.

The kids were still chattering with excitement, the younger ones darting through the air like whiskflies. Liana caught Tamin's ankle as he zipped past.

"Kids, calm down, all right? You've a busy night ahead and I don't want anyone getting too tired." They grumbled, but obeyed when Liana shooed them back over to their play area.

"Job tonight, huh?" I dropped into a chair next to Liana.

"Yeah. First in a couple days, so they're a little over-excited."

I knew better than to ask what the job was. Liana let me come around for old times' sake, but I didn't work for Red Dal anymore. He wouldn't take it well if I got nosy. My gaze lingered on Melly's dark red hair, bent over an intricate pattern of string as she chanted a rhyme along with Ness and Jeran. No telling how long she had left. I thought of the blood mage's smile, and suppressed a shudder. As an adult, I'd heard too many stories about Changed kids sold off to anonymous buyers, never to be seen again.

Liana followed my gaze. "Dev, about Melly…" She trailed off. My stomach knotted up at the unhappiness on her face.

"What's wrong?" Melly's Taint couldn't be failing already. Gods all damn it, not yet. Not when I had no chance of keeping my promise to her father.

Liana read my face. "Don't worry, her Taint's still strong. But…" She leaned in close, and whispered, "Morra said she saw Red Dal talking to a man wearing the badge of Karonys House."

Under the table, my hands clenched into fists. No surprise that Red Dal was already shopping Melly around to the top pleasure houses. Sethan had been handsome enough, but his daughter looked to surpass him by far. More, she'd inherited that crazy hair of his, the deep crimson of magefire flame—a shade rarely seen in Ninavel. Red Dal would make a mint, that was sure. But Karonys House… shit. They catered to highsiders with nasty kinks, and used taphtha juice to keep their jennies compliant. Melly'd be a vacant-eyed doll within days of entering Karonys, her mind burned away forever by the taphtha. I fought down nausea.

"Nothing's certain yet, Dev. Another house could outbid Karonys, easy." Liana sounded like she was trying to convince herself.

"Yeah." I didn't trust myself to say anything more. Hell if I'd let any pleasure house get their hands on Melly, after everything Sethan had done for me after my Change. I vowed silently I'd do whatever it took to complete Bren's gods-damned job. I'd never outbid Karonys, but my promised pay would be enough for other, riskier options. Red Dal or Karonys, neither would take well to theft of costly property, but with enough coin to cover our tracks, I could spirit Melly away and set her up proper in a new life far from Ninavel.

"I'm sorry, Dev." Liana put a gentle hand on my arm. "You all right? I heard about you and Jylla…"

I gritted my teeth. "Oh, for Khalmet's sake. You'd think someone had stood on top of the Alton Tower and announced it."

"But you two've been together since your Change! I don't understand. Just because she found a highside mark to squeeze dry…that kind of game never bothered you before." Concern was all over Liana's wide brown eyes and round face. I bit back a sour smile. Thank Khalmet, Liana didn't know the half of it. I shrugged and made an effort to sound cheerful.

"I'll be fine. I've got a job going, I'm heading out to Kost. That's why I came, wanted to say goodbye before I left."

"Oh good, I know how you love the mountains. But we'll miss you, me and the kids both." She gave me a little, wistful smile. "Take care of yourself out there, huh? Don't get eaten by wolves."

It always amused me what city people like Liana thought about the mountains. Wolves. Ha. More like avalanches and falling rocks and late-season storms. "Right. I'll make sure to fend off the wolves, and I'll bring you and the kids something from Kost."

Her eyes lit up, and for a moment I could see the skinny, shy little girl she'd once been. She always did love presents. I slipped a few coins into her hand. "Thanks for the news. Keep an eye out for Melly, huh?"

"You know I'll try," Liana said softly. I got up from the table, after another glance at Melly's fiery hair. *Grow slow, kid,* I urged her silently. *I just need a few more weeks.*

✳

(Kiran)

Kiran shifted from foot to foot beside a trellis covered in night-blooming jasmine. For the hundredth time, he stared up at the pattern of stars visible above Lizaveta's courtyard wall. The hour of his rendezvous with Dev was fast approaching. Yet without Lizaveta's promised aid, he dared not leave Ninavel. His magic was no match for Ruslan's. Ruslan would hunt him down with the lazy ease of a sandcat, the instant he realized Kiran had fled the city. Kiran plucked a moonflower from a nearby vine, then crushed the blossom in a fist. Lizaveta had told him to come to her garden, assured him of her help…but would she keep her word? She'd known Kiran since he was a child, but she'd known Ruslan far longer.

The patter of feet on stone made him whirl. A somber youth in the pale robe of a servant slipped through the courtyard gate. His eyes downcast, he handed Kiran a sealed packet. Lizaveta's personal sigil lay in glowing violet lines over the warded seal.

Kiran placed his hand over the seal. Power stung his senses, delicate and sharp as a cat's claws, and the seal cracked open. He unfolded the packet, which proved to contain a jeweled silver disc on a thin chain, and a note in Lizaveta's spiky handwriting.

The amulet will hide you so long as you abstain from magic. You have until dawn tomorrow before Ruslan returns. Use the time wisely.

Kiran let out a shaky breath. The servant was already retreating. "Wait," he said. Obediently, the youth turned. "Tell her—" Kiran stopped. Loss and regret tangled with gratitude in his throat. "Tell her, *athanya solaen*." A farewell, one of the scant phrases he knew of Lizaveta's native tongue. He'd heard Ruslan say it to her, once.

The youth bowed, and vanished into the darkness beyond the gate. Kiran balanced Lizaveta's note on his palm, and called fire from within. Blue flames devoured the note and remained, dancing, in his cupped hand.

Such a small thing, for the last act of magic he would ever perform.

The flames vanished as Kiran snapped his hand shut. Ruthlessly, he crushed the yearning they left behind. Alisa had lost her life. His own losses paled in comparison.

✳

The Aran Fountain stood still and silent, its stone bowl empty of all but starlight. Lord Sechaveh only ran city fountains on his favorite feast days; to do otherwise would be a shocking waste of water. The square appeared as empty as the fountain. Kiran's stomach sank. Where was Dev? Had he changed his mind?

On the far side of the fountain, a shadow moved. Kiran sighed in relief when it resolved into Dev's short, wiry form. He tried to force his muscles to relax. He had to prevent Dev from realizing the depth of his anxiety. Bren had assured him Dev wouldn't ask questions, but Kiran remembered Dev's uncomfortably sharp scrutiny in Bren's office. If Dev ever discovered the truth, he'd abandon Kiran in an instant. No untalented citizen of Ninavel would risk the wrath of a mage as powerful as Ruslan, no matter how high the pay.

Dev didn't speak as Kiran approached, only motioned for him to follow. He led the way through a maze of narrow alleys and darkened side streets, ending up in front of a cracked and splintered wooden door. The scent of animals, dung, and hay hung heavy in the air. Dev opened the door and ushered Kiran into a dusty room crowded with crates. The flickering light of a candle lantern illuminated a single rough table, covered in piles of leather straps and strange metal implements.

"Here's how this'll work." Dev pushed back his hood and dropped onto a crate, motioning Kiran to another nearby. Even in the low light, Dev's pale green eyes were as startling as Kiran remembered. Their color seemed completely out of place combined with the nut-brown skin and coarse dark hair so common in Ninavel.

"I've signed on as an outrider for the first trade convoy of the season. You're gonna be my apprentice. You're a little old for it, but I'll say your family's business failed and I'm taking you on as a favor." Dev studied him, head tilted. "Apprentice means you get food and water, no wages. And you have to work. Hard."

Kiran realized he was expecting a protest. "I can do that." Kiran had spent endless hours locked in concentration with Mikail in Ruslan's sunlit workroom, measuring out channel patterns for practice spells.

Surely mere physical labor would seem easy by comparison.

Dev looked skeptical, his eyes going to Kiran's hands, then back up to his face.

"If...I mean, if you'll show me what to do. I'm not familiar with..." Kiran eyed the tools on the table. He couldn't even guess at their purpose. "What does an outrider do, exactly?"

"What do you know about the route from Ninavel to Kost?" Dev sounded like he didn't expect Kiran to know anything at all. Kiran stiffened on his crate. He might not know much about untalented professions, but surely his knowledge of world geography far surpassed Dev's.

"It leaves the city to the west and crosses two high passes in the Whitefire Mountains before it reaches the border with Alathia. It's impassable in the winter from all the snow. The first group across is always a large one, because the merchant houses are anxious to sell."

Dev's one-sided little grin said he hadn't missed Kiran's indignation. "True, but that's not the only reason the first convoy is big. The route through the mountains isn't like some nice smooth city street. It's rocky, steep, rough, and winter avalanches and spring snowmelt mess it up pretty bad. Without repairs to the trail, wagons would never make it. So the merchant houses all chip in, money and supplies and labor, and the first convoy fixes the trail as they go. Anyone who doesn't contribute has to pay a toll, if they use the trail later in the season."

"An outrider helps with the repairs, then?"

"Nah. The convoy brings carpenters and stonemasons and their hired labor for that. Outriders work as a kind of scout. While the laborers work on one repair, we check out the terrain ahead and let the convoy boss know how badly the trail is damaged so he can plan properly for what's coming. Sometimes that just means riding up the trail a ways, but other times we need to climb up snow slopes or onto pinnacles to get a good view of the terrain. But checking trail damage isn't the big reason we're there. Our main job is the safety of the group." Dev's face had turned serious.

"You mean from bandits?" As a child, Kiran had spent hours reading adventure tales where brave soldiers fought off bandit hordes sweeping down from the mountains to prey upon wagons full of precious cargo.

Dev made a dismissive noise. "Too early in the season, and the convoy is way too big. Gangs'll wait 'til it's warmer, and you get single wagons going through. No, I mean safety from the mountains. Avalanches, rockfall, storms, the like. We look at the snow and weather conditions and tell the boss if we think it's safe enough for the teams."

"But how can you know for sure?" Did outriders use charms of some kind? Weather magic was chancy at best, and required careful control. Kiran had never heard of a charm detailed and flexible enough to allow an untalented man that kind of power.

"You can't." Dev spread his hands. "You know the mountains well, you can make a pretty good guess. It's still a guess, though. Sometimes we're wrong, and people get hurt. Or die."

"Have you ever…?"

"Been wrong? Not yet. I've seen it happen, though, when I was an apprentice. Twice. The first time, only one wagon was lost, along with two men and a team of mules. The second time was…" Dev inhaled, looked as if he were searching for a word. "Worse," he finally said, his voice studiously calm in a way that Kiran recognized.

"Oh," was all Kiran could think of to say. Dev sighed and leaned forward on his crate.

"Before we get to talking about gear for the trip, I need to know something."

"What is it?" Sweat sprang out on Kiran's palms. He'd always been better at lying by omission.

Dev hesitated, frowning slightly. "Look, I'm just the courier, and whatever your reasons for this, they're none of my business. But one thing is my business, because it affects how I do my job. You want to keep this little trip of yours quiet, that's fine. But what kind of attention are we talking about hiding from, here?"

Kiran took a careful breath. "Primarily the Alathian authorities at the border. But I also need to avoid drawing the attention of anyone in the employ of Suns-eye or Koliman House." Both were among the largest of the banking houses in Ninavel. With luck, Dev would assume his journey to Alathia was merely part of one the clandestine power maneuvers the great houses were famous for making. Should he tell Dev that he'd already taken precautions against magical methods of tracing? No, Dev would want to know what sort of precautions, and that would raise too many dangerous questions. Better to keep it simple.

"Exactly how intently will they be watching for you?"

"You needn't worry about any concerted effort on their part. They don't know I'm traveling to Kost. I only need to keep it that way."

"And that's all." Dev's eyes had narrowed. "You sure?"

Kiran met Dev's searching gaze. One heartbeat's worth of power, and Dev would believe anything he said. He throttled the urge. "Of course I'm sure."

Dev studied him a moment longer, then shrugged. "Fine. We'll only do some easy stuff, then." He tossed a small wax-sealed lacquer box to Kiran. "Hair dye. Rub that through your hair, and then I'll use a binding charm to set it. It'll turn your hair brown instead of black, make your coloring a little more like a northern Arkennlander's." The corner of his mouth lifted again. "Right now you stand out like a raven among sage hens. Oh, and we'll cut your hair some, so you look less highside."

Dev slid a small silver disc from his pocket, the size of a decet coin. "You'll need to wear this, either next to your skin or tied in your hair." At Kiran's questioning glance, he held it up in the light. "It's a look-away charm. Subtle, not flashy. Lots of us wear charms of one kind or another, nobody'll notice it." He indicated the silver bracelets on his own wrists, which Kiran recognized from the rune tracings as simple protective charms.

Dev held out the look-away charm. Kiran took it, gingerly. To his relief, the charm lay quiet in his hand, with no sparking or flaring coming from either it or Lizaveta's amulet, safely hidden under his clothes. Good. That meant Dev's charm was small and simple enough in purpose not to cause any pattern interference with the magic of the amulet. Kiran set down the charm and opened the box of dye. The pasty muck within smelled absolutely terrible.

Kiran forced himself to scoop up a handful. "Please tell me the stink goes away after using the binding charm."

For the first time since Kiran had met him, Dev laughed. "Think of it as practice for the trip, city boy. Have you ever smelled the shit from an entire convoy's worth of mules?" He laughed even harder at Kiran's reflexive grimace.

CHAPTER TWO

(Dev)

First time I'd seen a mountain convoy preparing to head out, only my fierce determination to impress Sethan kept me from slack-jawed gaping. The sheer number of men, beasts and wagons crammed into the staging yard was incredible enough, but it was the swarming efficiency of the preparations that had stunned me. Ganglords could only wish their crews were that fast and disciplined. When later I'd described my amazement to Jylla, a wry gleam had lit her slanted black eyes. *The toughest ganglord's not more than a sandmite in the eye of a highside merchant house,* she'd said.

Jylla. Gods all damn it, how long before every memory of her wasn't like a fucking knife to the gut?

I made sure my face was blank before I turned to Kiran, but I needn't have bothered. He was so busy goggling at all the commotion in the staging yard that I could have been wailing curses like a Varkevian demon singer and he wouldn't have noticed a thing. I checked him over one last time in the pale dawn light. His newly brown hair hung just below his collar instead of halfway down his back, grit lined his nails, and his clothes were old and ill-fitting but good tough leather.

Yeah, he'd pass for a streetsider. So long as he remembered to keep his mouth shut, anyway.

The westgate staging yard lay right inside the bulwark of the city's towering sandstorm wall, and the noise echoing off the smooth stones was deafening. Men were yelling to each other, mules braying, horses whinnying, all mixed in with the crash of crates being stacked and secured on wagons. I had to grab Kiran's arm to get his attention.

"Come on. We'll check in with the head outrider at our supply wagon, then pick up mounts from the horsemaster." I dodged my way through a trampling herd of burly packers hefting crates.

Kiran trailed after me. "You don't have your own horse?"

"Are you kidding? Do you know how much a horse eats? It'd be stupid to o͟n one when I only use 'em on outrider jobs. Pack mules are better if you're going solo."

We'd nearly reached the sturdy, weathered wagon painted with the outrider mark, indistinct black shapes resembling crossed ice axes. I recognized the tall, lean woman in sun-faded leathers who waited there. So, Cara had made head outrider? I'd never admit it to her, but I was impressed. Though Cara was a good six years my senior, she was young for the top spot on such a large convoy.

Kiran's face said he was dying to ask another question, but he shut his mouth as Cara strode forward. Good boy.

"Dev! I heard you were on for this job!" She caught me up in a spinecracking hug.

"Ease up, huh? I might need my ribs later." I pretended to gasp for air. Cara laughed and let go, her teeth flashing white in her deeply tanned face. Her blonde hair was bleached to the color of old bone, and with that tan, she must've spent her winter on the desert routes. I thumped her shoulder. "You've been working eastbound? Did you sign up when you were drunk? Those aren't mountains, they're sandhills."

"The climbing's no good, but the sandcat hunting makes up for it. At least I didn't sit on my ass in the city all winter. How do you stand it?"

"There are compensations," I said. She rolled her eyes.

"That's right, your she-viper of a business partner, I forgot. She still got you by the piton straps?"

Cara must be the one person in the entire city who hadn't heard, and I wasn't going to be the one to tell her. She'd never understood my bond with Jylla. If I had to listen to a chorus of "I told you so" all the way to Kost, I'd end up shoving Cara off a cliff. Fortunately, I had the perfect distraction.

"Cara, meet my apprentice, Kellan na Erinta." I gestured with a flourish to Kiran. I'd chosen his false name carefully. The first name was common as sand in Ninavel, yet close enough to Kiran's own to help him remember to respond. The last name used the old-fashioned Arkennlandish mode still popular among northern immigrants, to match his odd coloring.

Cara's pale brows shot up. "You? An apprentice? It's been, what, four whole years since your own apprentice days—you getting bored already?"

"His family's having trouble paying for their water rations. Bad times with their business, you know how that goes. I'm taking him off their hands as a favor." I put on my best virtuous expression.

"Hmm." Cara squinted at Kiran. I held my breath. The look-away charm would keep him forgettable and easy to overlook by the casual observer, but it wouldn't prevent direct scrutiny, and Cara had a keen eye.

After a moment's study, a wicked smile spread over her face. "You know, kid, if Dev throws you out, you can come to me. I'm sure we could work something out." She looked him up and down again, slowly and deliberately, and winked.

Well. First test passed, anyway. I glanced at Kiran, and didn't know whether to laugh or groan. His cheeks flamed and he looked about a heartbeat away from bolting. At least he didn't get all snooty and offended, highsider style. As it was, I gripped the back of his arm where Cara couldn't see, and squeezed. Hard. If he wanted to pass as a streetsider, acting like a sheltered sulaikh-maiden wasn't the way to do it.

"Need a bucket for that drool?" I asked Cara. "Must have been a long eastbound run. I hear those outriders turn into dried up old sticks, out there in all that heat and sun."

"This dried up old stick wants you to get your ass on a horse already. Meldon's about to order us to form up." Cara pointed at the convoy boss on his high platform overlooking the yard. As Kiran turned to see, she leaned over to me and spoke quietly. "Seriously, Dev, you'll have to keep an eye on him. Kid is too pretty for his own good, and it's clear he's got no clue how to handle it. Teach him how to say no nicely. I don't want any trouble, hear?"

I sighed. Cara's reaction to Kiran only confirmed what I'd suspected. Those high cheekbones and all that fine highsider skin and hair threatened to attract unwanted attention, no matter how many look-away charms I hung on him. No help for it but for me to keep him out of the way as much as possible.

"I've got it handled," I assured Cara. The horsemaster and his little group of spare mounts stood only a few wagons away. As Kiran and I headed over, I called back to Cara, "Who's our third rider, then?"

"Jerik." She pointed to a sinewy man with night-black skin who stood talking to an elderly drover. I hadn't recognized him from the back, but once Cara said the name, I knew him. Last I'd seen him, he didn't have the threads of gray streaking his braided hair. I'd worked with him once or twice back when I'd been Sethan's apprentice. Jerik was a good climber. Better yet, he was quiet and kept to himself. Perfect.

As we neared the horsemaster, my satisfaction disappeared in a hurry. Three wagons over, a thin-faced drover with a wild mop of curls was watching me as he checked the buckles of his mule team's traces. Khalmet's hand, what was Pello doing here? He worked for one of Bren's competitors in a different ganglord's district, but as a shadow man, not a courier. Merchant houses were always eager for privileged information on their competitors' shipments, and men like Pello made good coin sniffing out secrets. But shadow men stayed local, as a rule, haunting warehouses, stableyards, and taverns. It wasn't unheard of for one to work a convoy route, but the timing sure as hell made me suspicious. If he'd gotten wind somehow of this gods-damned little stunt, I'd have real trouble keeping Kiran's trip to Kost quiet. Not to mention the potential disaster at the border if Pello decided to sell me out to the Alathians.

"We'll be riding those?" Kiran was eyeing the shaggy ponies beside the horsemaster's wagon with a distinctly dubious expression.

Pello's gaze hadn't left us. I clapped Kiran on the back, and said loudly, "Don't worry, they don't buck. They're sturdy, patient sorts who don't mind a novice rider, and they'll carry you safe over rocky trails and through mountain storms." As opposed to the graceful, highstrung animals highsiders rode.

Kiran's abashed glance said he'd guessed my meaning well enough. The horsemaster turned, chuckling.

"New to convoy work, eh? Never fear, boy, I've the perfect mount for you." He urged Kiran toward a stocky bay gelding with a graying muzzle and a phlegmatic air.

I leaned against the wagon, met Pello's eyes, and nodded, deliberately casual. Pello returned the nod, a sly little grin creasing his coppery face.

I resisted the urge to grit my teeth. Damn it, I needed to talk to Kiran about Pello, and fast. But I couldn't do it in a crowded staging yard where anyone might overhear, and the convoy was about to leave. I'd have to wait until I could arrange a moment alone with Kiran on the trail.

The horsemaster returned with Kiran and the gelding in tow. After a quick discussion, I secured a pinto mare for myself, and a pile of tack. Kiran followed my instructions readily enough as I showed him how to check over and adjust the gelding's saddle. I watched carefully as he swung himself up. It wasn't smooth, or graceful, but he managed it without help, which I took as a good sign.

Cara was already mounted and waiting when we returned. "You and Kellan take the mid station, with the supply wagon. Jerik's on point, and I'll take the rear."

I nodded and tried to look grateful. Cara had seen Kiran's inexperience and was giving us a chance to let Kiran switch off riding the horse with riding in the wagon. But as long as we stayed with the supply wagon, we'd be in earshot of Harken, our wagon's drover. Harken had handled the outrider supply wagon for convoys longer than I'd been alive, and he was canny as they came, despite his laid back demeanor.

"At midmeal, Kellan and I can switch stations with you for a bit, if you want to eat in comfort while we get some exercise." I gave Cara a meaningful look, which I hoped she'd interpret as me wanting to work on my apprentice's shaky riding skills away from any catcalling drovers.

"Fine with me." The amused approval in her blue eyes told me she'd taken it the way I wanted. She turned her horse and trotted off along the snaking line of wagons.

Kiran watched her go with a little, puzzled frown. "Why aren't we all riding together?" His voice was low and hesitant. At my encouraging glance, he spoke a little louder. "You said an outrider's job doesn't truly start until we reach the high mountains…"

"Yeah, but rockfall's a danger even in the lower reaches of the canyons. Each outrider sticks with a different part of the convoy so if a bad rockfall or avalanche hits, then only one outrider gets injured or killed. If the convoy lost all its outriders, there'd be nobody to safely direct the search for survivors, or scout once the convoy moves on." He'd never know how cold that logic really was. I still had screaming nightmares about the terrible day Sethan had died.

Metal squealed, followed by a deep groaning sound. I straightened in my saddle, anticipation driving unpleasant memories into hiding. Far up ahead, the great western gate swung open, massive metal doors being pulled apart with a system of gears. My heart lifted as the mountains beyond came into view. The snow on their tops blazed fiery pink with dawn alpenglow, ridges and pinnacles standing out in sharp relief. The beauty took my breath away, and for a moment I felt like the luckiest guy in the whole world, forgetting all about Jylla and the job and all the rest of it. I couldn't keep a grin off my face as Meldon shouted, a hand bell rang, and the first teams of mules started forward in their traces. There's nothing like the thrill of starting a mountain trip.

❋

My horse plodded up the sandy trail after the outrider wagon. Harken appeared to be dozing on the wagon's frontboard, his broad-brimmed hat tilted down over his face, but I wasn't fooled. Soon as Cara returned, I'd drag my so-called apprentice off for our long-delayed private conversation. I'd been chewing over Pello's possible involvement all morning. No surprise that Kiran's little tale of banking houses wasn't the full story; I hadn't expected anything different. But if he'd lied to me about the level of scrutiny we faced, then highsider or no, I'd make him regret it.

Kiran sure didn't seem concerned now. He'd been snarled up tight as coilvine when we'd met at the fountain, but the stiff set of his shoulders had begun to ease the moment we passed the Whitefire gate. He almost looked relaxed, wedged between lumpy oilcloth sacks in the back of the wagon. His head was bent over some spare strands of rope as he diligently practiced the climbing knots I'd shown him earlier. It reminded me of Melly and the other kids with their string game, and I turned away.

Behind us, the remainder of the trade convoy stretched in a long line back down the trail. It had taken us all morning to cross the alkali flats outside the city walls. Now we'd reached gently rising slopes, covered in sagebrush and rabbitbrush, punctuated by occasional black lumps of whorled glassy rock and worn into folds by dry gullies. The only rain that ever fell in the Painted Valley came from rare but vicious summer thunderstorms that sent flash floods scouring over the parched soil, eroding it faster than a man could run.

It was hot already, the air shimmering and dancing above the alkali flats, making the city's shining white walls and pale spires seem to float above the ground. Ninavel always looks beautiful from the outside, and unreal. A mirage-city, completely out of place in the harsh heat of the deep desert valley. Behind the city towers, in the distance loomed the brown outlines of the dry, barren Bolthole Mountains that formed the eastern side of the valley, much lower and less rugged than the Whitefires. The haunt of sandcats with claws longer than a man's hand and the strength to crunch a man's skull into jelly; Cara was crazy for hunting them with nothing more than a crossbow fortified with a longsight charm.

I turned frontways again. Kiran's gaze had fixed on the city. His blue eyes darkened with something that reminded me of Red Dal sighing over a highsider house warded too well to risk sending Tainters inside. His fingers clenched around the half-finished knot, so tight his knuckles showed white.

So. Not as relaxed as he'd seemed, then. "Sometimes it's a hard thing, leaving the city," I said.

Kiran started. "What? Oh. Yes, I…I suppose." He fumbled at the knot again, his eyes darting to mine and then away. "Though it's… well, it's exciting, too. Traveling the mountains, like adventurers from a tale…I hadn't imagined I'd ever get to make a journey like this." A hint of wistful amazement touched his face.

"Oh, the excitement's just starting," I said, more curious than ever. Maybe he was only playing his streetside role, but I didn't think he was so good an actor. Highsiders had the coin to travel if they liked—but then, he'd implied he worked for a banking house, and certainly they were said to have rigid notions of a man's duties. A banking house even fit with Bren's covert instructions; they never trusted anyone. Hell if I could come up with any good reason for a banking house to try and sneak a person across the Alathian border, though. Banking houses loved their secrets same as all the other merchant houses, but I could think of a hundred less risky ways to pass private information or materials between Ninavel and Kost.

A jingle of straps and clomping of hooves filled the air, and our section of the convoy moved over to the side, allowing room for a Ninavel-bound mule train. This low down the trail was wide enough for two groups to pass easily, although the cloud of dust and sand kicked up by the passing mules sent Kiran into a coughing fit.

"Here." I tossed him my waterskin. "Remember, we're on strict water rations until we ascend out of the Painted Valley—so don't guzzle it all." Merchant houses hated to waste their weight allowances on water. Part of the convoy boss's job was to figure out the minimum amount of stores necessary to keep us all from collapsing of thirst before we reached the first high mountain stream.

Kiran took a careful few swallows. He capped the waterskin and handed it back, not without a last longing look at it.

"Where were those mules coming from? I thought we would be the first group coming through the pass?"

"From the mines." I pointed higher up on the valley slopes, where the sagebrush scrub changed over to broken cliffs. The rock there was scarred and dotted with the dark holes of mineshafts. Tailings piles streaked vivid colors across the dull tan slopes below. "Most of the mines are low enough they can be worked year round."

"What kind of mines?" he asked, and I stared. What kind of highsider wouldn't know the answer to that, let alone someone supposedly involved with a banking house? Most families who'd made it big in Ninavel had done so through the mines or the selling of their products. Banking house, my ass. Unless…maybe Kiran was newly come to Ninavel? But no, from the way he'd gaped around at the desert beyond the city gate like a Tainter on his first job highside, I'd swear he'd never set foot outside Ninavel in his life.

"Gold, silver, copper, iron, you name it, these mountains have got it." I kept my tone casual, but watched his face. "Why else do you think old Sechaveh went to all the trouble of building the city here in the first place?"

Just for a second, surprise showed in his eyes. But then they turned thoughtful, and he nodded. "Oh yes, I see. He founded the city here and then could make his money back from the mines."

"In vaultfuls," I said. What other reason could there be? The Painted Valley held nothing else but sand and sagebrush. Ninavel had to import or conjure everything needed to survive. Without the enormous wealth from the mines, the city would've failed in a season. Instead, Sechaveh and his heirs were now richer than the most outrageous tales of Varkevian sultans, and plenty of others had clawed their way to riches on his coat hem in the hundred years since he'd founded Ninavel. Sechaveh himself was a popular tavern topic streetside. Some said he had to be a mage, arguing no man could live as long as he had without magic. Others disagreed, pointing out his large numbers of descendants and the well-known fact that mages can't have kids. They said Sechaveh was so wealthy he could pay for immortality the way other men paid for healing charms.

"About the mountains…" Kiran's face shone with eager interest. I waved a hand at him to continue. So long as he stuck to questions any new hire straight from an inner district might ask, he could ask away. "What you said this morning—do you really go alone up there?"

"Yup."

His eyes went wide as a snow owl's. "But why?"

"Convoys only need real climbing outriders in the early and late seasons. In high summer, it's no problem to travel through. A man's gotta eat the rest of the year round." I didn't bother telling him the real reason for my solo trips. I couldn't imagine anything better than a summer spent climbing in the Whitefires. I'd long since given up trying to explain the allure of the high peaks to my city friends. Most of them just thought I was crazier than a rabid kitfox.

"But..." He frowned. "How do you make money, then, if you're not with a convoy?"

"The Whitefires hold plenty of profitable goods, if you know where to look." His confused frown didn't change, so I went on. "Take carcabon stones. Charm dealers'll pay good coin for any big enough to boost a charm's power, and the cliffs here are studded with 'em. Chefs drool over cloudberries, midwives want jullan leaves…you get the idea. I find stuff, bring it back, sell it and resupply, then head back up. Until the season's over and the winter storms come, and then nobody goes up there until spring."

"Oh! I never…" He cut himself off, real short. Then tried to hide it by rattling on. "What do you do in the winter?"

If he'd been about to say he'd never known where highside delicacies like cloudberries came from, then thank Khalmet he'd shut up in time. Old Harken wasn't even pretending to sleep, now. I realized Kiran was still waiting for my answer.

"If I have a good enough summer, I don't have to do anything in the winter." Which wasn't a lie, exactly, but I certainly wasn't going to get into details on the shadow games I played in the city. Especially since they'd all involved Jylla.

"Ho, Dev!" Cara cantered out of the settling dust cloud.

Fucking finally. "Come on, Kellan." I waited impatiently while Kiran climbed back on his horse. "I owe you one," I muttered to Cara.

She vaulted onto the wagon's outboard. "I know." Her smug smile said she'd collect on it, too. She flipped a hand in a mocking little wave. "Have fun, boys."

I had Kiran ride in front of me, ostensibly so I could watch how he handled the horse. In truth, I wanted to keep an eye on the drovers' reactions as the heavily laden wagons rumbled past us. Several drovers raised their hats to me, but their eyes slid off Kiran as if he weren't even there. His look-away charm was working, all right.

Pello's wagon was the second of five marked with the circle and hammer of Horavin House, near the end of the line. Pello himself sat slouched on the frontboard with his mule team's reins dangling idly from one hand. He studied Kiran with undisguised interest as we approached, unaffected by the charm. Kiran shifted uneasily in his saddle and shot a glance back at me. I willed him to stay silent.

"Dev, I never thought to see a man like you with an apprentice," Pello called out.

"There's a first time for everything, Pello." I'd wanted a clue about whether his interest in Kiran was specific or only the result of a shadow man's finely honed curiosity, and I supposed he'd given me one. Surely if he'd been hired to ferret out our plans, he wouldn't be so damn obvious about it. Unless he'd guessed my intent, and was playing to my assumptions? I cursed under my breath. Mind games like this had always been Jylla's specialty, not mine.

That thought didn't improve my mood any. I scowled at Kiran's back for the rest of the ride past the convoy. Soon as we passed the final wagon, I led the way off the trail and into a gully whose steep sides were dotted with spiny blackshrub. The syrup-sweet smell baking off the branches in the midday sun was chokingly strong. Nobody'd follow us here without good reason. I slowed my horse to an amble.

"We need to talk," I told Kiran, grimly.

"So I gathered." His shoulders had tightened up again. "What's wrong? Is this about that man who spoke to you?"

At least he wasn't totally oblivious. "Got any ideas why a shadow man's interested in you?"

He blinked at me. "A what?"

"Freelance spy. Sells information to the highest bidder, with a ganglord as middle man." Though in Pello's case, if he'd gone to all the trouble of joining the convoy, he must be on retainer for a specific job. "Pello's here for a reason, and I need to know if it's you. If there's anything you failed to mention back in Ninavel, now would be the fucking time."

Kiran looked honestly taken aback. "He can't be here because of me. I told you, no one knew I was leaving Ninavel."

Oh, for Khalmet's sake. He couldn't be that dumb. Right? "No one, huh? What about that banking house of yours? You know for a fact nobody let something slip by accident?"

His eyes had flickered at my sarcastic emphasis on "banking house," but he raised his chin and met my gaze straight on. "He doesn't know who I am. Unless *your* employer was indiscreet."

I snorted. Bren hadn't run a successful smuggling business all these years by being sloppy. "Fine, let's say Pello's here on another job. That won't stop him from seeking a little profit on the side. The minute he figures out you're no streetsider, he'll sell you out in a flash to Suns-Eye or Koliman, long before we reach the border."

Kiran jumped as if I'd stabbed him with the business end of a piton. "You mean, Pello can send messages back to Ninavel? How? I thought convoy workers didn't have access to such powerful charms!"

Interesting. Back in the city, Kiran had claimed he was most concerned about the Alathians at the border. The horror on his face now told a different story. "Ordinary convoy men don't. But Pello spies on merchant houses for a living. He'll have something, all right. Maybe not powerful enough to send more than a few words, but with the right codes, that's all you need."

"Oh." Kiran swallowed, hard. "That would be…unfortunate." He fiddled with his reins, then burst out with, "Once we cross the border, I don't care what messages Pello sends. But if news of me reaches Ninavel before then, it'll…it'll ruin everything!"

I glared at him. "If you'd told me how *unfortunate* back when I asked, I would've done a hell of a lot more to hide you." A disguise charm powerful enough to wholly alter a man's appearance cost the moon, especially on such short notice, but I could have demanded Bren produce a second advance.

Kiran flushed and looked down. "I'm sorry. I thought if I stayed anonymous leaving the city, I wouldn't have to worry about word getting back…" One hand rubbed his chest, over his heart, in an odd, nervous gesture. "What do we do?"

I sighed. "For now, you act your part, and stay clear of Pello. His charm's likely only strong enough to send one message, maybe two. He won't use it unless he's sure he'll profit." Meanwhile, I'd have to come up with a plan to cover that scenario. Great. Pello was no fool, and as a shadow man, his experience dwarfed mine in fighting dirty. I scowled all the harder at Kiran. "Anything else you'd like to share, *before* it bites us in the ass?"

He shook his head, still staring at his saddle horn. Not exactly a response to inspire confidence. I leaned over and grabbed his reins. The gelding cast a reproachful eye at me as I yanked him to a stop. Kiran jerked his head up, blue eyes gone wide.

"You want to reach Alathia safe and sound, with no one the wiser? I can make that happen, but only if you tell me what I need to do my fucking job. Understand?"

"Yes." He had the solemn, earnest look of a Tainter being chided by his minder. I flung his reins back in his lap.

"Remember: lay low. Don't do anything to draw attention, from Pello or anyone else. And stick close to me—don't give him a chance to get you alone." If Pello forced Kiran into conversation, I gave Kiran five minutes tops before Pello sniffed out his highside origins.

He nodded, still all serious and intent. I aimed my horse straight at the gully's steep side. Time to play out the role of off-trail riding lesson, in case any curious eyes were watching. In the meantime, I could ponder what I'd learned from our little conversation. So far I'd mostly gained a whole new set of questions. Chief among them: who or what back in Ninavel had Kiran jumping like a frightened snaprat?

✳

(Kiran)

"Here. Have some breakfast." Dev tossed Kiran a lump of bread.

Kiran nearly fumbled the catch in the dim predawn light. He'd never seen a more unappetizing meal. The bread was dense as rock and studded with unidentifiable dark chunks he could only hope signified dates or nuts. A far cry from his usual fare of cinnamon spice cakes drizzled with peachflower honey, or perhaps savory rolls with diced kelnar nuts…his stomach rumbled.

Dev wore the little one-sided grin suggesting he knew exactly what Kiran was thinking. "Eat up, Kellan. You'll need your strength." He jerked a thumb at the horses they'd just finished saddling.

Kiran smothered a groan. His groin and legs already protested every time he moved. The memory of his blithe certainty the day before about the ease of physical labor was a bitter one.

Dev chuckled heartlessly. "Hurts, does it? Don't worry, you'll feel better after a few days. Just remember to stretch your muscles out like I showed you, any time we take a break." He stuffed a chunk of bread in his mouth and heaved a supply sack onto the wagon.

Despite the deceptively gradual ascent out of the Painted Valley, the convoy had climbed higher than the tallest towers of the city before stopping for the night. Ninavel glimmered on the vast emptiness of the desert plain below, magelights fading with approaching dawn. Kiran shut his eyes. Even with his mental barriers up at full strength, the roiling confluence of earth forces beneath the city blazed like a lake of fire in his inner sight. He'd never before seen the confluence from the outside, in all its wild, turbulent glory. Within the city, the bone-deep pulse of its shifting currents had been as much a part of life as the air he breathed. Only now could Kiran fully appreciate why only the strongest of mages could harness its forces, and even then, only at a remove.

The earth beneath his feet already felt dead in comparison. As for the mountains…Kiran turned. The Whitefires stretched skyward before him, their snowy peaks burning crimson. Beautiful enough, but completely inert, from a magical standpoint. From all he had read, Alathia would be little different. Kiran denied the longing ache deep within. He had no intention of casting any spells in Alathia and risking discovery by their Council. The Alathians weren't known for their mercy toward foreigners caught working illegal magic.

Crimson changed to gold as the sun slipped over the eastern rim of the valley. Kiran's heart thumped painfully in his chest. If Lizaveta's note was accurate, any moment now Ruslan would return to Ninavel. And when he found Kiran gone...

The bread was ashes in Kiran's mouth. He stood, abruptly. Too late, he noticed Cara watching him as she secured straps on the supply wagon.

"Hey, kid, you look a little rough today. You being mean to him already, Dev?"

"Mean? Me? You know I'm the soul of kindness." Dev assumed an expression of injured innocence. He darted a glance at Kiran. "He'll be fine. He's just not used to sleeping on hard ground yet, right, Kellan?"

Kiran nodded, trying to imitate Dev's relaxed posture.

Dev swung up on his horse with easy, thoughtless grace. "His family was in the bookbinding business, you know. City folk, nice and soft," he said to Cara.

Kiran clambered onto his horse, with considerably less grace than Dev. Abused muscles screamed as he settled into the saddle, and he nearly bit through his cheek in his effort not to cry out. Dev and Cara exchanged an amused glance, and Cara shook her head.

"Dev, only you would take a city boy on as an apprentice."

Dev shrugged. "Sethan did it for me, back in the day. And hey, we can't all have outrider parents."

To Kiran's surprise, Cara looked away, as if made uncomfortable by Dev's words. But when she spoke, her voice remained teasing. "You were a tough little brat, as I recall, and you could already climb like a whiptail. Soft, my ass."

"Couldn't ride for shit, though. I thought I was gonna kill Sethan when he made me get back on a horse our second day out." Dev directed a knowing grin at Kiran. "Bet you're cursing me to Shaikar's seventh hell and back right now."

"It's not so bad," Kiran lied. A thread of curiosity surfaced through his nerves. He tried to picture Dev as an awkward young outrider apprentice, and failed. Even though Dev couldn't be that much older than Kiran—five years at the most—Kiran couldn't imagine him without his air of casual competence. He'd assumed Dev had learned all his skills since earliest childhood, raised in some kind of outriding family, but apparently that wasn't the case. Perhaps he could find a way to ask Dev about it, without inviting any unfortunate questions in return. The last thing Kiran wanted to discuss was his own childhood.

"Aw, listen to him," Cara said. "Still all polite. Now there's a nice change from your foul mouth, Dev."

Before Dev could reply, a bell clanged out from the head of the convoy. The level of commotion rose a notch as wagons began creaking their way back onto the trail. Cara tossed her long blonde braid over her shoulder and vaulted into her saddle, the mockery gone from her tanned face. "You and the kid get the rear station today. Jerik's on point scouting the lower canyon, and I'm with the wagon."

Dev flicked a hand in acknowledgement. He turned to Kiran. "You ready?"

"Yes. Should I—"

Raw, unadulterated power slammed outward from the city. Invisible and inaudible, yet Ruslan's magic blazed forth with the screaming intensity of a sandstorm. Kiran's senses reeled as Lizaveta's amulet seared fire into his skin. Dimly, he was aware of falling; then an impact knocked him breathless. The surge of magic washed over him, seeking onward through the valley. Kiran was left sprawled in the sand with one foot still caught in a stirrup.

"I hate to think what's gonna happen when your horse actually starts moving." Dev leaned down from his saddle and freed Kiran's foot, his face full of amused disgust. Beyond, men continued to bustle around the convoy wagons, hitching mules and securing gear, as if nothing had happened. Kiran shook his head in amazement. He'd known the untalented couldn't sense magic, but this…how could they be so blind? His ears still buzzed with the sheer force of Ruslan's fury.

"Muscle cramp," Kiran mumbled to Dev. He waved Dev's offered hand away and staggered to his feet. "Sorry. Caught me by surprise." Awe and terror tightened his throat. That blast of magic had been Ruslan's alone, with no help from the great forces of the confluence. Kiran had always known Ruslan was powerful, but he'd never had quite so vivid a demonstration of Ruslan's strength.

"Told you, you should stretch." Dev's expression was bland,

though his green eyes were sharp as ever. Kiran wanted to inspect the amulet for any damage, but under that gaze he didn't dare. Dev was already suspicious enough of Kiran's cover story. If Dev realized a mage hunted them, he'd plead with Pello to send a message to Ruslan, in hopes of saving himself. Kiran bit his tongue in frustration. Finding and destroying Pello's charm would be child's play, if he used magic. But the instant he did, he might as well shout his location straight into Ruslan's ear.

Kiran remounted his horse. This time the ache in his muscles faded to insignificance under the weight of his nerves. Ruslan's initial salvo had been a matter of impulse, the equivalent of a single, visceral shout of anger. Now Ruslan would plan his spellwork in earnest. Mindful of Dev's eyes on him, Kiran suppressed a shiver.

CHAPTER THREE

(Dev)

"You sure you didn't crack your skull in that little tumble this morning?" I asked Kiran, as our horses followed the tail wagon of the convoy around yet another dusty switchback. "You've barely said two words all day."

"I'm fine." Kiran's head was bowed, his shoulders stiff. "It's just so hot."

True enough that the midday sun blazed fiercely enough to turn a man's brains to sludge. But yesterday's equally blistering heat hadn't kept him from a steady stream of questions.

"Well, good news: we've reached Silverlode Canyon." I pointed ahead, where the trail left the sagebrush to disappear into a narrow gash in the pale cliffs. "In Silverlode, the heat'll ease some. And we'll be done with this gods-damned sand."

"Oh. Good." Kiran's gaze stayed locked on his saddle.

So long as he hadn't thumped his head badly enough to get brain sickness, he could stay silent as a sand lump if he liked. Though after long hours spent wrestling with the problem of Pello and his charm, I could've used a nice distracting conversation.

35

Red Dal had taught me a whole host of dirty tricks for disabling charms, and the more inspired ones even worked without the Taint. Problem was, they all depended on direct access to the charm in question. A clever man like Pello was sure to use serious protective wards to hide his charm stash from prying eyes. I might search his wagon a thousand times and never find the message charm. And try as I might, I couldn't come up with a way to arrange an unfortunate accident for Pello that wouldn't risk killing other, innocent men. Maybe Jylla was right and Sethan had turned me soft, but I didn't much like the thought of killing innocents for my own gain.

I sighed as my mare clopped up the final rock-strewn incline leading to the canyon's mouth. No, there had to be a way to break Pello's wards. I'd learned in my Tainted days that a little creativity can go a long way. I just had to figure how to apply it right.

Within the confines of the canyon, sand changed over to jumbled boulders. Great cliffs reared skyward on either side, hiding the high peaks from view. The sight of those familiar awe-inspiring cliffs improved my mood considerably. Even Kiran perked up a bit, staring at the heights rather than his saddle.

As we wound along the canyon's north slope, the kreeling shriek of a banehawk echoed off the sheer wall above. I turned to Kiran, wanting to see if he'd flinch or grab for a charm. That faint accent of his...I'd once shadowed a group of Kaithan traders who'd come straight from the southern blight. The liquid slur of their speech was the closest match I'd come up with for Kiran's oddly inflected vowels. And southerners were all superstitious as hell. Varkevians, Sulanians, Kaithans...even the ones who scoffed at the vast southern pantheon of demons still wore devil-ward charms and turned pale at the sight of a banehawk.

Curiosity brightened Kiran's face as he watched the hulking black shape soar past. "What kind of bird is that? I've never seen one so large."

Ah. Banehawks were rarely seen in the city. I'd spied them on occasion perched near butcher shops and slaughteryards in hopes of snatching up offal, but I'd forgotten a highsider wouldn't have cause to visit such places, not with servants to buy meat for them.

"Banehawk," I said. "They eat carrion. Some say they've the souls of devils banished from Shaikar's hells, and their call's a death omen. Half the men in this convoy are snatching at devil-ward charms right now."

"Devil-ward charm?" Kiran peered at me like he wasn't sure if I was joking. "But devils are only stories. What would such a charm even do?"

Well. His accent couldn't be Kaithan, then. I snorted. "Nothing. They're just a way for streetside charmsellers to make easy coin. Slap together some loops of copper, etch on some fancy-looking sigils, and sell it to superstitious marks who'll never know it's got no magic."

Superstitious though they were, southerners did know how to tell a good story. Khalmet's their god of luck, and they say he has one hand of human flesh and one of skeletal bone. If he taps you with the flesh hand, your luck is good, but if he taps you with the other, no charm will save you from disaster. Any man who spends time in the mountains sees enough people die through no fault of their own for that to make perfect sense. But I'd never seen reason to believe invisible devils lurked about waiting to poison men's souls. In my experience, men were capable of evil enough on their own.

Kiran shook his head. "But any mage could tell them the charm was worthless."

I cast him a sharp, quelling glance. Thank Khalmet we were riding far enough back from the convoy that no drovers should've heard that little comment.

Confusion mixed with unease on his face. I leaned toward him and muttered, "Ask a mage? Right. Because so many of those live streetside. Besides, devils might be the stuff of campfire tales, but mages can kill you just as nastily. Ganglords and highsiders may think themselves clever enough to deal direct with mages, but ordinary streetside folk know to keep well clear."

Kiran winced. "I see," he said softly. His lips pressed together, his expression turning as stubbornly withdrawn as it had been before we entered the canyon.

I sighed. I hadn't meant to shut him up entirely. But then, better he rode in silence than make any more dangerous slips of the tongue.

Pello's wagon wasn't far up the line.

The afternoon wore on and the trail grew ever more rocky as we continued the relentless ascent. I kept an eye on the clouds overhead, which had started as occasional tiny puffs and were by now numerous and much larger. Still white, but I was guessing that would change soon. Sure enough, Meldon's bell rang out once we reached a spot where the upward grade of the canyon lessened enough for the drovers to safely halt the wagons. We hadn't reached the trees yet, but head high catsclaw bushes choked the boulder-strewn bottom of the canyon, which meant water lurked down there.

"We're stopping here?" Kiran asked.

"Yep. See those clouds? They've been building all day, and there's likely to be a storm. Cara's told the boss, and he's decided to stop for the night. Better to have plenty of time to cover everything nice and tight and set up shelter."

"But what about water? I thought you said we wouldn't stop today until we hit a stream?"

"We have." I pointed down at the silvery green sea of catsclaw. "Catsclaw only grows where it's wet enough. There'll be a trickle of water down there. It'll be a pain in the ass to bash through the bushes and fill the jugs, but it's possible. We've got enough water left in the barrels to last the evening, but tomorrow morning we'll have to replenish our stores." I peered at the sky again. "It may even rain some, but I doubt it. This side of the mountains, you mainly get hail and lightning."

A frown crossed Kiran's face at the word "lightning." He squinted up at the clouds, shading his eyes with a hand. "Is it normal to get this kind of storm?"

I shrugged. "Yeah. Usually it takes longer to build up again. The last one was maybe four days ago. This time of year, you usually get a week or two in between, but you never know. No doubt the southerners'll claim that banehawk brought bad luck on the convoy."

Kiran still looked concerned, which surprised me. Most city dwellers think lightning's only a fun fireworks show, like the ones Sechaveh commissions from the mages for holidays. With all the mage wards on the towers, nobody ever gets struck in the city. Up here it's a different story, but most don't know that.

"You worried about getting hit? Don't be. Lightning likes to strike the highest point, and we're well below the ridgelines, here."

"That's good to know," he said, but his expression didn't change.

"We gotta head back to the outrider wagon and give Harken a hand with covering the supplies." He followed me as I spurred my horse up the trail, but he kept glancing at the clouds when he thought I wasn't looking.

✳

(Kiran)

Kiran hung on to his corner of the oilcloth as a sharp gust of wind tried to rip it from his cramping hands. He was grateful Dev hadn't asked him to help secure the ropes lashing the oilcloth over the contents of the wagon. Kiran had seen how swiftly and nimbly Dev and the others tied their knots. He couldn't match their skill, even when his muscles weren't already burning with exhaustion. He only hoped Cara, Jerik, and Dev finished with the other end of the wagon before he lost his grip entirely.

The clouds had grown dark to the west. Massive thunderheads towered above the serrated rock of the western ridges, and wind gusts kicked grit and sand into the air, stinging Kiran's eyes. Far worse was the sting of power against his inner senses, crawling along his nerves. His initial suspicions had solidified into certainty: this was no natural storm, no matter what Dev thought. Magical power coiled and twisted through those clouds. Invisible and intangible to the others, but each lightning strike would slam that hidden power against his mental barriers with the force of a battering ram. And if his barriers failed... Kiran shuddered. Ruslan would have him, then, and he'd never get a second chance to escape.

Magic whispered against his senses, right behind him. Kiran started and nearly lost his grip on the oilcloth.

"Easy, lad, it's only me." Harken patted him on the shoulder, his dark eyes kind. "Storm has you on edge, does it? Same goes for the animals." He nodded to the tethered outrider horses, who were snorting and tossing their heads. "Even good-natured, steady sorts like these don't care much for thunder and lightning, so we drovers have a little trick…" He opened one blunt-fingered hand. A pile of thumbnail-sized discs, each bearing a single swirled rune, gleamed in his callused palm.

"Muting charms?" Kiran blinked at the harmless little charms, berating himself for reacting so strongly to their minor magic.

Harken smiled at him in approval. "Exactly, lad. Put one of these on a halter…" He moved to the nearest horse and deftly clipped a charm to the inside of the halter's cheek strap. "Even the nerviest of beasts will sit meek as you please through a nasty storm. It doesn't totally block their senses, you understand—they wouldn't like that much. Only dims them, so all the noise and light aren't so overwhelming." He pulled a knife from his belt, pricked his thumb, and smeared a tiny drop of blood on the charm to activate it.

Kiran's breath caught in his throat as an idea blossomed. "That's… very interesting. May I see one?"

"Sure." Harken tossed a charm onto the wagon's outboard. "I've got plenty."

Kiran released a hand from the oilcloth and snatched up the charm. Something so simple and small wouldn't interfere with his amulet, and though the charm couldn't possibly relieve the coming assault on his senses, it might take the edge off. Enough to help him hold his barriers fast, if he was lucky.

"Hey!" A sharp tug on the oilcloth yanked Kiran from his thoughts. Dev was scowling at him in exasperation from a few feet away, a length of rope in his hand. "Let go, already. I can't tie this last knot with you pulling like that."

"Sorry." Kiran released the oilcloth and shoved the charm into his pocket. The storm was still far enough away that the thunder was only a low grumbling, but each distant lightning strike sent fire racing along his nerves. Dev finished his knot and directed Kiran over to help him set up a camping tarp. He used a huge boulder as the anchor for one long side and pounded stakes deep into the ground for the other, forming a slanted shelter with open sides.

"I doubt we'll get rain, but it's best to be prepared," he yelled over a loud wind gust. Kiran gritted his teeth and tried to focus on the task and not the increasingly ominous sky. When Dev turned away to check the stakes, Kiran slipped the muting charm out of his pocket and under his sock cuff, against his skin. Thankfully, only the untalented had to activate charms with their own blood. Kiran sent a slender thread of power into the charm. His sight dimmed, the world turning gray. When lightning struck again, to his relief the fire burning his nerves raw lessened a fraction.

Dev pulled Kiran under the slanted shelter of the tarp and sat down on folded blankets. "Now we wait," he said, his voice faint and tinny sounding.

Kiran drew his knees up to his chest and wrapped his arms around them, hoping to hide his shivering. Lightning flashed outside, and the resulting crash of thunder was lost in the soundless white fire in Kiran's head. So much power, so close...even with the little muting charm's help, the sensations threatened to overwhelm his control. Under his clothes, the amulet sparked and burned against the skin of his chest, and he hoped desperately its protections would hold. Lightning struck again, closer yet. Power smashed against his barriers. He buried his head in his arms, choking back a scream. He had to stay hidden from Ruslan, regardless of the cost.

❋

(Dev)

The storm's fury raged outside the open end of our tarp. No rain, but we got near-constant lightning mixed with the occasional violent burst of hail. The clouds were thick and dark enough to give the scene the look of late twilight, even though another few hours remained in the day. The cracks of thunder sent booming echoes rolling through the canyon. I kept an eye on the canyon's opposite wall, watching for rockfall.

Beside me, Kiran sat hunched up in a ball, his head down in his arms so only a shock of brown-dyed hair showed. He'd been skittish as a kicked colt before the storm hit, although he'd tried to hide it. And when I'd pulled him under the tarp, his arm muscles beneath my hand had felt tight as guy ropes. He hadn't said a word, only curled up tight as a snail on the blankets.

As a searing flash lit the world outside, I noticed he was trembling. Huh. I had seen little kids and animals afraid of thunder, but never an adult, young or otherwise. But then, I'd once met an outrider terrified of the harmless little whiptail lizards that liked to sun themselves on courtyard walls in Ninavel. He'd told me he knew it was crazy, but he just couldn't help it.

Maybe Kiran was the same; or maybe it was yet another piece of the puzzle. I wished I could start fitting pieces together, but so far nothing about him or the job made much sense. What really confused me was Kiran's obvious inexperience in shadow dealings. Unless this was only a practice run—maybe his superiors weren't sure a person could be safely smuggled through the border, and wanted some evidence of success before putting their real plan into motion. But if they wanted to send someone expendable on this run, why a highsider? Why not some streetsider eager for coin and safely ignorant of highsider business? Then again, given Bren's instructions, maybe somebody back in Ninavel wanted Kiran gone and didn't much care if he ended up truth-spelled and spilling his secrets to angry Alathians.

A wide bolt of lightning struck a pinnacle jutting like a broken finger from the ridge across the canyon, in a stuttering flash so bright it left glaring afterimages printed on my vision. Thunder exploded, and Kiran flinched violently. He made a choked noise loud enough for me to hear over the echoes, but didn't raise his head.

A puff of vaporized rock rose from the pinnacle, and a shower of enormous boulders tumbled down the cliff face, sending up an even larger cloud of rock dust. A sharp, flinty smell filled the air. I coughed, trying to get the scent out of my mouth and nose before it brought up memories I didn't want to think about. Just as well Kiran hadn't seen the rockfall happen. If the storm scared him now, I'd hate to see his reaction if he realized we were easy targets for any rockfall from the cliffs on our side of the canyon. I grinned sourly to myself at the thought as the rocks smashed into the talus slopes at the base of the cliffs. The grinding roar of the collision mixed with yet more thunder.

Gradually, the storm moved off eastward, taking the light show with it. We got one more shower of hail that made the horses fling their heads and snort in protest despite Harken's calming charms, but after that the clouds started to break up. Cautiously, I poked my head outside the tarp. The sun had sunk behind the peaks during the storm, and the western ridgelines stood out clear and sharp against a rose-colored sky.

The city wasn't visible anymore, thanks to the twists and turns of Silverlode Canyon, but the eastern sky was a sullen black. Continual flashes lit up the clouds, accompanied by the distant growl of thunder. The cityfolk would get a real show tonight. That was by far the most powerful storm I'd ever seen this early in the season. Usually storms didn't get anywhere near this bad until the heat of late summer. Of course, any outrider knows the mountains can always catch you by surprise.

I ducked back under the tarp. "Hey. Storm's over."

Kiran raised his head, and I sucked in my breath, shocked. His face was bloodless, with shadows dark as coal dust under his eyes. His pupils were dilated so wide his eyes looked black in the low light, and his teeth were clenched so hard his jaw muscles stood out in ridges.

"Damn, kid, are you all right?" I reached for him. He jerked and scrambled backward as if I'd threatened to stab him.

"Don't touch me!" For the first time, he really sounded like a highsider, his voice full of arrogant command. But the impression was marred by the way the whites of his eyes showed, which made him look more like a trapped animal. I spread both my hands, palms out.

"Okay, okay, just calm—"

He jumped up and raced outside before I could finish. A pair of drovers crossed his path, and Kiran jinked sideways so hard he bounced off a wagon and tumbled head over heels. One drover called something to him, but Kiran only scrambled to his feet and took off again. He dodged between the wagons and disappeared down the slope toward the catsclaw thickets. The drovers stared after him with their mouths hanging open.

Well, shit. So much for staying unnoticed. What in the name of Khalmet was wrong with him? I sprang to my feet, then hesitated. If I went running straight after him, there'd only be more talk. No, I should delay a little, then ease over to the catsclaw and try and find him before it got dark, if he hadn't already come to his senses and returned to the convoy. At least he couldn't get truly lost in this kind of terrain—there was no place to go. But if he tripped over a catsclaw root in a blind panic and bashed his fool head in, I could kiss my promised payment goodbye.

I headed for the wagon. Cara and Jerik were already at work, unlacing knots and checking supplies. Cara cocked an eyebrow at me. "The kid's faster than he looks. Needs to learn some manners, though."

"City boy." I tried to sound disgusted instead of stunned and pissed off. "The storm scared the shit out of him. Literally."

Cara snorted. "Some apprentice you've got there. Sure you didn't bring him along just for some fun in bed?" I made a face and reached for a knot, but she stopped me. "Forget helping with the wagon. I want you to scout before the light fails. If rockfall hit the trail ahead, I'd rather Meldon knew it tonight, instead of waiting 'til a morning scout."

I swallowed a protest. I knew why Cara wanted me to go. Of the three of us, I was by far the fastest climber, especially on an untested route. To have a sightline all the way up the canyon, I'd need to climb a spire on one of the knife-edged rock ribs extending down from the heights. But gods all damn it, from the height of the ridge, even if I hurried I'd barely make it back to the convoy before nightfall. So much for my plans to track down Kiran. I cursed silently as I pictured myself fighting through catsclaw in the dark. He'd better have calmed down and come back by the time I finished.

"You worried about the kid? Don't be. Jerik and I will keep an eye out for him." Cara's blue eyes held a little too much curiosity for my liking.

"I promised his family I'd keep him safe, is all," I muttered, grabbing the supply crate that contained the pitons. Ordinarily I'd downclimb rather than set an anchor and rappel from the ridge—there's no challenge in rappelling—but a rappel would get me back to the convoy that much faster.

Jerik barked out a laugh from the opposite end of the wagon. "Safe? As an outrider?" His voice was low and gravelly, probably from disuse. Prying conversation out of him was like chipping holds in granite.

"Not every apprentice decides to stick with the trade," I said. Which was true enough; some would-be outriders changed their minds quick after their first close call in the mountains. A perfect excuse for my sudden lack of an apprentice, once we reached Kost.

I threw a set of pitons, a hammer, a hemp rope, my climbing boots, and a waterskin into a pack. "Bet you I make it back before Harken shares out dinner." At least I'd have a chance of spotting Kiran from the ridge, unless he'd worked his way too deeply into the thickets.

Cara surveyed the ridge, then grinned. "You're on. One free drink in Kost if you make it back before dinner, two free drinks if you make it back before we finish taking care of the horses."

I flicked my fingers in the old streetside gesture used to seal a bargain, shouldered my pack, and raced off, leaping from rock to rock up the steep slope above the trail. My breath came fast and hard by the time I'd scrambled up the boulders to the base of the ridge. I stopped to let my heart slow before starting the climb. Plenty of small ledges and flakes studded the mica-flecked rock in front of me, and I judged the route well within my ability to climb without protection. But Sethan had long ago hammered into my head that it only takes one instant of carelessness or overconfidence to kill a climber.

I braced my back against the rock to put on my climbing boots, careful of the sharp iron nails protruding from their soles. The vivid pink of the western sky was edging toward paler violet, but an hour or so remained before the light grew too dim for contrast. From my vantage point I had an excellent view of the long line of the convoy, and below the trail, the thick tangle of catsclaw. I scanned the head-high bushes as I laced my boots, searching for Kiran, or at least some signs of his passage. But catsclaw was tough and resilient, its interlocking branches difficult to bend and nearly impossible to break, and I couldn't spot any trace of him.

I was about to give up and start the climb when something else caught my eye. A drover, approaching the outrider wagon with a casual stride. And damn it, though I was too far away to make out facial features, from the man's height and coloring I was sure it was Pello.

He sauntered up to Harken and Jerik, waving a friendly greeting. The two men paused in the act of unloading a grain sack, and Cara's blonde head turned, though she didn't stop currying her horse. Their conversation was lost in the indistinct hum of voices floating up from the convoy, but Harken pointed up in my direction. I clenched my teeth. Pello was sure to find out Kiran had run off alone. Oh, this got better by the minute.

Sudden and unwelcome as rockfall, memories of Jylla overwhelmed me. She'd always been the one clever with people and plans, even back when we were a pair of desperate, angry kids just past our Change. If she were in my place, she'd outfox Pello without even trying. *Dealing with people's no different than Tainting a mage ward,* she'd told me once. We'd been lying sprawled in a tangle of sheets, her slender fingers tracing lazily down my spine. *Find their weak spot, and push them the way you want.*

Yeah, just like she'd pushed me. How could I have been so dumb as to think she saw me any different? I spat and banished the image of Jylla's golden curves and teasing eyes. I might not have her cunning, but I'd never yet failed on a job. Shadow man or no, Pello wouldn't keep me from earning my pay.

Still no sign of Kiran in the catsclaw. This time I felt only relief. I turned back to the rock and flattened my hands on the stone. Shoving all my worries away, I concentrated on the gritty texture under my palms until nothing else existed. Then I moved, stepping smoothly up onto the rock while my fingers searched out ledges.

For a glorious interval, the entire world consisted of me and the cliff. My body flowed up the rock, every muscle perfectly under my command, my mind locked in absolute focus on each succeeding set of holds. When I reached the ridgetop and wedged myself into position straddling a block of stone, my grin stretched nearly as wide as Bren's. My nerves sang, and the stark beauty of the surrounding ridgelines and snowcapped peaks made my heart swell. The satisfaction deep inside was almost—not quite, but almost—as good as my childhood memories of my lost Taint.

My exhilaration faded at the thought. I surveyed the terrain ahead, recalled to duty. My perch gave me a hawks-eye view of the upper reaches of the canyon, all the way up to the edge of the wide basin below the pass. I traced the pale line of the trail. About a mile upcanyon from my ridge, a pile of freshly fallen boulders blocked the path. Some of them were big, too, wagon-sized or more.

I set about hammering pitons into cracks in the rock to anchor my rappel, unwelcome thoughts of Pello and Kiran creeping back into my mind. When I leaned out to throw the rope down, I stopped short. The catsclaw thickets below the convoy now lay deep in shadow, but a few circular patches appeared unnaturally dark, as if the bushes themselves had turned black. I squinted, trying to make them out, but the light was fading fast. I gave up and reached for the rope. I'd have another chance to take a look when we bashed our way through the catsclaw for water in the morning.

By the time I returned to the outrider wagon, twilight was giving way to darkness. The storm still blotted out the eastern sky, far enough away now that only silent sourceless flashes lit the horizon. Overhead, the first stars glimmered amidst stray wisps of cloud. Cara straightened up from lighting a candle lantern and clapped her hands, slowly. "Well, you win one drink, at least. Harken and Jerik are about to dig out our dinner rations."

"You'll want to talk to Meldon. I spotted major rockfall on the trail, about a mile up. Probably a full morning's work to clear." I shrugged out of my pack and tried not to be too obvious about looking around for Kiran.

"Figures, after that little show we had during the storm." Cara glanced across the canyon to the lightning-struck pinnacle, a sharp black outline against the darkening sky. We squatted down together next to the lantern and I drew a quick diagram in the dirt for her of the rockfall's position and extent.

Cara stood and brushed off her hands. "I'll head up to Meldon, fill him in before I eat. Oh, and the kid's back, safe and sound—he took your gear up to your tarp. Looked kinda wobbly, though. You sure you're feeding him enough?"

"He's just tired. Long day, for a city boy." Relief made my voice light. If Khalmet really favored me, maybe Kiran had even managed to avoid Pello. I'd have to think of some innocent way to ask Cara about Pello's little visit.

"He can sleep in some tomorrow, thanks to that rockfall. I doubt the convoy'll move before noon." Cara peered at me, her blonde brows drawing together. "You look like you could use some extra sleep yourself."

"Not my fault if Kellan snores." It wasn't entirely a lie. Kiran didn't snore, but he certainly was a noisy sleeper. Lots of thrashing and sighing and whimpering. From the sound of it, his dreams weren't much more fun than mine.

She grinned and strode off. I hurried over to the tarp, my nerves keying up a notch. When I ducked under the edge, the glow of a lantern illuminated our sleeping blankets, laid neatly out beside our personal gear. Kiran sat cross-legged beside them, staring at his hands laced together in his lap. He raised his head when I squatted down in front of him. Cara was right, he did look a bit unsteady, though that was a big improvement from the last time I'd seen him.

"What in Khalmet's name happened with you?" I demanded.

His eyes slid away from mine. "Nothing. I just don't like storms."

"Right." I drew the word out. His chin lifted, and I got another glimpse of a highsider's usual arrogance. Judging by the stubborn, mutinous look on his face, I could wait until all the snow melted off the Whitefires before he'd explain. I clenched my hands on my knees to keep myself from shaking some sense into him. "Remember how you agreed to lay low and stay close? Was I somehow not clear? Or in highsider talk, does laying low mean running screaming from a simple thunderstorm in front of half the convoy?"

"I wasn't—!" He shut his mouth so fast I thought he'd bite his tongue off. His gaze dropped back to his hands. When he spoke again, his voice was carefully controlled. "How much of a problem will this cause?"

"Did Pello find you? Talk to you, at all?"

He shook his head. My relief didn't lessen my anger. "He could have, easy. You gods-damned idiot! You think just because you're highside, you can ignore anything I say? You pull another stunt like this, and you can go to hell on your own."

"I'm sorry, all right?" His blue eyes were stricken. "Have you never acted out of emotion without thinking first?"

I opened my mouth to deny it, but couldn't manage the lie. Not with memories of my final night with Jylla so raw and recent. If I'd kept a cool head, I might have bargained with her and saved myself from losing everything. But no, I'd let my fury take my tongue, and done my level best to rip her apart. You don't live with someone as long as I had with Jylla without learning what will cause the most pain. Of course, that goes both ways. By the end of that night, we'd both said things we could never forgive or forget. And look where that had gotten me.

"Next time, think twice," I growled. "This isn't some fucking kids game. At the border, we'll be playing with our lives."

"I know," he said quietly. My anger faded at the sincerity in his voice. I studied the dark circles under his eyes, frowning.

"You okay, now? You still look a little..." I waggled a hand.

"I'm fine." The stubborn look reappeared.

"Whatever," I muttered. I shoved myself to my feet. "Come on, then. Time to eat."

Dinner wasn't much, without spare water for proper cooking. When I handed Kiran his ration of jerky, hardtack, and dried fruit, he released a sad little sigh. Harken and I chuckled, and even Jerik's mouth twitched.

"Last night of dry rations, lad." Harken gave Kiran a sympathetic look. "Tomorrow night we'll be high enough the stream will be in full flow, and I promise you won't be disappointed in my cooking." He leaned back from his seat on the wagon's outboard and reached into the stacks of supplies. "In the meantime, I brought a little something extra to share around." He produced a fist-sized sack which proved to contain Sulanian seedcakes sweetened with peachflower honey and dusted with cinnamon.

"You're a marvel, Harken," I mumbled through a mouthful of seedcake. Harken grinned at me, the warm golden glow of the lanterns softening the years etched in his face.

"You outriders aren't so different than the horses. Give you a treat every now and then, and it keeps everybody happy."

Footsteps crunched on rock, and Cara's high, clear laughter pierced the night air, followed by a man's indistinct murmur. I peered into the darkness beyond the lanternlight. That male voice sounded all too familiar.

"Hope you boys saved me something." Cara stepped into the light, her companion trailing after. Gods all damn it, I knew I'd recognized Pello's voice. Couldn't he mind his own business for one night?

He nodded to us all, friendly as could be, but my annoyance grew when his eyes lingered a fraction longer on Kiran than the rest of us. "I thought I'd return your awl before morning," Pello said to Harken, handing him the tool. "Many thanks for the loan." He sketched an exaggerated bow to Cara, his face full of wry humor. "And Suliyya's grace upon you, for the delight of your company on the way."

Cara's eyes sparkled with mocking amusement. "I love a man with a smooth tongue."

I stifled a disgusted snort. It hadn't taken Pello long to figure out the perfect excuse to come lurk around our camp. Cara was happy to flirt with anything short of a rock bear. Though she always held to her rule about not mixing bedplay and outriding, it didn't stop admirers from hoping. I had no doubt Pello would eagerly play the part.

"Glad I could help," Harken told Pello as he handed Cara her dinner ration. At least he didn't offer Pello any of his seedcakes. "Nasty storm like that, I'm surprised more tarps weren't damaged."

Pello's expression turned serious. "Perhaps you outriders could answer a question for a man new to the westbound route. Is it natural to get a storm so strong this early in the season?"

Beside me, Kiran went still. When Pello had first showed up, after one quick sidelong glance at me, Kiran had stared at the ground, picking idly at small rocks as if bored. Now I sensed him listening intently, though he didn't raise his head.

Cara dropped to sit against a wagon wheel, her hands full of food.

"It's not the usual way of things, but weather can be strange up here. I've seen it snow in midsummer."

To my surprise, Jerik spoke up. "The question's a fair one. A storm that bad before summer takes hold...it reminds me of the weather some twenty years ago, during the mage war." A frown marked his dark face.

"You worked that year?" Cara sounded impressed. "Must've been a hell of a trip."

"It was," Jerik said, shortly.

My respect for Jerik shot upward. I didn't remember anything from the mage war, since I'd only been a toddler at the time. I'd heard the stories, though; we all had. There'd been a falling out among some powerful mages, and they'd got to fighting. Lord Sechaveh had ignored it for a while, keeping to his hands-off policy. But when the magic thrown around got to the point of damaging the city and killing crowds of unfortunate bystanders, he'd gotten mad enough to draw the line.

The stories differed on what he'd done—some said he'd had the mages involved killed, others that he'd banished them. Nobody agreed on how he'd managed to do either, but the end result was that life in the city went back to normal. Still, it had been a crazy few months, and all that messing around with magical forces had screwed up the weather in a big way. I'd heard stories of storms with colored lighting bright enough to blind anyone foolish enough to look at it, and hail the size of a man's head.

I glanced at Kiran, wondering if his reaction to the storm had something to do with the mage war stories. He was several years short of my own age, so chances were good he hadn't even been born when it happened. Maybe somebody had told him the more gruesome stories as a kid and scared him good, but it was hard to imagine that making him go rabbiting off into the catsclaw. I had a sudden flash of the horror on his face when he'd realized a message might reach Ninavel. Had he thought the storm meant a mage was after him? Surely not. Even a highsider would know how dumb that idea was. Whatever mages want, they get, and they don't fuck around about it, either. If a mage wanted to stop him, Kiran would be dead already.

No, it had to be something else.

Kiran didn't look scared now; far from it. His fascination was plain as day, and I could practically see all the questions jamming themselves up in his throat.

"Mage war." Pello spoke as if he were savoring the words. "Now there's a thought to disturb a man's sleep." An odd undertone colored his voice, and I shifted forward, wishing his eyes weren't in shadow.

"Surely so," Harken agreed. "I worked a convoy traveling all the way to eastern Arkennland that year, so I missed all the excitement, but from the tales my sister shared, I'm not sorry. She lost her husband and two nephews—stonemasons, all of them. They were on a job repairing the southgate wall when one of the fights flared up. The whole wall came down, killed their entire crew in an instant."

Jerik stood, his back rigid. "I'll check the horses before I turn in," he announced, and headed off into the night without a backward glance.

Pello's mobile face creased in theatrical disappointment. Cara cuffed his shoulder. "Don't expect any campfire tales out of Jerik, not without a lot of sarkosa wine to soften him up first. The man's got a mouth tighter than a snare trap."

"I'll keep that in mind," Pello said. His gaze swept across us, and his smile held more than a hint of irony when he nodded to me. I suppressed a scowl as he made his farewells and finally disappeared down the line. Cara watched him go with a small, contemplative smile on her face that made me want to hit her.

"For Khalmet's sake, Cara, can't you manage one trip without any lovesick drovers mooning after you?"

She smirked. "I'd wondered where your tongue had got to. Who says I'm the main attraction?" She aimed a soulful look at Kiran. "Hard to compete with the likes of you, kid. You must have had herds of city girls throwing themselves at your feet...and plenty of boys, too, I'd wager."

Kiran looked like he wished the earth would split open and swallow him, but he managed a stiff little shrug. Cara ignored my pointed glare and flicked a dried fig at him.

"No need to be so shy. What, you have a lover back in the city?

Someone you miss?"

Kiran hurriedly ducked his head, but not before I saw the way he'd squeezed his eyes shut, as if in pain. "No," he muttered.

Well, that little reaction added new weight to my theory that someone back in Ninavel wanted him gone. I didn't know the rules for highsiders' love games, but maybe he'd chosen the wrong lover to chase after, and now he was paying the price. I felt a twinge of sympathy, but pushed it aside. Time to distract Cara. Teasing Kiran about his love life was one thing, but from the growing curiosity in her eyes, her next questions might be more dangerous. Anything she learned about his supposed past was sure to end up in Pello's ears.

"Have a heart and leave the poor guy alone, Cara. Can't you see he's tired after an entire day in the mountains?"

"Oooh, an entire day, and all he did was ride? Dev, you *are* going soft. As I recall, Sethan had you climbing laps your first day out." Cara stuffed another fig into her mouth. A reminiscent grin spread over her face as she chewed.

"Yeah, up and down that overhanging crack near the second bend of the canyon. I thought my fingers would fall off by the time he finally let me quit." I'd been mad as a stinkwasp. Later, I'd realized Sethan had been teaching me in his quiet way that endurance was as important as technique for a mountain climber.

"Gods, you were such a cocky little bastard, bragging that you could climb anything. Sethan had to shut you up somehow, or the rest of us would have strangled you by midmeal." The look on Cara's face said she was still savoring the memory.

Harken gave one of his low chuckles. "If we're telling tales, I remember one about a blonde-haired little loud-mouthed chit who insisted she could climb the Darran Spire." He leaned down to poke Cara's shoulder with one wide finger.

To my delight, Cara's cheeks reddened, an event nearly as rare as rain in the Painted Valley. "Oh yeah, let's hear that one," I said eagerly.

"Think I'll save it for a special occasion." Harken levered himself off the wagon's outboard. "Would one of you be good enough to help me put the food away? It's late, and this old man needs his rest."

"Sure." I jumped up. "Just show me where you want it, and Kellan and I'll take care of it for you."

Kiran scrambled after me with obvious relief. He darted glances my way as we stowed the food back in its warded container, but he held his tongue until we reached our tarp. "Pello's trying to find out about me, isn't he?"

"Oh, you noticed?"

He winced. "What are we going to do?"

And by "we," he meant me. "Take care of that damn message charm of his, for one thing."

"If you steal his charm, won't he know it was you?"

"Who said anything about stealing? I'll fix it so the charm seems to work, but any messages he sends go nowhere." Deadblocking a charm was one of Red Dal's best tricks, and one he held close to the chest. He'd always claimed no other handler knew the secret. I hoped a Varkevian-born man who'd never even been Tainted wouldn't know it was possible.

Kiran was looking at me like he'd never seen me before. "You can affect a charm's magic? How?"

"A little trade secret I picked up from a specialist. Nothing a highsider like you needs to know."

Frustrated curiosity was all over Kiran's face. His mouth worked, as if he wanted to ask a question but couldn't think of how to phrase it.

"Disabling the charm's the easy part," I told him. "Finding Pello's stash, that's hard. But I've got a few ideas. Give me the night to think them over."

"Anything I can help with?" Now he had the hopeful air of an eager young Tainter. It set my teeth on edge.

"Not unless you know how to peek an active hide-me ward."

I'd meant to shut him up, but a thoughtful frown creased his brow. "Do you mean, reveal the ward's location?" He fumbled in his hair. When he lowered his hands, the look-away charm lay glinting in one palm. "My...father once showed me that if a charm and ward are similar in purpose, yet have a different maker, the interference of their magic may cause visible effects if the charm passes too near the ward."

He'd choked on the word "father" like he had a mouthful of

cactus spines. Bad blood there, perhaps? I pushed speculation aside. I knew what Kiran meant. Every kid in Ninavel knows that party trick, though it's not very useful in practice. Crawling all over a house waving a charm takes hours; somebody's sure to discover you before you're done. Pello's wagon was a more reasonable area to search, but a bigger problem remained. "Yeah, a look-away's enough like a hide-me, but that charm's way too small to flash the ward."

"Didn't you say the cliffs here have carcabon stones?"

My mouth dropped open. Boosting the look-away charm with carcabon could actually work. I wouldn't get anything so obvious as sparks, but all I needed was the tiniest shimmer of air over the ward's location. No, wait, I didn't have any silver to properly bind a stone to the charm…my eye fell on my warding bracelets. If I tied both stone and charm against a bracelet, that might be enough.

"Huh. That's smart," I said. Maybe a brain lurked in that highside head after all.

Kiran's whole face lit up. Khalmet's hand, if Cara ever saw him smile like that, she'd keel over from sheer lust.

"Don't get too excited," I warned him. "We still have to find a decent stone." The nearby cliffs had been picked clean long ago. Except one. My blood tingled with a familiar thrill. Nasty, overhanging, with holds no bigger than sandmites and cracks too thin for pitons…no outrider had ever climbed Kinslayer crag. Word was the name came from an outrider whose brother had died attempting a climb. I'd scouted Kinslayer once and thought I could piece together a workable route, but Sethan had talked me out of trying it. Well. Sethan wasn't here now, and Kinslayer was the best chance within miles for a stone large enough to help us. I'd scout it again, see if the route I remembered was real or only the product of a cocky kid's ego. And if it was real…my heart pounded. What a climb that would be! But I couldn't deny the risk. If I fell, I'd sentence Melly to a living death.

CHAPTER FOUR

(Kiran)

Sunlight warmed Kiran's face and burned red through his closed eyelids. He opened his eyes, expecting the familiar sight of his bedroom's pale stone ceiling etched with the swirling lines of ward patterns. Instead, only the sun-bright blank canvas of Dev's tarp greeted him. He threw an arm over his eyes, a lump in his throat. He'd never see his bedroom in Ninavel again, with the stargazing charm he'd created for Mikail perched gleaming on his writing desk, and his favorite books of adventure tales hidden amongst the stacks of treatises on magical theory.

The adventure books had been gifts from Alisa. Kiran's eyes stung. How Alisa would have loved this trip! She'd pored over explorer journals and dreamed of traveling as an envoy for her merchanter family when she reached her majority. Grief and guilt turned the lump in Kiran's throat hot as molten silver.

The sound of voices outside the tarp recalled him to caution. Kiran hurriedly swiped at his eyes and sat up in the pile of blankets. He blinked in confusion at the sight of Dev's gear already packed up in neat little bundles. Why hadn't Dev awakened him? He yanked his boots on and stepped outside.

The sun was already high, and the white rock of the canyon walls shone bright enough to make Kiran's eyes water. The convoy wagons still stood in their unbroken line along the trail. A small group of drovers sat in a loose circle nearby, talking idly.

"Hey, lazybones!" Dev waved from his perch on top of the massive boulder that anchored the high side of the tarp. "Thought you'd sleep forever."

"Why didn't you wake me? I thought you said last night we'd have to fetch water while the rockfall gets cleared?" Had Dev spent the morning hunting for a suitable carcabon stone?

"Since I'm such a nice guy, I took care of the water duty myself. You looked like you needed the sleep. Besides, I figured you'd had enough of bashing through catsclaw." Despite Dev's casual sprawl and easy grin, his eyes raked over Kiran from head to toe with a calculating curiosity that made Kiran wince internally.

"Um. Thanks." Kiran fought to keep his expression neutral. The aftermath of Ruslan's storm was not a pleasant memory. The deceptively innocent-looking catsclaw had proved a nightmare to navigate, with thick, tightly woven branches that refused to bend and gave vicious scratches when he'd forced his way through. Worse, his barriers had been wavering on the edge of collapse. He'd been terrified Dev would chase after him before he could safely rebuild them. If Dev saw him draw power, he was certain to realize the extent of Kiran's lies.

"Not to worry, we'll keep busy, now you're finally up." Dev looked up at the cliffs above the trail, shading his eyes with a hand. "High time my apprentice learned some tricks of the climbing trade."

Ah. If Dev had indeed searched for stones that morning, he'd been unsuccessful. A climbing lesson would provide the perfect excuse for Dev to scour another cliff. Kiran smiled at him. "I look forward to it."

A sardonic gleam showed in Dev's eyes. "I'll remember you said that." He jumped down from the rock and went over to rummage in the wagon. "Grab something to eat, then we'll go."

Kiran choked down a handful of hardtack and jerky. Dev assembled their packs with a simmering energy completely at odds with his relaxed posture of a moment before. Despite his apparent confidence, he surely shared Kiran's relief about taking action to prevent messages from reaching Ninavel.

"Time for your first lesson—walking on talus." Dev jerked a thumb at the jumble of boulders covering the steep slope leading up to the cliffs. "Take it slow, and watch out for loose rocks. Use your hands to steady yourself, if you need to."

Dev strode up the talus as if it were no more difficult to navigate than a flagstone-paved courtyard, but Kiran found it a continuous struggle to keep his balance. By the time he and Dev reached the base of the cliffs, his leg muscles ached and he was gasping for breath.

"Sit down and rest a minute," Dev told him.

Kiran tried not to resent the way Dev wasn't out of breath at all. He sat down, gingerly. In the shadow of the cliff, the rocks underfoot were smaller, pebble to fist sized—what Dev had called scree. The scree slid and shifted under Kiran with a rattling hiss every time he moved, giving him the uneasy sensation that any minute he might tumble down the slope. He twisted to eye the cliff looming over his head.

"You think there's carcabon here?" The cliff looked impossibly steep. Kiran had no idea how anyone would get up it without the use of magic.

"On something this easy? Hell, no. Anything useful is long gone. But it's a good approach to the spot I have in mind, and it'll make a perfect practice ground for you."

"You mean I have to *climb* that?" Kiran's mouth went dry. He'd imagined practicing more knots and ropework while Dev pretended to give him a climbing lesson by example.

Dev chuckled. "What, did you think you'd get to laze around? I told Cara and Jerik I'd be training you today, and they'll be watching. We gotta put on a proper show before I do any prospecting."

"Oh." Kiran struggled to hide his dismay. He didn't mind the physical effort, but he was more than a little worried about his instinctive reaction if he fell. Even the tiniest use of magic outside his barriers, and Ruslan would find him.

Dev was watching him with his head tilted. "I'll show you the

basics down here first, and when you climb, you'll be safe on a rope."
His green eyes measured Kiran's face. "But if you think you're going
to have some kind of breakdown halfway up, tell me now."

Kiran flushed, hearing the unspoken *like you did last night.* "I'll
be fine." He wiped his sweaty hands on his leathers. He'd survived
Ruslan's storm. He could handle a simple training climb.

✳

Kiran clung to the cliff, his fingers wedged in a crack. His forearms
burned, and tremors wracked his calves. His right foot threatened
to slip off its precarious hold at any moment. He glanced down and
immediately wished he hadn't. The sharp-edged boulders far below
reminded him of the teeth of some storybook dragon, ready to rend
and maim. His instincts screamed for him to call power to save
himself. Grimly, Kiran concentrated on holding his barriers firm. He
refused to break under a mere physical threat. But if he fell—

"Hey!" The rope at his waist tugged upward. "You planning on
moving any time this century?" Dev's voice floated down from a ledge
high overhead.

Kiran repressed the urge to blast Dev to ash. "If…I move, I'll…
fall!" he panted.

Dev's brown head poked over the rim of the ledge. "So fall. You're
not going anywhere, I promise." The pull on Kiran's makeshift rope
harness increased. "Trust me!"

Trust. Kiran wheezed out a bitter laugh. Hardly any existed between
himself and Dev. Yet he'd never doubted Dev's competence at his job.
Kiran inhaled through clenched teeth and hauled himself upward.

Overtaxed muscles cramped. One hand popped free of the crack,
then the other. Kiran yelped and pitched backward, only to stop
short as the rope snapped taut. His chest smacked into the rock hard
enough to bruise, but he moved not an inch downward. Kiran leaned
his forehead against the rope and tried to calm his racing heart. He'd
held his barriers. Barely.

"See? Falling's not a problem," Dev called. "Brace your feet against
the rock and rest your arms."

"H-how long can you hold me like this?" Kiran tentatively pushed his body away from the cliff with his feet.

"Long as I need to." Dev leaned over the ledge's rim again. "You're tied in to the rope, remember? No need to clutch it like a southerner with a devil-ward charm. Shake your arms out, it'll help them recover faster."

Finger by finger, Kiran released his white-knuckled grip. The rope remained reassuringly taut. He swallowed and let his arms drop to hang at his sides. Dangling from the rope wasn't at all comfortable— his knotted harness dug painfully into his upper thighs and groin, and already his legs tingled with impending numbness—but the relief to his forearms and hands was immediate.

Kiran peeked again at the dizzying void beneath him. He'd once been accustomed to placing his life in another's hands. *The trust between focus and channeler must be absolute,* Ruslan had always said. Kiran had believed him; had trusted both Ruslan and Mikail without reservation.

What a fool he'd been. Worse, Alisa had been the one to pay the price. Guilt tore at him. If he hadn't loved her, if she hadn't trusted him…the terrible memories crowded in, full of blood and screaming. Kiran shook his head, violently. If he didn't escape Ruslan, Alisa's death would only be the first of many.

He scrabbled at the rock and managed to cram his fingers back into the crack. "I'll try again," he yelled.

"Ready when you are." Dev sounded pleased. Kiran summoned his concentration. He'd watched Dev climb, and years of channel pattern exercises had honed his memory. *You place your feet right, the rest is easy,* Dev had told him. So where had Dev put his feet? Kiran examined his memory and compared it to the cliff face before him. Ah—there. He balanced one foot on a rounded protrusion, wedged the other in a crack, and pressed upward.

Without the fear of falling overshadowing every move, the rest of the ascent was only an exercise in endurance. His muscles trembled with fatigue again by the time he wormed his way onto the broad ledge where Dev waited. Kiran settled himself cautiously in the spot Dev indicated and slumped back against the cliff with a sigh of release.

"Not bad for your first time." Dev's fingers flew as he tied a second, shorter length of rope from Kiran's harness to a nearby piton. At Kiran's skeptical glance, he nodded. "Seriously, I mean it. You did better than most would."

A tendril of warmth stole through Kiran. He rubbed his aching forearms. "If that was an easy climb, I don't ever want to see a hard one."

Dev's mouth twitched. "Don't worry, showtime's over. Now you get to relax a while." He glanced down at the head of the convoy, where the steady flow of men and tool-laden mules on the trail continued unabated. Their destination was out of sight around a bend, but the clink of tools on rock and the wavering tones of a Sulanian chant song echoed back down the canyon. "Let me stow some gear, and then we'll talk carcabon."

The sun-warmed rock felt good against Kiran's sore back. He flexed his hands, the burn in his muscles finally relenting. The canyon was oddly peaceful. Somehow colors seemed stronger and more vivid than in the city. The craggy cliffs forming the opposite canyon wall were blindingly white, with only occasional streaks of rust-red or gray or brown marring their purity, and the sky overhead was a deeper blue than Kiran had ever seen.

To Kiran's relief, the azure depths of the sky contained not even the smallest puff of cloud that might build into a storm. Ruslan couldn't know for certain which route Kiran had taken out of Ninavel. Since his storm had been unsuccessful at forcing Kiran to reveal himself, Kiran might have a few days' grace while Ruslan hunted in other directions. Or so he devoutly hoped.

A rattling noise called him from his thoughts. Dev was running his fingers over a set of pitons on a rope sling, as if counting them. But his eyes were fixed high above on the cliff, and his expression was oddly remote.

"What are you looking for?" Kiran asked.

Dev blinked and set down the sling of pitons. "The red bands of rock are where you find carcabon. I think that one's our best bet." He pointed to a red streak slashing across a sheer section of cliff, high and to the left of the ledge.

"Please tell me you're joking!" The angle of the rock edged past vertical, and Kiran couldn't see a single crack or ledge blemishing the sunlit stone. "We can't possibly climb that!"

Dev's one-sided grin appeared. "Well, you're right about the 'we' part. You'll stay right here, so you can quit twitching like a roundtail in a snare." He stood and shucked off his shirt. Then untied the rope from his harness.

"What are you *doing*?" Dev had impressed on Kiran in no uncertain terms that the rope was his lifeline, never to be untied while on a climb.

"Kinslayer's not the kind of climb that lends itself to pitons. Without 'em, a rope's only dead weight." Dev stretched his arms overhead and rotated his wrists. "Once I reach the carcabon, I can set a piton in the crack between the rock layers. I'll tie off with a sling, chip out any decent stones, and then climb an ascending traverse off the overhang. When I'm done, I'll downclimb back to you." He spoke as casually as if he planned a stroll down a city street.

"You're going to climb something called Kinslayer without a rope?" Had Dev gone insane?

Dev made a noise halfway between a snort and a laugh. "Don't let the name bother you. Outriders always make up dramatic names for crags. Makes for a better tavern story."

Kiran eyed the smooth expanse of rock leading up to Dev's chosen streak. A vivid vision of Dev's body plummeting through the air to splatter on the ground far below brought sweat to his palms. The ledge suddenly seemed a far more precarious perch than it had a moment ago. Kiran didn't even know how to get back down the cliff safely without Dev, let alone cross the Alathian border. "What if you slip? Forget the carcabon! We can find another way to deal with Pello."

Dev crouched down until his eyes were level with Kiran's. "Look. I've been climbing since I was knee high to a mule. I know what I'm doing." He slapped the pale stone of the ledge. "I wouldn't try Kinslayer if I thought I might fail. Without a carcabon stone, I can't find Pello's wards to break them. Kinslayer's the best chance for a stone. You want to stop Pello from sending any messages, this is the only way."

Dev was wrong, of course. There was another way. If Kiran were the one to search Pello's wagon, he could sense the location of any wards, even through his barriers. If he pointed the wards out to Dev, and then Dev used whatever trick he'd planned to break them... but no. How could Kiran possibly explain an ability to sense wards, without arousing Dev's suspicion? If he claimed he carried a special charm...no, Dev would want to see the charm, perhaps insist on using it himself instead of Kiran...

Kiran pinched the bridge of his nose. "Can't you at least get me back down first?" If only he had more time to think!

"What, and leave you alone where Pello can find you? Nope. You're safer here." Dev uncoiled from his crouch and locked his hands behind his back. He arched over in another stretch. "If Khalmet touches me, and I fall...you sit tight. Cara and Jerik will come for you. Stick with the convoy until just before the border. Then make up some excuse to stay behind, and send a message through with one of the workers, to Gerran's import house at the river docks. Gerran'll handle it from there." Dev hesitated, his eyes traveling over Kiran's face, as if he might say something else. Instead, he turned away.

"Was that supposed to reassure me?" Kiran cast about desperately for a tale that might convince Dev without revealing the truth. His mind remained stubbornly blank.

Dev paced to the end of the ledge without a backward glance. Kiran cursed himself for ever having suggested a carcabon stone as an option. "Wait, maybe we can—"

"Shut up," Dev said mildly. "I need to concentrate." He flattened his hands on the rock and bowed his head. Kiran recognized the intent stillness in his stance. He'd seen it hundreds of times in Mikail, preparing to cast a channeled spell. Kiran opened his mouth, then shut it again. Perhaps the climb was well within Dev's abilities, and Kiran was agonizing over nothing.

Yet if Dev had misjudged the difficulty...Kiran could halt any fall with ease, if he chose. Was Dev's life worth the cost? Kiran imagined Ruslan hot-eyed with predatory triumph. His stomach rolled over. If it were death Kiran risked, the choice to save Dev would be easy. He would have welcomed death at Ruslan's hands. Kiran pressed a hand against the hidden lump of the amulet and grimaced. Lizaveta's aid had not come without price. That escape was lost to him.

Dev raised his head. Kiran had one glimpse of the meditative calm on his face before Dev was gone, climbing away from the ledge with languid, flowing grace. He moved up the cliff as freely as if the ground waited mere inches away instead of a hundred feet below. The utter confidence in every line of his body eased the churning of Kiran's stomach.

Dev's pace slowed as the angle of the cliff increased. He shifted only a single hand or foot at a time, with precise, unhurried control. Kiran still couldn't understand how Dev could cling to such a sheer surface, let alone ascend it. But Dev twisted, and reached, and stepped, all with that same sinuous grace. Kiran began to relax as Dev neared the red seam.

For the first time, Dev hesitated. He leaned back, the muscles standing out like ropes under the brown skin of his back and arms. Reached a hand out, then withdrew it. Stretched upward, and slid his fingers over the rock, as if searching for a hold.

Kiran clenched a sweaty hand around a piton. He remembered the fiery ache in his forearms and hands after mere minutes of ascent. How long could Dev cling to such tiny imperfections in the cliff face? How long before even the most well-trained muscles must give way?

Dev held still for an agonizing interval. At last he straightened his arms and sank down into a twisted crouch. He rocked once, twice… and sprang upward, his body fully extended in the air. Kiran's breath froze in his chest. Clearly he'd been right, before. Dev was *insane*.

At the apex of his jump, Dev's reaching fingertips locked with unerring accuracy on the crystalline lip of the red layer. His arms flexed, taking his weight—and one hand lost its grip. Dev's body jerked. He swung from his remaining hand, clawing at the rock with his feet.

Kiran's heart leapt into his throat. He scrambled to his knees. He had only to release his barriers… He raised a hand; then dropped it, and sank back. Sick certainty cramped his gut. He couldn't face the unceasing hell that awaited, should Ruslan reclaim him. Kiran covered his face with his hands. Alisa would never have condoned a man's death, for any reason. Yet another way in which he'd failed her, though not the worst.

He'd dreaded the sound of Dev's scream, but the loudest sound remained that of his own thudding heart. Kiran peeked through his fingers.

Dev hung from the edge of the red seam in a contortion of limbs. One foot was wedged high over his head, the other leg doubled up beneath the hand he'd jammed between the rock layers. With his free hand, he was busily working a piton into the crack.

Kiran sagged against the cliff. The relief that swept over him did nothing to erase the shame that still seared his heart.

Dev grabbed the slender hammer hanging from its knotted sling around his waist. The high-pitched ring of metal on metal shivered through the air. Another agonizing pause followed as Dev snatched up a second sling tied to his harness, threaded the free end through the piton ring, and tied a one-handed knot. Sweat sheened his back as he worked. Kiran dug his nails into his palms, and willed Dev's grip to hold.

Dev swung one foot down, then the other. The sling drew taut as his weight settled onto the piton. The piton held.

Dev threw his head back and laughed. The sheer joy in the sound made Kiran's breath catch. He dropped his head to his knees, heat pricking his eyes. *Our nature is the same*, Ruslan had shouted. Kiran had spat at his feet and denied it. And yet in the moment of truth, he'd proved Ruslan right.

✳

(Dev)

I climbed back down to Kiran with my blood still buzzing like I'd drunk an entire cask of firewine. I felt light on my feet as a full-fledged Tainter. Almost, I believed I could step off the cliff and float free in the air the way I'd used to. Gods, I hadn't felt this good in years.

"Got us a decent stone," I announced. Kinslayer hadn't disappointed.

Several thumb-sized lumps of red crystal waited in my belt pouch. One to peek Pello's wards, and the rest I could sell for a tidy little sum once back in Ninavel. The more coin I had before trying to slip Melly from Red Dal's grasp, the better.

"You nearly died." Kiran's voice was flat. The tight curl of his body reminded me of the way he'd huddled during the storm, but his eyes were narrowed, rather than wide with fear.

"Aw, did that little slip scare you? Trust me, I've come closer to Shaikar's hells than that." Not much closer, in truth. I inhaled and stretched, remembering the cold shock of my hand breaking loose. Every fleck of mica on the granite had blazed into knife-edged clarity, every beat of my heart loud as thunder. I'd never felt more alive.

Kiran's eyes narrowed further. "It wouldn't have mattered what I said beforehand, would it? You wanted to do that climb."

"Of course I wanted to do the climb." What outrider wouldn't? I surveyed my route up the gleaming arc of cliff, and sighed in satisfaction. Sun winked off my single piton, still jammed in the fingers-width crack beneath the carcabon layer. Every outrider who traveled this canyon would know someone had conquered Kinslayer.

"So it's all right for *you* to endanger everything," Kiran snapped.

I took in his clenched fists and the sweat drying on his temples. Well, I was no stranger to fear-fueled anger. I shrugged back into my shirt. "Difference is, I didn't take a risk for no reason. Now we can take care of Pello's charm. You'll feel better then, you'll see."

Kiran twitched and turned his face away. I blinked, puzzled. Anger I could understand, but now he had the shifty-eyed look of a Tainter who'd screwed up an important job. Was he so touchy over his panic after the storm?

"How do we get down?" he asked. He still wouldn't look at me.

I started shaking out the rope. "I'll lower you, and then I'll climb down after you. Just face in to the rock, push your body away from it with your feet, and walk down as I let out the rope."

Kiran glanced over the edge and swallowed.

"Don't worry, it'll be a lot easier than the climb up." I made sure the rope ran properly through the system of pitons and around my waist, ready for the belay. "When you were, uh, *exploring* the catsclaw yesterday, did you notice anything unusual?"

"Like what?" His shoulders hunched up even higher.

I waved a hand at the silver-green mass of catsclaw far below. "See those black patches?" I'd confirmed early this morning while getting water that my eyes hadn't been tricked by the fading light of evening. Whole groups of bushes had died, their leaves withered and blackened as if burned. "None of us have seen anything like it before, not even Jerik."

"Could it be from...lightning strikes, perhaps?" Kiran wore a frown, but the guilty expression had faded. His twitchiness wasn't over last night's disappearing act, then.

"Maybe. But I heard Harken telling Cara this morning that some of the drovers are worried about their mules. Seems they're off their feed, like they're sick. And from up here, looks to me like the sick mules are from wagons closest to those burned patches."

Now he looked upset. "Will they be all right? The mules?"

"Who knows?"

Kiran leaned over to peer down at the convoy, biting his lip. "Will this delay us in reaching Kost?"

His worry was so evident that I relented. "Nah. From what Harken said, the mules are still able to pull. Just seems odd. You sure you didn't see anything in the catsclaw?"

His shoulders relaxed a little. "No," he said softly. "I didn't notice anything. I was...a little distracted, at the time." He glanced at me. "By the way, Cara's coming up the talus."

I leaned over, and made a face. She sure was. Stomping up the boulders like she meant to grind them into powder, in fact. No doubt she'd prefer to crush me instead. "Brace yourself. Soon as we're down, she's gonna flay me raw."

"She cares about you." He said it low, but I still heard the bitter undertone. Yeah, somebody had burned him, and recently, too. The lover he'd denied? Or the father he'd choked over? Regardless, I didn't bother to correct him. He'd learn soon enough that Cara's fury wasn't over my personal well-being. I'd broken the main unwritten rule of outriding—no risky climbs while on a job unless absolutely necessary—and as head outrider, she had to make me regret it.

I cast another fond glance at Kinslayer. Ah well. A climb like that was worth an ass kicking, even without the carcabon stones.

"You ready?" I asked Kiran.

He nodded. I helped him ease himself around to face the rock. He took a deep breath, and his face settled into the grim concentration I remembered from when he'd first crawled onto the ledge. I suppressed a grin. I'd seen that same determination on Sethan once, as he struggled with ice-coated holds on a difficult route.

The rope inched through my hands, and Kiran disappeared over the edge. The sharp focus I'd needed for Kinslayer hadn't yet faded, and in that cold, clear light, my half-formed suspicions about him solidified into certainty.

Kiran had an enemy back in Ninavel. Not just some faceless opposing merchant house, but someone specific he'd crossed. Someone Kiran believed didn't yet know of this little venture—but rich enough that if he found out, he could hire a mage to target Kiran. Maybe a relative, maybe a rival in love…either way, someone Kiran both feared and couldn't avoid within the city. Kiran hadn't wanted to leave Ninavel, that much was plain. No, he'd signed on for this trip out of desperation strong as mine.

I knew why, too. Once Kiran reached Alathia, not even a Ninavel mage could touch him—the Alathian border wards were rumored to be impenetrable, an invisible barrier surrounding the entire country that no spell and no foreigner could breach. Gods knew Bren had spent years trying to figure out a direct way through, without success. He was stuck using couriers like me to smuggle a trickle of goods past the Alathian guards at the few border gates. And within the border, all Alathia's cities lay smothered under a blanket of detection spells meant to alert their Council the instant anyone tried any magic more powerful than simple household charms.

But until Alathia, Kiran would be fair game. No wonder he was jumpy as a scalded polecat, and trying so hard to hide it. I ought to be mad as hell. Only thing was, I had a powerful hunch Kiran's enemy didn't need a mage. Bren's covert instructions made plenty of sense, if he and Gerran had worked a side deal with someone who wanted to both profit from Kiran's venture and ensure he never returned from

Alathia. Now I understood why Bren had been so insistent on my silence. He'd likely known I'd figure out this much. And he'd made it clear that if I warned Kiran, I'd forfeit all my pay.

Gods all damn him, anyway. If it came down to Kiran's safety against Melly's, I knew which one I'd choose. But I sure didn't like it.

The rope went slack in my hands. Kiran had reached the ground. An indistinct murmur of voices drifted up. Then Cara's yell came, loud enough to shatter stone.

"Dev! Get your ass down here!"

She sounded ready to rip my limbs off. Well, I'd stalled long enough. Time to face the minder.

CHAPTER FIVE

(Dev)

Cara lit into me before I'd even gotten both feet on the ground. "What the hell was that?" She stalked past Kiran, who flinched back like a man faced with a scorpion. I didn't blame him. The scowl on Cara's face could have melted lead.

"A climbing lesson?" I said. No good starting with an apology right off; that'd only rouse Cara's suspicions. If she realized I'd made a deliberate plan to climb Kinslayer for my own profit, she'd fire me on the spot.

Her fists clenched, and I hurriedly dropped my pack. I had to play it brash, but not so cocky that she fired me out of sheer annoyance.

"I know, I shouldn't have made the climb. But I was training Kellan, and I happened to spy a route, and I couldn't resist..." I tried to look contrite, but a grin pulled at the corners of my mouth. I threw my arms wide. "A first ascent of Kinslayer, Cara! Come on, you know you would have climbed it in my place."

Cara's gimlet-eyed glare only intensified. "Shaikar take you, Dev! If I'd realized you hadn't outgrown this kind of shit, I'd never have signed off on hiring you. You're not on some solo jaunt—you've got a responsibility to this convoy! You think because we're friends, I'll overlook whatever brainless stunts you pull? You can gods-damned well think again!"

"I got stupid, okay? I admit it. But, Cara…" She was a climber, same as me. Surely underneath her anger, a hint of sympathy lurked. I let the memory of the climb swallow me. Mind and body and stone, locked in perfect unity… "It was *glorious.*"

I had one instant to realize it was Kiran who showed a glimmer of wistful recognition, not Cara. Then Cara's fist slammed into my jaw.

I staggered sideways into the cliff. One hand darted to the boneshatter charm hidden in my belt, before I caught myself. "What the fuck?"

She advanced on me with a murderous look in her eye. "Glorious? I saw that slip of yours. It's only by Khalmet's choice you're standing here at all! You think I want to scrape your bloodsoaked carcass off the rocks, the way you did with Sethan? Did you forget how glorious that was?"

Blood pouring black from Sethan's mouth, gleam of bones poking through his side, and I didn't want to look lower, oh mother of maidens, how could he still be alive? I clenched my jaw, and welcomed the white-hot stab of pain where Cara's fist had landed.

"Leave it, Cara." She hadn't watched Sethan die. What the fuck would she know about it?

Cara jabbed a finger at my chest. "The hell I will. Accidents are one thing; we all feel Khalmet's touch in the end. But this! You'd be dead through your own gods-damned stupidity. At least Sethan's death wasn't his fault!"

"No, it was your father's," I snarled.

Cara's head rocked back. Hurt flared in her eyes, before they went hard as granite.

My anger died to ashes. Shit. Clearly I hadn't learned a thing from my fight with Jylla. I scrubbed a hand over my face, praying I hadn't just destroyed a years-long friendship.

"Cara…I didn't mean that. Truly. Denion made the best call he could. Nobody could've predicted a rockfall that big, after such a brief storm." My buoyant energy from Kinslayer leaked away, leaving me weary and a little sick. I knew how bad it had burned Cara when no convoy would hire her father again, despite his forty years of experience. How she'd flinched when tavern gossips proclaimed Denion's incompetence had killed all those men, as if they knew anything about weighing risks in the mountains. Gods damn me, why couldn't I rule my tongue? Jylla had deserved every harsh word, but Cara was only doing her job.

My apology made all the impact of a pebble thrown at a glacier. Cara eyed me with a frozen disdain that was worse than any of her anger. "Maybe money's the only language you'll understand, Dev. I'm docking half your pay for this run. If I catch you jeopardizing your safety or that of the convoy again, you're out of a job."

"Fine." My pay as an outrider was a pittance compared to what Bren had promised me. She could dock it all, if it'd thaw the ice in her eyes.

"One more thing," Cara said, still in a voice colder than a snowmelt stream. "Hand over those carcabon stones."

"What?" Damn it, she might have let the stones slide, if I hadn't ripped her so hard. "You dock my pay, that's fair. Taking my property, that's not."

"You think I'm going to let you profit from this?" She folded her arms. "If you want to stay on with this convoy, hand them over. Or head back to Ninavel. Your choice."

Behind Cara, Kiran was twitching like he'd stepped on a fire ant nest. He opened his mouth. I scowled at him. Last thing I needed was for him to stumble in and make things worse. Thank Khalmet, he took the hint and subsided, although the glare he directed at me nearly matched Cara's.

I slapped my belt pouch into Cara's hand, and prayed she wouldn't search my pack. "There. You happy?"

"Not in the least." She opened the pouch and checked the contents. Aimed another freezing stare my way, then rounded on Kiran. "You want to be an outrider, kid? Then learn this lesson well. The lives of everyone in the convoy depend on us. If you can't put that responsibility over your own desires, do us all a favor and stay home. Got it?"

Kiran's mouth tightened to a thin line. He stared at the ground and jerked his head in a nod. Khalmet's hand, you'd think he'd been the one caught climbing Kinslayer. He'd better learn to control that face of his before we faced the guards at the Alathian border.

"Crews are almost done clearing the trail. I'd better see you two back on station at the convoy before we move." Cara stalked off down the talus.

I blew out a breath. "Well, that could've gone worse."

Kiran raised his eyes to give me a disbelieving look. "I don't see how. You risked your life and our cover in the convoy, and we don't even have a stone to show for it!"

"Oh, relax." I slid a hand deep inside my pack and retrieved the carcabon stone I'd stashed there. "Why d'you think I made sure to chip out more than one stone?"

A gratifying mixture of surprise and relief flowed over his face. "You knew she'd take them?"

"I like to be prepared." Too bad nothing else about the conversation had gone the way I'd planned. My jaw throbbed like a demon singer's drum. More, I had a sinking feeling Cara's forgiveness would be a long time coming.

I tossed Kiran one end of the rope. "Coil that, and I'll pack up the rest."

He began looping the rope over his shoulders. Without looking at me, he said, "When we were on the cliff, you didn't tell me nobody had ever climbed Kinslayer before."

It had the sound of an accusation. I slammed a set of pitons down with a resounding clang. "Didn't we go through this already? I climbed it. We've got a stone. End of story."

"No, I didn't mean…" He hesitated. Twisted a section of the rope in his hands. "I only wondered how you learned to climb so well."

Meaning, he wanted to ask me about Sethan, but he didn't quite dare. Damn her eyes, why'd Cara have to drag the past up in front of him?

I shrugged. "Learned it young, that's all." And not from Sethan. No, for that I could thank Red Dal. He made sure all his Tainters learned to climb. A Taint thief can float more loot down from highside spires if he doesn't have to lift himself, too. I'd been better at it than most, just like I'd been more Tainted than most. Yeah, Red Dal had been over the moon about me in my Tainted days. I'd been so proud to earn his jubilant smiles and fatherly hugs. Shame I'd been too young and dumb to realize he didn't care two kenets about me, only for the profit I brought him. He'd sold me off without a second thought the moment my Taint failed.

Not a subject I wanted to discuss, either. Good thing I knew a quick way to shut Kiran up.

"How about you? What kinds of things did you learn as a kid?"

Kiran's face went shuttered and still. "Things from books, mostly. Nothing like climbing." He bent over the rope again.

Ha. Better than a silencing charm. It wasn't until he finished with the rope that he spoke again.

"When will we use the stone?"

I laced my pack shut and stood. "Once again, there's no 'we' here. You stay clear, and I'll handle Pello."

Kiran heaved an exasperated sigh. "All right, when will *you* hunt for Pello's charm?"

"Soon as I know for sure he'll be away from his wagon a nice long while." Something that'd be a bitch to arrange, for a man as wary as Pello. Before I moved, I hoped to gain one vital piece of information on his charm stash. And unless I missed my guess, Pello himself would provide it.

❋

(Kiran)

Kiran reached out a hand to feel the spray of the stream on his skin. The water tumbled through a rock slot in a white roar of foam. Never in his life had Kiran seen so much water, moving so quickly. The sheer wonder of it eased the bitter tangle of his thoughts and brought new energy to his aching body.

Even Dev's mood seemed improved by the sight. He'd been stone-faced and silent all the long afternoon ride. As they'd set up camp for the night, he'd spoken only in terse orders. But when he and Kiran emerged from a pine grove to confront the stream, the grim cast to his face softened.

Dev straddled the stream, his feet braced in rocky crevices. His arm muscles stood out in sharp relief as he held a jug against the force of the water. "Nothing like this in the city, huh? Wait 'til we get over the pass—then you'll see lakes."

Lakes. Kiran knew what they were, had seen illustrations and even scry-visions of them. But to see all that water with his own eyes—he found it incredible to imagine. He couldn't help a smile at the thought. Dev gave him an answering smile, one of his real ones, free of any trace of sarcasm or condescension.

Kiran's smile died as guilt clawed him again. Memory presented him with Alisa's voice, unwontedly serious. *Every life matters, don't you see? Rich or poor, we all have hopes and dreams, and people who love us.* Her words had struck a chord deep inside him, in a spot long left uneasy by Ruslan's harsher teachings. He'd agreed without hesitation, captivated as much by Alisa's ideals as the radiance of her smile.

Yet today on the cliff he'd have sacrificed Dev as surely as if he'd used a knife.

Kiran cast a stone into the stream with a vicious twist of his hand. He vowed silently that next time would be different. Next time, he'd make a choice worthy of Alisa, and accept the cost.

Within his mind, a small voice spoke—not in Ruslan's mocking tones, but in Lizaveta's gentle ones. *Make all the vows you like,* it whispered, fond and pitying. *You cannot change what you are.*

Dev was staring at him. Kiran hastily schooled his face and asked, "Where does all this water come from? And how can it be here with no one using it?"

Dev chuckled, though his gaze lingered. "It's not here long. This is snowmelt from the east side of the highest peaks. You only see this in the early season, and the water disappears into the soil of the lower slopes before it ever reaches the Painted Valley. The really heavy snows happen west of the mountain crest, so most of the water flows to the west. That's why Ninavel doesn't get any."

Dev handed the filled jug over to Kiran. He untied the dustcloth from around his neck, bent and wet it in the stream, then pressed it against the spreading bruise that darkened his jaw. His eyes shut in obvious relief.

"Didn't you bring any healing charms?" Kiran had never used such things himself, but he'd heard from Alisa that the untalented mended their injuries with charms and herbal potions.

Dev slanted a wry glance his way. "Healing charms don't come cheap. I wouldn't waste one on something this small." Dev hopped back over the water. "C'mon. We're helping Harken with cooking duty tonight, since we've finally made it to a decent campsite."

Reluctantly, Kiran left the marvel of the stream. At least the pine trees surrounding their camp were nearly as fascinating. Trees were rare in the city, even in the largest of gardens. The only pine tree he'd ever seen in Ninavel had been head-high with thin branches and sparse clumps of silvery needles. These trees reached more than three or four times that high, with gnarled heavy branches bristling with deep green. Pine cones and fallen needles littered the ground around the ever present rocks.

When they reached the wagon, Dev dug in a box and produced a set of fire stones. After clearing out stray pine debris from a small ring of rocks, he set the glossy black stones within. He pulled a knife from his belt and pricked his finger, letting a drop of blood fall and muttering the charm's activation words. Magic rippled against Kiran's barriers, gently enticing. Kiran clamped his hands on his knees. One day, the temptation would fade. He refused to believe otherwise.

The stones flared with red and blue flames. Dev sat back in satisfaction.

"Good. Last time out, we had a set where the damn mage who made them hadn't cast the charm properly, and I had to trade a good vermin ward to a stonemason to get hot food." He handed a battered tin pot to Kiran. "Here, fill this with water and set it on the stones."

Harken ambled over, a small brass chest cradled in his callused hands. "My thanks for fetching water, lads. I'll handle it from here." He opened the chest, and the pungent aromas of curry and crushed carrow seeds rose into the air. Kiran's mouth watered. It felt like years since he'd eaten anything but hardtack and jerky.

Harken stopped Dev as he passed. "Here, take this." He pressed a thin copper disc traced with dark runes into Dev's hands. "I brought it to treat sandfly bites, for the horses. Near wore it out, back in the desert, but it might have a thread of power left. It'd be a shame if that jaw of yours was too sore to chew my famous rasheil-nut curry."

A hint of red tinged Dev's brown skin. "Thanks," he muttered. He smeared a drop of blood on the charm and held it to his jaw. Kiran tried to unobtrusively shift position to get a view of the runes. Ruslan had dismissed healing charms as unworthy of study. *A mage has no need of such trivialities, and should you injure one of the* nathahlen *beyond repair, simply obtain another to suit your purpose. Men without magic are common as grains of sand.*

Kiran flinched, thinking of Dev on the cliff. Oh yes, he'd learned Ruslan's lessons well.

The tiny flutter of magic as Dev's bruise faded to a shadow conveyed little information. Dev flipped the charm back to Harken before Kiran could think of an excuse to inspect it.

Jerik emerged from the trees with another full water jug. Behind him strolled Cara and Pello, talking and laughing like old friends. Dev greeted them as casually as ever. Cara jerked her chin in a stiff, brusque nod, and walked to the opposite side of the fire. Pello's gaze flicked between them. His smile edged wider.

Kiran's stomach tightened. He took care to sit in the shadow of the wagon. Dev showed no sign of nerves around Pello, but Kiran didn't trust himself to manage the same.

"Real food, thank the gods." Cara inhaled with a beatific expression. She turned to Pello. "Want to join us for dinner? Harken's a hell of a cook."

Pello shook his head. "Much as that would please me, I should return to my own wagon." He ran his hands through his mop of curls with a longsuffering sigh. "I must inventory my supplies tonight. I fear I didn't lace my wagon cover tightly enough this morning. An animal got in while I was away working on the rockfall."

Kiran barely stopped himself from jerking in surprise. He glanced at Dev, who was leaning against the side of the wagon watching Pello with a blandly civil expression. Dev had worked alone that morning, while Kiran slept. He could have searched Pello's wagon—but why, before they'd secured a carcabon stone? Surely he wouldn't be so foolish as to put Pello on his guard before they had a real chance of finding the charm.

Dev's face provided no clues. Kiran tore his gaze away, hoping Pello hadn't noticed.

"Marmots are the spawn of Shaikar," Harken said. "Next time, bring a stronger vermin charm. The kind cityfolk buy keep out rats well enough, but not bigger animals."

"But if you do, remember to stash it this side of the border." Dev's one-sided grin made a fleeting appearance. "The Alathians have no sympathy for a convoy man's troubles."

Had Pello's eyes flickered? Kiran leaned forward.

Pello made a rueful face. "Ah, the things one learns too late. We have no such troubles on the southbound route."

"Yeah? So what brings you westbound?" Dev said, all polite interest.

Pello smiled at him, his dark eyes glinting. "A favor to a friend, as it happens. One of his regular men became unreliable, and he asked me to fill in." His smile sharpened. "I'm sure you understand, Dev, after your recent experience with unreliable friends."

"What's this?" Cara looked back and forth between Dev and Pello. Dev's expression stayed polite, but Kiran saw his fist clench, low at his side in the wagon's shadow.

"Surely you heard the sad tale?" Pello's eyes locked with Dev's. "It was all over Acaltar district before we left, how Dev's partner cast him aside like a burned-out charm."

Cara straightened, her mouth falling open. "Mother of maidens, Dev, that bitch finally cut you loose? No wonder you—" She stopped short.

Dev's breath hissed out through his teeth. "Yeah, Jylla and I split," he said, sharply. "Not that it's anybody's business but ours." Kiran winced in sympathy. From the look on Dev's face, he'd rather crawl through magefire than discuss whatever had happened. Kiran knew how that felt. He bowed his head, fighting back thoughts of Alisa.

"Ah, but when lovers are business partners, that's where the sadness comes in." Sympathy dripped from Pello's voice. "I heard she played you like a wind pipe. You did all the work, while she dallied with half the men in the city. Then she took your accounts and—"

Dev shoved away from the wagon. "Don't believe everything you hear," he growled, and advanced on Pello.

Cara sprang to her feet. "Enough!" She pointed at Dev. "You, back off. I'll have no fighting here." Dev grimaced and slouched back against the wagon. Cara turned to Pello. "You, out. I didn't invite you to our fire so you could provoke my riders."

"My apologies if I offended." Pello dipped in an ironic bow. "I'll leave you to your dinner." He vanished into the darkness.

Cara broke the awkward silence. "Whatever bad blood's between you and Pello, Dev, that's the last I want to see of it on this trip."

Dev didn't answer. He was scowling after Pello, but to Kiran's surprise, his eyes looked more thoughtful than angry. Kiran nudged him.

Dev blinked and bared his teeth in a grin at Cara. "I'll keep out of his way, if you keep him out of mine."

"Food's ready," Harken announced, leaning over to look in the pot. Kiran wasn't the only one who let out a sigh of relief. As Jerik set out bowls and Harken ladled portions, Kiran edged closer to Dev. Under the rattling of Harken's spoon in the pot, he whispered, "Why did—"

"Later," Dev muttered sharply. Kiran sat back in frustration. Later, when? Dev had warned him earlier the other tarps would be too close that night for safe conversation.

Cara handed round the filled bowls. When Dev took his, she leaned down and spoke quietly. "If that little sand adder ripped her fangs out of you, I get you're still working out the poison. Must be tough, leaving someone after so long. But for Khalmet's sake, don't fuck up the rest of your life over it."

For a moment, Dev looked weary beyond bearing. Then his face smoothed out, all expression vanishing. "Are we scouting tomorrow morning?" he asked, loud enough for everyone to hear.

Cara shook her head and muttered something under her breath.

She raised her own voice. "Yeah. First thing, too, so nobody stay out too late." She glanced at Kiran. "Kid, you'll join us. We'll be scouting avalanche conditions before the convoy crosses Broken Hand Pass—one of the most important parts of the job. You stick close to Dev tomorrow and pay attention."

As Cara retreated to the far side of the fire, Dev whispered, "Wait for the scout."

Kiran nodded, grudgingly. If Dev thought it necessary to be so cautious, Kiran would choke back his questions until morning. But he didn't see why they couldn't simply return to the stream and depend on the noise of the water to cover their conversation. Perhaps Dev thought Pello would anticipate such a move, and follow them? Kiran stabbed his spoon into his bowl. For the hundredth time, he regretted the necessity to hold his barriers. Without them, he'd sense Pello's presence no matter how well he hid, the man's living *ikilhia* energy burning bright as magefire flame in Kiran's inner sight. As it was, he could hardly feel the flicker of Dev's *ikilhia*, and Dev was sitting right beside him.

No one seemed eager to restart the conversation. Spoons scraped bowls, punctuating the rush of the stream in the distance. Kiran ate mechanically, barely tasting Harken's concoction. Cara's soft words echoed in his ears: *Must be tough, leaving someone after so long.* The truth of it intensified the ache in his heart. He'd spent his entire life with Ruslan and Mikail. Despite the horror of Ruslan's true nature, and Mikail's betrayal...a part of him missed them, badly. Childhood memories ran through his head, bright as sunlight. He bit down on his tongue hard enough to draw blood. The life he remembered was nothing more than a lie.

CHAPTER SIX

(Dev)

I sat cross-legged on a flat topped chunk of talus and soaked in the view. Below me sprawled the broad rock strewn basin at the head of the canyon. Dawn's light painted the surrounding peaks a vivid gold and softened the contours of the icy snowfields that spilled from their heights. To the west, between two rugged peaks lay the saddle of Broken Hand Pass, blown clear of snow by the high winds of spring. Out eastward, beyond the jagged pinnacles surrounding the deep gash of Silverlode canyon, the pale white rock of the ridges dwindled into steep gray and brown slopes and leveled out in the low sandy expanse of the Painted Valley. Ninavel was visible on the desert plain, tiny and toy-like at this distance, the firefly radiance of magelights sparkling in the valley's shadow. The splendor of the scene and the bite of the chill morning air helped to clear the cobwebs from my head.

Gods, I was tired. Though Kiran looked far worse. I eyed him as he struggled over the wagon-sized boulder below mine, his chest heaving in great gasps. Bluish circles stained the skin beneath his eyes, and his cheekbones stood out sharp as the ridgeline above us.

After all the yelling and thrashing he'd done in his sleep last night,

I thought it a miracle he had the energy to walk at all. Tonight I meant to go buy some yeleran leaf extract off Merryn, the convoy's healer. If Kiran refused to swallow it, by Khalmet, I'd pour it down his throat. Yeleran would knock him out for sure, and gain us both some much-needed sleep.

Kiran collapsed beside me with a groan. "*Now* can we talk?" he panted.

I turned to check on Cara and Jerik. High above on the slope, two dark forms squatted on the outflung arm of a snowfield. Sun winked off metal as they swung their ice axes. I had to admit, this apprentice thing had its benefits. Without Kiran, I'd be up there chopping a pit deep enough to check layers in snow still frozen from the cold of night. But Kiran couldn't match our pace on talus, even when he wasn't dragging from lack of sleep, and Cara had given me leave to hang back and watch out for him. Of course, I'd had to promise that I'd do all the heavy work on the next snow pit, when the sun would be high enough I'd be sweating like a rock bear on a sand flat.

"Yeah, we can talk," I told Kiran. "So long as you keep your voice down. Sound carries more than you'd think up here."

Kiran didn't waste another second. He blurted, "Pello was angry with you—did you search his wagon? If so, why would you do that? You can't have found his wards without the carcabon stone. Now he'll be suspicious of you, so how can you get to his charm? If he tells the Alathians about us—"

"Whoa, hold on! Take a breath before you pass out."

He sucked in a huge draught of air, and promptly doubled over in a coughing fit. I thumped him on the back and handed him a waterskin.

"Yeah, I searched Pello's wagon while he was working the rockfall. For two reasons. First, imagine you're Pello, and you come back and realize someone's pawed through the very place where you've hidden a warded charm stash. What's your first move?"

Kiran blinked at me, still red-faced. "I'd...make sure the wards remained intact and none of the charms had been taken."

"So, Pello checks his charms, finds them all still there, and then reactivates his wards. Which means they're nice and fresh and fully powered."

Kiran's mouth rounded into an "oh" of understanding. "A recently activated ward should react more strongly to the look-away charm."

"Exactly." Even with the carcabon to boost it, the look-away was such a minor charm that I wasn't entirely sure it could flash the ward. I wanted all the advantage I could get.

"What was your second reason, then?"

"Insurance, in case the carcabon's not enough to find his stash. A man's reaction to a threat can tell you a lot about what he's protecting. You saw how he tried to twist my tail after I poked him about the Alathians. If he only carried personal charms, he would've been a hell of a lot more subtle about his warning. Nope, he's carrying contraband meant for profit. Good news: it means he's got to keep clear of the Alathians, same as us. Better yet, now he knows that if he sells me out to the border guards, I'll happily return the favor the instant they put me under truth spell."

Kiran pulled off his woolen cap. He turned it over in his hands, thoughtfully. A tiny, dry smile pulled at his mouth. "What did he learn from your reaction?"

I snorted. "Nothing he didn't know already." Hell, Pello'd even done me a good turn. Now that Cara thought I'd climbed Kinslayer out of some misguided desire to lift my mood after Jylla, she might thaw a bit. Much as I hated the prospect of her lecturing me all the way to Kost, that had to be better than frozen, awkward silence.

The only part that bothered me was how Pello knew a bit too much about me and Jylla for a man who hailed from Gitailan district, not Acaltar. He must've checked up on me before the convoy left Ninavel. Maybe he'd only done it out of a shadow man's natural caution, since he knew I worked the route as Bren's courier. Or maybe it was a clue he really had signed on to sniff out our plans. All the more reason to take care of that damn message charm.

As if reading my thoughts, Kiran said, "But what about the message charm? Won't he be even more careful, now?"

"Probably." Too bad Pello wasn't the sort of man who'd assume himself safe after an apparent failure on my part to cross his wards.

"But he's on repair crew again day after tomorrow. Past Broken Hand Pass, the trail will need a lot of work; and Goranant House's lead stonemason owes me a favor. I'll get Gaven to claim Pello for rocksplitting duty—that should keep him away from the convoy long enough for me to flash and break his wards."

"Two days…" Kiran's fingers dug into the wool of his cap. "Isn't there a way you can search sooner?"

"Not a good way," I said.

Kiran's head tilted. "But there *is* another way."

Yeah, there was. One I'd considered during my sleepless night, and rejected as too dangerous. "Trust me, safest to wait for his next work shift."

Kiran gave me an urgent, pleading look. "Two days is too long! If you have another option, at least tell me what it is."

No question he was scared shitless of that enemy of his in Ninavel. I sighed. "Fine. What's the one thing guaranteed to pry Pello away from his wagon and hold his attention?" I poked Kiran's shoulder. "You. If he saw you wander off alone, he'd slink right after you, in hopes of cornering you into a conversation."

Kiran brightened. "So I would draw him away, while you disabled the charm…what's wrong with that idea?"

I scowled at him. "Shadow men are clever bastards. The moment you open your mouth, Pello will mark you for a highsider. And the longer you talk, the more he'll learn. He'll twist the conversation on you, make you reveal things without even realizing it. It's too risky."

"I'll answer him with nods and shrugs. He can't learn much from that." Eager determination shone in Kiran's eyes. "If he can't send any messages, and he's wary of Alathian interest…then even if he does realize I'm not from a lower district, the harm should be minimal."

Yeah, right. Kiran had no idea of a shadow man's wiles. Then again, a full inventory of Pello's contraband in my hands would go far towards ensuring his silence. And if Kiran's fear of his mystery enemy back in Ninavel was so strong he jumped at the chance to play bait, that was a warning I shouldn't ignore.

I'd scouted Pello's wagon already, which saved me time. Assuming the carcabon could boost the look-away enough, I figured on twenty minutes to flash and break his wards, disable the charm, and cover my tracks. Pello could find out far too much in twenty minutes. Unless… maybe I could arrange it so he'd waste time chasing Kiran down, first. Make sure the conversation was so short Kiran might have a chance of keeping his mouth shut. I thought for a moment, then fixed Kiran with a forbidding stare.

"You want me to disable that charm so bad, then listen close. If we cross the pass today, we'll camp at Ice Lake tonight. Nobody'll think it odd for a city boy like you to run straight to the lake the instant you're done with chores. If you go alone, Pello's sure to follow. You keep moving around the lake, and stay ahead of him best as you can. When he does catch up, no matter what he says, you keep your mouth shut, hear me?"

Kiran nodded, emphatically. "That won't be a problem."

"I'll come interrupt the moment I'm done with his wagon. If he starts pushing you too hard before then, then you leave, straight off. Don't worry about holding him there." Even if Kiran never said a word, Pello would read in his body language that he had something to hide—but he'd surely guessed that already.

"If you can disable that charm tonight, the risk is worthwhile," Kiran said softly.

"I hope so," I muttered. If he was wrong, I knew who'd have to handle the mess.

Cara and Jerik had left the snow pit and begun kicking their way up the snow slope, toward the broken rock tower resembling a man's upright hand that gave the pass its name. The summit of the Hand would give us an excellent view of the avalanche chutes beyond the pass. If we ever reached it.

"We gotta get moving," I told Kiran. "Snow climbing's easy to learn, but it's exhausting work."

A hint of the same fascination he'd shown at the stream joined the determination in his eyes. "Snow…does it truly freeze your skin if you touch it barehanded, like the stories say?

"You're about to find out."

※

Cara clapped when I helped Kiran onto the tilted blocks of stone forming the Hand's broad summit. "Congratulations, kid." She gave him a companionable whack on the back that nearly knocked him to his knees. "Wasn't sure you'd make it, after all your hollering last night. Did you decide the mountains were too quiet?"

I suppressed a sigh. I hadn't realized how much I'd miss Cara's cheerful mockery until none of it was directed at me. Even if Pello's tale-telling had spared me any more icy glares, the laughter still died out of her eyes whenever she glanced my way.

For once, Kiran didn't stiffen or blush at her teasing. He probably hadn't heard a word she'd said. He was gaping with eyes wide as kenet coins at the frozen sea of sharp peaks that stretched to the horizon. Immediately in front of us, the rock slabs dropped away in a thousand-foot cliff to another barren high basin full of boulders and snow. Once we crossed Broken Hand Pass, we'd have several days travel over an alpine plateau full of sharp ridges, subpeaks, and cirques before the trail plunged into the deep trench of Garnet Canyon and then made the long climb up the canyon's western wall to Arathel Pass. Beyond Arathel Pass waited the heavily forested western slopes of the Whitefires, and eventually, the Alathian border.

"How'd the snow layers look?" I asked Jerik. I might be the fastest climber, but Jerik's years of experience made him the uncontested expert in avalanche behavior.

"Nice and bonded," Jerik said. "Only one layer I didn't like. Must've had a warm spell after that snowfall. But the layer's well packed, and deep. It won't slide easy. Though if it did, we'd get a devil's lash."

Kiran turned. "A what?"

"A monster avalanche," I said. "Most avalanches happen when the top layer of snow breaks. The slide's maybe a few hundred feet wide. Enough to take out plenty of wagons. But if a deep layer breaks, the force can set the whole slope moving, maybe even all the way to bare ground. Avalanches that large can wipe out entire convoys."

"They're rare," Jerik added. "Last one was before my time."

Kiran's expression hovered somewhere between worried and fascinated. "But if you saw a dangerous snow layer…how do you know it won't slide?"

Cara laughed, not happily. "No guarantees in the mountains, kid. But don't you worry, we don't leave it entirely up to Khalmet. Layer bonding is only one of the telltales we check. Speaking of…" She slid her spyglass out of her pack and handed it to Jerik. "Let's take a look at those chutes, boys."

Jerik held the glass up to one dark eye and scanned slowly across the rugged terrain. "Shaikar's Tongue slid maybe a few days ago," he said.

I squinted at the chute he meant, a wide couloir dropping down from the upper slopes of a mountain with a distinctive double summit. Avalanche debris lay scattered at the bottom, but the slide hadn't reached as far as the trail.

Jerik lowered the glass. "Nothing more recent, and the Gate of Amaris looks good." He handed the spyglass to me, and I repeated the survey. I paused as I passed over a peak whose upper ridges were marked with streaks of darker rock.

"More snow on Iblanis than usual," I said.

"Didn't spot any big cornices, though," Jerik said. I studied the peak through the glass, carefully following the ridgelines above the chutes.

"Me neither." I finished my survey and handed the glass back to Cara. While she took her turn, I moved to Kiran's side. I nudged him and pointed down at a steep-walled semicircular bowl of rock just north of the pass. "Ice Lake's there, at the bottom of that cirque."

The lake in question was small and still choked with ice, but the pale green of melted water showed in patches near the edges. The convoy would have plenty of water without needing to melt snow. When the drovers all rushed off to fill their barrels before dark, I'd have the perfect opportunity to revisit Pello's wagon unobserved by any of his neighbors.

Perfect, so long as Pello didn't rattle Kiran into talking. If he did, the time for veiled warnings would be over. I'd have to confront Pello straight on. And if direct threats didn't work, I'd need to swallow my scruples and play a darker game, no matter the cost to others. Not a pleasant thought.

"The high mountains seem so…so stark. There's no life up here," Kiran said. His gaze tracked across the basin, a frown appearing on his face.

"You'd be surprised," I told him. "Birds, hopmice, all kinds of creatures live here. Later in the season after the snow melts, there'll even be flowers everywhere." A wistful pang shot through me as I remembered summer afternoons spent lazing beside cliffs amidst a riot of wildflowers. If I finished this damn job and at long last fulfilled my debt to Sethan…then I planned on disappearing into the Whitefires and letting clean stone and sunlight scour these last few Shaikar-cursed weeks from my head.

Kiran's face said he didn't believe me about the flowers. "Why are all the peaks named after southern demons?" he asked.

"Because they're beautiful, unforgiving, and can kill you on a whim," Cara said, grinning at him.

"They're not all named after demons," Jerik said. "But before Arkennland claimed this territory, the only people who came up here were southerners. Sulanians, Varkevians, even a few of the Kaitha. They named most of the peaks on the eastern side of the range, and their names stuck. Our name for the mountains, Whitefire, is actually a translation of an old Varkevian word for lightning. They saw the summer storms and thought it must be demons fighting."

It was the longest speech I'd ever heard from him. Cara gave a small, surprised snort. "History lessons aside, I think the convoy's safe as far as Ice Lake. We'll do some fracture testing and another layer check on the lakeside slopes, but so far the risk past the lake looks low. Agreed?"

Jerik nodded. "If deep layers go, it's usually earlier in the season."

I nodded my own assent. The risk was small enough that Meldon was sure to choose to continue. Thank Khalmet, we'd have no delays in reaching Kost. Every day brought Melly closer to her Change. The faster I finished this job and got back to Ninavel, the better.

"What would happen if you thought it was dangerous?" Kiran asked me.

"Depends on how dangerous," I said. "Medium risk, Meldon might send wagons through with much wider spacing. That way if a slide happens, hopefully you only lose one. High risk, we might wait at the lake a couple extra days, try and give things time to settle."

Cara handed Kiran the spyglass. "Here, Kellan, take a look." She looked at me. "Go on, tell the kid the signs to watch for."

It was the first thing she'd said direct to me in hours. At least she was meeting my eyes now. Progress, of a kind.

I did my best to repeat what Sethan had told me on my first trip out, while Kiran surveyed the couloirs with studious precision. Sethan had been a patient and careful teacher, with a real gift for explaining things in ways that made sense and were easy to remember. I knew I was way too impatient to match his skill in that area. Fortunately, I didn't really need it for this little charade Kiran and I were playing out, though Kiran was an excellent listener. He never twitched or fidgeted or sighed, and his attention never wandered. The intensity of his focus actually unsettled me. It didn't seem natural for a highsider. Though in truth the only other highsiders I'd met were drunken idiots who'd stumbled down streetside for gambling and cheap jennies.

Kiran, on the other hand...after I'd seen his fine clothes and smooth hands in Bren's office, I'd dreaded the idea of dragging him across the Whitefires. I'd figured either I'd be stuck listening to an endless stream of complaints, or he'd collapse under the demands of real work. Instead, so far I had to admit he'd done a decent imitation of a real apprentice. Hell, sometimes I even caught myself having fun showing him the ropes, and anticipating his moments of bright-eyed wonder. I scowled, reminding myself that it didn't matter. So he was better company than I'd imagined—so what? In the end, this was a job like any other, and I'd better keep it straight in my head that he was only another package to deliver.

✳

(Kiran)

Kiran clambered over the enormous boulders that choked the approach to Ice Lake. He darted a glance back toward the cirque's mouth, but the ragged sea of rocks blocked his view of the convoy's camp beside the trail. Traversing talus this large was more difficult than he'd anticipated; he might as well be crawling rather than walking. If Pello possessed any of Dev's easy agility, he'd surely catch up at any moment.

A thread of unease wormed through his chest. Kiran suppressed it, firmly. Pello was untalented, blind to the distinctive blaze of a mage's *ikilhia*. He couldn't possibly identify Kiran as a mage from a few short minutes of conversation, no matter how observant he was. The rest of what he might learn was trivial by comparison.

Kiran heaved himself onto the gently angled top of another giant boulder. He started to his feet, thoughts of Pello momentarily banished by wonder. He'd reached the lake.

So much water! And so different from the illustrations he'd seen. Books portrayed lake water as blue, or perhaps clear. But this water was a strange, milky green, like sunlit jade. High peaks surrounded the lake on three sides, their snowfields stretching down unbroken to the ice that still covered much of its surface. The ice was smooth and snow covered on the far end of the lake, but buckled and broken and fluted into strange shapes where it turned to open water.

Though the sun still stood a handspan above the western peaks, the air was already cooling fast, and a chill breeze wafted off the lake. Kiran shivered and pulled his overjacket tighter. He scrambled forward to the boulder's edge. The water rippling against the rock below was too far down to reach, but perhaps from the next boulder he could—

"An amazing sight, isn't it?"

Kiran froze. He'd had no warning of Pello's approach—curse the man, how could he move so quietly over such difficult terrain? He turned, careful not to lose his balance. Pello stood only a few feet away on the boulder's broad top. A water jug dangled from one hand, and a patchwork wool cap contained most of his curls. Though his grin was friendly, his dark eyes were fixed on Kiran with an intensity that prickled Kiran's skin.

Pello gestured with his jug at the lake. "Not even the hanging gardens of Reytani can compare to such a wonder…or so I'm told."

Kiran shrugged, carefully. His face felt rigid as stone. Of the thirteen highside districts, Reytani was the one Ruslan called home. Had Pello mentioned it at random? Kiran's unease swelled.

"Shy of me, are you? Never fear, I carry no scorpion's sting." Pello sauntered closer. Kiran couldn't help a glance over his shoulder. No retreat that way; only the lake. The long drop off the boulder's top to the fanged rocks on either side was more than he dared attempt. Pello blocked the only route off the boulder. He'd trapped Kiran as neatly as a thrice-spiraled ward.

Out of the roil of his emotions, power uncoiled, silent and seductive as a courtesan's dance. *No.* Kiran smothered the flame deep within. He focused grimly on the scuffed leather of Pello's boots.

"I once saw a man with skin and eyes as pale as yours," Pello said, in a musing tone. "In Prosul Varkevia, when I was a child. But he had hair black as Shaikar's heart, not brown, and spoke no civilized tongue—the shuka dancers whispered he hailed from far over the eastern sea."

Kiran raised his eyes before he could stop himself. He'd long known that his looks were unusual in the city. He'd once spent precious stolen hours searching without success through the contents of Ruslan's library for any mention of a people that might hold his heritage.

"Ah, that caught your attention." Satisfaction shaded Pello's smile. "Were you a talented boy, then? Sold off by the mother you never knew, as Dev was?"

Talented. Kiran's stomach curdled. Deliberate word choice, or not? Regardless, Pello now skirted terribly close to the truth. Silence was no longer an option—Kiran had to quash this line of thought. He recalled the cover story Dev had insisted he memorize, and lifted his chin.

"My parents are bookbinders, in Kulori district." A sliver of curiosity pricked through his anxiety. Had Dev truly been sold as a child? And if so, to whom, and why? Dev's *ikilhia* was dim as that of any untalented man.

Pello clapped his hands. "He speaks!" He cocked his head. "Bookbinders, you say...and what distant city left such a unique stamp on your family's tongue?"

Kiran knew his speech bore the influence of Ruslan's gliding vowels and harsh-edged consonants. Remnants of Ruslan and Lizaveta's native language, from a city Lizaveta had told him was no longer remembered except in tale and song.

He jerked his shoulders in another shrug. "I should get back," he mumbled. Even if he hadn't bought Dev enough time, he dared not linger. Had he really been so arrogant as to think his identity safe because Pello lacked mage talent? He truly was as prejudiced as Ruslan.

"Of course," Pello said genially. "Forgive my curiosity. Dev rarely keeps such interesting company." He took a single step to the side.

Kiran squeezed past, doing his best to ignore Pello's proximity. He sat down in preparation for sliding down the steep rock slope to the top of the next boulder.

A hand skimmed through Kiran's hair to settle on his shoulder. In a flash, Kiran was back in Ruslan's workroom, fear and fury clouding his vision. With a shout he tore himself away, raising one hand to strike even as he thumped painfully down onto rock.

"Hey!" Dev's yell slashed through his panic, dispelling the fog of memory. Kiran yanked his hand down, his heart pounding. Dev stopped short a few rocks away, staring at Pello, who pushed to hands and knees from his awkward sprawl on top of the lakeside boulder. "What in Khalmet's name is going on here?"

Kiran clenched his hands to still their trembling. His barriers still stood firm. He'd used no magic outside them, nothing Ruslan could detect. But Pello had been touching him when Kiran's power had flared, and the shock of unbridled magic had knocked him flat. Would he know a mage had felled him?

Pello staggered to his feet. His eyes met Kiran's, full of stunned realization. Kiran's heart stuttered in his chest.

He knows.

CHAPTER SEVEN

(Kiran)

The magnitude of Kiran's error paralyzed him. Time seemed to slow as Pello raised a hand to point straight at him, anger twisting his face.

"Keep a Shaikar-cursed leash on him, can't you?" Pello snapped to Dev. "Sparking a bane charm when I only offered him a helping hand…in Varkevia, a man might claim blood-right for that."

Kiran's thoughts wheeled like startled birds. The recognition in Pello's eyes, quickly as he'd masked it, had been unmistakable. Pello knew how close to death he'd come, and not from any defensive charm. Did he conceal the truth out of pure fear, or had he realized Dev's ignorance and held his tongue for reasons of his own?

Dev gave a contemptuous snort. "Yeah? We're not in Varkevia. You don't want to get charm-stung, how about you keep your gods-damned hands to yourself?" He turned a ferocious glare on Kiran. "And you—who said you could run gape at the lake when there's work yet to do? Get your lazy ass over here."

Kiran climbed silently over the rocks to Dev's side. Dev, at least, was playing out the script they'd planned. Kiran cast a glance back at

Pello, who watched him with a flat, speculative stare that raised the hairs on Kiran's neck. His hope that Pello feared his anger withered under the weight of that gaze. If Pello was even half as clever as Dev claimed, he must suspect that something prevented Kiran from magic. Otherwise, Kiran would have cast against him long before now.

Pello jumped down from the boulder. "How fortunate for you that I am a forgiving man." His tone held no hint of sarcasm.

Dev's eyes narrowed. "So long as you remember that I'm not." He and Pello stared at each other, their eyes cold and considering. At last Dev turned away and shoved Kiran into motion, back toward the convoy.

Kiran scraped and stumbled over the talus with Dev dogging his heels. Possible consequences paraded through his mind, each more unpleasant than the last. If Pello confronted Dev with the truth in an attempt to extort a bribe...if he struck a deal with the Alathians... or worst of all, if Dev hadn't succeeded in his mission...Kiran's blood ran cold. He snatched at Dev's shoulder.

"Did you disable the message charm?" he hissed in Dev's ear.

Dev glanced back toward the lake. Kiran followed his gaze. Pello had moved off along the shore, his patchwork cap bobbing into and out of view as he dodged between rocks. Dev dragged Kiran down to crouch beneath a boulder's overhanging face.

"Yeah, I took care of the damn charm. That part went smooth as Sellen wine."

Kiran's knees went weak with relief. Though disaster still loomed, it wouldn't be immediate. No hint of his location would reach Ruslan.

Dev glowered at him. "But you—what the fuck happened with Pello? 'Oh, I can keep my mouth shut, no problem'...what part of that involved a bane charm? Stinging a shadow man—Khalmet's hand, are you trying to get yourself killed? And you might as well wave a sign in his face saying you're no streetsider!"

Kiran returned his glare. "It was an accident," he said, tightly. "He startled me, and I...reacted."

A reaction that might cost him any chance of safety. Dev thought Pello's secret cargo would prevent him from going to the Alathians; that might have been true before, but no longer. The Alathians would gladly forgive a cache of illegal charms in exchange for news of a foreign mage sneaking across their border. Kiran's gut twisted. The Alathian Council would treat him no more gently than Ruslan, though doubtless their methods would be less inventive.

Dev's scowl deepened. "Tell me exactly what Pello did that upset you." When Kiran hesitated, he added, "It's important."

"He…" Blood heated Kiran's face. In retrospect, revealing himself as a mage over nothing more than a stray touch seemed unbelievably foolish. "He ran a hand through my hair. Then touched my shoulder."

"Your hair? Of course." Dev groaned and shook his head. "I'll bet you a thousand kenets he snagged enough strands that he can scout you with a find-me charm. Plus, now he'll figure out your hair's dyed, and the true color."

Kiran winced, remembering the conversation. Pello hadn't needed a hair sample to discover that. At least his stolen strands of hair would do the man little good. Lizaveta's amulet would confound any locator charm with ease.

None of it mattered, in the face of the true danger. Kiran fought to master his fear and think. There had to be a way to salvage the situation and silence Pello. But how, without magic, and without revealing himself to Dev?

Dev eyed him with a jaundiced air. "Let me guess, there's more bad news," he said. "What else did Pello find out?"

Kiran's knuckles whitened in his lap. If ever he were to reveal the truth, now would be the time. No more lies, no more careful evasions…oh, the thought was tempting. But reason triumphed over temptation. Dev would never continue helping him, if he realized the true danger he faced.

Perhaps he might disclose his identity to Dev, but pretend no other mages were involved. No, he'd never succeed in the type of elaborate lie required to keep Dev ignorant of the full truth. If only he possessed Mikail's stolid-faced, impenetrable calm!

Yet perhaps he could gain Dev's assistance without risking betrayal. Dev didn't know about the protection Lizaveta's amulet afforded.

"My employer is counting on my anonymity in Kost. Now you say Pello can track my movements there?" Kiran let his very real fear show. "He gets more dangerous by the day. We have to do something about him!"

"We are doing something," Dev said. "Or did you mean, something permanent?" A sharp, mocking grin spread over his face. "Don't think I haven't considered it. Want to know why killing Pello is a bad idea?"

Kiran shifted, uneasily. His streamside vow echoed in his ears. "I didn't mean kill him." *One touch,* a dark voice whispered. *That's all it would take…your barriers would stay intact, and you'd be safe.* He stifled the thought. Pello would never be so careless as to allow him within touching distance again, anyway.

"Uh-huh." Dev's grin remained. "Look, if Pello dies by knife, or charm, or even simply vanishes, the other drovers from Horavin House will insist Meldon investigate, and we'd all end up under truth spell. And trust me, arranging a believable accident for someone as canny as Pello is harder than you'd think. Unless you don't care who dies along with him." He gave Kiran a hard, searching look.

"No! That's not what I want! But…" Kiran floundered to a halt. What did he want, if not Pello's death? He wanted the last half hour never to have happened. No, he wanted to turn time further back, to the days when Alisa yet lived. When magic was Kiran's deepest joy, untainted by guilt and death. His throat tightened. Nothing could give him that. And now Pello stood ready to destroy his only hope of escape.

"Pello rattled you hard, and that'll make any man jumpy," Dev said. "I know it's tough on the nerves to play a slow game. But slow and subtle is the best way, here." He cuffed Kiran's shoulder. "No need to panic about the hair he grabbed. We've got at least a tenday before the convoy's in striking distance of the border. Plenty of time to set a plan, and I know dozens of ways to fool a find-me."

Kiran clenched his teeth on a protest. He didn't dare press any harder, lest Dev suspect he'd kept something back. And Dev was right, a little time yet remained. Enough, perhaps, to first attempt a solution on his own.

He had to stop behaving like the naïve child he'd once been, always relying on others for guidance and protection. He'd have no such luxury in Alathia. The sooner he embraced independence and learned to solve his problems unaided, the better. There had to be a way he could intimidate Pello into silence—the man was too smart not be wary of mages, even if he did suspect Kiran's handicap.

Besides, if he failed, then as a last resort he could still go to Dev. Tell him the truth, weather Dev's inevitable fury, and then beg, promise, threaten…whatever it took, to convince Dev to help him instead of betray him. By then, he'd have nothing to lose.

Dev was watching him thoughtfully. "Before he touched you, what questions did Pello ask?"

Back to dangerous territory. "He talked about the lake. Then he said I reminded him of someone he used to know, and asked about my family. I told him they were bookbinders." An idea occurred. "Oh, and he talked about you."

"Did he." Dev bit off the words like he'd tasted something sour.

"He said you'd been sold as a child—is that true?" It wasn't hard to let his curiosity take over.

"Pretty much." Dev leaned back against the boulder, putting his face into shadow. "Did he bring that up before or after you said your parents were bookbinders?"

"Before," Kiran said, slowly. "Why?" He wished he could see Dev's expression.

"Helps me scout his thought pattern."

Kiran devoutly hoped Dev wasn't following Pello's line of thought. "But, what he said…why were you sold?"

Dev's head tilted, his green eyes glinting in the shadow. "You weren't born in Ninavel, I take it."

"Why does—oh!" The meaning of Pello's reference to Dev as a talented boy suddenly came clear. "You were Tainted…" A thousand questions crowded Kiran's mind. The cook's boy had been Tainted, but only enough to rattle a cup from across the room, or inch pebbles around the courtyard without touching them. Kiran had been fascinated, regardless. When Mero moved a pebble, Kiran felt nothing, no matter how tightly he focused his inner senses. *You feel nothing*, Ruslan had said when asked, *because there is no magic to feel. The great forces of the confluence are powerful enough within the city's confines to affect the* nathahlen *in the womb, but the result is merely a*

*crude, fleeting ability to manipulate objects solely on the physical plane,
and only in proximity to the confluence. Magic is subject to no such
limitations.* Ruslan's dismissal hadn't lessened Kiran's interest, but
soon after, Mero had disappeared, and the other servants wouldn't
look at Kiran or Mikail, much less talk to them.

"What did the Taint feel like?" he asked Dev.

"I don't remember," Dev said flatly. He stood. "Unless you'd like
to try rock hopping in the dark, we'd better get moving. Soon as the
sun sets, it's gonna get colder than a demon's smile." The last rays of
the sun tinged the snow-laced cliffs above the lake with sullen fire.

Kiran fell silent, his relief at diverting Dev's attention tinged with
regret. The itch of his curiosity would have to go unsatisfied, for now.
He levered himself to his feet, his thoughts circling back to Pello. For
all Pello's clever deductions, he couldn't know if Kiran was working
alone. If Kiran approached him, privately, and threatened magical
retribution from a partner in Ninavel if Pello interfered in any way…
it might be enough.

"One more thing," Dev said, as he boosted Kiran up the face of
a hulking boulder. "Whatever charms you choose to carry is your
business. But I'm warning you now, you can't wear any more powerful
than household simples when we cross the border. Anything strong
like that bane charm, you'll need to hand over to me. I'll stash it safe
in the specially warded container I use to get Bren's goods past the
gate."

Kiran paused mid-scramble, dismayed. He carried nothing but
Lizaveta's amulet, which he had no intention of removing. The
amulet's protections should hide its presence from even the most
powerful of detection spells. But thanks to Pello's story, now Kiran
would have to come up with yet another convincing lie. "Fine," he
said shortly.

They made the trip back to the convoy in silence. Dev's weather
prediction proved accurate. As soon as the sun disappeared, the
temperature plummeted. Kiran had never been so cold in his life.
Even sitting as close to the fire ring as he could get, with a warm meal
in his stomach and wearing every stitch of clothing Dev had provided
for the trip, the chill seeped through to his bones.

The others seemed to feel it too. Even Jerik huddled close to the fire. Conversation during dinner was subdued, though perhaps more from the continued absence of Cara and Dev's friendly banter than the freezing night air. Kiran suspected the strained friendship bothered Dev more than he wanted to admit. Though his face and manner showed no hint of disquiet, his eyes sought out Cara whenever her attention was elsewhere.

To Kiran's relief, there was no sign of Pello. Doubtless he'd first attempt to send a message about Kiran's identity to whoever in Ninavel held the twin to his charm. Then he'd wait for his contact to exploit the information and reply. How long, before Pello realized no response would come? One day, two? Kiran had to confront him again before then, and without Dev knowing it. No easy task. Dev was a light sleeper, and during the day he rarely left Kiran's side. Perhaps during the morning bustle of packing up tarps and gear, Kiran could slip away and put his plan into action.

His resolution wavered at the memory of Pello's sharp eyes and knowing grin. He'd have to choose his threats with care, and deliver them with every ounce of arrogant confidence he could muster.

Well, he'd had an excellent role model in that regard. All his life he'd watched the untalented cower under Ruslan's burning gaze. Surely he could imitate enough of that mixture of supreme confidence and utter contempt to convince Pello the menace was real.

✳

The outrider wagon jounced out of the shadow of the cirque's cliffs into bright midmorning sunlight. Kiran pulled off his woolen cap and turned his face up to the sun, reveling in the sudden warmth. The day had dawned clear and bitterly cold, and he'd shivered his way through his chores with many longing thoughts of Ninavel's sunbaked heat.

The morning had brought no chance to seek out Pello. Dev's eyes never left Kiran, and he stuck closer than ever, as if he had some inkling of Kiran's intent. But at breakfast, Cara had announced that Dev and Jerik would do separate, solo climbing scouts that evening. Dev hadn't looked happy, but he'd had no choice but to agree. Kiran had resolved to seize the opportunity. Throughout the long morning ride, he'd imagined countless paths the encounter might take, and considered hundreds of carefully phrased threats.

The wagon jerked to a halt, nearly unseating Kiran from the outboard. He snatched at a supply sack to regain his balance. "We're stopping again?" He couldn't help the pained tone of the question. He'd already lost count of the number of stops they'd had as the convoy crawled along the southern side of the basin. At this rate, they wouldn't see the border for weeks.

"Told you there'd be lots of repairs today." Dev stood in his stirrups and peered over the wagon's stacked crates. "We've hit the Desadi Couloir. That's a wide one, still full of snow. Maybe an hour's work for today's crew to compact the snow and put down planks so the wagons can cross." Dev slouched back in his saddle and began idly retying a broken cord on one of his waterskins. His pinto mare stood patiently, her eyes half-lidded.

Kiran leaned back on a bulging sack. Towering rock crags loomed above, their massive heights buried in snow. The sky was a deep and dazzling blue, in stark contrast to the blinding white of the ridge. On the steep slope below the trail, oddly contorted pinnacles twisted skyward from the talus like isolated monoliths. Any other day the grand scenery would capture all of his attention. Instead, his thoughts turned back to Pello. What would a shadow man find most intimidating?

A faint wash of magic rippled past his barriers, like the echo from a distant shout. Kiran scrambled upright, his heart accelerating. He strained his senses. Had Ruslan—

A sharp crack split the air. Dev jerked to attention in the saddle, the waterskin falling from his hands. He twisted to stare at the peaks above. The drovers on the wagon behind him mirrored his frozen pose, faces all pointing up and leftward.

Kiran's inner senses were silent. "Dev, what—"

Dev cut him off with a harsh gesture. He kept his gaze on the peaks, one hand shading his eyes. Kiran saw only rock and snow and a small puff of cloud, spiraling upward to the indigo sky.

"Suliyya, mother of maidens..." Dev whispered. The fear in his voice stiffened Kiran's spine. He opened his mouth, only to be silenced by a piercing whistle from Dev. The shrill sound was echoed by another, and a bell clanged out an alarm from the front of the convoy.

Avalanche! With terrible clarity, Kiran saw Ruslan's intent. Unless he could reach safety in time, he'd have no choice but to use magic. He snatched for his horse's tether.

Dev smacked Kiran's hand away and gripped his arm. "Get up behind me," he ordered, his voice tight.

"But my horse—"

"Shut up and get on, damn you!" Dev grabbed Kiran's belt, lifting and pulling. Kiran barely got his leg high enough in time to slide it over the mare's back. Dev pulled his belt knife and slashed Kiran's gelding's tether free of the wagon. He tossed the tether over stacked crates to Harken, shouting, "No time to clear the slide path—ride for a pinnacle!"

Kiran caught a single glimpse of Harken's sallow face and wide eyes before Dev drove his heels into their horse's side. The mare squealed and exploded into motion. They pounded along the trail past braying mules and shouting men. Kiran risked a look up at the ridgeline. The formerly innocent cloud puff had swelled to tremendous size.

Dev cursed and jerked their mount's head to the side. The mare leapt down off the trail toward one of the twisted pinnacles below, this one broader than most. Dev drove her onward, straight up the steep scree field on the pinnacle's side. She slowed, snorting and struggling for footing on the sliding fist-sized rocks. Now that the clatter of hooves on stone was no longer deafening, a deep rumbling trembled the air.

Kiran yelled into Dev's ear, "What about the wagons—"

"Too late," Dev spat back over his shoulder.

Kiran twisted around again. The cloud was larger, and lower, sweeping down the mountainside straight toward the long string of the convoy. Frantic figures fought with horses and scrambled away from wagons.

"But all those men are—"

"I know." Dev's voice was flat. "Nothing we can do. If we live, we'll dig for survivors."

The rumbling grew loud enough to cover any screams from below, but a different voice screamed in Kiran's memory. A kaleidoscope of images whirled in his head: Ruslan's longfingered hands, black with blood; Lizaveta's cool, remote smile; Alisa's amber eyes, shimmering with terrified tears; Dev, clawing desperately for purchase on Kinslayer.

Hundreds of men would die, if Kiran surrendered to fear as he had on the cliff.

Kiran released Dev's waist and threw his weight sideways. He slid off the horse and landed in an ungainly tumble.

"What the fuck are you *doing*?" Dev screamed, struggling to turn the horse. He snatched for Kiran's arm. Kiran dodged and ran back down the scree slope in great plunging steps, barely keeping his balance.

He'd have the best chance of saving the convoy if he could place himself between the avalanche and the wagons, but would he have enough time? Worse, his need for power far outstripped his own store of energy, yet the only other source within reach was the *ikilhia* of those at the convoy.

With precise enough control, he might be able to draw *ikilhia* only from the livestock and exclude the people. He had to try. Fear churned in his guts and darkened his thoughts. The instant he worked magic, he lost all hope of remaining hidden. But if he didn't, the cost of his safety would be far too high to bear.

Kiran regained the trail and darted between two wagons. He scrabbled his way up the talus and snow on the far side. The onrushing wall of snow roared loud as thunder. No more time; he'd have to act now.

Kiran flung himself to his knees in front of a sharp-edged boulder protruding from the snow. He ripped down his barriers. Pulses of *ikilhia* burst into his perception, strung out all along the line of the convoy like a series of candles. Dull, muted pinpricks for the mules and horses, and vivid flames for the people.

In one swift movement, Kiran sliced his palms open on the boulder's ragged edge, then buried his bloody hands in the snow. The shock of connection blazed through him, and the life-lights snapped into sharper focus in his head. Hurriedly, he visualized a rough-meshed net, with holes too small for the larger lights to pass through.

Kiran threw open the gates to his innermost self and called power. In a distant part of his awareness, he registered heavy thuds and agonized squeals. *Ikilhia* flooded into him, sweet and burning.

He took as much as he dared in the few instants he had left. Magic danced in his blood, sweet as water to a thirst-parched throat, brilliant as sunlight after endless dark. Grimly, he hung on to his focus. No time for anything subtle. He would have to use brute force and hope it was enough.

Kiran raised his bloodstreaked hands. With a shout, he funneled a column of power forward. Magical energy slammed into the avalanche. The collision of forces sparked white-hot agony throughout Kiran's body as power splashed back along the conduit. He forced every shred of power back out, keeping the barrier solid, until at last the strain overcame him and he fell into blackness.

CHAPTER EIGHT

(Dev)

I fought to stay on the plunging, snorting mare as she struggled for footing. My own fault, for trying to turn her too fast—what the fuck had gotten into Kiran? The mare stumbled again, badly, and for a frantic moment I was too busy to worry about anything else.

By the time I got her sorted out, the avalanche's rumbling had died away to silence. I dreaded what I'd see when the white fog of spindrift cleared. That avalanche had been massive enough to bury the entire convoy. Countless men dead…and Kiran lost along with them, if he'd run back into the slide path. My best chance of saving Melly, consigned to Shaikar's hells.

Cold, sick foreboding filled me as I strained to see through the haze. I'd have to direct a search along with Cara and Jerik, assuming they'd survived. Dig out the crushed bodies of men I knew, their blue-tinged faces drawn in airless screams.

Slowly, the spindrift settled. The sight it revealed brought a rush of stunned relief so great it near knocked me from the saddle.

The majority of the convoy sat unharmed on the trail. Halfway down the couloir, the avalanche had split in the middle, sweeping down the edges instead of the center. The righthand river of snow had missed the convoy completely, spilling harmlessly across the trail a hundred yards in front of the lead wagon.

The lefthand slide had caught the convoy a few wagons short of the end. Scattered pieces of metal and wood poked up through the snow, all that remained of the wagons in the avalanche's path. I drove the mare back down the pinnacle's side, urging her to the fastest pace I dared on the unstable rocks. Any men buried in the thick snow of the avalanche had only minutes to live.

Deep gouges in the scree marked Kiran's running footsteps. They led straight back to the trail. I scanned the intact wagons, quickly. No sign of him, and damn it, no time to look further.

A sharp whistle pierced the air. Jerik's dark figure stood on a crag beside the slide path. He pointed first to himself, then to the broken remnants of wagons. As the closest outrider to the scene, he'd direct the first hasty search for survivors.

I whistled in reply, and stabbed a hand at the convoy to indicate I'd collect more men for the search. A third, fainter whistle echoed from the head of the convoy. I sighed in relief. Thank Khalmet, Cara hadn't been caught by the opposite end of the slide. As the mare clattered back to the trail, I glanced up at the couloir. Nothing unusual showed at the point where the avalanche had split. No rocks, no ice lumps, nothing to explain the avalanche's bizarre behavior.

Shouting, pale-faced drovers milled around wagons knocked askew by panicked mules trapped in their traces. Mid-line, many of the mules had fallen, and appeared to be so badly tangled that they couldn't rise. I burst onto the trail, and yelled loud enough to silence those within earshot, "Get down the line! Avalanche hit the tail end, we need probe teams!"

Men ducked their heads and hurried off. One man with the copper skin and dark curls of a Varkevian grabbed my stirrup, his other hand clamped around the spiked bronze loops of a devil-ward charm. "Khalmet spared us, but our mule teams are dead!" He pointed.

I rode to the front of the wagon. The mules lay collapsed in their traces, eyes staring and tongues protruding. What in Shaikar's hells?

The drover had followed me. "Neriyul said men are down too,

dead without a mark on them. The banehawk, the storm, and now this—surely we're demon-cursed—"

"You can't help dead men, but those buried in the slide still have a chance. So quit whining about demons and get the fuck down the line!" Not much hope Jerik's teams would find anyone to save, not with an avalanche as monstrously powerful as this one, but we had to try.

He swallowed and bobbed his head. Another drover, younger even than Kiran, came racing up the trail. He skidded to halt in front of me. "Jerik says he's got enough gear to hunt survivors, but he needs more probe poles and shovels before teams can search for salvageable goods."

"Tell him I'm on it." I spurred the mare back up the trail toward the outrider wagon. My heart pounded as we passed more sets of dead mules and a few limp bodies of men. What in Khalmet's name had happened? And where the hell was Kiran?

A familiar scuffed boot poking out from behind a boulder caught my eye. I hesitated, then jerked the mare to a halt. Damn it, if Kiran was dead like those mules, I had to know. I scrambled around the rock.

He lay sprawled face down. Blood stained the snow red around his outflung hands.

I dropped to my knees and reached for the pulse in his neck, sending up desperate prayers to both Khalmet and Suliyya.

His pulse beat steady under my hand. I passed shaking fingers over my eyes, then ran my hands over his body in a rapid search for wounds. I found none other than the cuts on his palms. From the blood streaking the edge of a rock above him, maybe he'd tried to catch himself as he fell.

I eased him over onto his back. He was completely unresponsive, his face ice-pale. Whatever had struck him down, a healer would have to sort out. I'd take him back to the outrider wagon, and send word for Merryn while I unpacked the poles and shovels.

I hauled him up and over my shoulder. Thank Khalmet he was so skinny. He was tall enough to be awkward for me to carry, but at least he wasn't very heavy. I staggered down the talus, one question repeating over and over in my head. Why the fuck had he run back to the convoy?

No answer to that unless he woke. The minute he recovered, I'd kick his scrawny highside ass so hard he'd never dare to leave my side again. I slung him over the mare's saddle with a grunt of relief, and swung up behind. As I urged the mare onward, I glanced up at the couloir.

The split in the avalanche path was directly in line with where I'd found Kiran. Icy shock stopped my breath.

Highside or streetside, no charm I'd ever heard of had the power to stand against an avalanche. But a mage...yeah, a mage could pull that off.

All at once, the nagging little discrepancies about Kiran reshuffled themselves into a terrible new pattern. Oh, no. Oh, fuck, no. How could I have been so fucking stupid?

I'd always thought of mages as living in their own arrogant, unknowable world, for all they shared the city with the rest of us. Gods knew even the lesser ones either stalked past like ordinary folk mattered less than sandflies, or drifted along with an eerily distant expression that was scary as shit. I'd never imagined a mage as a naïve soft-spoken kid, desperate to leave his troubles behind.

Unless that was only a role Kiran had played, for some strange reason of his own. I eyed the limp form draped over my saddle, warily. But then why divert the avalanche and save the convoy, when he'd been safe at my side?

Twisted metal and shattered wood filled my mind's eye. He hadn't saved all of the convoy. And Pello's wagon was one of those hit.

Last night, at Ice Lake...the odd tension I'd seen beneath Pello's show of anger, and Kiran's white-faced insistence that I do something about him...oh, shit, of course. I'd thought Pello merely excited over marking Kiran as a highsider, but he must have marked him as more than that. And Kiran...when I'd refused to act, had he decided to take matters into his own hands?

An even more unwelcome thought piled in. Assuming Kiran's nerves hadn't all been an act, and he did have an enemy back in Ninavel...not some rich highsider, but another mage? Khalmet's bloodsoaked hand! One thing to risk some wealthy bastard *maybe* hiring a disinterested mage to fire off a spell…another thing entirely to face an angry mage with a personal grudge.

I swallowed, my throat dry as bone. If I was right about any of this, then taking this job was the biggest mistake of my life. *Better to dance barefoot in a scorpion pit than play a mage's game,* the streetside saying went. Bren's money would do me no good if I didn't survive to use it.

Maybe I was wrong. Maybe I was so spooked from the avalanche that I'd read far too much into a simple coincidence of position. I had no proof, damn it, and no more time for speculation. Not with so much urgent work to do. Mage or not, I had no choice but to dump Kiran at the outrider wagon for now and worry about the truth of his identity later.

When my laden mare cantered up to the wagon, I found Cara already digging through crates and throwing probe poles into a stack on the ground. Deep lines bracketed her mouth, and the shadow of her father stood in her eyes.

"Mother of maidens, not the kid, too?" She hurried over and helped me lift Kiran into the back of the wagon.

"What d'you mean, 'too'?"

"Found Harken two wagons down, with Bartel and Korro. All three of 'em barely breathing and limp as dead shiftmice. Merryn says he can't wake them." She tossed me a blanket and the box of old cloth strips Harken used for quick bandages.

"Damn it, I gave Kellan's horse to Harken, told him to ride." My voice came out all rough. Proof be damned, my gut insisted this crazy mess had something to do with Kiran. In which case Harken and all the other downed men were my fault, for bringing him along on the trip. An awful weight settled beneath my ribs.

"Bartel's two sons showed up on Kellan's gelding just as I left," Cara said. "Harken must have passed the gelding off to them. You know he and Bartel are friends from way back."

"Khalmet's hand, what a crazy thing to do. If that avalanche had run true, they'd never have had time to get clear." I twisted a ragged strip of linen around Kiran's palm with unnecessary force.

"Good thing it didn't, then." Cara's voice was tight, and I knew she was thinking of the catastrophic casualties if it had.

"You didn't make a bad call." I shoved a wadded blanket under Kiran's head. "Conditions weren't right for the couloir to slide." That was as close as I dared come to my suspicions. That sharp crack right beforehand, almost too loud to be natural...sign of a magical trigger?

The bleak look didn't leave her eyes. "Maybe not, but men are dead anyway." She dropped a hand on my shoulder. "Merryn's moving down the line, tending to the injured. He'll help Kellan if he can. I need you to come work the probe teams."

"I know." I snatched up a pair of shovels. When Kiran woke up, I wanted answers. If he woke. I pictured Harken lying crumpled and silent, and my throat closed. No, damn it. Surely they'd all recover.

The avalanche debris formed a vast white wall across the trail, dwarfing the remaining wagons. Soon as we reached it, the first thing I saw was Pello, sitting on the trail wrapped in a score of blankets and surrounded by a group of excited drovers. I fought to look happy over a successful rescue, instead of disgusted. How in Shaikar's name had Pello survived? Gods all damn it, the man was like a cockroach.

Jerik kicked his way down a set of boot-packed steps from the surface of the slide. He jerked a thumb at Pello. "We saw his foot sticking up through the snow and dug him out first thing. No other survivors, so far."

Cara eyed Pello and shook her head in amazement. "Somebody owes Khalmet a favor."

Yeah, and it sure as hell wasn't me. I cursed under my breath.

Pello didn't glance our way. One arm was braced over his ribs, and his copper skin had a sallow tinge. He was the very picture of a shaken survivor; but when an anxious drover offered him a flask of heated tea, the abruptness of his reach spoke more of anger than of nervous relief.

I knew the feeling. If Kiran was a mage, he was a fucking incompetent one. Men dead, wagons destroyed, and for what?

The rest of the day was long and frustrating. Cara, Jerik, and I spent hours leading men in carefully spaced lines down the path of the avalanche debris, stabbing our poles into the snow as deep as we could. All we found were two dead bodies and a few splintered crates. The rest was buried too deep. If the summer proved a hot one, enough snow might melt off by season's end for later groups to find more, but with debris this thick, maybe not. The drovers plied their poles in grim-faced silence. Some of them wore so many charms they clinked as they walked.

It was near sunset by the time Cara called a halt to the search. Meldon waved her over to the last intact wagon for a long conference. Jerik and I sat silently, watching and waiting as men straggled back to their wagons. I spent the time turning over theories, none of them good.

Most of what I knew of spellcasting came from street rumors and kids' stories, not the most reliable of sources, but I'd always heard magic took a lot more work than using the Taint. I'd been with Kiran all that morning. Surely if he'd cast a spell to trigger the avalanche, I'd have noticed. But the more I considered, the more certain I became that Kiran's enemy was responsible for the slide.

Kiran had jerked upright like he'd sat on a pin, *before* the crack had sounded. Maybe he'd sensed the magic, somehow. He'd let me carry him out of harm's way—but then he'd had the idea to use the slide to kill Pello, and run back to cast his own spell. The only part I wasn't sure of was what had happened to kill the mules and men. Maybe Kiran's enemy had sent along a death spell just in case the avalanche wasn't enough to destroy his target.

Cara returned, her face set in hard lines. "Ten men died in the avalanche, and six others were found dead mid-line. The drovers report twenty dead mule teams and four dead horses. Seven men are still unconscious including Kellan and Harken, six were unconscious for a while but woke up while we were searching, and as many as thirty more are complaining of feeling weak and sick."

She looked back to where Meldon stood, his gray-haired head lowered and his thick arms crossed. "Some of the drovers are afraid of another avalanche and want to retreat to Ice Lake to get out of the slide zones. I told Meldon the avalanche debris is thickest behind us, so I recommend going on to Pero Lake in the next cirque over. I estimate it'll take us a day to fix an onward route, and two or three days if we tried to get through what's behind."

The seams in Jerik's weathered face deepened. "We need to talk," he said. His eyes cut left and right, as if checking to see if anyone else was in earshot. Cara motioned impatiently for him to go on.

His voice lowered to a growl. "That was no natural avalanche. A layer that deep shouldn't slide after a night so cold. And you both heard that crack, loud as thunder—no layer would break so loud! More, all these dead men and animals—I've seen it before." He twisted a snow pole in his hands, looking nearly as spooked as the charm-clutching drovers. "During the mage wars, in the city. When the mages fought, sometimes afterward there'd be whole areas of animals and people, laid out like they'd dropped in their tracks. Most of 'em dead, but the ones on the edges might just be unconscious for a while. Some claimed the deaths were a deliberate scare tactic, but others said ordinary folk die whenever they're too close to a powerful spell casting."

Cara stared at him, a frown line between her blonde brows. "No surprise that magic's involved here—nobody's wanted to say it, but we're all thinking it. But you're saying somebody here in the convoy cast a spell, and the act of casting killed the men and mules nearby? I've never heard of magic working like that."

"Me neither," I said. "Hell, there'd be nobody left in Ninavel if people died every time a mage cast a strong spell." All sorts of mages came to Ninavel, with a multitude of ways of working magic. Purified metals, crystals, wind pipes, complicated formulas and rituals, knives and blood…all those had featured in one story or another. None had mentioned death as a side effect. But if Jerik was right, maybe it happened when a mage got sloppy, casting a spell in a hurry as they must have done during the mage wars. That fit all too well with my theory about Kiran making a snap decision to use the slide against Pello.

"You both know that avalanche didn't run true." Jerik's knuckles whitened on the snow pole. "I figure a mage started the slide and then directed it right where he wanted."

"Son of a bitch," Cara hissed. "The bastard responsible for this deserves to be thrown off a cliff."

I hid a flinch. More than ever, I needed to know the truth of Kiran's involvement. Preferably before Pello decided to denounce us both to the rest of the convoy.

"You said the deaths happened when mages fought. Maybe one mage started the avalanche, and another tried to save the convoy," I offered. Better to start laying some groundwork now, in case of trouble. Maybe I could paint Kiran as having saved lives instead of taking them.

Jerik snorted. "Funny how none of Horavin house's wagons were saved, then." He shook his head. "I figure a rival house decided to get creative and hired a mage to ruin Horavin."

"That's crazy," I protested. "Horavin's too small. Any house wealthy enough to pay for a spell that powerful could've bought Horavin flat out. Easier, cheaper, and a lot less chance of nasty retaliation from Horavin's allies."

"Then maybe the head of Horavin looked cross-eyed at the wrong kind of mage," Jerik said. "I've seen them destroy men for less."

"Khalmet's bones, I can't believe this." Cara pressed her fingers to her forehead and rubbed. "Shaikar take all mages! How are we supposed to know if some asshole's about to bring down another slide on our heads?"

"Nothing the likes of us can do about magic." Jerik jabbed his pole into the snow as if he imagined it piercing a man instead. "You'll have to warn Meldon and let him weigh the risk."

Cara sighed. "I'll go talk to him, but you're coming with me. I want you to tell him exactly what you remember."

"I'll head back to the wagon and set up camp," I said. I needed some time to think. Cara nodded, absently. She squared her shoulders and strode back to Meldon's side. Jerik stumped after her. I didn't envy them. Meldon wasn't going to be pleased.

Overhead, wispy clouds faded from the pink of sunset toward the gray of twilight. I hurried past groups of men dragging dead mules off the trail. Cara had said earlier that Merryn had taken Harken and a few of the other unconscious men back to his wagon, saying their pulses concerned him, but he'd thought us competent to tend Kiran. Last she'd heard, Kiran hadn't woken yet. If Khalmet favored me, I'd get a chance to search both him and his gear before Cara and Jerik returned. I didn't know if I'd find anything, but I sure wasn't going to miss the chance to try.

The wagons nearest ours were abandoned and silent, their drovers either downed like Harken, or away helping with clean-up work. I rounded the back corner of the outrider wagon and stopped dead.

Pello stood bent over Kiran's limp body. His eyes were rimmed with white, and metal glinted in one hand.

"Get the fuck away from him!" I shoved Pello back without stopping to think.

Next thing I knew, I was face-down on the trail with my arms wrenched up behind my back and Pello's knee planted on my spine. I heaved against his hold. He jabbed his fingers into a nerve in my neck. Red agony unstrung my muscles.

I gasped a curse into the dirt. Should've struck first with my boneshatter charm, if I meant to tangle with a shadow man. I'd never been much good at fighting—you don't need fists when you're Tainted. I'd learned a few dirty tricks after my Change, but I'd spent far more time climbing than brawling.

Pello snarled into my ear, "You think a few years stealing trinkets qualifies you to play shadow games? You don't even know what board you're playing on."

"I'm not the one Shaikar nearly took today," I gritted out. He yanked my arms higher, and stabbed the nerve again. Black spots danced in my vision.

"If I killed you now, I'd be doing you a favor, little thief." Pello's laugh held a bitter edge. "But today, I am in no mood for favors. Far more satisfying to leave you to face the truth of how foolish you've been."

All at once, his weight left me. I rolled and freed the boneshatter charm from my belt, but it was too late. He'd already vanished beyond the dark bulk of the next wagon, and I wasn't dumb enough to try chasing him down in front of other drovers.

I rubbed abused arm muscles. Fucking shadow man. Did he really think I hadn't figured out this was a mage's game? I spat between forked fingers, and turned to Kiran's pale, still form. The blankets were unwrapped, and Kiran's clothes looked rumpled. Pello must have searched him. Maybe he'd taken anything there was to find, but I'd search again anyway.

The light was fading fast. I lit a candle lantern and began a methodical check through Kiran's pockets. I'd finished with his pants and was moving up to his shirt when a glint of metal caught my eye. A few links of a thin silver chain had spilled out of his shirt collar. I untied the top lace of his shirt and pulled the chain out.

My breath stopped for the second time that day. A silver amulet the size of my palm dangled from the chain. The complex, whorled design was studded with seven gems, all different in type and color. Two of the gems were blackened, the silver around them marred by dark streaks. I reached to pick it up for closer study. Warning sparks stung my skin, and I jerked my hand back. From the feel of those sparks, the amulet had a warding powerful enough to kill anyone who tried taking it off Kiran.

I didn't know what the amulet was for, but I sure as hell knew what it meant. This thing made my warding bracelets look like kids toys. I doubted even the wealthiest of highsiders would have access to so powerful a charm.

Confirmation then, of everything I'd feared. Kiran was a mage, and even if he hadn't started the avalanche himself, it had still happened on his account. More, Pello certainly knew it. Question was, what the hell was I going to do?

I ground the heels of my hands into my eyes, trying to think. I could run. Abandon Kiran and the convoy, and wash my hands of this entire Shaikar-cursed mess.

Yeah, and then what? I'd never work as either an outrider or a courier again, after pulling a vanishing act like that. And I'd never find another way to earn the coin I needed before Melly Changed.

Footsteps crunched on rock. Shit! Gritting my teeth against painful shocks, I stuffed Kiran's amulet back down his shirt. Then threw the blanket over his chest, for good measure.

A lanky, long-faced man I recognized as one of Bartel's two sons plodded into view. His eyes were red, and his mouth compressed in a hard, thin line.

I started to my feet, my nerves jangling. Had Pello begun spreading tales?

"Thought you outriders should know," Bartel's son said. "Harken's dead."

"What?" My knees gave way and dumped me back on the outboard. "Last I heard, Merryn was tending him!"

"Merryn was. Said he used every charm and potion he could think of, but Harken just slipped away, like his heart was too wore out to beat any more."

Nausea swept through me. Harken had been unfailingly kind, even when I'd been a loudmouthed city brat most other drovers would have happily drowned in the nearest stream. "Suliyya grant him rest," I said, my voice thick. Oh, mother of maidens, I should never have taken this job.

"He was a good man." Bartel's son shifted his weight. "I've got to get back. My father's still down. Merryn keeps saying he might recover, but..." He shrugged, helplessly.

I swallowed. "I hope your father makes it."

Bartel's son nodded. He turned and left, his shoulders drooping.

Beside me, Kiran stirred. His eyes stayed closed, but one hand clenched on the blanket, and he made a small, pained noise.

I palmed the rune-marked oval of the boneshatter charm. Soon as Kiran woke, I'd demand answers, even if it meant he cast against me in response. And if he'd killed Harken, then somehow I'd make him pay.

CHAPTER NINE

(Kiran)

Kiran struggled back to consciousness. His head throbbed and every muscle in his body felt packed with broken glass. He must have miscalculated the channel pattern for a spell exercise and succumbed to magical overload. Ruslan would be angry.

A rustle of movement caught his attention. He fought to speak.

"Mikail?" His mouth was so dry. Mikail would bring him water, and something to dull the pain. He'd mock Kiran for botching a spell so badly, but his hands would be gentle.

"No." The voice wasn't Mikail's. Kiran opened his eyes, confused. The young man leaning over him had a lean, brown face punctuated by a pair of furious green eyes, a far cry from Mikail's flat features and gray eyes opaque as stone. The soft glow of lanternlight illuminated stacked crates and the rough wood of a wagon bed. He pushed himself up, ignoring the pain stabbing through his muscles.

"Dev," he said hoarsely.

"That's right." Dev's voice was cold as a mountain night. "Now you're awake, let's get something straight. I don't know what game you're playing, but I'm done being your blind token. I want answers, or I'll let Pello tell every last man in this convoy you started that avalanche."

Memory came crashing back: the oncoming wall of snow, the burning rush of power, the shock of impact. Realization drove the air from Kiran's lungs. Ruslan was coming. "Oh, no. No, no, no…" He fought free of the blanket with a wild flail of his arms.

Dev backed a pace, his body tensed and his hands spread. Rune-marked silver glittered in one palm. "Don't like that idea, do you? You did cast a spell, then. Don't fucking try to deny it, because I've seen your amulet. Nobody but a mage could spark a charm powerful as that."

Kiran mastered the panicked impulse to ignore Dev and run. The runes on Dev's charm identified it as a crude but effective pain inducer. If Dev used it against him, the effort to block even so minor a charm might send him unconscious again in his weakened state. He'd lost enough precious time already.

"Yes, all right? I used magic, but not to start the avalanche! You don't understand, I—"

Dev's mouth twisted. "I understand Harken is dead, without a scratch on him. So are six others. Want to explain that to me?"

Horror chilled Kiran to the core. That inrush of power, so deliriously sweet…his gorge rose. Generous, amiable Harken gone forever, and Kiran hadn't even realized whose life he'd stolen. "I never meant for anyone to die," he said, his voice ragged. "The avalanche, it would have killed everyone…I tried to divert it without harming anyone, but I had to work so fast!"

Dev's eyes turned hard as agate. "Never meant for anyone to die, huh? Except Pello, and anybody else near him when the avalanche hit. Forget about them, did you?"

"What?" Kiran felt as if he'd missed a step on a tower stair. He twisted to look at the intact stacks of supply crates. "What do you mean, when the avalanche hit?"

"Don't play dumb with me," Dev snapped. "At Ice Lake, Pello marked you for a mage, right? You wanted him gone, and you found a way. Maybe you started the slide, maybe you only jumped on the opportunity…either way, you made sure it destroyed his end of the line. But you couldn't even get that right, you incompetent asshole—

Pello survived, and you killed all those men for nothing!"

"I didn't try to kill Pello!" Kiran faltered on Pello's name. One slip in focus as he'd channeled the power against the avalanche, and darker desires might well have contaminated his intent. He thrust the thought away. "I acted to *save* this convoy! And to do it, I threw away my only hope, my only protection—" He choked, his panic rising.

Dev's eyes narrowed to green slits. "Why in Suliyya's name should I believe you? You've done nothing but lie to me from the start."

Kiran fought to regain control. He had no illusions that he'd be able to cross the mountains on his own. He needed Dev's knowledge and expertise, or running would merely delay his capture. "You're right, I've lied to you, and I'm sorry. I'll tell you the truth now, if you'll only listen!"

Dev crossed his arms, his eyes still cold and unyielding. "Go on, then."

Kiran sucked in a steadying breath. "I didn't lie about wanting to reach Alathia unnoticed, but I'm not worried about banking houses. I was hoping to hide from another mage."

"Oh, that part I figured out all on my own." Dev's voice held an edge sharp as obsidian. "Now you'll say this other mage started the avalanche in hopes of killing you. And you think when he figures out you're alive, he'll try again."

"No, you don't understand! Ruslan doesn't want to kill me. He wants to find me. My amulet, the one you saw—it hides me from his magic. But the amulet can only conceal me if I don't use magic myself. When I blocked the avalanche, for Ruslan it was like…like a signal blaze in the Aiyalen Tower. Now he knows exactly where I am, and he'll be coming, as soon as he can prepare and cast a translocation spell." Kiran couldn't keep his breath from coming faster. "You have to get me away from here. The amulet can still protect us, if we hide in the mountains. He won't be able to find or strike at me directly with magic—or you, so long as you stay near me. But the amulet won't help if he can see us in the ordinary way! We have to run, right now!"

"You mean *you* have to run." Dev glared at him. "I agreed to help you sneak past the Alathians, not escape from a mage ready to dump a mountainside on my head!"

"He'll find out you helped me leave Ninavel. He'll kill you for that, if you don't run with me. Not a fast or easy death, either. Magic can bring agony greater than any you can imagine. And Ruslan is… inventive." Alisa had screamed long after her voice gave out, her mouth gaping in agonized, airless cries. The sight haunted Kiran's dreams.

"Maybe I'll offer to help him, instead of you." Cold calculation gleamed in Dev's eyes. "You're too weak or too afraid to use magic right now, aren't you? Otherwise you'd be casting spells on me instead of talking. Seems to me my best chance of survival might be in joining the guy most likely to win."

Kiran's chest constricted. All his fears were coming true; and Dev was right, he didn't dare attempt a working in his weakened state. Chill sweat trickled down his back. He had to convince Dev; he had to. "I know you need money. You'll get none from Ruslan. If you'd sent him word of me before the avalanche, he might have rewarded you then. Now, all you'd receive is your life, and perhaps not even that."

Kiran leaned forward and drew out his amulet. "If you guide me the rest of the way to Kost, you can have this once we cross the border. I know it's worth a lot. Between that and Bren's money, you'll gain a fortune if you help me."

Dev stood silent, his head lowered. Kiran's pulse drummed in his ears.

"Tell me something," Dev said. "If you're so desperate to hide from this guy, why'd you go mess with the avalanche?"

"I couldn't let all those men die." Kiran hesitated. "I know what you must think of me, after…after Harken, but I'm not like Ruslan. I'm not a murderer!"

"Wish I could believe that," Dev muttered. He studied Kiran, a deep frown line etched between his brows. "You claim Harken and the other deaths mid-line were—what? The result of some kind of fuck-up of yours in the spell casting?"

Kiran swallowed. He was fortunate that Dev knew too little of magic to understand what the deaths implied about Kiran's methods. It was true enough that if he'd drawn power with more skill, the men might yet live. "Yes. I told you before, I had to work too fast to block the avalanche. If only I'd had more time to cast the spell…but if I hadn't cast at all, far more would have died." Why couldn't Dev see that he'd saved far more lives than he'd taken?

Dev's frown remained. "Why's this Ruslan so hot to find you?"

Kiran twisted the crumpled blanket in his hands. He'd have to tread cautiously, to have any chance of Dev's help. Perhaps a series of carefully chosen truths, rather than a lie…

"When two mages work together, spells can be cast beyond the ability of either alone. Joining mind and power so closely with another is difficult and dangerous, but I have certain…skills in this area. Ruslan wants my cooperation in his spellcasting. But the spells he casts…he seeks power without any regard for others, and kills for the pleasure of it. I'd rather deny my magic than use it in service to him!"

Kiran halted; tried to gain control of his breathing.

"Let me guess, Ruslan's not the sort of guy who takes no for an answer," Dev said.

"His strength far exceeds mine; I can't hope to stand against him. If he finds me now, he won't ask. He'll simply rip my mind apart until I have no will left to resist him, and make me his creature entirely." Desperation filled Kiran at the thought. "You have to help me, please!"

Dev was silent again. At last he huffed out a sharp breath. "Fine. I'll run with you, do my best to get us safe to Kost. But not because I think you deserve help—all I want is my payment."

Kiran shut his eyes, dizzy with relief. Dev could think what he liked, so long as they escaped Ruslan. "I understand." He gathered his strength, and tottered to his feet. "I'm ready to leave."

"Not yet, you aren't." Dev scowled at him. "I get you think this Ruslan could spell himself here any minute, but there's no way in Shaikar's hells I'm leaving without proper supplies. I'll work fast as I can, but I need time to pack."

"But—"

Dev cut him off with a sharp slash of his hand. "I mean it. Otherwise, go throw yourself off the nearest cliff, because that's a better way to die." He heaved a supply sack down off the wagon bed. "I want to warn Cara and Jerik about him, anyway—"

"No, you can't!" Kiran grabbed Dev's arm. "The less they know, the safer they'll be. Ruslan will search their thoughts when he arrives. It won't be pleasant for them, but if he finds they know nothing of my identity and weren't involved, they'll survive the experience."

Dev wrenched his arm from Kiran's grasp. "Fuck that! Ruslan's gonna be mad as a stinkwasp when he finds you gone. They deserve the chance to get the hell away before he comes, same as us!"

"You'll guarantee their deaths. Ruslan will hunt down any who leave the convoy, and they'll have no way to hide, or defend against his magic. I know you fear for them, but truly—their best chance of survival is to remain here, unknowing."

Dev raked his hands through his hair, and glared at Kiran. "You'd better be right, damn you. Harken's death is on your head already; don't think I'll forget."

Guilt stabbed Kiran again. "I won't either," he said, wearily.

"By the way, I wasn't kidding about Pello, earlier. He thinks you tried to kill him, and he's not a happy man. He searched you while you were out; I stopped him from anything more, but I hope you're not missing anything important."

Pello had become the least of his worries. Nevertheless, Kiran put a hand to the amulet. Glowing lines of force traced delicate spirals on his inner sight. The pattern remained intact and the energies flowed unhindered. "The amulet is the only charm I carry, and it shows no sign of tampering."

Dev's scowl didn't lessen. "Pack your gear, but stay in the wagon. If you hear anyone coming, pretend you're still unconscious." He pointed at the amulet. "And for Khalmet's sake, put that thing away."

✳

(Dev)

Gods, I had to be out of my mind. Running for the Alathian border with an untrustworthy, half-assed excuse for a mage, while some scary bastard hunted us with the gusto of a hungry sandcat...I'd taken some crazy risks in my time, but this had to top them all. Slim chance of a payoff, but slim was better than none. Melly's fate still lay in my hands, and I owed Sethan far too much to break my vow to him out of simple fear.

On the bright side, leaving the convoy would solve another problem. Kiran's panic had clearly shoved all other concerns clean out of his mind, but I knew better than to ignore the threat of an alive and angry Pello. The bastard was probably accusing us to Meldon right now. And whenever Ruslan showed up, Pello'd be happy to help him hunt us.

On a solo trip three seasons ago, I'd discovered a climber's shortcut across the high peaks barring the way on the other side of Garnet Canyon. The route wasn't easy. I remembered miles of steep scrambling over unstable talus, and one serious climb. I'd never tried the route this early in the season, when treacherous snow coated the cliffs. But nobody else in the convoy should know of it, not even Cara, and it'd let us reach the border in days, rather than the week it'd take for even a flat-out ride on the trail.

I thought of Kiran's sunken cheeks and unsteady hands, and grimaced. I had serious doubts about his ability to handle the rugged terrain off the trail, let alone climb in his condition. Damn it, I'd haul him by main force if I had to. If he was so desperate to reach Kost, he'd find a way to manage.

I sorted through equipment, throwing gear down into a pile on the ground. A full length rope, ice axes, extra cords, short lengths of rope to make harnesses, a set of fire stones, heavy clothing, food, waterskins...the pile grew. I snatched up our largest pack and jumped down off the wagon.

A flat, arid voice spoke from behind me. "What the fuck are you doing, Dev?"

My hands spasmed on the pack straps. I turned to see Cara's lean form standing in the shadows at the edge of my lantern's glow.

Shit! I'd counted on the sound of her horse warning me of her return. Of all the times for her to walk back instead of ride! Kinslayer had damaged our friendship; this would destroy it. Coward that I was, I'd hoped to be long gone before she realized, so I wouldn't have to face the look in her eyes.

Maybe I could still delay the moment of truth. "Kellan woke up, and the avalanche rattled him so bad he's panicked over another slide hitting us while the convoy's stuck here. I thought I'd take him on an overnight scout, give him something else to think about. We'll need to know the conditions up ahead, anyway."

"Don't, Dev. Just…don't. How stupid do you think I am? You've got enough food there for a week. You mean to leave the convoy, right when I need your help the most." Each word was barren as the Gosashen blight.

"I have good reason—!" I choked back the truth that crowded my throat. Cara's life was worth more than our friendship.

She strode forward. The lanternlight fell on her face and revealed the bleak fury she'd kept from her voice. "Good reason! Gods damn you, Dev. Kinslayer was bad enough, but this! Is the profit from your smuggling truly worth more to you than anything else?"

I froze, too taken aback to even blink. Anger warred with contempt in her blue eyes.

"Did you really think I didn't know about your little sideline? I've turned a blind eye because I know how Ninavel works. If it wasn't you, it'd only be somebody else. Better if it was you, I thought, because I believed you'd never let it interfere with the safety of the convoy." She directed a meaningful look at the supplies sitting on the ground between us. "I guess I was pretty fucking stupid after all."

"Cara, I—"

She rode right over my words. "What, you think you'd better cut and run like Pello, because whatever you're smuggling might've earned you the ire of a mage? They'll say you were in league with Pello, that you brought the avalanche on our heads same as he did. Hell, I'd agree with them if I hadn't seen you two face off like sandcats marking territory."

"Wait, what? Pello—what?" I goggled at her, wondering if I'd completely misheard.

"He stole my horse not twenty minutes gone. Rode her down into the basin like a man demon-marked, and crossed the snowfield below the slide, heading west. Meldon ordered us to let him go, says we're safer without him. He's sure the avalanche was on Pello's account, that he must've been carrying contraband stolen from a mage and now he's running for Alathia in hope of saving his worthless skin."

Or in hope of selling information on Kiran to the Alathians. Shit. Ruslan might chase him down and drag him back for questioning, but I didn't dare count on that.

The skin around Cara's eyes tightened, her mouth thinning. "The way the drovers are talking, if Pello ever shows his face back in Ninavel, he'll get strung up for the vultures. You want to join him, is that it?"

Pello's move made little sense to me, given he must've known he'd take the blame for the avalanche, but I'd ponder his reasons later. If he reached the border before us and spilled his tale to the Alathian mages, we'd never make it through. All the more reason to get moving.

"Look, Cara, ganglords aren't exactly patient or forgiving. I promised a delivery date for my goods, and I've got to keep that promise. I can't wait around for days while we dig out the route. Soon as I get to Kost, I'll tell the importers about the avalanche—they can send Meldon a relief party with replacement mules." Twenty dead mule teams meant Meldon would have to cache some cargo, even if he distributed as much as he could amongst the surviving teams. Merchant houses never left much weight margin, and the convoy still had to make the steep climb over Arathel Pass.

"Meldon needs experienced outriders right now a hell of a lot more than he needs mules, and you know it. You talk of promises— what about the promise you made when you signed on with the convoy?" Cara's fists tightened at her sides. "What the fuck is wrong with you? That little bitch tossed you out on your ass, so now you've got to prove you're just as selfish and cold as she is? Congratulations, you're doing a great job."

I flinched. *You selfish, backstabbing bitch!* I'd shouted at Jylla. *When your Taint burned out, your soul went with it! All you have left is ashes and greed!* Her eyes had glittered, her mouth curling. *You think you're any different?* she'd sneered. *Your precious Sethan taught you to pretend, but inside you're dead as Shaikar's eyes.*

It wasn't true, damn it. "You think I want to leave? You want to curse me for taking a ganglord's money, go ahead. I've been cursing myself plenty today. But what's done is done!"

"You're right about that," Cara snapped. "Leave, and you'll never work as an outrider again."

"Don't you think I know it?" I couldn't hide my own anger. I'd give up more than outriding for Melly's sake, but the loss was bitter as blackroot.

"Then in Suliyya's name, tell me why!"

I shook my head, mute with frustration.

Cara gripped my shoulders, hard enough to bruise. "Sethan believed in you, trusted you—after all he did to help you, how can you repay him like this?"

Furious, I struck her hands away. "Fuck you, Cara. If you think Sethan was so perfect, then you didn't know him too well."

"What's that supposed to mean?" The mixture of outrage and disbelief on her face snapped my last thread of self-control.

"This whole thing is Sethan's fault! I wouldn't need the money if he'd had the sense not to—" My brain finally caught up with my mouth, and I swallowed the rest before I could blurt out something I'd really regret. Anything I told Cara might end up in Ruslan's hands. I couldn't risk a vindictive mage finding out about Melly. Cold sweat dampened my neck at the mere thought. I turned away from Cara, digging my nails into my palms in an effort to calm down.

"Dev…" There was a new, softer note in her voice. "Just tell me what's going on."

I kept my back to her. "Forget it, Cara. I'm leaving, and I don't care what you think about it."

"Go, then." The softness had vanished; each word was cold and precise. "But you lay one hand on those supplies, and I'll cut it off. Hell if I'll let you walk away with half our gear without even an explanation. You take your personal gear, and that's it."

"Damn it, I'll pay for what I take! I've got the coin, just let me—"

"No." Resolution hardened her voice. "You still don't get it, do you? Lives depend on these supplies—that's a hell of a lot more important to me than your Shaikar-cursed money." She dropped one hand to her belt knife, her pale eyes bleak as winter.

Khalmet's hand, just when I thought this day couldn't get any worse. Cara was no shadow man—I'd have a fair chance of taking her down in a fight. It'd be messy, though, and even if I didn't use the boneshatter charm, one or both of us was liable to get badly hurt. I hesitated, weighing the risk of delay. Maybe if we left and I doubled back later that night to steal supplies...

Behind Cara, a shadow moved, stretched to touch her arm. She crumpled to the ground. I rushed forward, yanking the boneshatter charm from my belt.

Kiran hastily backed away from Cara, his hands upraised. "I didn't harm her, I promise! The effect is temporary."

"What the fuck did you do?" Cara's pulse beat steady and strong, and her breathing was regular, though her skin felt worryingly cold to the touch. "You said you didn't dare use magic!"

He shrugged, watching me. "That wasn't magic. Touch creates a conduit to a body's energies. I...dampened hers, that's all."

Not magic. Yeah, right. A chill prickled my skin. What did I really know about Kiran? Only what he'd told me, and he'd proved himself a liar ten times over.

"She wasn't going to yield, and you said we needed the supplies." He shifted on his feet, blue eyes wide and urgent. "She'll wake within minutes, I swear to you. We've delayed long enough already—we need to go!"

For an instant I hovered on the edge of telling him to go fuck himself. He'd killed Harken, done gods knew what to Cara, and I was supposed to help him? But Melly's youthful face hung in my mind's eye, the crimson flame of her hair and her eager smile the very image of her father. *Whatever it takes*, I'd vowed.

"Fine," I snarled. I slid my arms under Cara and heaved to my feet with an explosive grunt of effort. Kiran started forward, as if he meant to help. I showed my teeth. "Don't you fucking touch her again."

His mouth tightened to a thin line, but he backed off. I laid Cara on the wagon bed, gently as I could, and wrapped a blanket around her. Put a hand to her cool, still face, and stood there with my throat knotted tight.

Kiran gave an anxious little cough. I gritted my teeth and left Cara's side, praying to every god I'd ever heard of that I wasn't making another terrible mistake.

✳

(Kiran)

Kiran gnawed on a thumb as Dev shoved climbing equipment into a pack with vicious efficiency. How long had it been, now? Long enough for Ruslan to make the necessary preparations for a translocation spell?

Translocation is difficult and dangerous, Ruslan's voice said in his memory. *There are many avenues for error, and enormous power is required for even the smallest distance. This power must be channeled carefully and properly, or the mage risks failure or even death. For this reason, it is not used lightly.* He'd shown Kiran a channel diagram of stunning complexity. Hundreds of channels spiraled and crossed in dizzying tangles, careful annotations marked above each dense cluster. *Have you ever cast it?* Kiran had asked, looking wide-eyed at the spell. Ruslan had smiled at him, gently. *Let us say there have been certain situations in which the benefits outweighed the risks.*

Kiran shivered, wrapping his arms around himself. No question Ruslan would consider this such a situation.

Dev thrust a pack at him. "Put this on."

Kiran obeyed. Dev buckled a far larger pack shut and stood, a small pouch clenched in his hand. He strode over to the back end of the wagon, where Cara lay. Kiran heard a heavy clink, as of coin. When Dev returned, he was empty handed, his face dark and shuttered. He stomped past Kiran and surveyed the expanse of the basin, black and silver in the light of the rising moon.

"We'll scramble down to the basin floor, then make our way west to the edge of Garnet Canyon. Once we drop into Garnet, we can't be spotted from the trail, and trees will give us cover." Dev stabbed a finger at Kiran's chest. "You said that amulet of yours will protect me if I stay close. How close, exactly?"

Kiran called the amulet's pattern into his head. A spell powerful enough to obscure the bonfire of a mage's *ikilhia* was too strong to be tightly localized. The energies would spill over, spreading beyond Kiran's immediate location and fading with distance. Not enough to hide a second mage, but a *nathahlen* like Dev...Kiran considered the dim glow of Dev's *ikilhia* and made a rapid calculation.

"You should stay within five hundred yards."

Dev's scowl deepened, but he jerked his head in a nod. "Fine. Move quiet as you can at first. I'll tell you when we're far enough from the convoy that we can pick up the pace." Dev settled his pack with a furious wrench of his shoulders.

Following Dev through talus was hard enough, but following Dev through talus in the dark when every muscle in his body ached fiercely and his head was pounding proved to be almost more than Kiran could manage. The tiny amount of *ikilhia* he'd drawn from Cara was but a sand grain in the vast desert of his body's need. The pack on his back felt full of lead, his lungs burned, and with each jarring hop between boulders, the pain in his muscles rose another notch. He clung to the thought that every step he took reduced the chance Ruslan would find him.

The convoy receded with painful slowness. Scattered magefires glowed like muted stars along the line, and indistinct murmurs of voices drifted through the night air. Dev negotiated the slope with a leashed violence in his movements that made Kiran wince. *I'm sorry,* he wanted to shout. *I didn't want any of this to happen.* Instead, he concentrated on moving without knocking any rocks loose.

At long last the slope's angle eased, and Dev turned to him. "Forget being quiet. Now we move fast as we can."

Kiran fought to churn his aching legs more quickly, stumbling over the rocks. Dev led him westward until a broad snowfield blocked their path, gleaming in the moonlight. A line of deep pockmarks stretched from their side to the far edge.

"That's where Pello rode across?" Kiran whispered, pointing at the tracks. At Dev's swift, dark glance, he added, apologetically, "I heard your conversation with Cara."

"Then you know he's making for the border," Dev said. "I hope to beat him by the shortcut I have in mind." He stamped on the snow. No mark remained when he lifted his foot. "The crust has frozen hard already. Our tracks won't show, but watch yourself—we can't use ice axes or boot spikes if we don't want to leave a trail. Take small steps, and move slow." He eased out onto the snow, then turned.

"Maybe Pello only took off because once he saw that pretty amulet of yours he feared you'd try to bury him again if he stuck around. But running for the border straight away like that makes a lot more sense if he knew Ruslan was coming. Any thoughts?"

"I don't see how he could know of Ruslan in specific," Kiran said, slowly. Most untalented men who met Ruslan didn't live to tell the tale. "But perhaps he thought as you did that another mage had tried to kill me with the avalanche, and might try to strike the convoy again."

"Maybe." Dev didn't sound convinced, but he turned and continued edging across the icy expanse.

Kiran shuffled after him. The snow felt terrifyingly slick under his boots, and the surface was patterned with awkward lumps and ridges that made balance difficult. By the time they reached snow-free ground again, Kiran's legs trembled with tension and fatigue.

"How much farther until the canyon?" he asked Dev.

"About two more miles."

Two more miles! Kiran didn't know whether to laugh or to cry. His body was already screaming at him to stop. He'd never done anything like this during a recovery period, and he had no idea what the long term effects would be. If he drained his strength too far, would he lose the ability to hold his barriers? Or merely fall unconscious again, in which case, would Dev abandon him?

Dev eyed him. "You want to take a break?"

Yes, his burning muscles insisted. But high on the dark bulk of the eastern ridge, the dim pinpricks of convoy magefires were still visible. Kiran gathered his concentration to block out the pain. "We should keep going."

Dev shook his head, but made no comment. He led Kiran across endless undulating fields of boulders. The moonlight painted everything in shades of silver, gray, and black, and the world seemed eerily silent except for the harsh sound of Kiran's breathing and the painful pounding of his heart.

Without warning, the night split apart. Magic boiled over Kiran, seething against his barriers. Silent lightning clawed his nerves and blotted out his vision. For an endless moment he hung trapped in fire, the amulet a blazing star on his chest.

Somewhere, someone was calling his name. Kiran blinked, the world reforming around him. He was huddled on his knees, one hand braced on a rock, the other clenched so tightly around Lizaveta's amulet that his fingers cramped and tingled.

"Hey! Kiran!" Dev's voice was sharp with worry. He reached out a hand to Kiran, then yanked it back, frowning.

Kiran straightened. Rocks dug painfully into his shins. He took a deep, tearing breath, and released the amulet. He waited for panic to swallow him whole, but all he felt was a bone-numbing cold.

"What the hell happened with you?" Dev demanded, as Kiran climbed to his feet.

"Ruslan." Kiran's voice shook despite his best effort to steady it. "He's come to the convoy."

CHAPTER TEN

(Dev)

"Ruslan? Shit!" I glanced across the moonwashed basin to the pale streak of the Desadi Couloir. All was silent and still, the view unchanged from moments ago. Now I understood why southerners clung to their devil-ward charms. What else could you do, in the face of an invisible threat that could strike at any moment? "He attacked you? Damn your eyes, you said the amulet would protect us—"

Kiran made a noise that might have been a laugh. "It did." He staggered forward, as unsteady as a miner on a five day tavern crawl. I grabbed his pack strap and dragged him onward, glancing again over my shoulder.

"You call that protection?" Khalmet's hand, I felt like a target sigil was etched right into my back.

Kiran sucked down another ragged, harsh breath. "The translocation spell...it requires tremendous power, and Ruslan didn't...didn't bother with containment wards. Deliberately, no doubt. The amulet shielded me from the worst of the overspill, but even so...if I'd been closer, his arrival would have knocked me unconscious. At this distance, it merely…disoriented me."

Disoriented. Ha. From his choked-off cry as he'd fallen, and his wide, blank eyes, he'd come closer to complete collapse than he wanted me to know. No choice but to keep moving, and pray his legs didn't give out before we reached Garnet Canyon. So long as we traveled the open ground of the basin, far too easy for Ruslan to spot us by spyglass. My back itched more fiercely than ever.

We struggled up a boulder-strewn rise. Beyond, the ground sloped away into a great yawning darkness. Stubby trees poked up through the rocks, and a faint sighing of wind through pines drifted up from the void. Thank Khalmet, the canyon at last. I hurried Kiran down the slope, letting out a relieved breath as we dropped below the sightline from the trail.

The moon still stood high overhead in the star-spattered sky. The trees on the canyon's slope wouldn't be thick and tall enough to block the moonlight until right before the first set of serious cliffs. Even if Ruslan was breathing right down our necks, I'd never succeed in setting a series of tricky rappels in the dark. But by going slow and careful, we might continue down until then. I wanted every inch of distance from the convoy I could get before we had to stop and wait for dawn's light. I eyed Kiran, who still wavered on his feet with every panting breath he took.

"This next bit's gonna be steep, but you make it down, we'll be in nice thick trees. Think you can manage?"

His white, drawn face turned to mine. "I'll crawl, if I have to."

"Good," I muttered. I didn't know how much of Kiran's story I believed, but I was certain of one thing: his terror of Ruslan was real. Last thing I wanted was to meet a mage capable of inspiring that much fear in his own kind.

I took a firmer grip on Kiran's pack strap, and tugged him through gnarled dwarf pines. As the slope steepened, the talus changed over to broad, curved slabs of polished granite, ghost-gray in the moonlight. Kiran edged down them at a snail's pace that made me twitch with anxious frustration. I didn't dare push him to move faster, not with the way his legs wobbled. A misstep here would mean broken bones, or even a snapped neck.

Though a snapped neck might be preferable to what we'd face if Ruslan caught us. I'd seen a man once who'd crossed a mage. He'd been writhing on bloodsmeared flagstones, his skin bubbling into red ruin as he screamed loud enough to crack glass. The wind mage who'd cast the spell on him hadn't even bothered to stay to watch him die. She'd stalked off with no more expression than if he'd been a blackfly she'd crushed.

Gods, if Kiran was wrong, and Ruslan hurt Cara...I should have told her everything, convinced her to run with us.

Yeah, so she could die right alongside me, when Ruslan hunted us down. My estimate of our chances, never high, was dropping fast. Maybe that amulet meant Ruslan couldn't strike at us directly, but after watching Kiran nearly collapse from the guy's gods-damned travel spell, I had a nasty feeling the amulet's protection didn't mean half as much as he'd claimed.

Kiran was still breathing hard as we negotiated a dirt gully coated in slippery pine needles, but I judged him steady enough to speak again. I caught his arm.

"So Ruslan shows up, finds we've left the convoy. You say he can't track us with magic. What's his next move?"

Kiran braced a hand on a pine trunk. He stood a moment with his head lowered, breathing in deep gulps. "He'll question those at the convoy, in hopes of discovering our intended route, and likely send men to hunt for us. He'll also try and...force me to reveal myself again. Target possible routes, and cast spells to trigger avalanches or rockslides...but powerful spells take time to prepare. If we cross the mountains quickly enough, I'm sure we can reach Alathia." He sounded like he was trying to convince himself as well as me.

Alathia...an awful thought surfaced, as we shuffled down another moonlit slab. "So he can't track us, what difference does that make? He's gotta realize where we're headed. What's to stop him from warning the Alathians about us, to keep us from crossing the border?" Message charms didn't work through the Alathian border wards, but a mage surely had other ways of communication.

"Ruslan won't contact the Alathians," Kiran said, like it was a fact set in stone. "He doesn't want me captured by them. I'd be of no use to him then."

That sounded awfully optimistic. I let it slide, for now. "Okay, what if he spells himself to the border ahead of us and waits near the gate to ambush us?"

"He can't translocate there, not from the convoy. I told you, translocation takes tremendous power, and the mountains here are magically inert. He'd have to return to Ninavel first before he could cast another such spell."

"But he could ride to the border, same as Pello...shit! Can he contact Pello, use him to set an ambush?"

Kiran bit his lip and nodded. "But you said we could beat Pello to the border..." He looked at me with the hopeful eyes of a Tainter seeking reassurance. I scowled.

"My shortcut'll get us there faster than a normal rider on the trail, but can Ruslan cast spells on a horse? Keep it from faltering, or tiring?" I'd thought we had a fair time margin, but that assumed even a hard-driven horse would need rest and food on the trail. If a man rode straight for the border without any stops or slackening of pace, that'd narrow our margin to a whisker.

Kiran stumbled, caught himself against another pine. "Perhaps, but he'd need a complex spell to alter a living creature that way—one that would take a day or more to prepare."

His hands were trembling on the pine trunk, and strain tightened his voice. I shut up, not wanting him to waste energy on talking. Another half mile to the cliffs, I judged. Already, tree branches stretched across the sky, filtering the moonlight to a dim haze.

I had to help Kiran more and more often as the shadows closed in. His breathing grew labored, and he clutched at tree trunks and branches for support. When we came to a hollow amidst a cluster of twisted pines, I pushed him down onto matted needles.

"Rest here," I told him. "We have to wait for dawn before we tackle the cliffs above Garnet River." No matter how my badly my nerves twitched at the idea of Ruslan's searchers gaining ground.

Kiran slumped over on his side without speaking. He didn't move, his body limp, as I tugged off his pack and threw a blanket over him. I cursed, silently. If he needed something more than sleep, we were screwed, because I sure as hell was no healer.

This had to be the stupidest thing I'd ever done. I pressed my hands to my temples, then grimaced and settled back against my pack. No point in stewing over it; I'd made my choice. I needed rest, especially if I'd have to haul Kiran over tomorrow's rougher terrain.

Sethan had long ago taught me how to block out nerves to gain a sound sleep the night before a tough ascent. Focus on the memory of a favorite climb, calling up every move, every sensation in exact detail until everything else fades away...the trick had never failed me before. But despite all my attempts to call up happier times, the image that chased me down into broken, troubled sleep was Cara as I'd seen her last, sprawled on the wagonbed with her pale hair straggling out of her braid and her face marked with lines of stress and sorrow.

❋

Dawn's light and the twittering of whitelarks woke me. I sat up and rubbed my aching side with a muffled groan. In my sleep, I'd slid from my cushioning pack onto a tangle of knobby pine roots.

Yeah, and if that was the worst discomfort I suffered on this Shaikar-cursed trip, I could count myself favored by Khalmet. I thought of Harken and the other dead back at the convoy, and my throat tightened. Their friends would burn the bodies, using the flashfire charms Merryn carried for that purpose. Sing death chants to call Noshet's spirit guardians, and erect a few rock cairns draped with personal mementos that might last a season or two before storms demolished them. Not much to show for a life spent in the mountains, though the tale of their death would doubtless long be recited around convoy campfires.

Assuming Ruslan didn't kill everyone in the convoy, out of sheer spite. My hands clenched. The bastard wouldn't, surely. Not if he wanted men and provisions for hunting us.

I glared down at the source of all the trouble, wishing I'd never laid eyes on him. Kiran lay curled on his side, so tightly wrapped in his blanket that only the tip of his nose showed. He didn't stir when I called his name. I grabbed a fallen pine branch and poked him, not gently. He rolled away with an unintelligible mutter.

"Time to move," I announced.

He sat up slow as a man ten times his age. I didn't much like the bluish-gray tinge to his skin, and the circles under his eyes had darkened to near black.

"How bad off are you?" I asked. Khalmet's hand, if I had to carry him the whole way, we'd never escape Ruslan.

He darted a wary glance at me. "I'll be able to walk, if that's what you're asking." He started to stand, and nearly fell. "I'm only a little stiff. Give me a minute." He tottered away through the clustered pines. I muttered a curse. Just a little stiff, my ass.

But when he emerged from the trees a few minutes later, he looked a lot better. His face was merely pale, rather than sickly gray, and though he still moved like every muscle hurt him, he was at least walking at a reasonable speed. Even more interesting, the cuts on his hands had vanished, the skin of his palms unmarked under the dirt. Maybe he'd done some kind of mage healing ritual back there in addition to relieving himself.

I handed him his pack and a handful of jerky. "Eat while you walk. Once on the cliffs, we'll be visible for miles down the canyon. We've gotta do the rappels fast, before any searchers get low enough in Garnet to spot us."

He nodded, his face set in determined lines. Slung on his pack, and clambered over jackstrawed logs after me, chewing as he went.

My thoughts slid back to the convoy like iron filings to a lodestone. Ruslan, questioning Cara and Jerik, casting spells on them...every dreadful tale I'd ever heard of angry mages cycled through my head, punctuated by images of Cara contorted in agony.

Damn it, if I kept this up my nerves would fray away entirely. Time to employ another of Sethan's little mental tricks. He'd always said the best way to stop fretting over a problem you can't solve was to focus on one you could.

The border crossing, for instance. Assuming we survived Ruslan's pursuit, sneaking Kiran past the Alathians wasn't exactly a trivial matter. Khalmet's hand, I'd thought the task hard enough when I'd believed him only an ordinary highsider, but now? Half the spells at the Kost gate were meant to detect what the Alathians called "unregistered mages."

I turned to Kiran as he slithered down a boulder. "Not telling me you were a mage…didn't you think that might be a *tiny* problem when we hit the border? How exactly did you expect me to sneak you through without knowing what I was doing?"

Kiran laid a hand flat on his chest. "A mage has a distinctive aura, true, but the amulet should conceal mine from the gate wards in the same manner it conceals me from Ruslan."

"You're telling me that charm is so powerful you can walk right past another mage, and they won't notice a thing?" Hard to believe, but it'd sure make my life easier if so.

Kiran stiffened. "There's an actual mage at the border?"

My foot twitched with the desire to kick him. How in Khalmet's name could a mage be this dumb? "Of *course* there's a mage! Who the fuck did you think enforces all those ridiculous rules about magical imports?"

He glared at me as he eased down another slick gully. "The books I read about Alathia only discussed the border wards," he said, tightly. "When I asked Bren if a crossing was possible for me, he didn't seem to think there'd be a problem."

"Bren knew you were a mage, then."

Kiran nodded. I remembered Bren's broad, smug smile, and scowled all the harder. Shaikar take that weaselly bastard! No wonder he'd rolled over on my demand for more profit. I should've known he was hiding a complication dangerous as this.

Then again, maybe Bren's knowledge was a much-needed spark of good news. He wouldn't have agreed to arrange passage if a crossing wasn't possible. Unless he'd never meant us to make it…but no. If the Alathians caught us at the border, when they put me under truth spell they'd find out all about Bren and Gerran's illegal trade, and Bren would lose a fortune. Besides, he wouldn't have bothered with those extra instructions and warnings on discretion if he didn't think I'd get Kiran into Kost.

A sharp line had formed between Kiran's brows. "Do you believe there's a way for me to cross the border?"

Oh, *now* he'd figured out Bren might've lied. My reasons why Bren hadn't weren't fit to share, based as they were on his covert instructions. Instead, I spoke with as much confidence as I could muster.

"There's always a way. The border itself might be stronger than the walls of Shaikar's innermost hell, but the detection spells at the gate aren't exactly foolproof." Though I wasn't so sanguine I could figure how to fox them well enough to sneak a mage through before Ruslan hunted us down and burned me to ash.

I squeezed between two close-set pines and stopped short. The granite slab beneath my feet ended in thin air. Beyond, the slope dropped away in broken cliffs to the heavily forested floor of the canyon. Tatters of mist trailed off treetops in a sinuous line that marked the course of the river hidden beneath their boughs. The western side of Garnet's great U-shaped trench held no cliffs, but the slope was wickedly steep nonetheless. Red fir and bristlebark pines crowded the lower slopes, thinning out and disappearing some thousand feet below the serrated ridges of the peaks that stretched to meet the brightening sky.

"Where do we go once we get down?" Kiran sounded daunted.

I unlaced my pack and pulled out harnesses and rope. "We'll ford the river, then climb out the canyon to the cirque below Bearjaw Peak." I pointed to a hulking mountain with a host of spires sticking up from its north ridge like crooked fangs. "On Bearjaw's north ridge, see the little notch between the two largest spires? That's what we're aiming for."

Kiran's gaze followed my finger. "That looks, um." He paused, and I could see him rejecting all the words like *impossible* and *insane*. He finally settled on "Steep."

"The climb to the notch isn't as bad as it seems." Hidden behind a buttress was a protected rock chimney with plentiful, solid holds, a climb even a novice like Kiran should be able to manage with the occasional assist. Khalmet willing, we'd make the cirque tonight, then ascend to the notch early the following morning while the avalanche danger was lowest. "I've never met anyone else who knew Bearjaw has a viable route. When Ruslan asks, he'll hear about the easier unnamed passes down south of the trail. If Khalmet favors us, he'll assume we've headed for one of those, and send his searchers that way."

Not something I intended to count on, though. I scanned the canyon as I worked, searching for any telltale glints from a spyglass. Ruslan's searchers shouldn't have reached the depths of the canyon yet, but Pello could've, with his head start. Hopefully he'd stuck to the trail, which switchbacked down a slope far to the south, but if he hadn't…I sighed, and dropped my clutch of pitons back into my pack. Far slower and more difficult to use natural anchors like trees to set the rappels, but I didn't dare leave a trail of metal pitons, not to mention the noise of hammering them into rock.

Kiran put on his harness and began uncoiling the rope. I caught another glimpse of the healed skin of his hands. Far as I could tell, not a trace of the ragged-edged cuts remained.

"What kind of mages are you and Ruslan, anyway?" I didn't know what the different types of mages called themselves, but streetside storytellers had long ago come up with a bunch of nicknames loosely based on the materials mages used to fuel their spells. Wind mages, earth mages, metal mages, crystal mages, song mages…the list was endless, and gods knew I was no expert. But for one of the major types, maybe I could sift enough truth from tavern stories to give me an independent idea of what I was dealing with.

"What?" His hands slackened on the hemp coils.

"How do you raise power?" In Ninavel, you knew right off by the style of sigils on a mage's clothes. Without that obvious clue, I was lost.

Kiran lowered his head and attacked the rope again. "I was trained to use forces that exist deep within the earth."

Earth mage or sand mage, maybe. Only middling powerful, if you believed the stories—and without the horrific reputation of the strongest mages. Yet even a middling powerful mage was dangerous beyond any enemy I'd faced before. My stomach set to jumping all over again. "And Ruslan?"

Kiran's mouth thinned. "He is the same."

"But stronger and more experienced," I said, sourly. At least I hadn't made an enemy of a bone mage, or worse—a blood mage. I hid a shudder, remembering the contemptuous malice I'd seen in the smile of that cold-eyed bastard on Eranya Street.

"Yes." Kiran gave a vicious yank on his harness belt knot. "I'm ready."

I stepped into my own harness, after a last glance up and down the canyon. The sooner we finished the rappels and got back under cover in the trees, the happier I'd be.

✳

Sunlight flooded the canyon by the time we made it down the final cliff. Kiran handled the rappels far better than I'd feared, though his exhaustion was plain in the cautious slowness of his rope handling and the shadows under his eyes.

No telling if anybody had spotted us. The instant we stowed the climbing gear, I set out over the canyon floor toward the river. The forest here was easy terrain, the last we'd have for a long while. The trees were all bristlebark pines, ancient and stately, with trunks too broad for one man to reach around. The lowest of their branches soared twenty feet over our heads. On a job once as a kid I'd snuck into the Temple of the Burning Moon, high in the airy sweep of Kahori Tower. The echoing marble chamber with its rows of massive columns had made me feel no bigger than a sandflea; my first sight of bristlebark forest had brought much the same sense of awe. Almost, I wished I could've seen Kiran's reaction to it at a time untainted by our fear of pursuit.

As it was, Kiran hurried along after me with his head down. Occasionally he trailed a hand across a shaggy bristlebark trunk, as if to assure himself its girth was real. Otherwise he hardly seemed to notice his surroundings—until we reached Garnet River. That stopped him dead in his tracks, his eyes wide with a mixture of wonder and dismay.

"How do we get across?" he asked.

Garnet River was only a baby compared to the great waterways of Alathia, but it made the white roar of the stream back in Silverlode Canyon look like a mere trickle. Ten wagonlengths wide and deeper than a man was tall, the river swept along in a deceptively smooth flow that could knock a man off his feet in seconds. The water was clear as daylight; I could see speckled fish hovering in the pebbled shallows. The steep-sided banks were already green with knotweed and fiddlenecks. In a few weeks when the wildflowers blossomed, they'd blaze with color.

"We gotta find a place where we can rock hop, since I'm guessing you can't swim."

He gave me a quizzical look. "Can you?"

"Yeah. Not well, though, so don't count on a quick rescue if you fall in." I led him through the pines above the riverbank, hunting for a spot where enough scattered boulders poked through the water's surface to allow a crossing.

"How did you—"

"Another outrider taught me, in mountain lakes." Which explained why I wasn't that good. Even in high summer, the lakes that dotted the Whitefires' cirques could freeze a man's blood in moments. Sethan had insisted swimming was an important skill for an outrider, but I hadn't wanted to spend one heartbeat longer in icy lakewater than absolutely necessary.

I hopped down the bank onto a glossy, rounded boulder that overhung the river. Beyond, the water swirled and foamed past the exposed tips of a ragged field of rocks.

"We'll cross here," I told Kiran. "I'll go first, and carry your pack. Once I make the far bank, I'll let you know if any of the rocks are unstable. The rocks will be slippery, so step slow and make sure each foot is solid. If you slip and fall in, try not to panic. Turn on your back and keep your feet pointed downstream—better for your feet to hit a rock than your head. The river will eventually sweep you into an eddy, and then I can reach you."

"Can't we use a rope?" Kiran eyed the river with a distinctly nervous expression.

"If you were tied to a rope and you fell, the force of the water would hold you under, and the rope might get tangled in the rocks. You'd likely drown before I could pull you to shore. I can't set a handline, either, because the path across zigzags too widely, and the water's too deep and fast to use a branch as a pole."

His knuckles were white on his pack straps. Time to play the confident minder. "Look, you've done fine on talus and cliffs, and this is easier. No question about where to put your feet. Just take it slow, and you'll be safe on the riverbank before you know it."

I made short work of the crossing. Only one rock was dangerously slick, coated in slimy river-weed. I pointed it out to Kiran, shouting over the noise of the water, and waved for him to start. He hopped from rock to rock with tight-faced concentration, his hands spread for balance. One foot slipped when he landed on the weed-covered rock, but he recovered nicely and kept coming. He was only two jumps away from the bank when he stopped short, his head cocked as if he were listening.

I called to him, but he didn't respond. His body jerked, his eyes rolling up to the whites.

Fuck! I'd seen this last night. I sprang out onto the nearest rock. He was already tipping over. I snagged a sleeve with a desperate lunge, and pulled. He collapsed half onto me, half in the river. The current nearly tore him from my grip, but I heaved backward with a shout, and we toppled onto the bank.

I shoved Kiran off me, and winced, my hand shooting to my left side. From the soreness there, I'd strained a muscle. Gods all damn it, that was just what I needed. I eased to my feet. Nothing else felt more than bruised, at least.

Kiran coughed and pushed himself to his knees, water dripping from his soaked left side.

"Whatever happened to 'powerful spells take time'?" I dumped a blanket on him. "Dry off with this and then tie anything wet to the outside of your pack. The sun will dry it as we go."

Kiran put a shaky hand up to his temple. He seemed dazed, but not nearly as bad off as he'd been in the basin. "Ruslan can't have prepared a properly targeted spell this quickly. He must have brought something general in nature…" He trailed off, his brow furrowing. I waited, but he tugged off his overjacket without speaking again.

"Khalmet's bloodsoaked hand, don't shut down on me now! What kind of spell did he cast?" Whatever Ruslan had done, I was sure we'd soon regret it.

"I don't know," he snapped. "With my barriers up, I can't *feel*—!" He made a violent, frustrated gesture with one hand.

"Fine, so you can't tell exactly. Can you make a guess, at least?"

Kiran's hands locked tight on the blanket's edge. His gaze turned inward. After another moment, he said slowly, "The magic seemed oddly diffuse, like he meant to spread it over as broad an area as possible. A weather spell, perhaps."

The sky overhead was pure, innocent blue, though we certainly didn't have an unobstructed view beneath the screening bristlebark branches. "Weather spell—for what? Rain, lighting, snow, wind?"

He shook his head, his face grim. I sighed. Any of those would be dangerous on a route as exposed as ours, but we couldn't wait around to find out what Ruslan had in mind. I'd watch the sky for threats as we climbed out of the canyon, and think up a bolthole in case a storm hit.

Kiran bent to tie his wet overjacket to a pack strap.

"Wait—what's that?" I reached for his shoulder, where a dark stain spread over the wool of his shirt.

"What?" He clutched at his chest as if he thought he might've lost the amulet to the river, though the chain still glinted at his collar.

I touched the wet ends of his hair, then sniffed my fingers. "Gods all damn it, your hair dye's coming out."

He shrugged, looking relieved. "You used a binding charm to set the dye. The binding was probably disrupted when I pulled power to block the avalanche. Surely it doesn't matter now?"

"Ruslan already knows you're in the mountains, yeah, but you can't go around dripping hair dye all over everything. It stains, and that'll make the Alathians suspicious." Damn. Washing it fully out would take far too long. But if Ruslan sent a storm our way, Kiran might stain half his gear.

I decided to compromise. I'd dump a few bowls worth of water over his head now, get the worst of the dye out. Any stains from what remained should be faint enough to explain away.

"Come lean your head over this rock," I told him. "The river's not done with you yet."

※

(Kiran)

Kiran's teeth chattered as he scrubbed a blanket over his freezing head. He'd been so disoriented from the lash of Ruslan's magic that he'd barely noticed the river's icy grip when Dev had dragged him off the rocks. But after enduring multiple bowls of frigid water poured over his head, his entire scalp burned with cold, as badly as if he'd been singed by a backflaring channel.

"You'll warm up fast once we start walking." Dev tapped his fingers impatiently on his pack straps.

"I h-h-hope s-so." Kiran gave up trying to warm his skin and stowed the blanket. The instant Kiran settled his pack on his shoulders, Dev strode off through the sunlit trees. Kiran lagged a careful distance behind, and veered to touch pine trunks. The flicker of *ikilhia* he drew from each tree was but a taste of their dark, ancient lives. His abused body cried out for him to drop his barriers and suck in power in great draughts, but he knew better. Ruslan wouldn't feel *ikilhia* drawn by touch while he wore the amulet, but only so long as his barriers held firm.

Power…what had Ruslan done, to fuel his spell without access to the forces of Ninavel's confluence? He might have brought and used *zhivnoi* crystals, warded reservoirs of stored energies…but Kiran recognized that as a foolish hope. Weather spells were challenging and chancy, but they required delicate control more than raw power. With the proper preparations and ritual, Ruslan would only need the *ikilhia* of a single life, perhaps two, to fuel the spell. He'd welcome the chance to kill, both to vent his anger and to intimidate those he intended to question.

He wouldn't choose Cara, or Jerik, surely. Ruslan would consider their knowledge of the mountains a useful resource. Wouldn't he? Guilt weighed Kiran's steps. He stole a glance at Dev, who radiated determination with every stride up the slope.

"I'm sorry," Kiran blurted.

"For what?" Dev's expression was wary. "Near falling in the river? No help for that."

"No, for...for everything. Ruslan coming, and...that you had to leave the convoy." Kiran remembered the thinly concealed pain in Dev's voice when he'd shouted at Cara. "When I asked you to help me, I didn't know it would mean you couldn't ever work as an outrider again."

Cynicism gleamed in Dev's eyes. "Would it have made a difference if you had?" At Kiran's conflicted silence, he snorted. "I didn't think so. Spare me the false apologies, then."

Stung, Kiran protested, "It wasn't false! You think I don't know how it feels, to be forced to give up something you love?" Never again to feel the glory of magic coursing through his blood, lifting his soul into light...sometimes he could hardly bear the thought.

Dev shot an odd, slanted glance his way. "You're talking about magic, I take it." He frowned. "You mean to hide in Alathia for the rest of your life?" His tone made it clear he didn't think much of that plan.

"Until I can discover some other means of protection." For all Ruslan's volatile temper, he also possessed the cold patience of a nightclaw lizard. Kiran had no illusions he would give up the hunt simply because his quarry had temporarily escaped beyond his reach. But Ruslan would never imagine him capable of giving up magic completely. He'd expect Kiran to hide far from the Council's seat of power, in hopes of using his magic in secret. Whereas Kiran intended to head straight from Kost to Tamanath, the largest city in Alathia and the stronghold of the Council, where their detection spells were strongest. By staying quiet, anonymous, and never casting so much as a first level spell, he might remain safely hidden from both Ruslan and the Council for years. Time enough, perhaps, to find a different, more permanent solution.

Dev's face had darkened. "Ruslan holds a grudge that long, does he? Shit! I can't hang around in Alathia forever, I've got important business back in Ninavel!"

"You won't have to," Kiran said. "I told you I'd give you the amulet. Wear it while you return to Ninavel, and then once you're in the city, stay away from Reytani district. Ruslan won't bother to hunt you if you don't cross his path. He thinks of untalented men as tools to be used or cast aside, not enemies worthy of attention."

"What a guy," Dev said.

"Maybe you won't have to give up outriding," Kiran said earnestly. He couldn't help those back at the convoy, but perhaps he could lessen the price Dev paid. "Once this is all over, you should tell Cara what happened. Say I forced you into helping me. She knows you've no defense against magic—surely she'd forgive you. I'll even write a letter saying as much, if you think it would help."

"It's Meldon who'll make sure I never work again, not Cara." But the grim set to Dev's face eased. For the first time since the avalanche, his glance at Kiran was merely thoughtful, rather than edged with wary hostility.

"Not all magic's outlawed in Alathia, only that not sanctioned by the Council. You'll need a false identity in Alathia anyway—why not get a forged birth-token to show you're Alathian-born, and join up with the Council's crew of mages?"

"The Council doesn't rely on anything so crude as tokens," Kiran said. "Alathian mages are taken as children and schooled both in magic and loyalty to the Council. And once each year, adult mages must submit to an examination of their thoughts and memories to prove they've held to the Council's laws."

"What happens to the ones that fail?"

Kiran shrugged. "The treatise I read said it depends on the severity of the offense. Some are executed, others mind-burned and exiled…"

"Yeah, the Alathians are all heart." Dev's scowl returned.

Kiran winced, wishing he'd had the sense not to remind Dev of the harshness of Alathian justice, and retreated into silence. He soon needed all his breath to match Dev's pace. Climbing out the unrelentingly steep slope of the canyon was far more difficult than the descent had been. His thigh muscles burned and quivered, yet he and Dev still marched through thick trees. He didn't even want to think about how much farther they had to go.

Sweat dripped from his temples and his breath came in great gasps by the time the trees thinned. The matted pine needles underfoot gave way to polished slabs of angled stone like those Kiran remembered from the opposite side of the canyon. Dark lines streaked the pale rock, and a stream of water slid down one slab in a thin smooth sheet.

Dev called a break. Kiran rubbed his aching muscles while Dev filled the waterskins. Kiran drank eagerly, feeling as if he'd sweated out an entire water jug's worth of moisture. Dev peered at the sky, a frown line between his brows.

Kiran saw only some high thin clouds, forming streaks and wisps above the western mountains. "Can you tell what Ruslan did?"

"No question something's building, but it's too early to tell what kind of storm, and how fast it'll reach us," Dev said. "Keep going, and I'll let you know when I figure it out."

Kiran struggled onward at a pace that felt little more than a crawl. Dev's progress was made with his usual abundant energy, but in rapid spurts. He would race up the rock, then stand staring at the sky while Kiran puffed his way up the same distance.

By late afternoon, Kiran's legs trembled with fatigue even though he'd been surreptitiously stealing snippets of *ikilhia* from trees at every opportunity. Finally he had to ask Dev for another break. Dev eyed him for a long moment, then nodded. Kiran collapsed gratefully onto the rock, his chest heaving.

Dev squatted beside him. "Your friend Ruslan doesn't do things by halves. See that cloud?" He pointed at a long, contoured and strangely smooth cloud that ran the length of the sky. The wispy clouds in the west had spread into a hazy veil over the sun. "Means we're going to get one hell of a storm. It's building faster than I've ever seen."

"A thunderstorm?" Kiran blanched. His exhaustion was so deep he doubted he could hold his barriers under a prolonged magical assault like the one he'd endured in Silverlode Canyon.

"If only," Dev said. "No. Haven't you felt the temperature dropping?"

Now that Kiran was no longer sweating his way uphill, the air felt much cooler. He'd assumed that was simply a result of gaining altitude. But if the temperatures plunged to the depths they'd reached at Ice Lake, and a storm hit... "You mean, it might snow?"

"Yeah. A lot, and soon, so we need to find shelter quick. Good news is, I know a protected spot up high where we can ride out the storm."

"Wouldn't it be better to stay down in the trees?"

Dev shook his head. "Deep snow will be too soft in the trees, where it's protected from the wind. Pushing through snow like that is exhausting, slow work—it'd take us days to climb out of the canyon. Higher up, the wind'll freeze the snow crust solid; we can use boot spikes and travel onward once the storm passes. Besides, I figure Ruslan expects us to run for low ground. Then after the storm, all he'd have to do is move up the bottom of Garnet Canyon until he either found us or picked up our trail in the snow."

"I see." Kiran steeled himself to ignore the burn of his overtaxed muscles.

"One thing I need to know first…" Dev prodded the overjacket and blanket tied to Kiran's pack. "Thank Khalmet, your gear's dried out. But once the storm hits, we'll need a way to stay warm. Can he detect the magic from a fire stone charm?"

"A magefire should be safe so long as I remain nearby with the amulet," Kiran said. He glanced across at the opposite wall of the canyon, and promptly wished he hadn't. Timberline seemed impossibly high above their current position. "How far to this place you're thinking of?" He dreaded the answer.

"It's a ways," Dev said. "But I think we can make it there by dark." *If you'll get off your ass and start walking,* was the unspoken sentiment plain on his face.

Kiran stood and suppressed a groan as the weight of the pack settled back on his shoulders. "All right. I'm ready to continue."

As he took one slow step after another up the gently curving slab of rock, he thought back to the surge of magic that had struck him at the river. To generate a storm so large, Ruslan must have cast a fully channeled spell. That required both a channeler and a focus, and that meant Ruslan wasn't alone.

Kiran's stomach twisted. He knew who Ruslan had brought. "Mikail," he said softly. His mage-brother, his closest friend and confidant, joining Ruslan in the hunt…his heart hurt at the thought, even as new tendrils of fear curled down his spine. Breathing harder, he tried to move faster.

CHAPTER ELEVEN

(Dev)

By the time we reached the barren expanse of Bearjaw Cirque, the sky had turned a leaden gray. Snowflakes small as sand grains swirled through the air, and the icy bite of the wind promised much worse to come.

Somewhere along the base of Bearjaw's southern cliffs, a cave waited. It wasn't even a true cave, only a spot where a massive chunk of rock had long ago broken away from the cliff and left a deep hollow beneath an overhang. Later rockfalls had piled boulders over the hollow, but a slender gap remained, just wide enough for a man to slide through to reach the enclosed space beyond. Within, we'd be well protected from the wind and snow.

The trick would be finding the cave again. I'd spent a few nights there two summers ago while I chipped carcabon stones from a nearby cliff, but back then I'd approached from the western side of the cirque. Things were bound to look different when coming up from the east. I figured our best bet was to climb straight south to the base of the cliffs and then work our way westward until we reached the cave.

Kiran plodded through the rocks toward me. His face was white and set, exhaustion plain in every slow, dragging step.

I yelled over a gust of wind, "Not far now—the cave's in those cliffs." I pointed at the forbidding southern wall of the cirque.

His shoulders slumped. The distance wasn't that great, only a mile or two, but it was all over talus, some of it steep.

"Rest here a minute," I told him. "Eat something, and put on everything warm you've got. It's only gonna get colder."

Kiran sat down without speaking. He gnawed on a piece of jerky like he was almost too tired to chew. I tried to ignore my unease. We were almost there, damn it. He could make it.

Even in the short span of our break, the snow picked up significantly and so did the wind. The flakes remained small, not a good sign. This storm meant business. I sighed and fixed the position of the cliffs firmly in my mind. Between the snow and the lateness of the hour, soon I wouldn't be able to see them at all. If we got lost, we'd wander through the rocks of the basin until we froze to death.

Thinking of that, I got out one of my short lengths of rope. When Kiran clambered to his feet, I tied one end around his waist and the other around mine. "Keep this on and we won't lose each other," I yelled into his ear. If he replied, I didn't hear it, muffled as his face was in his hood, hat, and scarf. I started walking, holding the rope up behind me to keep it from snagging on rocks.

The snow fell thick and fast, turning the talus into a slick, treacherous obstacle course. The wind whipped icy flakes into my eyes with painful force. I grew steadily more worried about Kiran. He weaved from side to side as he stumbled after me, and he fell often. At first he struggled back to his feet on his own, but as time wore on, I had to haul him up, making my strained side muscles ache and cramp in protest. After about the tenth time of that, I shortened the rope to an armslength and towed him up the talus.

When we reached the cliffs, the world had dimmed to gray, the air choked with blowing snow. Kiran braced his back against the rock and slumped down into a crouch. His eyes were closed, snow frozen on his eyelashes and the ends of his hair. Yelling didn't budge him, and I resorted to kicks to get him moving again. I dragged him forward, praying desperately to Khalmet that the cave wasn't far and I would recognize it in the failing light. I began cursing Kiran, the job, Bren, and most of all that damn mage who'd brought on this storm, spitting my words into the howl of the wind.

At last, miracle of Khalmet, a familiar pile of boulders loomed out of the whirl of snow. I untied the rope from my waist, yanked Kiran around in front of me, and by dint of pushing and screaming, got him up to the narrow crack of the opening. The gap was partially blocked with snow and ice. I knocked it clear with one hand and forced Kiran through with the other.

Once inside, the relief was immediate—no more wind, and the ground was dry. The cave was black as a mineshaft, but I'd made sure our fire stones waited at the top of my pack, and I had plenty of practice in lighting a magefire by touch alone. Blue and red flames flared into life and illuminated Kiran, lying curled in a tight ball and shivering violently.

If he was still shivering, he was better off than I'd feared. Once a man stops shivering, death isn't far away. I snatched up a blanket from my pack.

"Kiran! Hey, listen to me! You gotta get out of those wet clothes, if you want to get warm." He didn't respond. His eyes were squeezed shut and his skin waxy-pale.

I hastily stripped off my own snow-crusted outer layers and started working on Kiran. I had enough trouble peeling off his overjacket with him shaking like a palsied drunk, but when I started on his woolen undershirt, he jerked away and batted at my hands.

"Hold still!" I reached for the shirt again.

He shook his head, saying something I couldn't understand through his chattering teeth, and rolled away.

"Hold *still*, damn your eyes," I growled, and dragged him back. I'd seen this before. Men caught out too long in the cold got irrational or even delusional, and attempts to reason with them only wasted time and breath.

He tried to fight me, but I was stronger and far more coordinated. In no time I had him pinned flat on his back, his wrists trapped in one of my hands. I yanked his shirt over his head, got it free of his wrists, and reached for the blanket.

I froze mid-reach, my eyes fixed on his bare chest. Not on the amulet, dangling on its chain, but on the mark etched into the skin over his heart—

The red and black sigil of a blood mage.

I sprang backward. "*You're a fucking blood mage?*" The force of my shout tore my throat raw. All the terrible stories crowded my head, full of sadistic, gruesome torture and death. Cold horror rimed my spine.

Kiran was still shivering too hard to move easily, but he tugged the blanket around himself with trembling hands, covering the sigil. He bowed his head, wet black strands of hair falling forward to hide his face. Too late; I'd already seen the stark, despairing guilt printed there, good as any confession.

My chest felt like a boulder was crushing it, my lungs unable to draw air. When Pello had searched Kiran, the sigil must've been what he found. Sign of the most deadly and powerful mages in Ninavel… this, not the amulet, had sent Pello running for the border like a man chased by demons. *You don't even know what board you're playing on,* he'd said. Shaikar curse him, he'd been right.

Yet my horrible certainty faltered, as other memories rushed in: Kiran's wide-eyed wonder at the sight of the stream, his bright, eager smile when I'd called his carcabon idea a smart one, his painfully earnest expression when he'd offered to write Cara a letter. I couldn't wrap my mind around the two concepts: Kiran as I'd seen him on this trip, and the blood mages of legend. Was he that good of an actor? I found myself bending over him and asking, "The stories people tell… are they true? Blood mages torture and kill to fuel spells?"

He winced, and huddled deeper into the blanket. "Yes." His voice shook as badly as his hands. "But I don't—I've never—"

"Never killed anyone for a spell?" I welcomed the sullen fire of anger growing within, burning away the frozen weight in my chest. "Remember Harken? Pollis? Jacol?"

He flinched with each name I shouted at him. It only fed the flames of my anger. He'd made their deaths sound accidental, a byproduct of his haste in casting; and the stories of blood mages talked of slow and lingering death, the kind to give a man screaming nightmares, not the instant collapse of those killed at the convoy. But did he think I was such a fool I couldn't make the connection, with that sigil staring me in the face?

"Oh, you murdering bastard—I should have known that crap about 'the forces of the earth' was a lie! I should've seen you for what you are the moment you killed Harken!"

Kiran's head shot up, his eyes wide. "It wasn't a lie! The *akheli*—blood mages, you call them—in Ninavel, they *do* use forces within the earth to fuel spells…but the forces are too dangerous and wild, they can't be channeled by a mage's own energies alone, you need another source of power to harness them—"

"So you kill people. Steal their lives to use for your *harness*." Disgust and contempt near choked me. "And what, the torture part's just for fun?"

"No." His voice was low, and hoarse. "Death gives power, but… violent death gives more. But I didn't lie to you—I'm not like Ruslan, I only meant to save lives, not—"

"Ruslan! He's a blood mage too, isn't he? Fuck!" Cara and the others at the convoy, in the hands of a mage who carved people into bloody shreds for his spells—and he'd cast one already. Oh, gods! "How many did he kill to make this storm?"

Kiran put his hands over his face. "I don't know," he said, haltingly. "I hope…not more than one. He wouldn't choose anyone—anyone possibly useful to him, like Cara or Jerik."

"As if that makes it all right! You sick son of a bitch, don't try to pretend you care. I've seen the look in your eyes when you talk about magic. I know how bad you want it—you can't wait to murder someone again, can you?"

"You don't know anything!" He dropped his hands, his eyes wild beneath the tangles of his dark hair. "I never wanted it, not this way!" The last part came out in a strangled shout.

"What the fuck is that supposed to mean?"

"I told you, I'd rather deny my magic forever than use it as Ruslan does!"

"That's right, your little sob story about you and Ruslan—what vital facts did you leave out of that? Let me guess, you were happy to kill people so long as you were in control, but then he showed up and demanded you play his game instead, and that stuck in your throat—"

"No!" His voice cracked on the word. "Ruslan is…was…my master from the start. But I didn't understand what blood magic was like, not until it was too late! After that I tried to renounce it, but Ruslan thinks he owns me, he'll never let me go—"

"Oh, come on! You trained for how long to work blood magic, yet you claim you didn't know?" What kind of a gullible mark did he take me for?

"I never—!" Kiran checked his shout. He dragged shaking hands through his hair, and drew in a slow, uneven breath. "Ruslan raised us, and he kept us isolated from most other people. He blocked our magic, except under carefully controlled conditions—he said unfettered spellcasting was too dangerous until we came of age. We only learned theory, and did exercises. There's a ritual he performs, when we reach adulthood…" He faltered, and shut his eyes. His face turned the color of curdled milk. "The *akhelashva* ritual…takes a lot of power. It was the first time I saw true blood magic being worked."

I frowned. He made Ruslan sound like a glorified version of a Taint thief handler. Gods knew Red Dal leashed his Tainters tight, and kept them ignorant until the end. Not to mention all this "us" and "we" business…"How many kids does Ruslan keep?"

Kiran opened his eyes, looking surprised. "None, now. Mikail and I were his only apprentices. None of the *akheli* ever take more than two," he said, as if it were self-evident.

"Why not?" I'd have thought a blood mage would want plenty of lackeys to lord it over.

"Complex spells require two mages working as one, and the skills aren't simple to master. Easier for two apprentices to learn and practice together, as Mikail and I did. But the talent is rare, and a master *akheli* like Ruslan does not share power lightly." Bitterness filled his voice.

I leaned against the cave wall. Ruslan did sound like Red Dal, who also thought of his kids as being his property. But if a Taint thief died on a job or ran away, Red Dal could always buy or steal another

Tainted kid to replace them. Every kid born in Ninavel's got some trace of the Taint, though for most it's hardly noticeable—maybe one in a hundred is Tainted enough to be useful. But a mage-born kid with enough talent to attract the interest of a blood mage must be a hell of a lot harder to find. Plus, a month or two of training was all a Tainter needed, while it sounded like Ruslan had spent years training Kiran. Made sense he'd be both furious and determined to find his wayward apprentice. I could even—grudgingly—get why Kiran was so desperate to escape.

Assuming Kiran wasn't lying through his teeth. Again. He knew I'd been Tainted. The leap to my childhood profession wasn't a long one. Maybe he'd come up with this little tale hoping to gain my sympathy. Even if his story was true, it didn't excuse the deaths he'd caused, or the way he'd left those at the convoy to face a furious blood mage without so much as a warning. I eyed him, coldly.

"You wanted to run, fine—you should've had the guts to do it solo. A score of men are dead, thanks to you. How many more will Ruslan kill?"

"I didn't know what else to do!" Kiran gave me a desperate, pleading look. "The *akhelashva* ritual bound me to Ruslan, in a way I cannot break. He can control my magic as his own, rip down my defenses with a single thought, find me no matter how far I run…the amulet blocks the bond, but it won't stop him for long. The Alathian wards are my only hope of real protection, but I didn't know how to cross the border undetected, let alone the mountains! I needed a guide. You."

Me, the Khalmet-touched fool now stuck in this cave while his friends faced a mage who specialized in agonizing death. A spike of renewed fury pierced me. "You should've told me the truth," I snapped. "I'd never have taken you with the convoy if I'd known—!"

"You wouldn't have helped me at all," Kiran said, with bleak certainty.

Damn right I wouldn't have. If I'd known even half of this back in Ninavel, I'd have thrown Bren's offer in his face. Triple pay plus charm-grade gems, my ass. What fucking good was money to a dead man? Even if I survived Ruslan, that still left the Alathians. They didn't fuck around when it came to blood magic. If they caught me helping a blood mage, they'd burn me alive on the spot.

Watching me, Kiran paled further. "Dev, don't—don't do anything rash. Everything I told you at the convoy was true, I swear it on my blood and *ikilhia*." His fingers clenched on the blanket. "If you abandon me, Ruslan will find you, and you'll die at his hands. Even if you give me up to him, he won't spare you. Not after you helped me run from the convoy. You don't know his skill at flaying flesh and soul, prolonging torment beyond all bearing—" He choked, and pressed his hands to his eyes. His chest heaved in a juddering gasp.

Fuck. I recognized the sight of someone fighting off a dreadful memory. Kiran might be lying about his own motives, but I doubted he was lying about Ruslan being a vindictive, sadistic bastard who'd slaughter by inches anyone dumb enough to cross him. That part matched right up with every tale of blood mages I'd ever heard.

I whirled and paced the length of the cave, struggling to shove anger aside and think. I couldn't cut and run with Ruslan on the prowl, no matter how badly I wanted to. Not yet, anyway. But if we reached the border...easy enough for me to ditch Kiran and cross alone to safety. Forget the money, forget this entire godsforsaken mess...

Forget Melly, who'd pay a terrible price for my cowardice. Fail Sethan, who'd saved not only my life, but my very soul, and never once counted the cost.

Kiran had recovered himself enough to square his shoulders and meet my eyes, though his breath still rasped in his throat. "If you need more coin, or anything else...once we're safe in Kost, I'll get it for you."

I snorted, still pacing. "Yeah, right. How, without your magic? You think I don't know you'd say anything to get yourself across that border?" Didn't keep him from being right about my lack of options, damn him. If Sethan was watching from Suliyya's gardens like the southerners claimed, I sure hoped he appreciated the shit I was crawling through for Melly's sake.

"I'd find a way." The dark determination on his face checked me mid-stride. He'd played it so mild in the face of my accusations, I kept forgetting how dangerous he truly was. His fear of Ruslan might keep him from using the full strength of his magic, but he'd proved with Cara that he was far from helpless, even so. What might he do, if he believed I meant to abandon him?

Gods all damn it, I'd cast myself straight into a viper-infested cesspit this time. If only I hadn't needed Bren's money so badly—

Bren. I rounded on Kiran, as a nagging tendril of a thought burst into full bloom. "When you bought passage from Bren, did he know you were a blood mage?" Khalmet's bloodsoaked hand, I'd rip out Bren's sly, oil-soaked tongue if he had.

Kiran shook his head, with a wary frown. "I told him I was a mage, but not what type. Why?"

"Good to know which of you was the worse viper," I muttered. Kiran might believe Bren ignorant, but I had my doubts. I'd thought Bren's instructions meant he and Gerran had made a side deal with Kiran's enemy, but after hearing the whole story on Ruslan, that no longer fit so well. I thought it far more likely they intended to sell Kiran out to the Alathians through a safely anonymous intermediary. Handing a blood mage over to the Council would earn them a nice bonus, and also ensure their own safety, in case Kiran later decided to cover his tracks. If they gave Kiran up to Alathian justice…well. Maybe that'd be Shaikar's judgment on him, for what he'd done to Harken and the others.

I blew out a long breath, and straightened.

"You've made a decision," Kiran said quietly, eyes still locked on my face. The cramped curl of his body near hummed with tension. "What do you intend?"

"Let's get something straight." I crouched in front of him, just beyond his reach. "If I didn't need Bren's Shaikar-cursed money, I'd leave you to rot, and cheer when Ruslan showed up to kick your lying ass."

Kiran's eyes narrowed. One hand twitched, his fingers flexing. I mastered the urge to scramble backward. Showing fear would only invite a more direct threat.

He said, "But…?"

I scowled at him. "I do need that money. So. I'll still guide you to the border, and gods willing, get you through. But the instant we cross, we're done, hear me? You're on your own." No matter what unpleasant surprise Gerran had in store.

Pure relief washed over his face. He slumped against the cave wall. "I never expected anything different."

"Good." I stood. The magefire had warmed the cave enough to halt Kiran's shivering, but he still looked badly chilled. We were losing heat out the entrance, aided by the occasional icy blast of wind that spat swirls of snow through the crevice. I'd need to fix a tarp to try and block the gap. "This storm could last days. We'll need to conserve energy and food. If I were you, I'd sleep as much as possible. We'll have a hard climb to the notch once the storm clears."

Kiran sighed and tilted his head back against the rock. The firelight softened his pallor, making him look very young as well as unhappy. I turned away from the sight. No need to like him, or even believe him. I just had to get him across the border. That'd be hard enough.

✳

(Kiran)

Kiran shifted closer to the magefire as Dev pounded pitons into the rock near the cave entrance. The wild howl of the wind outside made him shudder with remembered cold. His physical exhaustion was deeper than any he'd experienced before. His entire body hurt, not with the sharp fire of magical overload, but with a deep, pounding ache. His eyelids seemed weighted by lead. Sleep promised welcome oblivion, but the chill hostility in Dev's eyes kept jerking him back from the brink.

If only Dev hadn't seen Ruslan's *akhelsya* sigil! Anger or fear, either one might easily grow to outweigh Dev's desire for payment. But how could Kiran prevent betrayal to Ruslan or the Alathians? He could think of no argument he hadn't employed already. Money seemed a frail thread to hang all his hope on.

His thoughts slowed despite himself, his body surrendering to sleep's ever more insistent pull. For a time, exhaustion kept his sleep dark and dreamless. But as the hours passed and his body slowly recovered, the inner darkness faded, replaced by memories.

"What is it that has upset you, little one?" Lizaveta looked up at him from where she reclined on a low couch. Her jasmine-scented black hair slid in a heavy fall over one smooth brown shoulder to pool on the crimson folds of her robe.

Kiran was too agitated to sit. "You have to help me, khanum Liza, please. I can't live like this, I won't! Can't you undo the binding?"

Her kohl-lined eyes followed him as he paced. "You know the answer to that, Kiranushka. The mark-binding is forever. No one can undo it." She sat up and reached for his hand. "Can you not see how much he loves you? All these years he has waited for you to take your place with Mikail at his side."

Kiran stopped short, baring his teeth. "Loves me? Loves me? How can you say that, after what he did?"

Her face remained placid, though a shadow moved through the liquid depths of her eyes. Gently, she drew him down to sit beside her. "Ruslan is sometimes…hasty. He only meant to teach a lesson. Can you not forgive him?"

He jerked his hand from her grasp, feeling the bitter sting of tears. "I will never forgive him. Never. He is a monster." He swiped at his eyes. "I refuse to be one. I'll kill myself, if that's what it takes to free myself from this." He gestured furiously at his chest, where Ruslan's mark lay.

Lizaveta's delicately painted lips curved. "Ah, Kiran. Always so dramatic." She sighed. "I told Ruslan as much when he first brought you to me. This one, I said, this child does not have the right temperament for our life." She traced a finger down his cheek. "But your life-light burned so brightly, so full of power, so eager and so loving—how could we not love you in return?"

"I mean it, khanum Liza. Help me, or I'll seek the only release left to me."

"Very well, little one. I will help you, on one condition." She paused, her eyes on Kiran's face.

"What?" Kiran said, unwillingly.

"You must give me a binding blood-promise: you will not kill yourself,

by direct or indirect action, no matter what should occur."

Kiran glared at her. "No! If I do that, you'll just hand me back to him, the moment I step out your door."

Lizaveta's eyes grew hard, her face stern. "Give me this promise, and I will help you leave Ruslan. I have said it. Do you doubt my word?" Her voice cut through the air like a whip.

"I...no." Kiran bowed his head. "I'm sorry, khanum Liza."

"Then what is your answer?"

He was silent for a long moment, biting his lip. At last he met her eyes. "I will promise."

She rose and glided over to an ornately decorated side table, her bare feet silent on the thick carpet. A sigil glowed to life on a chest carved with spineflowers as she approached. She removed a silver knife and bowl from the chest, and padded softly back to him. Seating herself gracefully on the couch, she placed the bowl between them, and held out a hand, palm up. The knife waited, gleaming, in the other.

Slowly, he extended his own hand. With practiced, rapid motions, she cut matching lines first on his palm, then hers, following the lifeline. Blood welled up to coat the silver blade. She clasped his hand, and he drew in a sharp breath as blood met blood and her magic rose to envelop him. If Ruslan was all blazing red fire, she was something much more dark and subtle, a deep violet vine twining through his consciousness. But for all her subtlety, he could feel her strength, ancient and powerful, equal to her mage-brother's.

With her magic sinking roots throughout his mind and soul, she looked deep into his eyes and said softly, "Make the promise."

He obeyed. The power flared as he spoke, searing the words into his heart. Satisfied, she withdrew. With their hands still clasped, she drew him forward into a kiss. He resisted, memories of Alisa rising to drown him. But she was patient, her mouth sweet as the lira berries she loved to eat, and long habit made him yield. After a timeless interval, she released him. He turned his hand over to find the cut vanished. She'd worked a restorative binding so smoothly he hadn't even felt it.

She smiled at him, gently. "Ah, Kiranushka. I will miss you." She rose. "Come to me in a day's time. I can provide you with means to hide yourself from Ruslan, and I will give you the name of a man who can arrange passage for you out of the city."

"Thank you." Kiran hesitated. *"Ruslan will be angry with you, if he discovers you helped me—"*

She put a finger on his lips, a wicked gleam in her eyes. "Angry will be an understatement, little one. But fear not. In the many long years we have known each other, Ruslan and I have been angry with each other countless times, and it has not destroyed us." She sighed, her smile fading. "This is what you are too young to understand: that for the akheli, *family is all."*

Kiran woke to Dev shaking him by the shoulder. A suspicious wetness lingered in his eyes. He rubbed a hand over them and hoped Dev wouldn't notice. "What is it?"

"Storm's over," Dev said. "Time to pack up and go." The tarp lay in a neat bundle beside the cave entrance. Snow caked Dev's boots, and his cheeks were red with cold.

"Already?" Kiran peered at the darkness outside the crack. "I thought the storm would last longer."

"It's been a full day."

Kiran blinked. He'd slept for an entire day? No wonder hunger pains cramped his stomach and his mouth felt dry as bone. He reached for his waterskin. The deep ache had gone from his body, though his muscles still felt sluggish and stiff.

Dev busied himself with his gear with sharp efficiency. Kiran's worries returned at the sight of his impassive face. Dev would want to reach the border to escape Ruslan, but he might easily have lied about his intent to help Kiran cross.

"When we reach the border…you said before 'there's always a way,' but what will you do to find one?" Specifics would be a good sign, but if Dev brushed the question aside with vague assurances, that would be a clear warning.

"While you were sleeping, I did some thinking." Dev sat and strapped a set of small but wickedly sharp metal spikes to the instep of one boot. "When I bring Bren's usual goods through, they're in a box sealed with a special ward that damps down their magic, to a level so low it fools both the mage and the gate spells. The box goes in a hidden compartment, so the guards don't see it in their search. Works every time. I figure a mage shouldn't be far different. Hide you from the guards, find a way to suppress your magic same as Bren's charms, and I can get you through."

Kiran relaxed a fraction. "Suppress my magic…" He frowned, thoughtfully. The amulet worked by misdirection, not suppression. "May I see your ward?"

Dev extracted an oilskin bundle from his pack. Gently, he unwrapped layers of cloth to reveal a thin copper square inset with gleaming gold lines.

Kiran laid a hand on the copper and cocked his head in surprise. Rather than fiery swirls of cleanly contained energies, the ward contained a chaotic darkness unlike any magic he'd sensed before. "What kind of mage made this?"

Dev shrugged. "Dunno. Got it from Bren when I first started working his route. He called it a blackshroud ward."

Kiran released the ward. Extend that dark void over a group of charms, and he could well believe them undetectable by ordinary methods. But his own aura dwarfed that of any charm. "I doubt this type of ward would be enough to conceal me."

"I didn't think it'd be so easy." Dev rewrapped the ward. "I've got an idea, though. The Alathians aren't much on magic, but you wouldn't believe what they can do with herbs. I heard an Alathian say once that one way their Council controls magical offenders before trial is to force drugs on them that cut off their magic. Bet you they'll have a drug that'll do the trick, in combination with your amulet and my ward."

"But how would you obtain such a thing?" A drug that cut off magic…Kiran supposed that was possible, since mind, body, and magic were inextricably linked. Surely the effects wouldn't be permanent. Though if they were…he crushed the protest in his heart. He'd chosen the moment he left Ninavel to trade magic for a life free from Ruslan.

"Gerran'll know. When we reach the border, best if I first scout the gate and make a trip into Kost to talk with him, before we try taking you through."

Kiran tensed. "You'll go into Kost alone." A solo trip into Kost would give Dev the perfect opportunity to either betray him to the Alathians or safely abandon him to Ruslan.

Dev darted a sardonic glance his way. "Want a guarantee I won't sell you out, do you? Too bad. Seems to me I've had to take your word for all kinds of shit on this trip. About time you had to take mine."

Kiran subsided, reluctantly. With his life at stake, he couldn't afford to merely take Dev's word. Perhaps if he approached the problem from another angle...Dev needed money, but why so badly? Based on his words to Cara, Kiran was certain it wasn't out of simple greed. If he could learn why, he might discover another, stronger inducement to offer.

It wouldn't be easy. Dev was nearly as reticent on personal matters as Kiran. Kiran yanked his pack shut. If there was a way to get Dev talking, he'd find it.

CHAPTER TWELVE

(Dev)

Icrested Bearjaw's ridge and flopped onto the snow with a
heartfelt groan. My strained side was on fire, and my back felt
like someone had been thumping it with rocks. Snow and ice
had turned the easy climb I remembered into a lethally slick ascent
near as difficult as Kinslayer. Kiran hadn't a prayer of managing
it. I'd got him up ten pitches worth of rock one inch at a time, by
hauling on the rope with all my might every time he made even the
slightest advance upward. Khalmet's hand, I hadn't worked so hard
on a climb since the time Sethan had broken his ankle on a three-
day ascent of Nyshant Peak.

Kiran struggled up my bootpacked steps in the final snow slope. He
eased himself down onto the snowbank next to me. "Are you all right?"

"Yeah, yeah. Just resting." The view westward from the notch was
spectacular. Snow-dusted spires dropped down to lines of thickly
forested ridges that glowed a lush green in the late afternoon sun. In
the distance, a break in the trees marked the deep gorge of the Elenn
River, twisting southward through the foothills. The Alathian border
lay on the other side of the Elenn, guarded by the invisible barrier

164

that prevented foreigners like us from crossing anywhere other than a border outpost like Kost.

I'd tried crossing in the wild once, just to see. Even though I'd inched through the seemingly empty forest clearing, hitting the border felt like I'd slammed face first into a cliff at the speed of a charging rock bear. I'd tumbled backward onto my ass with my head throbbing, blood leaking from my nose and ears, and not even a shimmer in the air to show I'd troubled the wards. Of course, that was only for an ordinary guy like me. Word was the barest touch from a foreign mage like Kiran would fire the wards in truly spectacular fashion: empty air blazing into a wall of magefire, joined by the instant appearance of a horde of grim-faced Council mages eager to destroy the unfortunate intruder. Not a scenario I cared to risk.

Kiran pointed to the sunwashed hills. "Is that Alathia?" Wary hope glimmered in his eyes.

I nodded. "Kost lies southwest of here, where the Deeplink River meets the Elenn. We'll head down to treeline, then cut south across the ridges until we can drop into the gorge."

"It's so green! Look at all those trees..." His voice was soft with wonder.

I wasn't falling for that wide-eyed act anymore. I pushed to my feet and said sharply, "Come on. Not much light left in the day."

If I'd needed any more proof that Kiran's master had spellcast that storm, I would've had it by the relative lack of snow on the west side of the ridge. Ordinary storms dumped their heaviest loads on the Whitefires' western slopes, resulting in the abundant Alathian waterfalls and rivers. But only a hundred yards west of Bearjaw's ridgeline, the snow thinned to scant inches deep, instead of the several feet we'd fought through in the cirque. Too bad—I'd been hoping for a nice easy glissade down a snow slope, and instead we had to clamber over slippery talus.

I had to lower Kiran down another cliff, while I took shallow breaths and tried to ignore the pain stabbing my side. I downclimbed the same section, placing my feet with care thanks to all the meltwater dripping down the cliff face. Sporadic rattles of rockfall echoed through the basin as the meltwater loosened rocks in the couloirs. I kept an eye on the narrow couloir directly above, praying no sharp-edged missiles would catapult out before we could clear the fall zone.

Just as I reached the ground, Kiran exclaimed, "Oh! What are those?"

A group of mountain goats perched on the cliff's edge, watching us. The adults were shaggy and disheveled, their thick winter coats falling out in clumps. Several fuzzy, bright-eyed babies peered down from between their mothers' legs.

The sharp knock of bouncing rocks sounded from the couloir. The goats scattered.

Shit! "'Ware rock!" I yelled, and ducked, my arms going up to shield my head. A sudden violent shove from behind sent me sprawling into a snowbank. Amidst the whining buzz of rocks flying past, I heard a dull thud, and Kiran cried out.

I thrashed free of the snowbank, my stomach dropping into my boots. A rock strike to the head would kill Kiran instantly, magic or no magic. If all this had been for nothing—!

He lay curled on the ground clutching his left arm. Blood trickled between his fingers, but he was alive. The force of my relief near dropped me into the snowbank again.

I squatted beside him. "Let me see your arm."

Wordlessly, he took his hand away. The rock had gouged a deep cut, and his lower arm was bent at a strange angle.

"What the hell were you thinking? You should've stayed clear," I growled, digging through my pack for my charm stash. I didn't own anything near so powerful as the convoy's precious store of bonemender charms, but my little pains-ease and skinseal charms were better than nothing.

"A rock was going to hit you. I could see it," he said, in a small voice. "I didn't know what else to do."

So he'd taken the hit instead, from a rock big enough to kill if it'd hit my skull or spine. I should've been grateful, but instead I felt unsettled, even angry. Far easier to remember he was a liar and a murderer when he didn't pull stunts like this.

Damn it, his saving me didn't mean he was a nice guy. He'd only feared his chance to cross the border would vanish if I got too badly hurt to continue.

I reached for his arm, and he pulled it away with a hiss of pain. "Don't touch it!" His voice broke and wavered on the words.

"I have to clean and bind it," I said as patiently as I could, and reached for it again.

He leaned away from me. "No! If you do, I don't know if I could stop, I—"

"Stop what?" I snapped. We'd already wasted enough time on the climb to the notch, and now this.

His eyes looked almost black, his pupils were dilated so far. "It hurts and it wants to heal, and I need power to do it, and up here there's only you."

Horror froze my tongue. I stumbled backward, as if that would make a difference. He hadn't needed a touch to steal Harken's life.

A bitter grimace twisted Kiran's mouth. "I won't take from you. Not on purpose. But if you touch me, you'll bypass my barriers, and it might happen...accidentally." His eyes dropped away from mine on the final word.

I shuddered. Khalmet's hand, but the thought of my life draining away with me helpless to stop it was a nasty one. In my mind's eye I saw the staring eyes of the dead mule teams. An idea made me straighten.

"What about the goats? Can't you, uh...*take* from them?" Even if we could no longer see them, they wouldn't be far.

He gave a tiny shake of his head. "I'd have to drop my barriers, and that's dangerous. Ruslan can reach me, then. The only way to draw power and remain safe from him is by touch."

"Damn." I edged closer and peered at his arm with my hands clasped firmly behind my back. "That's a bad break. If I can't touch you, you'll have to fix it up yourself. Awkward, but I've got a pains-ease charm that should help some—"

"A healing charm won't work on me, not while I hold my barriers." Kiran twisted to look down the valley. "If we can reach the trees, I think I could safely take enough *ikilhia* from them to heal it myself."

"Yeah, well, that's a good couple hours of walking. You've got to bind the arm and put it in a sling, or you'll pass out from pain long before we hit treeline," I told him. "Then we'd be well and truly fucked, because I sure as hell can't carry you without touching you. Unless…" I peered at him. "You were out cold after the avalanche, and I hauled your skinny ass back to the convoy without dying of it."

"My collapse then was from pressing my magic too far, not a physical injury." Kiran looked down at his misshapen arm. His next words came out thin and airless. "I told you of the ritual Ruslan performed, when I came of age. That ritual did more than bind me to him. A whole and healthy body has a specific pattern—and mine is now linked directly to my magic. Any marring of that pattern, and my magic seeks to repair it, as instinctively as breathing."

I swallowed, my mouth gone dry. "You're saying that to *not* take power to heal yourself is like deliberately holding your breath."

He nodded, eyes still downcast.

Every time I thought this trip couldn't get worse, Khalmet proved me wrong. "How long can you…?"

"Long enough to reach those trees."

Gods. I tossed Kiran the waterskin, and prayed the confidence in his words was warranted. "Clean that cut off with some water while I make some bandages."

It took almost an hour, but eventually he got the arm bound up. I tied a rough sling for him out of a length of rope, and strapped his pack onto mine with another. My side felt like a rock bear had clawed it when I heaved on the doubled pack. "Mother of maidens, what I wouldn't give for a mule," I muttered. I'd need that pains-ease charm myself by the time we stopped again. Assuming I wasn't a drained husk of a corpse.

The sun was already sinking into the haze above the forested hills. We'd never make the trees before it set. I sighed, heavily. Another grueling march in the dark, under a looming threat I had no defense against. Gods, I'd never thought the day would come when I couldn't wait to get the hell out of the mountains.

At least we'd already made it over the worst terrain. Soon after we started walking, the valley widened, talus fields mixing with marshy tundra dotted with old snowbanks. A stream appeared from under the snow, gurgling downward through the rocks, the water shining white in occasional tumbling falls.

At first Kiran moved along in silence, his face pinched and inward-looking, his arm cradled in the sling against his chest. He wasn't able to walk very fast, but I wasn't exactly sprinting either, with my side screaming and the weight of both our packs crushing my spine and shoulders. We'd been going maybe an hour when Kiran spoke up.

"Do you think you could…talk about something?"

"What? Why?" I certainly didn't feel like talking.

"I think it would help me," he said, sounding apologetic. He was looking white around the mouth, and he wouldn't meet my eyes.

I tried to sound casual, and not like every instinct was yammering at me to run. "Uh. Fine. What do you want me to talk about?"

He started to shrug, and stopped with a gasp, his face lined with pain. "I don't know. Something—something interesting. How did you learn to climb, and be an outrider?"

I considered making up a tale, but I felt too tired and nervous to bother. He'd likely guessed most of the truth, anyway. "When I was a kid, I was a Taint thief. My handler taught all of us to climb. He thought it made us better at the job."

"A Taint thief, truly? That's why you were sold? I'd read of such things, but only in children's tales…" He sounded fascinated. I guessed the distraction thing was working. "What did you steal?"

"Jewelry, coin, charms…whatever our handler asked us to get." Which had sometimes included far stranger things than coin or charms. Though Red Dal did plenty of freelance work, he made the biggest money from jobs on commission. Between highsiders, merchant houses, and ganglords, he had no shortage of customers desperate to get their hands on valuable goods protected behind wards. I'd lifted everything from intricate Sulanian bone sculptures to a spymaster's secret records.

"I've never met anyone strongly Tainted. Could you truly fly, and shatter ward patterns, like in the tales?"

Mother of maidens, but the memories burned like salt in a wound. "Yes."

He checked at the bitter violence of the word. "I'm sorry, I didn't mean to…I was only curious."

"I know." Most were, even Ninavel natives who'd had some trace of the Taint themselves. Didn't make talking about it any easier. Before I could come up with a change of subject, he spoke again.

"What happened, then, after you…after?"

"My handler sold me to someone else." Another set of memories I didn't care to revisit. Those first weeks in Tavian's hands were a black blur. Some Tainters never surfaced from the soul-destroying depression that followed the Change, and ended up dead because they just didn't care anymore. That might've been me, but for Jylla. Her handler had sold her off to Tavian scant weeks before me. Somehow, we'd pulled each other through, our shared shock turning first to anger, then determination.

I'd thought we'd had a bond nothing could break. Yet she'd stolen every kenet I owned and cast me aside like all we'd shared meant nothing. I kicked steps over a mud-smeared snowbank with sullen violence.

"Your handler sold you to an outrider?" Kiran asked.

"Of course not. What in Shaikar's hells would an outrider want with a newly Changed city brat?" Tavian's gang had sold taphtha, lionclaw, and other addictive drugs to merchant house men who preferred to keep their vices secret. Tavian had wanted a runner boy who could slither into unlikely places for drops, and knew how to keep his mouth shut.

Jylla, he'd had other uses for. The old, sick anger twisted in my gut, no matter that Tavian was seven years dead.

"But then, how did you…?"

I reined in my tongue with an effort. Not Kiran's fault he'd dredged up memories so bitter. "You've heard us talk of Sethan, right? Some two years after my Change, I met him on the street one day." And by "met," I meant "tried to steal from." I'd had this crazy idea in those days that I'd prove you didn't need the Taint to steal. I'd become the best thief in Ninavel, and then Red Dal would take me back. Gods, what a fucking idiot I'd been.

I'd known better than to pick pockets; too dangerous without the Taint, if the mark wore warding charms. Instead, I'd resorted to simple snatches from busy street markets. Once my chosen mark was distracted in a conversation, I'd grab his parcels, take off down a side alley, and climb straight up to a roof. Most people never thought to look up, and I'd had no idea that adults who weren't handlers could climb.

Yeah, and then I'd tried that on Sethan. Gods, I'd nearly fallen off the wall when he swarmed right up after me. We'd ended up in this crazy chase all over walls and rooftops. No matter what I did, I couldn't shake him. He'd finally caught up just as I started a suicidal jump across a blank section of wall, some hundred feet above a flagstone courtyard. I'd known that without the Taint the jump was too far, but Red Dal had hammered into my head that death was preferable to capture. Sethan had grabbed the strap of my rucksack and somehow managed to jerk me back and keep his own precarious hold. He'd dragged me onto a roof, ignoring my kicking and biting, and yelled at me not for stealing, but for nearly killing myself.

"We got to talking, and he invited me to come climbing with him on real rock," I told Kiran. Once he'd stopped yelling, Sethan had told me I was a hell of a climber, and I'd heard in his voice that he meant it. It was the first time since my Change anybody'd told me I was good at anything.

"It was just some easy cliffs next to the Juntar mine, but I wasn't even halfway up before I knew I wanted to spend the rest of my life climbing." The dizzy elation I'd felt on the cliff had been a drug strong as any Tavian sold. I'd never thought to feel like that again, Changed as I was. "Sethan and I kept climbing together, got to be friends, and the next year he took me on as apprentice." After Jylla and I had killed Tavian; though Sethan had never known that part.

"He taught you outriding…and then later he died, in a rockfall?"

"Right." I didn't stop the word from coming out curt and cold. It'd be a bright day in Shaikar's hells before I talked about that rockfall to anyone, let alone Kiran.

If he heard the warning in my tone, he didn't heed it. "But if Sethan is dead…why do you need money for his sake?"

Gods all damn it, I'd forgotten he'd overheard my fight with Cara. I stopped dead and fixed him with my fiercest glare. "That's none of your fucking business." Hell if I'd spill my secrets to a liar like him, especially when I wasn't certain whose ears they might end up in if Gerran sold him out.

"Isn't it?" His expression wavered between defiant and pleading. "My life depends on your need for that money. But without knowing why you need it, how can I trust it's truly so important to you that you'll not betray me?"

"Use your gods-damned eyes! You think I would've abandoned the convoy, given up outriding, and risked death at a blood mage's hands if that money wasn't fucking vital to me?"

He winced. "I truly am sorry it's cost you so much to help me. My offer stands—if there's anything I can do for you, after reaching Kost—please, just tell me."

My gaze lit on his bandaged arm, and my anger faded. Regardless of his motives, he'd spared me injury or worse today. "If I think of something, I'll let you know," I said, and walked on.

He took a breath, but before he could raise another unpleasant topic, I blurted out the first question that came to mind.

"You said Ruslan raised you—how young were you apprenticed?" I had no idea how that worked for mages, and I had to admit I was curious.

"Five, perhaps six years of age? I'm not exactly sure." Kiran sighed. "I don't remember anything before Ruslan. He always said it was because my life only truly started when I came to him."

"Huh." What a crock of manipulative horseshit. Red Dal trotted out similar crap with his Tainters, and we hadn't seen through it either. I quashed an unwilling pang of sympathy. "Was it hard, learning to do magic?" Using the Taint had been easy as breathing, but street stories said spellcasting was different, even for powerful mages.

Kiran started to answer, then fell silent as we negotiated a stretch of talus and he had to concentrate to keep from jostling his arm. His voice was breathless when he next spoke. "Sometimes. There's a lot to learn, both to design spells and cast them. Even a tiny mistake in a channel pattern can result in enough spillover to destroy both of you in an instant."

"Sounds lovely," I muttered, then paused. "Both of you? Is that like what you said before, that it takes two mages to do a difficult spell?"

"Yes. One to control and direct the power within the channels, and the other to focus it through the lens of his will and cast the spell."

"What's it like?" The question slipped out before I could stop it. Gods, the Taint had been pure joy. Savage longing tore my heart at the very thought.

Kiran was silent for a moment. "Glorious," he finally said. I recognized the echo of my description of Kinslayer, and the pain in his voice, twin to my own.

Damn it, when he talked of magic, he didn't mean anything so innocent as either climbing or the Taint. "How many channeled spells does a blood mage cast?" I figured that was a nicer way to put it than *how many people do you kill?*

He didn't answer right away. "I only cast practice spells, where we didn't use full power. But I think…I think Ruslan casts channeled spells often."

I wondered what "often" really meant. How many people disappeared in a city the size of Ninavel? I thought of the streetside slums, all the beggars and whores and gangs. All the immigrants that flooded into the city, hoping to strike it rich and failing more often than not. Ninavel must be a perfect haunt for a blood mage.

The sun had set while we talked, the haze on the horizon glowing a dusky, burning orange. Through the twilight, I spied a clump of twisted dwarf pines amidst a set of rocks.

I pointed. "Will those work?" If so, we might be spared hours of stumbling in the dark.

"They'll help." Kiran's eyes were dark holes, his expression indistinct in the gathering gloom. The careful way he held himself told me his arm was hurting him badly.

"Then we'll stop there for the night. I'll run ahead and set up camp before the light fails completely," I said. He nodded, and I picked up my pace, glad to put extra distance between us.

When I reached the trees, I found a nice dry patch of ground between two boulders big enough to act as windbreaks. I set up the tarp, and lit the fire stones the moment Kiran arrived.

He didn't say a word, just went straight for the nearest tree and grabbed a branch like it was a lifeline. I don't know what I'd expected. A flash like a mage ward would give, or a sound, or something—but there was nothing like that. His head fell back, his eyes closed, and the look on his face made my skin crawl. I'd seen that same slack-jawed pleasure in lionclaw addicts when they swallowed a dose.

The needles of the tree withered to brown, then curled and blackened as if burned.

"Khalmet's bony hand," I breathed, suppressing a shudder. Those charred-looking patches of catsclaw before Broken Hand Pass… Lightning strikes, my ass. It had been Kiran. I remembered his wild-eyed desperation right after the storm, and felt an uncomfortable shock of recognition. *Don't touch me,* he'd said, much as he had after the rockfall. I swallowed hard at the thought of how close my hand had been to his shoulder. I'd always thought the Alathians a bunch of priggish idiots for their restrictions on magic, but this trip was changing my mind fast.

Kiran worked his way through the entire clump of trees. When he returned, his arm still lay in the sling, but the pinched look had gone from his eyes and mouth, and he sat without wincing.

"Is it better?" I wanted to ask, *is it safe,* but I didn't want him to know how unsettled I really was.

"Not all the way." He poked his arm. "I'll have to wait until we reach more trees to finish the healing. But it feels much better."

"Good." I tried to sound matter of fact, and not look at the blackened husks where living trees had once stood. "We're over the worst terrain, so no more climbing or rappelling. But we're still two days out from Kost. How long do you figure we have before Ruslan tries something else?" How long, before he murdered some other Khalmet-touched convoy member? I struggled to blot out an image of Cara, bloody and screaming.

Kiran rubbed his forehead, looking unhappy. "Two days…I think he'll cast again, in that time. If he believes we're still above timberline, he may try a series of earthquakes to trigger rockfalls and avalanches over a broader area—or if he realizes we've reached the western slopes, perhaps wildfires…"

Wildfires. Great. I'd better make sure we stuck close to streams.

Kiran hastily added, "The closer we get to the border, the safer we'll be—the wards are so powerful they'll disrupt other workings."

"We'll rest up for a few hours, then, and keep going once the moon rises," I said. If we headed straight west, another half day's walk would put us at the rim of the Elenn gorge, as close to the border as we could get until Kost. I prayed that'd be close enough.

✳

(Kiran)

"There it is, the border with Alathia." Dev stood balanced on a prong of rock that jutted out over the dizzying chasm of the Elenn Gorge.

Kiran had no intention of joining him on a perch so precarious. He edged closer to the rocky rim. Far below, the shining silver ribbon of the Elenn River twisted along the narrow canyon bottom. The leaden gray cliffs of the gorge's steep sides had a stern, foreboding aspect after the bright rock of the high mountains.

The forest on the far rim appeared no different than that on Dev and Kiran's side. Yet when Kiran concentrated, even through his barriers he sensed a deep, soundless thrumming, warning of quiescent power. He wished he dared release his barriers and examine the border properly. When he'd researched the Alathian wards, every scholar he'd read had agreed on the wards' strength, but none had any certain knowledge of their design, or the source of their enormous power.

Kiran had his own theory, based in part on a disparaging comment Ruslan had once made about Alathians being narrow-minded fools using forces they barely understood. Certain historical treatises spoke of strange artifacts found in the far west, the remnants of a vanished ancient civilization. Most were useless or broken, but the few that worked were said to be curiously powerful, as if a vast host of mages had worked together to create them. Kiran suspected the Alathians had found such an artifact and discovered a way to exploit its power for their own use. Yet even with that assumption, the potential design of their wards still eluded him. How could any passive, charm-bound spell generate a barrier of that extent and strength? Not even the purest of metals could hold so much energy.

Perhaps if a mage were to construct a spell that spiraled back on itself, like one of the eddies Kiran had seen in Garnet River…

"Kost lies downriver, to the south," Dev said, dissolving the fascinatingly elegant pattern taking shape in Kiran's head. "The gorge widens out beyond the next bend, and we can scramble down a side ravine to the Elenn."

Dev paused. His green eyes turned calculating, in a way that rekindled Kiran's nerves. "Back at the convoy you said I've got to stay within five hundred yards of you, or else Ruslan pounces on me. How fast, exactly, would Ruslan find me? Far safer if I could stash you somewhere well clear of the gate, before I go through to talk with Gerran. Otherwise, we'll have to risk an Alathian spotting you."

Kiran's nerves clamored louder. Dev wanted a way to leave him before they'd even reached the gate? He glanced involuntarily across the gorge, at the silent forest beyond.

He was so close to safety—closer, in truth, than he'd ever thought to reach. To have freedom jerked from his grasp now would be all the more terrible, yet he'd failed to discover anything specific to offer Dev that might ensure he kept his word. Kiran had thought last night a promising start, but ever since he'd taken *ikilhia* to heal his arm, Dev had retreated into blank-faced efficiency, refusing all attempts at more than casual conversation.

If only he might offer Dev a way to regain the Taint! Dev's yearning had been startlingly clear. But so far as Kiran knew, not even magic could provide that. He'd rejected the idea of a lie—even if Dev believed him, when Kiran didn't follow through on his promise in Kost, Dev might easily go to the Alathians in revenge.

Yet if Dev meant to abandon or betray him, he could do so just as easily with Kiran standing right outside the gate, as with Kiran hidden deep in the forest.

With a swooping, vertiginous feeling in his stomach, Kiran said, "An untalented man like you, traveling so close to a source of magic as powerful as that of the border wards—for Ruslan to isolate your *ikilhia* now would be like attempting to identify a single spark amidst a wildfire. He can do it, but not quickly or easily. You'd have half a day to reach the border, perhaps more."

Dev raised his brows. The faint twist to his mouth said he hadn't missed Kiran's reluctance to share the information. Kiran braced for a sharp comment, but Dev only nodded and said, "There's an abandoned cabin partway down the ravine—we can reach it by midafternoon. If I leave you there and run straight for Kost, I'll pass the gate by sunset. I'll get everything arranged and return to the cabin by mid-morning."

A full night in Alathia. More than enough time to speak to the authorities and give testimony under truth spell. Unease gnawed at Kiran's gut.

"Wouldn't it be better for me to wait off in the woods somewhere? What if someone decides to visit this cabin?" If the Alathians came for him at Dev's instigation, he might be able to hide in the forest… though he had no idea what he might do after that.

Dev slanted him a glance. "Small chance anybody'll wander up a trailless, nondescript side ravine—but if someone comes, either hide, or tell 'em you're meeting up with a prospector. See, I've gotta take our camp gear with me. I'll be playing solo prospector at the gate, and the Alathians'll notice if I don't have a full set of supplies. At the cabin you'll have shelter, and a food storage locker. Bears roam these woods. I'm thinking you'd rather not try and beat one off with a stick, after it smells your food."

"Bears?" Kiran tried to decide if Dev was joking.

Dev's one-sided grin appeared, for the first time since the avalanche. "Yeah. Alathian prospectors don't carry charms powerful enough to keep them away, so they've gotten bold." He tilted his head, the amusement dying out of his expression. "I guess if a bear came, you could just, you know—" he made a vague hand gesture, and grimaced.

Kiran was startled into a disbelieving laugh. "Oh yes, I'll get close enough to touch a wild bear." He shook his head. "Any magic from a distance means releasing my barriers, and that means—"

"Ruslan crashes down on you like a two-ton boulder and makes the bear look like a fuzzy kitfox cub, yeah, I got it." Dev turned away. "Look, we've made it over the mountains, and you said Ruslan couldn't cast anything strong at us so close to the border, right? Try and relax a little."

Kiran swallowed a sharp reply. Though Dev's voice had brimmed with confidence, he knew Dev well enough now to see the tension in his stance that put the lie to his bravado.

He followed Dev back from the lip of the gorge into the forest. In a move that by now was almost habit, he brushed a hand across a pine trunk.

The forest in front of him abruptly shimmered, as if seen through a heat haze, and changed into a panorama of snow and rock. Startled, Kiran stumbled, and the ghostly image vanished. He rubbed a hand over his eyes. His barriers stood firm, and no hint of magic tinged the aether. Perhaps exhaustion was catching up with him.

Dev glanced back. "How's the arm?"

Kiran rotated his wrist. He'd been skimming off bits of *ikilhia* from trees all morning to finish the healing. Unmarked skin now replaced the torn, bruised flesh left by the rock, and the throbbing pain had gone. Better yet, the pulse of wrongness that last night had burned in an unceasing scream for power had now faded to a whisper so faint Kiran could ignore it with ease. "Almost completely healed," he told Dev.

Dev's eyes were narrowed and thoughtful. "Can you heal yourself of anything, that way?"

"Any physical injury, yes. But the greater the injury, the more power is required." Kiran didn't explain that the greater the injury, the more instinctive and uncontrolled the power draw. No need to make Dev more wary of him than he already was. He cast about for an innocuous subject that might ease Dev into further conversation.

"What kind of pine trees are these?" The trunks weren't quite as broad as those of the bristlebarks in Garnet Canyon, but these pines were far taller. Kiran couldn't even see their tops, his view blocked by heavy branches laden with blue-green needles.

"Cinnabar pines. See how red the bark is? It reminded people of cinnabar ore." Dev's face settled back into impassivity, and he picked up his pace.

Kiran sighed. His thoughts returned to the momentary visual distortion he'd experienced. Had it been a hallucination, brought on by stress and lack of sleep? He feared it signified some new assault by Ruslan, yet he'd felt no magic. He worried at the question, as he and Dev wound their way between cinnabar trees and hopped over trickling streams half-hidden by arching ferns.

The vision had happened just after he'd taken a flicker of *ikilhia* from a tree. Everything he knew about magic said touch-drawn power shouldn't affect his barriers…but just in case, he refrained from any further attempts.

Yet an hour later, it happened again. One moment he was trudging after Dev up the side of a gentle ridge, the next the world before him blurred and transformed. Not to snow and ice this time, but to a marshy meadow lined with trees of a kind Kiran had never seen, thin slender things with white bark and tiny fluttering leaves. Kiran stopped dead. He searched his barriers for any flaw, hunting for any suggestion of magic.

Deep within his mind, the tiniest twitch, so subtle it was barely detectable. The meadow scene dissolved back into cinnabar forest even as he isolated the sensation.

"What is it?" Dev had turned to stare at him. "Has Ruslan cast another spell?"

"No…" Cold descended over Kiran. That faint twitch, like the brush of questing fingers across a barred door…"Not in the way you mean. But I have a suspicion…tell me, where do you find trees with trembling, heart-shaped green leaves, and bark pale and smooth as stone?"

Dev eyed him with wary confusion. "Sounds like aspen. No groves in this valley, but down near Arathel Pass, the south-facing slopes are covered with 'em. What in Shaikar's hells does that have to do with us, or Ruslan?"

Arathel Pass. Kiran's chill grew deeper. He pressed a hand to the cold weight of Lizaveta's amulet. It lay silent and still under his shirt, without any warning twinges of heat or sparks. "Ruslan and I are linked. The amulet blocks that link. But just now, I saw a vision of aspen trees in a meadow, and earlier, a view of snowy peaks. Both times, it was as if I looked for an instant through someone else's eyes. I fear those eyes are Ruslan's—and that he might also have seen through mine."

Dev tensed. "You mean your amulet doesn't work anymore, and he can find us?"

"Not directly. Believe me, I'd know it if he'd circumvented the amulet completely." Kiran remembered all too well the crushing, inexorable pressure of Ruslan's will on his unprotected mind. "I think he's found a tiny flaw in the amulet's protections, like a hairs-width crack in a cistern cover. He'll try and widen it, to break through entirely. In the meantime, he'll glean what information he can."

"From whatever he sees through your eyes?" Dev frowned. "Did you have any warning, before you saw this—vision?"

Kiran shook his head, reluctantly. "I think I opened the way for Ruslan, somehow, by healing my arm—the first time it happened, I'd just drawn a little *ikilhia* from a tree. But the second time, I hadn't touched anything."

Dev thumped a hand on fissured red bark. "If he saw cinnabar forest, he'll know we've made the Whitefires' western slopes, but that's still a broad area to search. Thank Khalmet you weren't looking at the Elenn Gorge. Keep walking, and describe what you saw, exact as you can."

Kiran did his best to describe every detail of both visions. Dev listened with a thoughtful scowl. He said, "Sounds like Ruslan's in the Sondran Valley, maybe a mile below Arathel Pass. That's four days' ride from Kost in the ordinary way. Based on how fast he covered the distance to the pass from the Desadi Couloir, I'm guessing he can halve that. But we should still beat him to the border, if we cross tomorrow like I planned." He sounded cautiously relieved.

"It's not a physical race any longer," Kiran said quietly. "If Ruslan breaks through the block on our bond before I cross the Alathian wards, the distance between us won't matter." His breath shortened at the thought. Ruslan had proved after the *akhelashva* ritual that he could crush any resistance on Kiran's part with casual ease. Doubtless he'd first force Kiran to kill Dev, and not in any way as simple as draining Dev's *ikilhia*. A demonstration of his control, a removal of a source of interference, and a punishment for Kiran, all wrapped into one.

Not something he wanted Dev to realize, this close to the border, lest Dev abandon him in favor of safety. But Dev gave Kiran a sharp, wary look, as if he'd picked up on Kiran's thought. "How long do we have?"

"I have no idea. Days, hours, minutes...impossible to tell." Kiran held Dev's gaze. "Whatever supplies you need to purchase in Kost, get them quickly."

"Oh, I will," Dev said.

Kiran searched his face, but Dev's expression was as unreadable as Mikail's had always been when he chose not to share his thoughts. Sweat dampened Kiran's hands on his pack straps. He had no choice but to place his fate in Dev's hands, and hope Dev didn't betray his trust as badly as Mikail had.

CHAPTER THIRTEEN

(Dev)

I'd thought I'd seen Kiran twitchy with nerves before, but the hunched shoulders and restless hands I remembered paled in comparison to his behavior as we scrambled down the ravine toward the cabin. He near jumped out of his skin every time a twig cracked, and he alternated between squinting fearfully at cinnabar trees and staring holes in my back.

My own nerves weren't too quiet, either. It didn't take a scholar to figure out my lifespan would be measured in heartbeats if Ruslan weaseled his way past that amulet. I ignored the queasiness in my gut. Damn it, this wasn't far different than racing to finish a climb in the face of an oncoming storm. Panic was a fool's reponse that only led to deadly mistakes.

I stopped Kiran when we reached a gurgling rill of water bounded by a blaze of crimsonweed. "You had any more of those visions?"

He shook his head, his mouth a bloodless line.

"Ruslan knowing we're on the western slopes is bad enough, but if he spies a cabin, he won't need a wildfire to figure our position." I pulled out one of the cloth strips we'd used to bind Kiran's injured arm. "I'm gonna tie this over your eyes, and lead you the rest of the way. Should be only a quarter mile."

He didn't even speak, just bent his head. I knotted the strip tight, and took him by the arm. His muscles quivered under my hand, but he followed without hesitation.

I'd found the cabin on my way up to Bearjaw Cirque two summers ago. Its abandoned state had been obvious—half the roof had fallen in, and timbers were missing from several walls. I had no idea why anyone would have bothered to build a hideaway so far up a nondescript side canyon, or what had happened to the owner, but since the stout storage locker remained intact, it made a handy cache for food and supplies.

Kiran trailed a hand across the log wall as I led him toward the rusty-hinged door. He made a small, surprised noise. "The whole building is made of wood?"

I'd forgotten he'd likely never seen any structures not made of stone or adobe. "Wood's no scarce resource here."

"A shame. Stone, I could perhaps have linked to the amulet..." He sighed, heavily.

"No caves around here, either." Not that I wanted to spend any more time in a cave.

The door squealed like a hare caught by a hawk as I opened it, and we both flinched. I helped Kiran duck through into the dim, musty interior. The main room had once been some twenty feet long, but when the far section of roof had collapsed, the space was halved by a bristling wall of broken timbers. I tugged Kiran over to a corner and kicked aside mouse droppings. "Sit here. I know it's not much for comfort, but it'll keep out wind and wet. I'll leave your pack right beside you."

He sat down, cautiously, and drew his knees up to his chest. He tilted his blindfolded face up to mine. "Just...hurry. Please."

"Fast as I can," I promised, and backed away. His head tracked my movement. The desperate hope there made my breath catch. Gods damn him, he was a blood mage, not some scared little Tainter. He didn't need my protection.

The cabin's storage locker was a sturdy wooden substructure with a heavy cover secured by a sliding bear-proof latch. I sorted rapidly through the contents of my pack and threw our food and everything that didn't fit with my intended guise as a solo prospector into the locker. I latched it tight, and yelled to Kiran, "See you mid-morning." I didn't wait for a reply, just raced straight for the forest fast as a roundtail released from a snare.

The buzzing of my nerves eased a touch as I vaulted down boulder piles and zigzagged around fat cinnabar trunks. I hadn't realized how badly the need to hold myself to a pace Kiran could match had weighed on me. Not his fault he was slow, but gods, what a relief to cover ground at a decent pace. I made it down the ravine with the sun still a handspan above the gorge rim.

A rough trail ran along the floor of the gorge, past scattered log cabins tucked amongst slender molasses-scented syrup pines and massive cinnabar trees. Alathians weren't supposed to settle this side of the border, but King Arkenndren sure didn't bother enforcing the law way out here, and the Alathian Council only cared about their own rigid rules. If a few misfits and loners wanted to live on the Arkennland side of the border, the Council's attitude was one of good riddance.

Most of the cabins sat silent and shuttered. Now the winter snows had melted, most settlers would be out hunting, fishing, or prospecting during daylight hours. I made a mental note of the few cabins with horses grazing outside, or woodsmoke trailing from their chimneys. On my way back I'd need to find someone willing to rent a cart to me. Shouldn't be hard, since many settlers made a little extra money by renting spare equipment to hunters or prospectors. It was the other supplies I needed to find that might be tough to come by.

Two miles later, the trail spilled out onto the broad, rutted road coming up from the south to the Kost gate. The gorge widened as it met the gentle Parsian Valley and the Deeplink River joined its lazy, looping spirals to the green rush of the Elenn. Kost sat on the delta formed by the confluence of the two rivers. Tiered streets jam-packed with wooden buildings layered the valley's side, and the smoke from countless wood fires hung trapped in a dense pall over the town. I much preferred the clean white stone and magelights of Ninavel, but for once I welcomed the sight of the throat-clogging haze.

Kost's border gate lay on the far side of a broad bridge built of granite blocks and cinnabar planks that spanned the gleaming swirl of the Elenn. The gate itself was a wide freestanding arch some twenty feet high, carved from rock the faint yellow of old bone. Ward sigils covered the arch's surface, in inset lines of an odd, glassy black substance. Metal or crystal, maybe. I'd never managed a close enough inspection to find out. The Alathians didn't take kindly to gawkers.

I approached the bridge with the brisk stride appropriate to a prospector eager to wet his dusty throat at a riverside tavern. The buzz of my nerves was back, loud enough to set my neck muscles twitching. Gods, but I wished I could spare the time to study the way the guards handled entry inspections. If Pello had beaten us here, or if Kiran was wrong about Ruslan's willingness to involve the Alathians, the guards would be looking for men matching our descriptions.

But with Ruslan chipping away at Kiran's amulet like a miner hunting an ore seam—not to mention tracking me down in the bargain—I couldn't afford any delays. I'd have to trust to Khalmet that our shortcut over Bearjaw had given us enough lead time, and I wasn't only steps away from getting arrested.

I crossed the bridge just as a guard lit the great torches at the gate in advance of twilight. Three more guards lounged against the squat stone building of the gatehouse, and another two stood beyond the arch, their gray and brown livery melding into the shadows. The mage handling inspection duty wasn't in view. He was probably lurking in the relative comfort of the gatehouse, along with the guard captain.

When the guards came to attention, it was the half-hearted, lazy attention of men faced with a scruffy prospector of no importance. A trickle of relief lightened my stomach, as two of them ambled over to bar the way. The guard captain strode out of the gatehouse with his logbook under his arm.

"State your name and business." He sounded bored, but his eyes were a mite sharp for my taste.

"Devan *na soliin*, out of Ninavel." I used the old Arkennlander form that politely indicated I lacked a family name. I didn't dare lie about my identity, and not only because the mage would be listening for it. I'd been in and out of Kost too many times under my own name to chance not being recognized. Times like this I always wished Suliyya had seen fit to bless me with a pair of properly nondescript dark eyes to match my Arkennlander coloring.

The way to deal with Alathians was to tell the truth, just not all of the truth. "I've been up mountain-side, and I'm coming in to arrange sale of my wares," I told the captain. He wrote in the log, and I shrugged out of my pack and handed it to a waiting guard.

The mage finally deigned to appear from the gatehouse. He was a small, stiff-backed man whose olive skin had a sallow tinge, as if he rarely saw the sun. His dark hair was cut screamingly short in the formal Alathian style, the gold seal of the Council prominent on the chest of his gray and blue uniform. Unlike the guards, his every move was as rigidly proper as a soldier on a parade ground.

The mage stalked in a slow circle around me, his ringed hands spread. Long practice let me keep my expression bored as that of the guard rifling through my pack while the captain peppered me with questions. How long did I intend to stay in Kost, which importers did I mean to deal with, how many times had I crossed the border before...the usual annoyingly nosy list.

After a small eternity, the mage stopped his circling. He moved to my pack, and spent a further age fondling each charm in my much-reduced stash. I'd taken care to bring only those so weak as to be Alathian-legal. Too bad I couldn't have left them all at the cabin—but Alathians would never believe a Ninavel prospector who claimed to carry no charms.

"He can pass," the mage finally announced. Beyond him, the guard crammed my gear into my pack and nodded to the captain.

The captain scribbled another note in his log and handed me a token stamped with an identifying number and my date of entry. I slung my pack onto my shoulders and sauntered forward.

The gate arch loomed above, its wards dark and silent. With an effort, I kept my breathing regular as I crossed beneath it. There was no reason the wards should spark for me. But the way this trip had been going, I half expected the wards to trigger on general principle.

The gleaming black swirls stayed dark, and I passed the final pair of guards without incident. An immense wave of relief swept over me. Gods, it felt good to know no spell Ruslan cast could touch me now.

Temptation struck like lightning. I didn't have to go back. I could lay low in Kost, long enough for Ruslan to hunt down Kiran and drag him back to Ninavel. Sneak back to the cabin after a week or so, retrieve my stash, and only then go to Gerran. Tell him he couldn't blame me for losing against an angry blood mage, take my usual, much smaller fee for Bren's other items, and cut my losses.

This time it wasn't only Melly I saw in my mind's eye, but Kiran, blindfolded, white-faced and desperate. I scrubbed a hand over my face and sighed. I'd never taken the easy way out in my life; no point in starting now.

I hurried on past the boatyards to the stables, and secured the use of a sturdy little bay pony and a lantern. The oil lamps of shops and taverns lit Kost's main streets, but Gerran's office wasn't exactly on a main street. He did business out of a set of warehouses deep in the twisting maze of Kost's riverside district. Unlike similar areas in Ninavel, not many people wandered the riverside streets past sunset. Alathians did their business during the day and tended to congregate inside taverns and dancehalls at night, probably due to the winter rains that drenched the city for half the year.

Many of the buildings I passed were dark, but Gerran's office windows glowed warmly with candlelight. I'd figured the old bastard would still be there, working on his accounts in preparation for the Ninavel convoy's arrival. I tethered my horse to the rail outside and clattered up the wooden steps. When I pounded on the door, a burly man in gray workman's clothing answered, clearly Gerran's hired muscle. Gerran had new men every season, but the general type never changed. Big, bulky, and too dumb to get any dangerous ideas.

"Devan, out of Ninavel, to see Gerran," I told him. He disappeared inside and I heard a muted exhange of voices. When he returned, he opened the door for me without a word. I went through the front room full of boards with prices and exchange rates written on them and into Gerran's back office. Like Bren's, the outwardly plain room contained only a table, a few chairs and some boxes in stacks, but Gerran did all his real business here.

Gerran eyed me over his spectacles from his seat at the table. He was of an age with Bren. Gray haired and balding, his walnut-brown skin creased deep as saddle leather, but still with the powerful build of an athletic man. I'd heard he'd been a convoy boss for many years until he and Bren went into business together.

I had to hand it to him. A visit from me so far in advance of the convoy's arrival could only mean trouble, but no hint of dismay showed on his broad face, and his gravelly voice was calm as ever. "Dev. Did you run into trouble with your consignment?"

He was playing it careful, not sure how much I knew, not wanting to give anything away. I let the anger that had been lurking inside ever since I'd seen Kiran's blood mage sigil boil to the surface. "You'd better believe there's trouble." I planted my hands on his desk. "Let's discuss the special consignment, shall we?"

Gerran signaled with a twitch of his fingers. The hired muscle left the room, closing the door behind him. "Fine," Gerran said. "What's the problem?"

"How about the minor fact you forgot to inform me I was smuggling a mage? Not just any mage, but a fucking blood mage? And on top of that, a blood mage who's got another blood mage after him?" I kept my voice low, but the venom came through clear as if I'd shouted.

His eyes didn't even flicker, the bastard. That meant he'd known Kiran's full identity from the beginning, and so had Bren. The desk creaked protestingly under my hands. "What the hell are you and Bren thinking, playing against a blood mage?" I growled.

"Couriers don't need to know details." Not a shred of remorse showed in those dispassionate eyes.

"Details?" My voice rose, and I stopped, taking a moment to get it back under control. "You asshole. Thanks to your missing details, first the entire convoy almost died in an avalanche, and then a blood mage descends like Shaikar himself, looking for your gods-damned *consignment*. Who knows how many convoy members he killed?"

For the first time, he looked concerned. "You did bring our goods? All of them?"

Khalmet's bloodsoaked hand, I should've known that's all he

cared about. I bared my teeth at him. "Oh yes. Yes, I did. Left the convoy and ran flat out through the mountains in spite of a spellcast snowstorm to do it, no less. So you know what, Gerran? You won't see a single gods-damned charm until we renegotiate some terms."

Gerran leaned back in his chair and crossed his thick-muscled arms. "You know Bren and I don't work that way. You agreed to our terms back in Ninavel."

"Yeah, I took Bren's terms. That was before I had to abandon the convoy—you know what that means, damn your eyes. I'll never work as an outrider again, so by Khalmet, I want compensation for the lost income," I snarled.

"Bren and I have plenty of work for a man of your skills. You don't need to sign on with a convoy to handle our more special items," he said mildly.

"Yeah? What about the part where I've made an enemy of a blood mage? How are you gonna make that up to me?" My voice was rising again, and he frowned, glancing at the door.

"A mage won't concern himself with a mere courier, once the job's done. But if you want to play it safe, I'll gladly arrange work for you within Alathia's borders." He still used the calm, reasonable voice that made me want to grab one of his chairs and throw it at him.

"You think I'd take another job from you, after this? I meant what I said. You won't see a fucking thing unless I get ten spell-grade—not charm-grade!—gemstones per item. *All* of the items." I had all the leverage now, and I meant to use it. Spell-grade gems were near flawless in cut and purity. Sold to a highside supplier in Ninavel, the profit from so many would be a sum large enough to replace every kenet Jylla had stolen from me three times over. I might even be able to buy Melly straight out instead of working a scheme to spirit her away.

He considered me in stone-faced silence. "Seven spell-grade stones per item," he offered.

"Ten," I said flatly. "And I want the rest of my payment from you, immediately upon delivery, no waiting upon a return to Ninavel. If I need to lie low in Alathia for a while, I want all my money beforehand."

His eyes narrowed, and he opened his mouth to protest. I slammed a hand down on his desk.

"Don't fuck with me, Gerran. My terms, or no deal. I'll fucking give away the packages instead."

A muscle under his eye twitched. Yeah, he didn't like that idea. He crossed his arms over his chest again.

"Fine," he snapped. "Payment immediately upon delivery. Anything else you'd like? A musical fanfare, dancing girls?"

"Just an answer to one question." I removed my hands from his desk. "How in Khalmet's name did you expect me to sneak a blood mage across the border without triggering the wards?" Suliyya grant I'd guessed right that Gerran had a solution. I didn't relish the thought of wasting precious hours tromping around asking dangerous questions of apothecaries.

Gerran's expression was still sour as spoiled goat milk. "My scout's about to leave for the Sondran Valley to watch for the convoy. He'd have met with you and given you this." He reached into a drawer and tossed me a sealed glass vial. I held it next to the candles on his desk. The vial was full of a paste the sickly green of moldy bread.

I gave Gerran a dark look. I'd bet good coin his man wouldn't have told me Kiran was a mage, just ordered me to dose him. "What is this stuff?"

"I'm sure you've realized the only way to get a mage across the border undetected is to suppress his magic." Gerran pointed a finger at the vial. "This will do that. Give the dose two to three hours before you pass the gate. I assume you're capable of handling the rest."

One problem solved. But Gerran's words had brought an unpleasant possibility to mind. I didn't fully understand Kiran's talk of barriers and blocks, but I gathered he was holding Ruslan at bay somehow, in addition to the amulet's protection. If the drug suppressed his magic, would it leave him wide open to Ruslan's control? I had a nasty feeling only Kiran could answer that, and by then, we'd be out of time for other options. If any other option even existed.

"How's it work?" I asked Gerran.

Gerran snorted. "What do I look like, an apothecary?"

"Fine, then. What's it called?" At Gerran's scowl, I sighed in irritation. "I have to know, because I'll need to find out if it reacts badly with other drugs."

"Hennanwort," Gerran said shortly. "Very rare, and very expensive, so don't lose it, and watch who you discuss it with."

"Yeah, yeah." Thank Khalmet, I already knew of an herbalist with a reputation for discretion, who kept a shop near the taverns that catered to traders and convoy men. I'd simply have to find out as much as I could about the drug, and gamble that Kiran could figure a way to take it safely.

"Remember, you earn not a kenet unless you bring the full consignment straight here after passing the gate." Gerran's voice had gained a hard edge.

I slipped the vial into an inner chest pocket. "Nothing wrong with my memory." Unfortunately. The mixed fear and hope blazoned on Kiran's face back at the cabin wouldn't leave me. I hesitated, eyeing Gerran. My suspicion he meant to sell Kiran out was stronger than ever, but to whom? It couldn't be Ruslan. Gerran wasn't so big a fool as to think Ruslan wouldn't learn he and Bren had arranged Kiran's escape in the first place. Maybe if I came at it sidewise...

"Must be something wrong with yours, for you to risk a mage's game. Shaikar's hells, has it been so long since you've lived in Ninavel that you've forgotten what they're like?"

Gerran speared me with a look sharp as a piton spike. "You want to survive this? Then stick to the part of a token, and keep that gods-cursed nosiness of yours in check."

I should've known he was too canny for an easy slip, though I'd figured we'd get to threats in the end.

"I'll be clear, then: whatever you're playing at with this delivery, leave me the fuck out of it. You pay me fair without any double crosses—because if I meet with an unfortunate accident, a charm-sealed missive spilling every detail of your illegal trade will land in the laps of the Alathian Council." A protection I'd arranged years ago on Jylla's advice and renewed every season since, though I'd never needed it until now.

Not that it'd buy me more than a few days of safety before Gerran tracked down the arrangement I'd made at Korris House. But a day's grace was all I needed to sneak out of Kost and lose myself in trackless Alathian forest. Soon as I got paid, I meant to run for one of the far southern border gates, in case Ruslan was lurking outside Kost's. I'd cross back into Arkennland, wear Kiran's amulet, and loop back cross-country through the Whitefires to Ninavel and Melly.

Gerran's mouth pulled into a grim smile. "No need to get twitchy. You keep to my delivery instructions, and you'll walk away a live and wealthy man, exactly as agreed. Bren and I have always been men of our word."

True enough, in a twisted sort of way. One of the reasons I worked for Bren was his reputation for honesty in payment, if in nothing else. Gerran was angry over the change in terms, not a reaction I'd expect if he meant to kill me or sell me out. But I didn't like not knowing his intentions for Kiran, and I didn't trust him.

No profit in leaving him angry, though. "One thing you should know," I said. "I wasn't kidding about that avalanche. Five wagons were lost, all from Horavin House. I'd estimate two days delay to dig the route out, not including interference from a pissed off blood mage, or his gods-damned snowstorm. I'd say the convoy's a week out. Maybe more."

Gerran raised his brows, and nodded to me. By knowing the rough arrival date of the convoy and the news of Horavin's loss, he'd gain a certain advantage over the other brokers.

If the convoy arrived at all. I still carried the dark fear that Ruslan wouldn't limit himself to killing a few to fuel his spells. Though even a few was too many. I sent up yet another prayer to Suliyya for Cara's safety.

Gerran's muscle man showed me out, still without speaking. Only the brightest stars glimmered through the smoky murk overhead. Ugh. Though no doubt Kiran would've happily traded clear mountain air for the safety from blood magic I currently enjoyed.

I pictured him huddled in the cabin with his hands clamped white-knuckled on his knees—and banished the image with a muttered curse, as guilt pricked me. Damn it, Melly's fate was what mattered, not Kiran's. I'd warned him he was on his own after the border. Better to heed Gerran's warning and stay clear of his game. I faced enough risks already.

✳

(Kiran)

Kiran had never endured a more endless night. Once darkness fell, the cabin's interior was black as onyx, even without the blindfold. Scuttlings and scratchings emanated from the cabin walls, sounding far too loud to be produced by innocuous rodents, and he kept imagining he heard the crunch of stealthy footsteps outside amidst the moan of wind through the pines.

But far worse were the occasions when the black void dissolved into the cool glow of magelight, and he glimpsed shadowed forest under a starlit sky. The sneaking, questing tug in his mind grew stronger with each vision, to the point where he felt a constant, shadowy itch even when his sight was his own. He wove layer upon layer of frustratingly gossamer defenses from his own *ikilhia*, praying all the while Dev would return in time.

Once, he saw more than night-darkened forest. Beside a tree, a gray form turned, and a wash of silver magelight revealed Mikail's stolid face. Mikail's mouth moved in silent words Kiran couldn't read, and he gestured with fingers that glimmered an eldritch green. The image vanished as suddenly and completely as all the rest, leaving Kiran to stare into blackness with his heart pounding.

Ruslan must have directed Mikail to speed their travel, while he focused all his attention on exploiting the flaw in Kiran's protection. Mikail, always so reliable, so obedient…Kiran buried his face in his hands. Why had he been so blind as to believe Mikail his ally? Dark memories rose to gnaw at him.

"Brother," Mikail whispered. "Are you awake?"

Kiran raised his head from the cold flagstones, slowly. His eyes felt hot and sticky, his throat raw. Mikail stood just beyond the sullen red glow of the wards spiraling around him.

Mikail's breath hissed through his teeth. "You look terrible." He bent and slid a silk-wrapped packet across the ward lines on the floor. The lines flared, then settled. "I brought you some food."

The warm, buttery scent of kallas bread made his empty stomach cramp. "I don't want it," Kiran said, in a hoarse croak.

Mikail sighed. "I should have brought water, I see. But you should eat—you'll need your strength. Especially if you keep fighting Ruslan this way. Why do you do it? You know you can't win."

"You know why." Anger drove Kiran to his feet. "You were there. You helped him! How could you channel for him, knowing what he meant to cast?"

"Do you imagine I could have refused?" Mikail said evenly. "I was marked and bound years before you."

Kiran slumped back to the ground. "Every time I close my eyes, I see Alisa screaming, begging me to help her..." He pressed his hands against his face. "I can't bear this. I can't. I keep thinking, if only I make him angry enough—"

"You little fool!" Mikail's voice was sharp as a slap. "Even in his worst rage, Ruslan would never kill you. But if you keep provoking him, you'll drive him to destroy your will—is that what you want?"

"Better that, than living every moment with the knowledge Alisa died in agony because of me!" Kiran pounded a fist against a flagstone. Ward lines flared crimson with warning, and he snatched his hand back with a hiss of frustrated anger. "I'd thought I was so careful. But I must have slipped somehow, made a mistake. He'd never have known of her, otherwise. But I can't think what I did, and it tears at me so badly I can hardly breathe—" His voice cracked, and he broke into a racking set of coughs, his throat burning.

Mikail stood silent, watching him. When he spoke again, his voice was so low it was barely audible. "You were careful. It was I who told Ruslan you had a nathahlen lover."

"What?" Kiran's ears buzzed with shock. Mikail had vowed his silence. Had covered for Kiran for years, without a single protest. Had always been the one Kiran could turn to for help, for protection.

"I thought your nathahlen girl a harmless infatuation that you'd outgrow. But years passed, and you only became more entangled. When you started to parrot her ridiculous ideas about the worth of nathahlen lives, I feared a simple case of childish rebellion might turn into something more dangerous." Mikail shook his head, his eyes hooded and dark. "I

was right. Look what's come of this—it's nearly destroyed you! I should never have waited so long. Better if I'd told Ruslan years ago."

Horror combined with fury to darken Kiran's vision. "You told him, knowing what he would do?" He shoved to his feet, his body trembling.

"I knew he'd put a stop to it. I didn't know your reaction would be so...extreme." Mikail wore the slight frown of one who had made a minor but annoying miscalculation in a spell exercise.

"You're not even sorry..." Kiran whispered, staring at Mikail. His rage grew to a searing blaze so bright he could no longer contain it. Blind to everything else, he struck at his mage-brother with every ounce of magic born of fury and betrayal.

Only to collapse, gasping, as the wards encircling him blazed to life and reflected the strike in a burning backlash.

"You see?" Mikail said softly, as Kiran writhed in pain. "You're no nathahlen. The sooner you accept that, the better."

Kiran jerked his head off his knees. The dim light of morning filtered through cracks in the cabin walls. He must have slept, though he didn't feel rested. Anguish and grief still lanced his heart, Mikail's face alternating with Alisa's in his mind. He forced the images away, and reached for the blindfold lying in a tangle at his side.

Distant but approaching, a heavy clomping of hooves. Kiran sprang to his feet, the blindfold dangling forgotten from a hand. Awful certainty gripped him. Dev had betrayed him, exactly as Kiran had feared, and now the Alathians had come to arrest him.

The maddening itch deep within checked his instinct to draw power. Ruslan would pounce on even the slightest opening; and if forced to the choice, Kiran would prefer captivity in Alathian hands to Ruslan's.

Kiran hurried to the cabin door, braced to run for the forest in a last desperate bid for escape. But when he yanked the door open on squealing hinges, he saw not the uniformed Alathian riders he expected, but Dev, perched on the frontboard of a dilapidated wooden cart drawn by a sway-backed draft horse with a shaggy gray mane and legs thick as pine trunks.

Amazed, joyous relief sent Kiran racing across the clearing with an ear-to-ear grin. Dev had kept his word, and safety remained within

Kiran's grasp—it felt too good to be true. "You came back," he blurted.

Dev swung down off the cart with a bemused grunt. "I said I would, didn't I?" A fleeting, shadowed expression crossed his face. "Khalmet's hand, you look like you spent all night fending off bears." His eyes narrowed. "Turn and face the trees, not the cart. How close is Ruslan to breaking through?"

"The block yet holds," Kiran said, hastily obeying. "But we shouldn't delay." He frowned, thinking of the cart behind him. It was far smaller than the convoy wagons had been, with low sides and large wheels. He didn't see how he could remain hidden from the Alathian guards, let alone a mage.

"Turns out it's Sulanians, not Alathians, who make the right drug for the task." Dev held up a vial filled with an unpleasant-looking green paste. "Hennanwort. Word is, it'll suppress your magic, no problem. But will it mess with that block of yours against Ruslan?"

Kiran traced a cautious finger down the vial. He sensed no magical residue; a drug for the body only, then. "Does it truly suppress magic, or merely a mage's aura?"

Dev shrugged. "The herbalist I talked to wasn't sure exactly how it worked. She said it's grown by a religious sect in Sulania for their rituals. Apparently it distorts the senses for ordinary folk that take it, gives 'em weird visions the way gosha berries do. She said it alters the body's flow of energies, whatever that means. I figure that's good news for sneaking past wards. But she also said when mages take it, they can't do magic while the effects last."

"Magic is an act of will," Kiran said. "Any drug that affects the mind's ability to focus will interfere with active spellcasting." He poked the vial again. To release barriers was also an act of will, even if sometimes driven by instinct. Everything he knew said a physical drug shouldn't affect them...but then, he'd been wrong about the safety of drawing power by touch. "I think it's safe, but I can't be certain."

"Why'd I know you'd say that?" Dev muttered, looking grim. "There's a second part to this. I'm gonna fix up a hiding space for you within the driver's box of the cart. You'll be out of sight, but it won't be soundproof. Which means you can't make even the slightest noise." He pulled out a second vial containing a dark, sludgy liquid.

"A large enough dose of yeleran leaf extract will put you in a deep sleep and slow your heart and breathing to the point a casual observer might think you dead. It'll prevent you making any accidental noise, and it'll make you doubly hard for the mage to detect."

Kiran looked unhappily at the vial. He supposed he'd expected something of this nature, but it didn't make the prospect any more appealing. The thought of being so completely helpless during the border crossing brought his fear of betrayal roaring back to life. Then again, perhaps he could ensure the hennanwort didn't cause disaster—Ruslan couldn't use the link if Kiran were so deeply unconscious. "Can you give me the hennanwort after I'm asleep?"

Dev shook his head. "That's the thing—the herbalist said you've got to take the hennanwort first and wait for it to take effect before you can take the yeleran. Otherwise the hennanwort won't get absorbed right."

"There must be another way." One in which he wouldn't be so vulnerable.

Dev's brows lowered. "You want to get through the border, or not? Trust me, I'm not thrilled about this either. But these drugs are the only way I know for a mage to pass that gate."

After a long, silent struggle between competing fears, Kiran gave a reluctant nod. Though he'd had no more visions, the mental itch had swelled into a sharper, straining pull. The certainty of Ruslan's triumph outweighed all other worries.

The sharp line between Dev's brows eased. He pocketed the vials and thrust an armload of empty burlap sacks at Kiran. "Never mind that blindfold; better for us to pass the gate sooner than later, which means I need your help. I'm gonna work on the cart; you go somewhere out of sight of the clearing and fill these up with rocks. Any type, doesn't matter, but aim for stones about the size of your fist."

Kiran started off with the sacks, but called over his shoulder, "Why do we need rocks?"

"I'm playing prospector, so I need sacks of ore. Most ores don't look like much until they're refined, so those bastards at the gate won't be able to tell the difference."

The stony ground under the cinnabar pines yielded an abundance of loose rocks, but many were too large or too small to fit Dev's criteria. Kiran scrambled about searching while a racket of hammering and sawing disturbed the cool morning air.

Sunlight slanted through the cinnabar trees to pool golden on the forest floor by the time Dev called for him to return. Kiran staggered back to the clearing with a laden sack gripped in his arms.

Sweat stained the back and sides of Dev's shirt and piles of sawdust lay scattered on the matted pine needles, but when Kiran risked a quick glance at the cart, it looked no different. He said as much to Dev, diffidently.

"That's kind of the idea," Dev said. "No point in having a hidden compartment if it's obvious. Here, take a quick look." He handed Kiran up into the cart bed, and pointed at the boxy front section beneath the driver's seat.

"Looks like a standard driver's box, right?" Dev tapped the corner of a board sharply with his hammer. The back side of the driver's box fell outward, revealing a dark rectangular space. "That's where you'll be."

Dev pointed with the hammer at the forest. Kiran obediently turned to face the trees again. The hiding space hadn't looked very big. "How will I breathe?"

"It's not air tight," Dev said. "That's why you have to be so quiet." He jumped down from the cart. Kiran followed, slowly. Now that the moment of truth was fast approaching, his nerves shrieked louder than ever. His imagination cast up one dismal scenario after another. The hennanwort, dissolving his barriers…Dev, handing him helpless to the Alathians…

Yet if Dev had intended to tell the Alathians, he'd surely have done so during his night in Kost, and returned with them in force rather than alone. Instead of focusing on fears, Kiran ought to consider the future after a successful border crossing.

"Once we reach Kost, you'll take me to Gerran? Bren said Gerran would provide me the paperwork and supplies I need to travel onward."

Dev jerked his head in a nod. "I'll take you straight there. He'll stash you someplace safe to sleep off the yeleran. And once you wake up—whatever Bren arranged, Gerran will do." He spoke with an odd intensity that made Kiran wonder if Dev found it equally difficult to imagine a successful end to their journey.

Strange indeed, to think of traveling on without Dev as a guide. "When I wake up…will I see you, again?"

"No. I told you, once we cross, you're on your own." Dev's clipped tone and dark expression reminded Kiran all too well of their conversation in the cave. Regret seized him with surprising strength. He hadn't realized how badly he'd wanted Dev's black opinion of him to improve. Kiran told himself it didn't matter, not so long as Dev kept his word.

Besides, Dev's brusque manner might be merely from nerves. His surely rivaled Kiran's. After all, it was Dev who would die if Kiran was wrong about the hennanwort, and Dev who had to undergo the scrutiny of the guards and the mage at the border. Kiran was struck again by how much Dev was sacrificing and risking, to get him safely into Alathia.

"Dev. Um. I just wanted to say thank you. For everything."

Dev shifted, uncomfortably. "I'm sure as hell not doing this out of the goodness of my heart." He ran a hand over his face and turned away. "I'll load up the sacks, and then we'll go. Take a rest, and have something to eat. You won't want to take the yeleran on an empty stomach." Dev tossed a parcel to Kiran. "Got this in Kost for you."

Kiran untied the parcel to find a loaf of spiced bread, a small tin of jam, and an almond pastry. His mouth watered with painful force. He hadn't eaten anything since Dev had left the day before, too distracted by his fears. And before that, he'd had only jerky, hardtack, and dried fruit for days on end.

Dev flashed a wry grin as he strode past with another bulging sack. "Worst comes to worst, at least you'll have had a proper meal, right?"

Kiran bit into the pastry. He tried to focus only on the sweetness bursting on his tongue. If these were his last minutes of freedom, he wanted to savor them.

CHAPTER FOURTEEN

(Dev)

I let Kiran ride in the open cart bed until we were a quarter mile short of the settlement trail. When I pulled the cart to a halt, he stood with the grim intensity of a man waiting to be sentenced. I broke open the hennanwort vial and smeared the green gunk on a piece of seeded bread I'd saved. Khalmet's hand, I couldn't believe those crazy Sulanians ate hennanwort willingly. It looked like years-old mold and smelled like rancid oil. I handed the green-slimed bread chunk to Kiran, with a sympathetic grimace.

He stared at it long enough that I stirred, wondering if I ought to prompt him. But his mouth firmed, and he resolutely took a bite. "It doesn't taste quite as bad as it smells," he said, after a convulsive swallow.

"Thank Suliyya for small favors." I handed him a waterskin. He forced down the rest of the bread, coughed, made a face, and hastily gulped from the waterskin.

My own throat felt dry as a sandflat. If Kiran was wrong, and the hennanwort let Ruslan through his protections…what would it feel like, to die the way Harken had?

Ruthlessly, I buried the thought. No going back now. I'd made my play, and the outcome was in Khalmet's hands, not mine.

"How long until it takes effect?" Kiran was trying not to sound nervous, but his blue eyes were huge in his pale face, and his hands had locked in a death grip on the cart's side.

"Shouldn't be long." Or so the herbalist had claimed. "Why don't you get down and stretch your legs some while we wait?" Nothing for settling nerves like a little movement.

He scrambled off the cart and paced between cinnabar trees, his shoulders rigid as iron. I tied and re-tied idle knots in the reins, trying to ignore the rapid thudding of my heart.

Kiran stopped short and put a hand up to his head. "I feel dizzy." He swayed on his feet. I jumped down and crossed to his side.

"Come back to the cart and sit down." I reached for his arm, hesitated, then forced myself to take it. If Ruslan got hold of him, I'd die whether I was touching him or not.

"My head…oh, gods…" He staggered and fell to his knees despite my grip. "Dev, I can't—" his voice rose, the panic in it unmistakable.

"Shit!" I dropped his arm fast as a burning firestone. "Is it Ruslan?"

"No, my barriers hold, but…" his voice was slurring. His head fell back, his black hair coming away from his face. His pupils had shrunk to pinpoints, making his eyes look eerily blue. "I can't—" he repeated, and clawed at his temples.

"Kiran! Stop!" I grabbed his wrists. He twisted and thrashed in my grip like a panicked animal. I yelled at him, trying to make him focus on me. He quieted, though his breathing remained fast and shallow.

"Kiran. Listen to me. Is the drug suppressing your magic?" I tried to speak slowly and clearly. Obviously the hennanwort was doing something unpleasant to him, but I'd no idea if we could safely pass the gate wards.

He blinked at me, struggling to focus, and I repeated the question, even more slowly. "I think…yes…it feels…" he said finally, his voice thick. He shuddered hard, all over, and didn't finish the sentence, his eyes going wide and blank again. I sighed. Clearly that was all the reassurance I'd get. At least the hennanwort hadn't brought Ruslan down on us—or so I assumed, from the fact I was still breathing.

I coaxed Kiran back onto the cart with the soothing voice I'd once used on scared young Tainters. "Kiran, you're doing fine…now crawl on up…"

His teeth were clenched, and I had to pry open his mouth to pour in the yeleran extract. He tried to spit it out, but I forced his jaw shut and pinched his nose tight, so that in the end he swallowed. He fought me after that, but his movements were sluggish and weak. I had no trouble holding him still until the yeleran dragged him under.

I sat back and released the breath I hadn't even realized I was holding. Fuck, I hated this job. I sure wished that herbalist had mentioned hennanwort could cause a full blown panic. But then, maybe that was only true for a blood mage, or even just for Kiran— hell, what did I know? I wiped my hands on my leathers, as if by doing so I could erase my growing sense of uncleanliness.

Only the white of Kiran's eye showed when I peeled back an eyelid. He was well and truly out, his limbs limp as a doll's. Time to get this over with.

I arranged him comfortably as I could in the long, narrow space of the compartment. The ward-sealed box containing my personal charms and the rest of Bren's items went in the corner beneath his feet, beside the engraved plate of Bren's blackshroud ward. I pricked a finger and smeared blood on the blackshroud, packed hay around Kiran and the box as a cushion against the jolts the cart would take on the trail, then slid the main panel back into place.

I stacked the false ore sacks to cover the panel and made sure the sack openings were all easily accessible. If I had Khalmet's favor, the guards would open the sacks without bothering to move them around. I whispered the blackshroud's activation word. A flicker of carmine red raced over the wood of the driver's box.

Warded, sealed, and ready…but would the drugs truly fool the Alathian mage at the gate? Only way to know was to try.

The trip to the bridge went uneventfully, if slowly. I exchanged nods with a few passing riders on the settlement trail, who didn't give me or the cart more than a glance. But once we reached the main road and faced the bridge, I cursed under my breath. Five heavily laden wagons surrounded by dark-skinned riders in ornamented leathers waited in line at the gate. From the bone discs braided in the riders' hair and style of carvings on the wagons, they'd made the long journey north from Sulania along the western front of the mountains.

The herbalist had told me the hennanwort's effects would last a full day or more, but the yeleran would only keep Kiran out for four, maybe five hours. Inspections on foreign trade wagons could take long enough to push that margin razor thin. If Kiran woke up before we passed the gate, I'd be in trouble. But damn it, the guards had already seen us; they'd get suspicious if I turned around now. I pulled up behind the hindmost wagon, and settled in to wait.

The day wore on, slowly, and it took all my experience to pretend I was nothing more than bored. An argument broke out between the Sulanians and the Alathians over some piece of their cargo, and it dragged on until I wanted to throttle them all. In the end, one of the Sulanians tried to bribe the guard captain, a dumb move if I ever saw one. Preventing bribery was one of the reasons the mage stood watch, and the guard captain was well aware of it. He impounded the crate and ordered the arrest of the unfortunate Sulanian.

Angry yells erupted, and one idiot even drew a knife. The Alathian mage barked out a word. The glassy ward lines on the gate blazed white, and crackling silver light haloed the knife-wielder. He dropped like he'd taken a rock strike to the head.

The yells cut off into shocked silence. The mage stared round in challenge, but the other Sulanians were smarter than their comrade. They kept their eyes down and their mouths shut, as the guards hustled off the original offender and the limp body of his friend.

I took deep breaths, seeking to calm my uneasy stomach. Gods, I could've done without the reminder of what I faced if anything went wrong.

I'd hoped the guard captain would cancel the inspection and turn the Sulanians back, but the convoy's boss was a smooth talker. After a lot of bowing and apologetic gestures on his part, the captain grudgingly motioned for the guards to continue. The Sulanians stood by meek as hopmice while guards crawled over every damn inch of their wagons and the mage glowered over each piece of cargo. My calm stretched ever thinner. Just when I thought it would finally break, the guard captain finished off with a series of stern-faced warnings, and waved the Sulanians through.

Our turn, at last. As the Sulanian wagons creaked through the gate, my mind snapped into the knife-edged clarity I used for climbs.

The guard captain approached with his logbook. Both he and the mage were different men from last night, although I recognized a few of the guards on duty. I watched the mage without looking directly at him. With his pinched face and sour expression, he looked like he belonged in a banking house.

The mage paced around the cart, his hands held out, the metal of his detection charms winking in the sunlight. I summoned the memory of a day spent relaxing in the sunwashed expanse of Gelahar Cirque. Not a single care to trouble my thoughts, surrounded by the stark beauty of jagged ridgelines above blue-green lakewater…lazy calm spread over me as I answered the captain's questions.

The mage stopped near the front of the cart. I lost myself in cobalt sky and a sweep of gleaming rock; my breathing stayed even, my heart steady.

He scuffed at something in the dirt, frowning, and moved on. I didn't allow myself even a blink of relief.

The mage nodded to the captain, and moved off to examine my pile of Alathian-legal charms. Almost done, now. I paid the required tax as the guards retied my sacks of supposed ore. The mage passed back my charms, and the captain handed me the entry document that allowed me to sell my wares in Alathia. I ducked my head to him and twitched the reins.

We passed under the great arch and the wards stayed silent and still, without even a glimmer of life.

The moment we passed out of sight beyond the boatyards, I slumped and sucked in a lung-bursting breath. By Khalmet, I'd done it! Beaten both Ruslan and Pello to the border, and slipped Kiran past the Alathians…mother of maidens, I could hardly believe we'd made it.

But the job wasn't done yet. *Take him straight to Gerran's,* Bren had said. An order I couldn't ignore, if I wanted my hard-earned payment. I got a flash of Kiran's panicked, pale face, his body twisting feebly against my hold—and shoved it aside. No, damn it. Melly's life depended on me. I'd do nothing to risk the coin that would save her, not when I was so close to finishing this job I could taste it.

A muffled groan made me start. Shit, I should've known things were going too smooth. The delay with the Sulanians had cost us too much time, and the yeleran was wearing off. When Kiran woke, he'd find himself still disoriented by the hennanwort and confined in a cramped, dark space. No doubt he'd panic, maybe even start screaming. Kost wasn't Ninavel, where people knew to mind their own business. Alathians would come running, and call for the city guard. I had to get to Gerran's, fast.

I held my breath and prayed Kiran would stay under as we rattled through streets bustling with solemn-faced Alathians. I heard him shift a few times, but nothing more, thank Khalmet.

Soon as I drove the cart around behind Gerran's office into his packing yard, I jumped off the frontboard and started yanking sacks away. Kiran groaned again, louder. I cleared the panel and whacked it open.

Kiran's eyelids were fluttering and his breathing was accelerating fast. I dragged him out and braced him against a sack.

"Kiran, can you hear me?" I spoke right into his ear. He moaned, and opened his eyes. His pupils were tiny specks in a sea of blue, and his eyes met mine without any recognition.

"We made it. You're in Kost," I said.

He blinked at me with those vacant blue eyes, and said something so badly slurred I couldn't understand it. At least he wasn't panicking like he had in the forest. Maybe the grogginess from the yeleran was keeping him calm.

I reached for his amulet, gingerly. Kiran had said he'd released its warding, to prevent any chance of it spiking the detection spells. No sparks stung my skin, and I lifted the amulet over his head and pocketed it. He'd promised it was mine, once in Kost, and I didn't want any misunderstandings with Gerran.

A glimmer of sense returned to his eyes as he watched me retrieve my warded box and pack away the blackshroud ward. He straightened against the sack.

"We're safe?" he asked, the words heavily slurred but recognizable.

I nodded. The stark relief dawning on his face made my gut twist. I opened my mouth, not sure what would come out—and shut it, fast, as Gerran's back door opened and the massively muscled guy I remembered from the night before bounded down the steps.

"Gerran wants you two inside," he announced.

"I'm working on it," I snapped, and reminded myself sharply that Kiran wasn't my problem anymore. Or wouldn't be, soon as I got him off this damn cart. I hauled him to his feet. Just as I was eyeing the drop to the ground and wondering how to manage it without dumping Kiran on his head, Muscle Guy solved my problem by grabbing Kiran's belt and lifting him down as easily as if he were a stray kitten.

Muscle Guy looked like he meant to sweep Kiran up and carry him the rest of the way, but Kiran staggered backward, fetching up against the cart's side. "I can walk," he insisted. The effect was spoiled a little by the slur and the way he swayed like a fir in a strong wind. I exchanged a look with Muscle Guy, who shrugged. I sighed, shifted my warded box under one arm, and tugged Kiran's arm over my shoulders.

"Right, you can walk. Let's go this way." With a fair amount of help from me, he weaved his way across the yard, and after a few false starts, negotiated the steps.

Once inside, I thumped the box down on Gerran's desk and disentangled myself from Kiran, who kept his feet by clutching the desk's edge like a lifeline. Muscle Guy joined another man so like him as to be his twin, standing stolid-faced by the wall.

Gerran pushed his spectacles up his nose and leaned forward in his chair. "Any problems in the crossing?"

"Only a delay from some Sulanian idiots who thought they could get contraband through with a bribe." I pricked my thumb and pressed it to the center of the box's wards. They shimmered blue-violet and the lock clicked. I removed the leather bag containing my own personal store of charms, then nodded to Gerran.

He extracted Bren's charms and wards one by one, unwrapping their oilskin coverings and comparing each item against a ciphered list.

With each tick mark on his list, the satisfaction in his dark eyes grew.

"The delivery appears in order." He added the final charm to the glittering row already laid out on the table, and peered over his spectacles at Kiran. "Though I'll need to inspect the special consignment." He motioned to the first of the muscle twins. "Hold him."

Kiran's eyes went wide as the man pinioned his arms. He drew breath, but his captor clapped a broad hand over his mouth. Kiran's eyes rolled to mine in mute appeal.

My hands fisted, but I held my ground. Damn it, I'd known something like this was coming. Shouldn't matter if it happened in front of me instead of after I'd gone. Besides, the second muscle twin was watching me with flat, hard eyes. Gerran's insurance, in case I got any crazy ideas.

Gerran yanked Kiran's shirt up to his neck, revealing the red and black snarl of the blood mage sigil. He examined the sigil intently, comparing it to a sketch.

Over his shoulder, Kiran's eyes met mine, and it took every ounce of will I possessed not to flinch. Oh gods, the sick, stunned realization on his face…I felt lower than a mudworm. I concentrated fiercely on the thought of Melly, safe and happy. It didn't help.

Relief joined the satisfaction in Gerran's eyes. "Take him up to third-level storage, and restrain him until the buyer arrives."

Buyer? The sour taste in my mouth got stronger. I'd thought Gerran meant to set the Alathians on Kiran. Not a pleasant outcome, but one I might have stomached, for the sake of Melly and poor dead Harken. Kiran had made it plain he'd prefer the Council to Ruslan; and I'd told myself the Council might be lenient, once they heard his tale. Yet the shame burning my throat said deep down I'd known Gerran intended something nastier than a simple snitch.

As Gerran's man dragged him to the door, Kiran shut his eyes tight, his body tensing. I froze, images of dead mules and blackened trees flashing through my head.

Nothing happened, and I let out a shaky breath. The herbalist had been right about the hennanwort, then.

When Kiran opened his eyes, they were dark with despairing

fury. As the muscle twin hauled him out the door, I turned back to Gerran, careful to display none of my shame and anger. The second twin hadn't moved a hairsbreadth, his gaze still locked on me.

Gerran was busy opening his strongbox, without even a glimmer of concern. "Too bad you didn't keep him unconscious," he said, pulling out stacks of gold and silver bars.

"The delay at the gate was too long, and the yeleran wore off." Try as I might, the words still came out sharp.

"It was a difficult job, Dev, but you're being amply rewarded." He counted out a gleaming pile of gold bars and laid a plain velvet bag on top. "Your fee and your gemstones, as agreed."

I opened the bag and spilled out a sparkling rainbow of stones onto his desk. Silently, he offered me a jeweler's glass. I checked each gem for flaws, keeping a wary eye on the hovering muscle twin. "Tell your men to return the cart to a guy named Silas, at a cabin a mile north of the gate."

"Not a problem," Gerran said. "Here's the paperwork." He handed me documentation that showed I'd profited from a sale of silerium ore, and a second set naming me as a gemstone courier to Ninavel, which I'd need in order to safely store the gold and gems in a warded vault. The Alathians kept nearly as close an eye on their banking houses as they did on the border.

I wrapped up the lot, my nerves jumping. Gerran's promises notwithstanding, I half expected his man to leap on me the minute I turned my back. But I exited and crossed to the cart unmolested. Gerran's door remained shut, the yard silent, as I unhitched and saddled the horse. The first muscle twin was nowhere in sight. He must've stayed with Kiran, wherever they'd stashed him. I jerked my gaze away from the warehouses surrounding the yard. Whatever they'd done with Kiran was no business of mine.

I repeated that to myself as I rode away. A small fortune sat in the pack lashed to my saddle. I'd replaced all I'd lost to Jylla, and could finally give Melly the safety and the future Sethan had so desperately wanted for her.

Hell, I should be proud. I'd managed to complete the job in the face of avalanches, snowstorms, and angry mages. I ought to be going out celebrating tonight, damn it.

The thought only swelled the guilt gnawing at my guts. I clenched my hands on my reins. People were bought and sold in Ninavel all the time. Khalmet's hand, I'd been sold twice over, and it hadn't hurt me any. So what if I'd lied—so had Kiran. He'd been using me like I was using him, and he'd only told the truth when I forced it out of him. I didn't owe him anything. He'd murdered Harken and a score of others, endangered my friends, and cost me my future as an outrider.

None of it eased the memory of that terrible look in his eyes. Fuck. I kicked my horse into a heavy trot, but I couldn't outrun the other memories that chased me. His despair in the cave, when I'd seen the blood mage sigil; his white, pinched face after he'd pushed me clear of the rockfall; and worst of all, his blindingly bright smile when I'd first returned to the cabin.

Damn it, maybe I'd feel better if I made certain the mystery buyer wasn't Ruslan. I didn't see how it could be—why should Ruslan bother to pursue us across the mountains, otherwise? Yet I couldn't figure why anyone else would want a runaway blood mage apprentice so badly.

I'd been to Gerran's compound enough times over the last few years that I had a fair idea of his security measures. Breaking and entering in Alathia was far easier than in Ninavel, where anyone with enough coin could place seriously nasty wards. Gerran surely used deadly Ninavel-made wards inside his office, hidden from the Alathian authorities, but the wards scribed over his compound's outer fence met the Alathian legal standards and were laughably weak.

Gerran had placed his wards well, and no gaps existed in the protections on the sturdy fence. But the biggest failing of Alathian wards was their limited field of effect. I'd long since noticed that a good climber might scale the wall of a neighboring grain barn to a height that'd place him safely above the reach of the ward energies. One long jump would clear both wards and fence and give access to Gerran's storage yard. The barn wall was made of tightly fitted, weather sealed boards, making the climb a tricky prospect, but thanks to Red Dal, I'd had years of practice with exactly that kind of balance work.

Gerran had told his men to take Kiran to the third level, and only one of his warehouses had more than two floors. When I'd glanced that way after leaving Gerran's office, I hadn't seen any wards on the warehouse walls, only around the doors and windows. An old smoke vent sat high up under the eaves, a hole just big enough for a small, wiry person like myself to squeeze through into the maze of rafters beyond. Alathians rarely bothered with internal sealing for mere storage buildings, due to the expense, so likely there'd be cracks between ceiling boards wide enough for me to peek through to the rooms below. Soon as I'd secured my pay, I'd sneak into Gerran's compound and find where they'd stashed Kiran, take a look at the buyer...maybe even figure a way to provide Kiran a little anonymous help before I left Kost.

✳

(Kiran)

Ever since he'd taken the hennanwort, Kiran felt trapped in a nightmare. A terrible smothering numbness engulfed his mind, his inner senses vanished as completely as a severed limb. Wavering colored halos shimmered in disorienting array over his sight, and the distances between objects grew and shrank with no discernible pattern, as in some bizarre dreamscape. Every time he reached for power, he felt nothing but a sickening void, and his thoughts scattered and skipped like striderbugs in magelight.

He couldn't move. Sometimes he thought he was bound to a chair in a small, bare room with wooden walls. Other times he was certain he remained in Ruslan's workroom, held immobile by wards, and his memories of the mountains nothing but a dream and a lie. Had Dev betrayed him yet? He wasn't sure. Perhaps he was still huddled in the darkness of the abandoned cabin, waiting for the Alathians to come...

A squealing sound scraped across Kiran's consciousness like a file. A door, opening...he looked up with a sense of awful inevitability. Ruslan had come; he was certain of it. It was always Ruslan, in his nightmares.

For an instant he even saw Ruslan, tall and sardonic, a cold light in his hazel eyes. But as panic sliced through the haze in his head, his vision cleared, and Ruslan's image vanished. Instead, two men stood watching him, blurred by flickering halos. Muddy gray danced around an older, spectacled man whom Kiran recognized in a vague way, and a blaze of lurid yellow outlined a man he didn't know, slender and dark-haired, with the brown skin of an Arkennlander, though he wore formally cut Alathian clothes in shades of somber gray.

Alathia; he was in Alathia, yet still in danger. His surroundings wavered and solidified. Ropes crossed his chest, arms, and legs, binding him to a sturdy wooden chair.

The unfamiliar man's eyes met his, and he jerked against the ropes in uncontrolled reaction. The man didn't look anything like Ruslan, but his eyes burned with arrogant confidence the same way Ruslan's always had. He wore no sigils, but Kiran knew without a doubt he was a mage, and a powerful one.

The mage smiled at his flinch. Cold fear speared through the fog blurring Kiran's thoughts. Ruslan might have smiled so, faced with a victim helpless against his magic.

The mage reached out and ripped Kiran's shirt open downward from the neck, exposing Ruslan's *akhelsya* sigil. Triumph flamed in his eyes.

"Get out," the mage told the older man. The words bounced and echoed in Kiran's ears. The older man began a protest. The mage turned, and the other's face went ashen. He backed out of the room so fast he tripped on the threshold. The door squealed shut.

"What is your name?" the mage asked Kiran, his voice now cold and clear as if it rang form the icy heights of a mountain. Kiran took refuge in the thick, drowning folds of numbness, and didn't answer.

"I can see we'll need to get better acquainted," the mage said. With dreamlike slowness, he pulled a slender dagger from his belt. The sinuous writhing of the silver halos framing the blade entranced Kiran, until red stained them. His scattered thoughts abruptly focused. A thin line of blood streaked the mage's hand, and the knife now approached Kiran's arm, just above the ropes that bound it to the chair.

Blood magic! Kiran strained desperately against the ropes. He budged not an inch. The blade sliced his skin in a burning line. The mage's bloody hand closed tight over the cut, and Kiran cried out, miserably, as a sharp sting of power pierced the numbness enveloping him. Magic raced under his skin, freezing everything in its path. A silent flash seared his vision white.

Slowly, the world faded back into being. Kiran raised his head, cautiously. His inner senses remained numb, but the halos and odd visual effects had vanished, and the confusion of his thoughts had cleared.

"That's better, isn't it?" The mage's voice no longer echoed strangely. "Let's try again. What is your name?"

Kiran stayed silent. Names had power. Not nearly so much as blood, but enough to be dangerous.

The mage made a slight gesture, and Kiran's muscles seized, caught in the grip of a tightening vise. He heard his own voice speak in a ragged gasp. "Kiran."

"Kiran ai Ruslanov, I think you mean." The mage flicked his fingers. The pressure holding Kiran released. He slumped in the ropes, sick with realization. The mage had worked a binding on him through the blood-to-blood contact. Only a simple snare-binding, too minor of a working to trigger the Alathian detection spells, and yet impossible for Kiran to fight without access to his magic.

"I'm not Ruslan's. Not anymore," he said defiantly. The mage leaned forward to trace a finger over Ruslan's mark.

"True enough. Now you're mine, though I doubt you'll prefer it. Ruslan was always such an idealist about apprentices." The mage gave a contemptuous chuckle.

"You…you know Ruslan?"

"Oh, yes." The mage showed his teeth in a smile. "Thanks to your erstwhile master, I've spent the last twenty years exiled in this godsforsaken backwater of a country instead of enjoying my rightful place in Ninavel. A situation I intend to rectify, now that I have you."

The mage's expression softened in a way that lifted the hairs on the back of Kiran's neck. "You have no idea how delighted I am that you chose to run to Alathia." He stroked a hand down Kiran's cheek, then cupped his chin. "I'll enjoy this even more than I imagined. Ruslan has good taste, I'll give him that."

Kiran tried to jerk his head away, but the mage tightened his hold. "I won't be yours, either," Kiran spat through clenched teeth.

"You won't have a choice, I'm afraid," said the mage. "That's the difference between me and Ruslan." He touched Kiran lightly on the forehead, and the world went dark.

✳

(Dev)

I watched though a crevice between ceiling boards, my stomach churning, as Kiran went limp and the mage stepped back.

Shit. Now I had answers, all right, but I didn't much like them. Gods, the way the mage had smiled when he'd done—well, whatever he'd done, when he'd covered Kiran's cut arm with his bleeding hand. Kiran had keened and jerked like he'd been scorched by a burning brand, his head cracking backward into the chair so hard I'd winced to hear it. And all the while, the mage had worn the soft, contemplative smile of a man savoring a fine wine.

Below me, the creak of an opening door. I reapplied my eye to the crack, and nearly fell off my rafter when I spotted a familiar sharp-chinned, coppery face under a mop of dark curls. Pello! What the fuck?

"You summoned me?" He looked thinner than I remembered, and a hell of a lot more exhausted. No fucking wonder—he must've killed his horse under him to reach the border this fast. Even then, he shouldn't have made it, unless this bastard had somehow given him a helping hand.

"This is the boy you shadowed from Ninavel?" The animation the mage had displayed while talking to Kiran had vanished, leaving his voice cool and dry as a desert in winter.

Pello nodded. I grimaced. He'd been working for this asshole from the start?

"What evidence did you detect of a mage hunting him?"

Pello described with a shadow man's exacting eye for detail every damning incident from our time with the convoy. The unseasonally strong thunderstorm, Kiran's panicked flight into the catsclaw, and the blackened patches afterward. My searches of his wagon—Shaikar take him, he'd figured out I'd disabled his message charm, though he admitted he didn't know how. Kiran's reactions to his conversational goads at Ice Lake—gods, but Kiran had left a lot out of his account—and Kiran's accidental reveal of himself as a mage. For the first time, Pello's dry recounting took on an edge.

"You didn't warn me he was a mage, and a blood mage at that," he said, in a tone just short of accusation. Ha. At least I wasn't the only one who'd been kept in the dark.

The mage gave him a look, and I had to give Pello points for guts. He didn't back down, though his hands clenched at his sides.

"I might've died by that lake," Pello said. "I'd have taken more precautions, if I'd known the boy could kill with a touch. And the next day, the avalanche…" He described the diverted path of the slide, and his own near demise and rescue. The way he told it, Kiran's intent to kill him wasn't in doubt.

The mage shrugged. "My protection served you well enough, it would appear."

Pello's scowl said he wanted to dispute the point, but he went on with his tale. I wondered exactly what protection the mage meant. A charm? Something more?

When Pello described his search of the unconscious Kiran, and his discovery of both the blood mage sigil and Kiran's amulet, the mage held up a hand.

"This amulet you describe…he's not wearing it now."

I tensed. The amulet lay around my own neck. I'd thought it might help shield me from Gerran's wards.

"Gerran may have taken it. Or the outrider courier, Dev."

Trust Pello to bring my name to a blood mage's attention. I held my breath.

"No matter," the mage said. "I have seen its like before, and know its capabilities. The boy might well have escaped his master's control, wearing such a charm. Evidence indeed that he represents a genuine opportunity, and not a trap. Good." He stroked Kiran's bowed head, possessively, and waved a hand at Pello. "Continue."

"I thought the boy lost to you, and his hunter's arrival imminent," Pello said. "Your instructions said I must not be discovered, and I knew I'd never conceal my mission from a blood mage. I fled and used your *okalyi* charm to speed my travel, hoping I might survive to bring you news. I crossed the border not two hours past, and received your message to meet you here." He eyed Kiran. "I was surprised to learn the boy had arrived safely in Kost."

He'd left out our little scuffle at the outrider wagon. Interesting. Maybe he didn't want to admit he'd as much as warned me off helping Kiran. Once he'd seen Kiran's mark, he'd known a blood mage whose magic was unrestricted by the Alathian wards was about to descend on the convoy. He might've considered changing employers—not something he'd want this mage to know.

"Gerran says his courier is a resourceful man," the mage said.

"Apparently so. Perhaps you should have employed him instead." A sardonic glint lit Pello's dark eyes.

I didn't feel resourceful, I felt like a gods-damned idiot. All my efforts to keep Pello from figuring out my plans, when he'd known them all along…and the charm he'd mentioned, that'd let him reach the border faster than any man should—I hadn't seen anything near so powerful when I'd searched through his stash. Which meant he'd hidden it elsewhere, knowing I'd break his wards. Damn his eyes, he'd played me skillfully as Jylla had, and I hadn't had so much as an inkling of the truth.

"I required an independent observer. Your services have been adequate." The mage removed a leather pouch from his belt, and offered it to Pello. "Your payment. In gemstones, as you requested."

Pello didn't move to take it. His stance appeared casual, but I saw the way he was balanced on the balls of his feet, mere inches from the door. "Do you think me a fool, to come within your reach? You don't want the boy's master to know you have him. I'm sure you'd find it safer by far to let death stop my tongue, rather than relying on coin."

If anything, the mage looked amused. "Do you imagine distance will save you?"

"In Alathia? Yes," said Pello. "You dare not cast true magic here, under the eye of the Council. Yet I know the danger of a blood mage's touch."

The mage's eyes narrowed. "You know little of what I would or would not dare."

Pello's teeth showed in a sharp smile. "Do I not? I had time to consider, as I rode for the border. Shadow men hear much, and may piece together scattered whispers into a complete tale. I know who you are, and why you hate Ruslan Khaveirin. More, I know what you intend. You mean to break Lord Sechaveh's hold on Ninavel. Destroy him, and take the city as your own."

I sucked in a surprised breath. A blood mage wanting to rule Ninavel…was that the true story behind the mage wars? It made sense the other Ninavel mages wouldn't care for the idea of a blood mage replacing Sechaveh, and would've fought to prevent it. But damn it, I wished Pello had been a tad more specific. He might know who this bastard was, but I still had no idea.

The mage had listened to Pello's little speech without any further show of emotion. "You don't appear to be making a very good case for your continued survival," he said, drily. I had to agree. Whatever Pello's game, he'd taken a terrible risk.

Pello radiated sincerity. "I tell you this so there is truth between us. So that when I tell you I would gladly serve you in this goal, you might believe it."

Oh, the little rat bastard. I saw his game, now. Return to Ninavel as the right-hand man of the city's new lord, rather than a mere streetsider. What bothered me was that he wouldn't make the play if he didn't think this mage had a real chance of taking down Sechaveh. I couldn't figure why, given that Sechaveh had clearly won before.

A hint of contempt crossed the mage's face. "Why would I wish the service of an untalented man?"

"I have no magic, true. But even the most powerful of mages cannot be everywhere, and know all. I can obtain information on your enemies that your magic cannot."

Yeah, yeah, the standard shadow man sales pitch. I couldn't tell if the mage was buying it or not.

"And in exchange?"

"My life, of course. And your protection of it. When I fled the convoy, I made an enemy of Horavin House, and they are not merciful. Should I return to Ninavel, I would prefer not to spend all my time dodging assassins."

The mage's face was impassive. Pello waited in apparent unconcern, though inside he must've been wound tight as coilvine.

"I accept your offer." The mage held up a hand, as Pello brightened. "On one condition. You must allow me to search your thoughts, to verify the truth of what you say." A tiny, unpleasant smile touched his mouth. "One can never be too careful."

Behind his back, Pello's hands fisted so tightly I thought blood might drip from his palms. I grinned, fiercely. He'd thought he was so clever, yet he'd been trapped neat as a blacktail in a snare. If he let the mage touch him, gods only knew the result.

Pello's shoulders stiffened. He jerked his head in a nod. I pursed my lips in a soundless whistle. He might be a rat bastard, but he had balls.

The mage held out a hand, palm up.

Pello edged forward, reluctance clear in every line of his body. He hesitated, then extended his arm.

Swift as a striking snake, the mage clasped his bare wrist. Pello gave a strangled, agonized cry and collapsed, dangling from the mage's grip like a bone doll. I waited for the mage to cast his dead body aside, but instead the mage held his pose, his eyes distant and his hand locked over Pello's wrist.

He wasn't killing Pello, but searching his mind. My stomach lurched. Shaikar take me, this was what I'd left Cara and Jerik to face, back at the convoy.

Pello's face had gone gray, and blood trickled from the corners of his mouth. The mage's face stayed as serenely calm as a Varkevian idol's. At last he released Pello's wrist with a contemptuous flick of his hand. Pello dropped flat on his face, his body spasming in little hitching jerks. I winced, imagining Cara in his place.

The mage strode to the door and called for Gerran, who slid into the room with the wary caution of a man entering a sandcat's lair. The mage waved a hand at Kiran, unconscious in the chair, and Pello, who still lay twitching and gasping like a man brain-burned. "Have your men take them both to my carriage," he said, and stalked out.

I eased myself away from the crack in the boards. Oh, gods. I should never have come to Gerran's warehouse. Far from lightening the black weight in my gut, what I'd seen and heard had only made it worse. I hadn't only betrayed Kiran to a fate he'd rather have died than face. I'd handed a monster the key he thought he needed to bring a second war down on Ninavel.

CHAPTER FIFTEEN

(Dev)

I dropped my forehead against a roof truss, wishing to all the gods I could forget what I'd just seen and heard. Every instinct screamed at me to get the fuck away from the Shaikar-cursed blood mages before I got myself killed. I should run back to Ninavel, use my hard-won coin to free Melly, and get us safely out of the city before it erupted in magefire. I could warn my city friends a power-hungry blood mage meant to strike down Sechaveh and claim Ninavel—some of them might even believe me...and even if they thought me a sun-blinded, jabbering idiot, Sechaveh would surely win in the end, just like he had before. Right?

Yet the desperate defiance on Kiran's face and the agonized fear in his cry haunted me. If I left him to a slavery bad as anything Melly faced...what kind of man did that make me?

One every bit as soulless and cold as Jylla had claimed. If I ran, I'd prove her right, and earn every harsh word Cara had shouted at me.

But Melly...I'd promised Sethan I'd save her. No matter the cost.

My skin burned against the cold metal of the truss. Much as I didn't want to admit it, I knew full well Sethan would never have

219

wanted me to keep my promise to him this way. He'd have been horrified by what I'd done to Kiran, let alone the idea of me sneaking off while a blood mage worked to start a war that might kill thousands.

I could see the way he'd look at me with fierce, earnest eyes. *You can still make this right,* he'd say. Sethan had always believed in second chances. *All you need do is free Kiran, before the mage can make use of him.*

Yeah, sure. How the fuck was I supposed to do that? Even in my Tainted days, I'd stayed well clear of mages. Magic couldn't detect or prevent the invisible grip of the Taint, which gave Tainters a chance at breaking wards—but ward magic was passive, bound to a single purpose. Red Dal had warned us time and again that nothing could compete with active casting. And now I hadn't even the Taint to help me.

Pello's words whispered through my head. *You dare not cast true magic here.* This was Alathia, not Ninavel. A blood mage here would still be a deadly opponent, but the instant he cast anything stronger than a street-simple charm, he'd trigger the Council's detection spells and bring a host of their enforcer mages down on his head. Plus, the Alathians would never have agreed to let a blood mage live in exile within their borders—which meant they must not know about him.

A weapon I might use, though if I ran to the Alathians while Kiran remained a captive, I'd sentence him to death along with his captor. Now that I wasn't making idiotic rationalizations to myself, hoping for leniency from the Council for Kiran felt crazy as wishing for snow in Ninavel. No question Kiran was a blood mage, and the Alathians weren't known for making fine distinctions.

Besides, they wouldn't limit their questioning of me to safe topics. They'd find out all about my smuggling and Gerran's operation, and even if I didn't end up executed by the Council for my own crimes, my life wouldn't be worth two kenets when Bren found out who'd destroyed his business. But if I could find a way to break Kiran free and only then set the Alathians on the mage, anonymously…

Gods. I'd thought ditching the convoy to run with Kiran was crazy. Stealing him away from a blood mage was a whole new level of insanity. Yet the vicious knot in my stomach had already eased at the idea of a rescue. And if I'd learned one thing from my trip through the mountains with Kiran, it was that mages weren't the invincible creatures I'd thought. They were human like everyone else, and made mistakes. Mistakes that could be exploited. I hoped.

Best to treat it like any of the jobs I'd worked in the old days, and start with a thorough scout of the mark's location. I began crawling through the rafters, back toward the smoke vent. Damn it, I'd never sneak out of Gerran's compound in time to follow the mage's carriage, and I didn't have any hair or blood from either Kiran or Pello to key a find-me charm with.

Kiran, slumped in the ropes with his shirt torn halfway down his chest...I gripped a rafter with renewed force. His shirt, with the faint dye stains on the collar, left by his snow-dampened hair in the cave. And I still had a packet of dye from the same batch, sitting in my stash. I'd thought I might need it if I had to lie low in Kost. I'd never used dye to key a find-me, but it might work. So long as the mage didn't dump the shirt or burn it. I crawled faster.

At least I had one advantage. The mage had no idea I'd have any remaining interest in Kiran. He wasn't expecting me, and any Tainter worth their price knows that's the best advantage of all.

✳

(Kiran)

Kiran returned to consciousness the same way he'd left it, with the mage's hand on his forehead. He twisted away from the touch, his eyes flying open.

Instead of tied to a chair, he lay on a narrow but thickly quilted bed. The wood of the walls and ceiling was polished to a warm golden glow, and a patterned silken tapestry caught the light of an oil lamp hanging from the ceiling. Kiran pushed up, only to collapse back on the bed as sluggish muscles gave way.

The mage looked down at him dispassionately from his seat on an ornately carved chair beside the bed. "It'll be a while yet before that hennanwort wears off completely."

Even as the mage spoke, Kiran reached desperately for power, realizing the smothering numbness within had faded. Yet the moment he released his barriers, he slammed up against a force as solid and unyielding as a stone wall.

The mage gave a dry chuckle at Kiran's reflexive gasp. "Come, now. You cannot imagine I'd allow the drug to wear off without a better means of control." He pointed.

Intricate silver filigree twined over Kiran's forearms from wrist to elbow, the metal bright against his skin. Kiran's stomach sank. A charm strong enough to block a mage's power so completely must be thirteenth level, or more—well beyond anything Kiran had ever created. But if he could read the pattern... he touched silver, and cried out as needling agony swept over him.

A small smile played about the mage's mouth. "Surely Ruslan bound your magic as a child."

Kiran forced himself upright despite the trembling of his muscles. True enough that Ruslan had blocked both him and Mikail for years, claiming mere proximity to the powerful forces of the confluence would destroy the mind of any mageborn child without such protection. But Ruslan had used a specialized form of a blood-binding, not a physical charm.

"Who are you?" Kiran asked, his voice husky with disuse. Ruslan and Lizaveta rarely spoke of other *akheli*. Yet if they'd ever mentioned this man, perhaps he could recall something of use.

"My name is Simon Levanian." The mage sounded as if he expected Kiran to recognize the name. It meant nothing to Kiran.

Simon's brown eyes turned cold. "I should have known. How very like Ruslan, to assume in his arrogance that his apprentices need not know my name."

"Why should we know the name of some street conjurer exiled to Alathia?" Kiran imitated Ruslan's most derisive tone, despite the fear chilling his heart. If this man was anything like Ruslan, defiance would easily provoke him to anger. Anger might drive Simon to a mistake; or perhaps Simon would kill him in a rage, as Ruslan had not. Kiran thought of his blood vow to Lizaveta with bitter regret. Any effort toward death more direct than this would be impossible.

Already he skirted the edges of her binding, making it hard to speak.

Simon's eyes narrowed. Kiran felt a small, fierce surge of satisfaction.

Despite his narrowed eyes, Simon's voice remained calm. "Brave words, young Kiran, when I hold your soul in my hands."

"You hold nothing of the kind." Without the hennanwort blurring his thoughts, Kiran remembered quite well the supposed advantages of the binding Ruslan had cast on him during the *akhelashva* ritual. The mark-bond gave Ruslan near total control over Kiran; yet the bond's very nature meant no other mage could supplant or dissolve it, and it protected Kiran's mind and magic from many of the worst bindings an enemy mage might cast.

Though Simon could cast far nastier spells on Kiran's body than a mere snare-binding. Kiran shoved down memories of Ruslan's more vicious punishments, and kept his expression contemptuous.

"I'm not a fool," he told Simon. "You can block my power, or kill me, but you cannot touch my will."

"Did Ruslan tell you that?" Simon's gaze dropped to Ruslan's mark, half revealed by the ragged tear in Kiran's shirt. "What faith you have in him. He'd be so pleased, if he knew."

Kiran bit back his first furious denial. "I should have faith in your words instead? A powerless mage skulking behind the border, afraid to face the one who defeated him?"

He'd hoped to provoke Simon further, but Simon only looked amused. "The only powerless mage I see here is you."

Kiran refused to look at the hateful charms spiraling over his skin. "What do you want with me? I don't care what you claim, I know the meaning of a mark-bond. You can't control my mind, or use my magic against Ruslan."

"Not as long as you are mark-bound," Simon agreed, mildly. "But you lack imagination if you believe that is the only use I'd have for an apprentice of Ruslan's." He drew the slender silver dagger from his belt.

Kiran scrabbled backward on the bed. Simon flicked a hand. Power rippled under Kiran's skin. His muscles went slack, dumping him flat on his back.

Curse the man, of course he'd kept his snare-binding in place. Kiran watched in helpless frustration as Simon nicked his own finger. Simon traced a bloody rune on Kiran's forehead, and spoke soft words. The blood burned on Kiran's skin, power pressing inward. The room dissolved before his eyes.

"Ow!" Kiran yanked his hands back from the spell channel, his fingers already blistering. Magefire erupted in crackling arcs, only to subside as the exercise room wards blazed to life and damped the energies back to safe levels.

"Watch it, stupid." Mikail scowled at him from across the silver tangle of channels laid out on the floor. "What were you thinking, disrupting the channels like that? Now we'll have to start all over again." His aggrieved expression changed to one of concern, as Kiran hissed and sucked on his burned fingers. "Are you all right? Did I channel too much power for you to hold?"

"No." Ruslan's voice made Kiran start and jerk his fingers from his mouth. He hadn't heard Ruslan come in, but there he stood, leaning against the wall with folded arms. The ebbing fire of the wards turned his chestnut hair to burnished copper and cast shadows beneath the smooth golden planes of his cheekbones. "Mikail, you did well. The error was Kiran's alone." His voice grew stern. "Kiran, had this been a real spell, your lapse in focus would have meant death for you both."

Kiran flinched. Ruslan was right. He'd let his attention wander, just for an instant, and lost control. "I'm sorry," he said, looking anxiously at Ruslan. "I didn't mean to. It's just—the weather is so nice today—Mero said the baby songbirds would be hatching, and—" Too late, he noticed Mikail's subtle shake of his head.

Ruslan's expression darkened. He strode across the room and bent to grip Kiran's shoulders. "Mero? Who is this?"

Kiran swallowed. Mikail's expression made it clear Kiran had done something that would anger Ruslan far more than his error with the spell. "I…he…"

"He's the cook's boy," Mikail said hurriedly, his eyes on Ruslan's face. "We talk to him sometimes. When he brings food to our room. That's all."

Ruslan turned and looked at Mikail, then back at Kiran. "Is that all?" His voice was soft, but his eyes were anything but. Kiran knew it would only be worse if he lied. Ruslan always knew when they lied.

"I, um. Sometimes I play with him," Kiran admitted in a voice that was little more than a whisper. He liked Mero, who was friendly and talkative, unlike the rest of the servants. Mero knew all kinds of interesting things, like where the birds nested and the lizards hid at night, and he was happy to show off his Taint.

"Kiran." Ruslan didn't look angry now, only disappointed, his deep voice sorrowful. "What have I told you?"

"You said the nathahlen aren't like us and they're just stupid and we shouldn't bother with them, but Mero's not like that, he's nice—" Kiran's explanation stumbled to a halt as Ruslan's mouth tightened.

"I told you to keep yourself apart from them, Kiran, and you did not listen." Ruslan's voice was stern again, his hazel eyes cold.

"I didn't think you meant Mero," Kiran said miserably. He bowed his head, knowing what would come.

"It's my fault, Ruslan, I should have watched him better." Mikail's slanted gray eyes creased with anxiety. "Kiran's only little, he gets mixed up sometimes."

Ruslan raised his eyebrows at Mikail. "Your instinct to protect your mage-brother is commendable, but Kiran is old enough to know better. I fear I must reinforce the lesson." He lifted a hand. Kiran tried to brace himself, but it didn't help.

The world turned to fire, flames melting his skin and charring his insides as his screams tore his throat raw, the agony building until it threatened to rip his mind apart...

The pain ebbed at last, leaving Kiran in a crumpled, whimpering heap. Through a blur of tears, he saw Mikail backed white-faced against the wall, his hands over his ears.

Strong arms lifted him, enfolding him in solid warmth. "There, now," Ruslan said tenderly into his ear. "All over." He cradled Kiran against his chest, one hand stroking through Kiran's hair.

Kiran buried his face in the silken folds of Ruslan's shirt and cried. Ruslan hummed softly and rubbed Kiran's back in soothing circles, until Kiran's sobs died away to sniffles.

A tentative finger touched Kiran's shoulder. He lifted his head to see Mikail, his face still pale and his eyes solemn. Ruslan freed an arm and pulled Mikail in against his other side.

"You'll remember now, Kiran, yes? You won't make me hurt you anymore?"

Kiran nodded, gulping. Ruslan turned to Mikail. "And you'll set him a good example—no more idle conversations with servants."

"Yes, Ruslan," Mikail said earnestly.

"Good." Ruslan gave them both a last hug and stood. "Now. Perform the exercise again. If you hold your focus properly this time, Kiran, I'll heal your fingers."

Disorientation washed over Kiran as the memory abruptly receded. His fingers ached with remembered pain, his nose full of the jasmine and citrus-scented air of Ruslan's house in Ninavel.

Belatedly, he realized he could move. Simon had relaxed the snare-binding. Kiran quelled the urge to scramble backward again, knowing it wouldn't make any difference.

"What…what was that for?" From the *ighantya* rune still tingling Kiran's skin, Simon must have experienced the spell-triggered memory along with Kiran, using his existing snare-binding as a link. Again, too subtle of a casting to disturb the Council's detection spells. But what had Simon hoped to learn from such a commonplace childhood moment?

Simon only tapped a finger on the chair arm, his dark brows drawn together in dissatisfaction. "Perhaps some adjustments to the arcana," he muttered.

Ah. So subtle a spell was difficult to target properly. Simon hadn't wanted that memory, but another—which one, Kiran couldn't tell. Perhaps Simon imagined Kiran possessed knowledge of the complex, layered defensive spells that guarded Ruslan's mind and *ikilhia*. The idea startled Kiran into a bitter chuckle. If Simon thought Ruslan confided in his apprentices, he didn't know Ruslan at all.

Simon glanced at Kiran. "If you mock your master's indulgence of your disobedience, I share the sentiment." He shook his head. "What a fool Ruslan is. Why he didn't burn out your will the moment he took you as his apprentice, I'll never know. That ridiculous obsession of his with creating a family, I suppose." He gave a scornful laugh. "Not that I'm complaining. His weakness will mean his death."

Kiran's eyes widened. Simon's hatred for Ruslan had been evident from the start. But to kill Ruslan…not even in Kiran's darkest, wildest dreams had he imagined such a thing was possible. Ruslan was far too clever and strong, his defenses so thickly layered not even a channeled spell could penetrate them.

Yet Simon's sharp derision when he'd spoken of Ruslan and family…Kiran's mouth went dry. *Akheli* were exquisitely skilled in the art of torture. Did Simon think to gain advantage over Ruslan by threatening—or worse, enacting—some savage torment upon Kiran?

Torment is what you deserve, after the horrors I endured, Alisa's voice whispered within. Kiran fought to project only confidence. "You must know Ruslan would never bow to an enemy's demands, no matter what you do to me."

"True; not even Ruslan is so foolish as that." Dark amusement lit Simon's eyes as he stood. "Though you are wise to fear my casting. Ruslan's corrections will seem as love-taps compared to the agonies my wards will visit upon you, if you brave them." He tapped the black ward lines etched into the doorframe, meaningfully. The lines flashed a quick, vivid green as the door shut behind him.

Kiran concentrated. Even with his magic blocked by Simon's charms, he could sense a low, snarling mutter of power within walls, ceiling and floor. Not strong enough to kill, but enough to savage his nerves and blast him unconscious.

He studied the silver banding on his forearms. He'd never succeed in reading a spell pattern through pain so intense as Simon's charms could inflict, but if he could damage the filigree badly enough, he might shatter the bonds on his power.

Kiran scooted over to the nearest bedpost, a chunky wooden column broader than his hand. Bracing himself as best he could with one arm, he slammed the other against the post.

The charm flashed a violent blue, and agony blurred his vision. Kiran doubled over, gasping. Gradually, the pain ebbed. He peered at the silver, seeing it unmarked as he'd suspected. The flash meant the charms contained protective wardings to prevent damage.

The few room furnishings were heavy, carved wooden things. Kiran reached for the oil lamp overhead, hope rising, but Simon had anticipated him. The lamp was warded as strongly as the walls. Kiran growled in frustration and glared at the floor, covered in a thick, soft rug marked by subtle colors and patterns. Simon was wealthy despite his exile.

An exile he clearly believed would end, now he had Kiran. He must think Kiran's memory held some key to Ruslan's defenses, unlikely as that seemed.

New unease cramped Kiran's stomach, as he recalled Simon's amused condescension when he'd agreed about the mark-binding, and the covetous heat of his gaze when they'd first met.

The only release from a mark-bond was in death; but Ruslan's death or Kiran's, either would suffice to dissolve the link. If Simon killed Ruslan, afterward he could mark-bind Kiran for his own, if he chose. But why bind Kiran rather than simply kill him along with Ruslan?

In all Simon's talk of his exile and his plans, he'd said *I*, never *we*. Kiran straightened, in a blaze of certainty. Simon was alone. Without a partner mage, he couldn't cast channeled spells—of course he'd be eager to bind a trained apprentice.

But Ruslan's magic outweighed Simon's by a thousandfold, with Mikail and Lizaveta to channel for his casting while Simon cast alone. How could Simon possibly think to defeat Ruslan with such a handicap?

Yet if Simon destroyed Ruslan, and Kiran somehow escaped before Simon could mark-bind him… for an instant, Kiran pictured it: true freedom, the sort he'd barely dared to imagine. A dizzying vista expanded. He might seek out a different, more innocent form of magic. Travel to distant lands, the way explorers did in the tales both he and Alisa had loved.

The memory of Alisa's bright eyes and wistful smile closed Kiran's throat and brought him tumbling back to reality. Even if by some miracle he achieved freedom from both Ruslan and Simon, Kiran would remain one of the *akheli*. The *akhelashva* ritual had changed him in more ways than the mark-bond, and from everything he'd read, there was no way back. He'd always be a pawn to more powerful mages, and a dangerous but profitable commodity to men like Dev.

Dev. Kiran's hands clawed into the bedquilt. His other memories of Kost were hazy from the drugs, but his last moments with Dev stood out with painful clarity. Not a hint of surprise had shown on Dev's face when Gerran's man had grabbed Kiran. Dev had known it would happen—and he'd neither warned Kiran, nor lifted a finger to help him.

A black wave of anger crested. Kiran forced it down to a roiling undercurrent. Foolish, to feel so bitter. He'd known the chances of betrayal were high. But he'd been so relieved, when Dev had returned to the cabin—he'd let down his guard, started to trust.

Ruslan had always insisted the *nathahlen* could never be trusted. *They'll turn on you like jackals the instant they see an opportunity, jealous of your power.* Kiran hadn't wanted to believe him, preferring Alisa's far rosier view. But all his attempts to embrace her ideals had only led to disaster.

He shook off the thought. The only thing that mattered now was finding a means of escape. Otherwise if Simon did kill Ruslan, Kiran would only exchange one monstrous master for another. *Why he didn't burn out your will the moment he took you as an apprentice, I'll never know,* Simon had said. Kiran shivered, his gorge rising.

✳

(Dev)

Early morning in Kost brought thick veils of river mist drifting through the narrow, cobbled streets. Soon as the sun rose over the rim of the gorge, the fog would burn off, but for now it turned Kost into a dreamscape of half-seen shapes and odd echoes. I hurried up the terraced lanes of the city's southwest quarter, the silver band of my find-me charm pulsing warm on my bicep beneath the rough brown wool of an Alathian-style tradesman's jacket. Alathians did business at disgustingly early hours, and enough tradesmen making deliveries traveled the fog-choked streets to make my presence unremarkable.

The find-me charm was a simple one, too minor in nature to offend the Council's sensibilities. It operated on the same principle as the old kids' game of fire-and-ice. The closer I moved to the charm's target, the warmer the band grew. So far, my idea about targeting the dye on Kiran's shirt appeared to be working. The charm had led me from my room at a nondescript riverside inn up to this far more genteel district perched high on the side of the Parsian Valley, full of Kost's version of highsiders, exactly the kind of place I'd expect a mage to frequent.

Only problem was, the charm didn't hold enough power to work longer than a half-day at most, and the gods-damned streets twisted back on themselves like a tangle of sand adders as they climbed the hillside. Moving in the right direction was slow, frustrating work, requiring an eye-crossing level of concentration on subtle changes in the charm's warmth. My gut fizzed with a mixture of impatience and worry. If I didn't track down Kiran before the charm gave out, I'd never find him in this terraced maze of highsiders.

Instead of the cultivated courtyards and graceful archways that separated highsider dwellings in Ninavel, Kost's richer denizens stacked their houses in rows, side by side with no space in between. Looking down at lower terraces, I'd seen the houses had tiny courtyards in back, barely large enough for a few flowerpots. Down riverside, all the buildings were boxy, ugly things of plain wood, but up here, wood mixed with gray and brown stone, and some houses had slate roofs. Occasional steeply slanted parks lined with trees and lush flowerbeds crossed the gap between terraces.

The fog began to burn off, and wan sunlight seeped through the haze overhead. My head pounded with the effort of concentration. The charm's power was fading. Gods all damn it, surely I was close, now. I'd nearly climbed to the valley rim.

I raised a silent, relieved cheer when at last I narrowed in on a row of houses just past a slender, near-vertical strip of a park. I dawdled along a stone stair winding up through the park, pretending to admire a rainbow cascade of larkflowers.

The ten houses in the row didn't look much different from countless others I'd passed. Three stories tall and fronted with gray blocks of stone, they had narrow slots for windows, white lintels, and ornamental carving on the doors and eaves. Three of the ten had purely decorative woodwork with no sign of a family crest, meaning they likely weren't owned by natives of Kost. One of those three, midway along the row, had silver plaques inscribed with ward lines not only bracketing doors and windows, but strategically scattered over roof and walls as well. The wards were standard Alathian make, meant to paralyze an intruder rather than kill, but the placement was expert. Not a chink existed in their protection.

That had to be a mage's house. I weighed the risk of walking the row to confirm Kiran's presence—or at least, that of his shirt—with the last glimmer of the charm's power. The mage didn't know me from any other Arkennlander, but if Pello was in there and caught sight of me, he'd mark me no matter what disguise I wore. Damn it, I couldn't chance that.

Shaikar take Pello, anyway. Every time I turned around on this trip, there he was, making everything twice as fucking difficult. Why couldn't he have slunk off back to Ninavel instead of throwing in with the mage?

I'd have to shadow the house careful as a handler scouting a job. With wards placed so well, I'd never manage to sneak inside. But whatever the mage had planned for Kiran, it surely involved magic, and he couldn't do any serious magic in a house smack in the middle of Kost without running afoul of the Council. No, he'd have to take Kiran somewhere else first, and the first step in any rescue was to figure out when and where he intended to make his move.

The creviced gray limestone of the cliff that formed the foundation of the next higher terrace drew my eye. Plants grew out of the cracks, from ferns to scraggly, stubborn trees. And high up in the rock face, a round dark hole like an open mouth.

When the Alathians built Kost's terraced streets into the steep side of the Parsian Valley, they'd bored narrow tunnels through the rock to channel the runoff from the heavy winter rains and keep it from causing mudslides or ground erosion. The lower end of this tunnel looked just wide enough for a person to squeeze inside. It'd be cramped and awkward, but I'd be hidden from view, and I'd have a good sightline down to the house I wanted to watch.

A perfect spot for a deathdealer's ambush, if only I could shoot a crossbow bolt through Simon's heart. I knew better than to try. Aside from my lack of experience with weaponry, I'd heard far too many stories in Ninavel about idiots who tried to ambush powerful mages. Throwing knives, crossbow bolts, even Sulanian hand cannons…none of it could penetrate the invisible armor of a mage's defensive spells, no matter how sudden the surprise. Too bad. If anyone deserved a knife in the throat, it was a blood mage.

No, I'd need to find another way to deal with Kiran's captor, and that meant keen observation. I sighed. When Red Dal scouted a job, he sent kids in shifts so someone watched the house every moment of the day and night. No possible way to duplicate that, working alone. My contacts in Kost were all part of Gerran's operation, and gods knew I didn't want a single whiff of my intentions getting back to Gerran. I knew a few others here by name, but none I could trust.

What I needed, damn it, was Jylla. Since I'd Changed, I'd never worked a city job without her. That wicked glint in her black eyes when she'd worked out a clever plan…the way she'd dissolve my nerves before a tricky job by muttering sarcastic observations about passers-by until I near burst with suppressed laughter…I kicked a loose cobblestone, viciously. Jylla would never have joined me in something crazy as this. She'd have laughed her perfect little ass off when I told her my reasons, mocked me for being soft in the head, and then talked me out of it with a host of coolly practical arguments.

To Shaikar's hells with Jylla. I'd shadow the mage's house best I could, seize on any weakness I found, and pray for Khalmet's favor. I'd need the touch of his good hand to have a hope of foxing a blood mage.

CHAPTER SIXTEEN

(Kiran)

The creak of the door startled Kiran awake. He'd settled on the bed intending only a brief rest, his thoughts still consumed with the question of Simon's plans, but the muddy lethargy of his thoughts suggested he'd slept far longer than he'd meant. He shoved upright, hastily bracing for another confrontation with Simon.

Pello slid around the door with a plate of bread and cheese and a water jug balanced in his hands. Kiran's jaw dropped. "You! What are you doing here?"

A smirk spread over Pello's face. He set down the food. "Dev never realized I represented an employer within Alathia, then? How gratifying. Or…" The smirk turned sly. "Perhaps he knew, and didn't tell you."

Bad enough that Dev had handed him over to Gerran, but if he'd known about Simon, and what Kiran faced in Simon's hands…the bitterness that pierced him edged toward hatred. With an effort, Kiran leashed his anger. Regardless of what Dev had or hadn't known, he no longer mattered. Pello, however…"You traveled with the convoy at Simon's bidding? Why?"

"Simon Levanian is a cautious man." Pello ran a finger over the thickly clustered ward lines inscribed on the doorframe. They remained quiescent; Simon must have keyed the wards directly to Kiran. "An apprentice of his greatest enemy, obligingly running straight into his grasp…as the saying goes, beware your rival's touch, disguised as Khalmet's good hand."

Simon had feared his escape was some trick of Ruslan's? Kiran's heart quickened. Perhaps he could use that fear against Simon.

Sardonic amusement gleamed in Pello's dark eyes. "Yet anyone with eyes can see you have no guile. Such a disappointment for your former master, I am sure. Did you run to escape his heavy hand? Do you glory in the dreadful end Simon intends for him?"

Kiran's breath caught. If Pello knew Simon's plans, his quick tongue might be far looser than his master's. Kiran assumed an expression of utter confidence. "Simon will fail. Ruslan's magic far outstrips his."

"Cautious men do not gamble without the certainty the odds are in their favor," Pello said, with another twitch of a grin.

"What makes you so certain Simon has judged his chances correctly?"

Pello raised his brows. "What makes you believe he hasn't?"

Sudden insight struck Kiran. Pello didn't know Simon's plans either, and underneath his mocking assurance, a splinter of doubt must linger. "Dev claimed you were clever, but that must have been another lie. Choosing to serve Simon…a clever man would have realized the chances of survival are nonexistent. The *akheli* are not kind to untalented servants. Even if Simon should somehow prevail over Ruslan, you'll not last more than a year. You'll anger him one day, or he'll need a source of power and take what's closest to hand. But when Simon fails, your death will come far sooner."

Pello flipped a hand in dismissal. "I hardly think a mage so exalted as Ruslan Khaveirin would concern himself with the death of one so lowly as I."

Excitement sparked within. Pello didn't know…oh, careful, he must be careful. "You don't understand," Kiran said. "Simon bound you. Only a lock-binding rather than a full drone-binding, I'd imagine, but for an untalented man, completely vulnerable to magic…should Simon fall to Ruslan, the force of his death will blast through the link and snuff out your life as rapidly as a candle in a sandstorm."

No trace of mockery showed in Pello's eyes now. "I exchanged no blood with Simon."

"The *akheli* need no blood rituals to bind the untalented. Has he never touched you?" Kiran read the answer in the sudden rigidity of Pello's stance. "He can kill you now with a thought, and the Alathian wards won't sense a thing." Though only if the two men were in close proximity; a fact Kiran hoped Pello didn't know.

"All the more reason to devote myself to ensuring his success," Pello said flatly.

Kiran leaned forward. "A lock-binding can be broken or thwarted, with the right knowledge. Knowledge I have, and would share, if you help me cross Simon's wards."

Pello laughed. "Ah! A commendable effort, but a doomed one. To throw away all I might gain at Simon's side, when I have only your word such a binding even exists? I am not so gullible as you, to be led trusting as a calf to slaughter."

Kiran gritted his teeth. "You'll gain only death."

"So you say." Pello moved for the door.

"Simon will prove me right," Kiran said urgently. "He'll use the binding against you, the moment you disobey or even irritate him. When he does, think on what I've said."

Pello shot him one last narrow-eyed glance and slipped out. Kiran thumped a fist into the bedquilt. Curse it, if only he'd found more convincing words! Certain as the sunrise, Simon would use that binding one day—but perhaps not soon enough to help Kiran.

✳

Time dragged on in endless, silent hours, and Kiran's frustration climbed ever higher. He paced the room, tracing ward lines over and over, seeking even the tiniest of flaws in the invisible bars of his cage. He found none. Simon's wards were seamless, and his charms proved impervious to all Kiran's attempts to damage or remove them.

Kiran braved the shattering pain countless times, trying to read their pattern. The charms' protective wardings knocked him unconscious before he could get so much as a glimpse.

He could only guess at how long he'd been Simon's captive. His only means of measuring time was to count meals and the number of times he'd slept. That was no good guide, since he suspected Simon of sending meals at irregular intervals, and his body's natural rhythms had been disrupted by the drugs. He thought it had only been a few days, though it felt like more. Simon hadn't returned, and neither had Pello. His meals were brought by a dour-faced old woman who refused to even raise her eyes from the floor, let alone speak, no matter what Kiran said to her.

Despite all the time he'd had to think, he'd come no closer to understanding how Simon planned to strike at Ruslan. Physical harm would not suffice to kill an *akheli*, and if Simon truly lacked the ability to cast channeled magic, he'd never breach Ruslan's defenses.

Ruslan had once told Kiran the only danger a master *akheli* need fear was his own capacity for error when working with forces as immensely powerful as those of Ninavel's confluence. A mistake in channel design might easily send energies too great for any mage to contain surging through both channeler and focus, overwhelming all protections and burning both to ash in an instant. Perhaps Simon intended to trick Ruslan into an error of that nature—but Kiran couldn't imagine how.

The door opened. The ward lines glowed livid green, extinguishing Kiran's hope his visitor might be Pello.

Simon stepped over the threshold with the delicacy of a cat. He was dressed much as before, in somber but well tailored Alathian clothing, without any sigils or markings. Slender and of medium height, he had none of Ruslan's commanding physical presence. Only his eyes gave the lie to his mundane appearance. They swept over Kiran, coolly appraising.

"It appears you have made a full physical recovery. Good."

Kiran watched him warily. Plentiful sleep and food had erased the last traces of his exhaustion from the trip across the mountains, as well as the lingering weakness from the drugs. He felt healthy and strong, but it would do him little good against Simon's magic.

"Sit down." Simon put a hand on a chair. Kiran shook his head, backing up a few paces for good measure.

Simon sighed. "Why waste time with vain attempts at defiance?"

Because it irritates you, Kiran didn't say. Small hope that Simon's irritation would lead to a mistake in casting, but Kiran had to seize any hope, no matter how small. He shrugged.

"Suit yourself," Simon said, with a shrug of his own and a flick of his hand. Kiran fell sprawling onto the floor. Simon called, "Morvain!"

A gray-haired man with a scar bisecting his jawline poked his head around the open door. Simon pointed at Kiran, then the chair. Morvain entered and hoisted Kiran with broad, callused hands, depositing him in the chair with no apparent effort. Kiran recognized the stubbornly blank look on the man's scarred face. Ruslan's servants had worn much the same expression. This man had been with Simon far longer than Pello, and would know well the crushing grip of Simon's binding. A tiny spark of hope rekindled. If Pello had the sense to talk to Morvain, he might yet realize the truth of Kiran's words.

As Morvain hurried out, Simon drew up the second chair to face Kiran's. He sat, his silver dagger gleaming in one hand.

Kiran marshaled his concentration. If Simon meant to touch his memories again, he wasn't without defenses. Yet better first to wait and see which memory Simon's spell retrieved, in hopes of gaining insight into Simon's plan.

Simon sliced a finger and traced another bloody *ighantya* rune on Kiran's forehead. But this time, before he cast, he dabbed more blood on a thumb-sized chunk of amber and held it over Kiran's heart. The amber glowed like a miniature star as Simon spoke and the spell took hold.

Kiran stood tall in his white robe as Lizaveta draped a crimson length of rune-patterned fabric around his neck.

"Today you come of age, akhelysh. *Are you ready?"*

Kiran nodded, striving to match her solemnity, afraid his voice would betray his excitement if he spoke. He'd been waiting for so long. Mikail had undergone the akhelashva *ritual three years ago. Kiran had pleaded for Ruslan to perform the ritual for him as well, but Ruslan had only smiled and told him to be patient.*

Now at last the time had come. Ruslan and Mikail had been preparing for days and he hadn't been allowed to help. He'd asked Mikail a thousand times what the ritual was like, but Mikail always refused to discuss it. He'd shake his head and give Kiran a superior look, saying it was a secret only true akheli *might know.*

Lizaveta kissed him gently on each cheek, then took his hand and led him to the door of Ruslan's workroom. There Ruslan stood in full ceremonial robes, marked with the red and black sigils of his magical lineage. Lizaveta put Kiran's hand in Ruslan's and stepped back, her face grave but her eyes bright. Ruslan bound another piece of crimson fabric over Kiran's eyes.

"You go into this room sightless, soundless, voiceless…ready to be reborn," he said, his voice resonant. Kiran's senses faded as the spell took effect, his world narrowing to the feeling of Ruslan's renewed grip on his hand. Ruslan led him forward, and—

Kiran's mind recoiled, his entire being focused in rejection of the memory. He caught a flashing glimpse of Simon's intent face, felt the rune burn on his forehead. Simon spoke, harshly. Magic dragged at Kiran, yanking him back down into memory. Instead of fighting the pull, he reinforced it, casting himself down at a speed that rushed him past the *akhelashva* ritual, further into the past…

Kiran straddled the high stone wall, watching the kittens play on the sunlit flagstones beyond. They were feral cats and would be killed if noticed, but they lived within the walled sanctum of a very old, reclusive factor from Suns-Eye House who didn't seem to care that his outer courtyards were slowly falling to ruin. The sweeping mosaics patterning the flagstones were sand-dulled and cracked, and spineweed sprouted in the corners. Kiran rarely saw the mother cat, who was skinny and kept to the shadows, but the kittens were bolder. They ventured out onto sunwarmed stone, pouncing on each other and chasing whiptail lizards.

"What are you looking at?"

Kiran turned so quickly he nearly fell off the wall. A girl stood on the walkway below, watching him. She looked about his own age, somewhere in her early teens, her dark hair curling free from a single braid. Her loose shirt and trousers were clean but simple, bound by a brightly patterned sash around her slim waist, and she carried a woven basket with parcels inside. Kiran thought she was likely a servant or a shopkeeper's daughter, out on errands.

Kiran shrugged, hoping that if he didn't answer, she'd go away.

"You come here every week. I just want to know what's so interesting."

Kiran was startled into speech. "You've been following me?"

The girl shrugged, and set her basket down on the paving stones. She eyed the wall, hands on her hips, then grabbed one of the knotted karva vines clinging to the stone. She hauled herself high enough to thrust an imperious brown hand at Kiran. "Help me up."

Kiran hesitated, then took her hand and pulled. She heaved a trousered leg over the wall and settled, facing him. Wide amber eyes darted from his face to the courtyard. "Oh," she said, seeing the kittens. She sounded disappointed. "I was hoping it was something really good."

"Like what?" Kiran asked, curious despite himself.

She sighed, blowing a stray curl of hair out of her face. "I don't know. A baby dragon, maybe? Something exotic I could tell my family about. Ever since we arrived in Ninavel, they spend all day working on their precious business ledgers, and they hardly even notice me."

A merchant's daughter, then, despite her simple clothes. "There's no such thing as dragons," Kiran said.

"How do you know?" She gave him an arch look. "Plenty of mages live around here, you know. One of them could have made one. A magic dragon." Mischief sparkled in her eyes. "I heard when Sechaveh's great-granddaughter got married, he had his mages conjure her a team of unicorns to draw her carriage."

Kiran opened his mouth to tell her that it was likely mere illusion, that the amount of power needed to create some fantastical animal was impossibly huge, but that thought reminded him he shouldn't even be talking to her in the first place.

"I should go," he mumbled, and reached for a karva vine. If he didn't return home soon, Ruslan would want to know why a simple purchase of spell-grade silver had taken him so long. And if Ruslan decided he'd been too friendly with this nathahlen girl...his hands cramped around the vine.

"What's your name?" the girl asked. He shook his head, avoiding her eyes. She smiled at him, winningly. "Come on, don't be shy. I'm Alisa. My uncle warned me Ninavel boys aren't so well mannered as those back east, but surely you can see now you've got to tell me your name, or else it's terribly impolite."

He'd never seen someone smile like that, like she was lit from within. A queer pang squeezed his heart. Before he could stop himself, he answered, "Kiran."

Alisa rewarded him with another radiant smile. "Well then, Kiran, I'll see you next week." She winked at him and slithered down the wall to pick up her basket once more. Her head was high as she sauntered out through the archway that led to the main street. Kiran stared after her, rooted to the spot. Next week; suddenly, the time until Ruslan sent him out for more spell material seemed far too long.

This time when the spell released him, Kiran struck Simon's hand away and vaulted from the chair in one convulsive motion. "Stop it!" Alisa, vivid and beautiful and alive…pain seared him, worse than any magefire strike.

On Simon's face, surprise changed to dawning comprehension. "I see…your redirection didn't completely succeed. The two memories must not be unrelated. How interesting." He eyed the chunk of amber in his hand, thoughtfully.

"You seek my memory of the *akhelashva* ritual? *Why?* The mark-binding cannot be dissolved while Ruslan yet lives, and you must already know the ritual's forms!" The very thought of reliving it choked the breath from Kiran's lungs. Did Simon imagine Ruslan had exposed some vital weakness that day? Kiran swallowed a half-hysterical laugh. The weakness had all been his, not Ruslan's.

"I have my reasons." Simon's gaze lingered on Kiran's clenched hands. "The distress it causes you is only a side benefit, I assure you." He smiled, slow and cruel.

Kiran drew a steadying breath. So far Simon had cast only simple contact bindings and spells so minor they barely required a source of power. Proof that Simon had to tiptoe around the Alathian detection magic, and dared not attempt spells of any real strength. Against minor spells, Kiran had every chance of weaving mental defenses with his own *ikilhia* to keep the memory safely hidden.

He lifted his chin and locked eyes with Simon. "You think I haven't realized how weak you truly are? You're alone. No way to cast channeled magic...compared to Ruslan, you may as well be *nathahlen*."

"Ruslan certainly thought so, after he slaughtered my apprentices." Simon's smile sharpened. "Beautiful symmetry, isn't it? He destroyed my property, and now I'll use his to destroy him and regain all I lost."

Property. Kiran's hands clenched. "You'll never get that memory. I'll fight you with every spark of *ikilhia* I possess."

"Such passion," Simon said softly. "A shame to destroy it. But when I bind you as my own, I'll not make Ruslan's mistake of leaving your mind intact. Your capacity for independent thought is a small price to pay for your eager, unthinking obedience to my every desire." His gaze traveled Kiran's body. The dark anticipation in his eyes swept away all Kiran's restraint.

"When Ruslan tears you apart, I'll rejoice in your agony," Kiran snarled.

Simon chuckled. "At last, the cub bares his fangs. I'd wondered if you were truly *akheli*, but I see Ruslan did not choose in error."

Kiran clamped his teeth on a shout. Simon only sought to goad him further. Rage wouldn't help him; he needed cold, clear calculation, to construct mental blocks and shifting veils of misdirection that Simon's spells could never breach. He settled for glaring icily at Simon, who stood, amusement still shading his smile.

"Fight, if it pleases you," Simon said. "The end result will be the same. For all Ruslan's training, you are but a child in the ways of power."

Kiran held his tongue. Simon might have more experience, but he'd surely underestimate the strength of Kiran's determination. He'd rather die than relive the day that in one stroke had destroyed all he'd ever loved.

❋

(Dev)

The arrival of a major convoy was the only time Kost got half so lively as Ninavel. A chattering crowd of traders, merchant house factors, and bankers packed the cobbled square around me, all of them jostling for a view of the wagons undergoing inspection beyond the broad arch of the border gate.

Meldon's convoy had arrived at last, preceded by a host of wild, contradictory rumors brought by hard-riding watchmen from the Sondran Valley. Magic, death, destruction of trade goods…the merchanters looked tense enough to spit nails, while the independent traders craned their necks with gleeful curiosity.

I kept the brim of my hat pulled well down over my eyes. Joining the crowd was a risk, but I didn't care. Eight long days spent in vigil over the mage's house in a cramped drain hole meant I'd had far too much time to revisit all my fears. I wasn't going to wait one instant longer for news of Cara and Jerik's fate.

Eight days, and I'd dreamed up a whole host of possible plans to free Kiran. Too bad every single one ended up with one or both of us dead or in the Council's hands. The mage was a careful bastard, and no mistake. Not only was his house warded like one of Sechaveh's gem vaults, he personally inspected all deliveries, and allowed no one to enter except Pello and two others: an ancient crone of a housekeeper, and a gray-haired guy with the scars and grim competence of a former soldier, both of them tight-lipped as a prospector sitting on a rich ore vein. The only thing I'd overhead of interest was the mage's name, Simon Levanian. Not that it did me much good, other than to curse him properly.

I'd stayed well clear of Pello, but I'd shadowed the other two on errands. They'd visited feed and dry goods shops, stables, and a packing yard, all of which confirmed for me Simon meant to leave Kost, and soon. Good news, because then he might take Kiran out of that gods-damned vault of a house, but bad news, because I was running out of time.

If Simon wanted to work serious magic, he surely meant to cross the border back into Arkennland, and the Alathians were just as nosy with their exit inspections. To pass the gate wards and the Alathian mage, he'd have to use something like the hennanwort dose I'd given Kiran. The brief window of time between Simon taking hennanwort and a border crossing would be my best chance to intervene. Arrange a distraction to keep Pello and that ex-soldier busy, snatch Kiran, tie his amulet back on him to block any tracking charms, and run like Shaikar himself was after us.

Nice idea in theory, but the details were a bitch, all the way from the start. The best chance of keeping Kiran free of the Council was to act before Simon reached the gate. No way to know Simon's route in advance, so I'd have to catch them leaving the house. But I couldn't lurk in that gods-damned hole all day and night. The tunnel slanted at an awkward angle that meant I had to brace myself the entire time to keep from sliding out. Rest while on vigil was impossible. I was already running far short on sleep, and while I could maybe force myself to stay awake long enough to guarantee I'd be in place when they left, then I'd be so exhausted I'd be in no condition for the rest of the job. And that was only the first problem of many.

A full-throated cheer rose from the crowd as the first wagon creaked through the gate. I elbowed aside an annoyingly tall trader, straining for a view of the riders who paced alongside the mule team.

Blonde hair gleamed bright in the midday sun. My heart lifted with a force that near knocked me off my feet. Cara, alive…and a few horses behind, I spotted Jerik's sinewy shoulders and gray-streaked braids. I shut my eyes, sending a round of fervent thanks to the gods.

The slumped curve of Cara's back spoke of weariness, and her flashing smile was noticeably absent. A twinge of shame darkened my relief. Somebody had died, to fuel Ruslan's spells. I'd find out who, and make an offering to Noshet's spirit guardians, in their name—but that could wait. I ducked my head, preparing to fade back through the crowd.

Then froze, as a solution to my difficulties sprang full-blown into my head. All at once, I knew how to mark the mage's departure, safely shadow their carriage, and take care of any opposition while I grabbed Kiran.

It wasn't Jylla I needed. It was Cara. Cara, with her climbing skills, her deadly accuracy with a hunting bow, and her firsthand knowledge of Ruslan's visit to the convoy that could draw Pello like a sandfly to a honeytrap.

Cara, who'd probably gut me as soon as look at me, after the way I'd left. To gain her help would take a miracle of Khalmet. Besides, I'd already put her in danger once—last thing I wanted was to drag her back into this mess. I tried to shove the idea straight out of my head.

It wouldn't go. *You'd be the one to bear all the risk,* Jylla's voice whispered in my head. *She'd be fine. You want to win this fool's game of a rescue? Or are you gonna weasel out because you're too fucking gutless to face Cara again?*

Gods all damn it. I'd go, then, and talk to her. Assuming she let me get a word in before she threw me out on my ass. I had nothing to lose but my pride. Cara was honest and trustworthy as they came. No matter how furious she was, she'd not run her mouth about me to anyone else. I just had to figure out how to make her listen.

✳

Evening found me lying flat in the shadows on the roof of the Silver Strike's stables. It hadn't been hard to find where Cara was staying in Kost. She always took a room at either the Brown Bear or the Silver Strike, saying they were the only inns in Kost that served a decent dark beer. Like many from Ninavel, I much preferred wine or spirits, but Cara's family had emigrated from somewhere up north where beer was practically a religion.

The stable roof offered a perfect vantage point across the inn's muddy inner courtyard to the windows of the guest rooms in the main building. Cara's room was the twelfth one along, on the top floor. The room was dark; knowing Cara, she'd stay until late in the inn's common room, drinking and talking, and return with a bed partner. She claimed a tumble in bed was the best way to mark a convoy job's end, good or bad. A good journey called for a celebration, she said, while a bad one called for a distraction. No doubt she'd be looking for one hell of a distraction this time.

She was too wary of theft to allow a city lover to spend the night.

I meant to wait for her to have her fun, and talk to her once her lover of the evening had left. That way maybe she'd be too tired to kick me out straight off, and in as good a mood as I could hope for.

I had no fear she'd close the shutters to block my view of her room door. Cara had always said loud and long how much she hated to shut out the sky. Best of all, the windows didn't have any wards and neither did the roof. Most riverside inns left magical protection up to their customers rather than pay for the maintenance of exterior wards.

The only tricky part was staying awake. The stable roof felt like a feather bed compared to that Shaikar-cursed drain hole. I had to fall back on all the tricks I'd learned in my Tainted days to stave off the weariness that dragged at my eyelids. A Tainter learns fast and early how to keep alert on a long night's work, or face not only the anger of your minder, but the practical jokes of your denmates.

Just when I thought I'd have to resort to stabbing my palm with my belt knife, Cara's door opened, shedding a warm glow over the room. Cara and a man with the dark skin and brightly colored clothing of a Sulanian trader tumbled in, their hands already busy with each other's shirt laces. Cara pulled away long enough to light a single candle and shut the door. Then she was kissing him again, deep and hungry, her shirt slipping down to expose the smooth muscles of her back and shoulders.

I averted my eyes, hissing in annoyance at the heat rising in my own flesh. Damn it, I didn't need any distractions. Gods knew I'd had my share of idle fantasies about Cara over the years, but that's all they'd been. Jylla'd taken plenty of other lovers during my summers in the mountains, and I'd enjoyed casual bedplay of my own, but Cara had made it plain from the first day I'd met her that she didn't take outriders as bed partners.

Another glimpse of dark hands tracing tanned skin brought unwanted memories of Jylla cascading in. She'd been as energetic and cunning in bed as she'd been in everything else. Gods, the wild nights we'd spent together…I sank my teeth into my lip and fought the urge to bang my head against the roof in frustration. At least now I was wide awake.

Finally, Cara and her lover moved off to the bed, out of my line of sight. I dug my fingers into wood shingles and reined in my runaway imagination. After what seemed an eternity, Cara reappeared, thankfully dressed in her undertunic. She lit another candle, and the Sulanian strode into view, still lacing his shirt. One last kiss, and he was out the door. About gods-damned time.

I cat-footed my way over the roof and climbed the side wall of the main building's second story. I paused above Cara's room. If I knew Cara, there'd be no need to break in. She'd said plenty of times how she couldn't sleep in a room with no fresh air. Sure enough, a rattling echoed from below, followed by the creak of wood. I gripped the roof's edge and flipped off in a twisting arc that sent me straight through the open window.

Cara went for a knife before I even hit the floor. As I landed in a wary crouch, she advanced around the bed in nothing but her undertunic, fire in her eyes and a good seven inches of steel shining in one hand.

Shit. So much for the good mood. Time to talk fast.

CHAPTER SEVENTEEN

(Dev)

"Cara, ease up! I just want to talk." I dodged to put a spindly wooden chair between us, ready to snatch it up to block her knife hand.

"So you drop through my window in the dead of night like some kind of Varkevian deathdealer?" Cara slowed her advance, but the knife stayed raised and ready. "You thieving, lying little bastard! Whatever you've got to say, I don't want to hear it. Get the fuck out."

Yeah, this was going well. "You've every right to be angry. But please…" I showed my empty hands, and bowed my head. "*Please*, Cara. I'm begging you, hear me out. Then if you want, I'll go, and never come back."

"You think you can abandon your duty, charm-sting me, steal vital supplies, and then waltz in here wanting a chat? Fuck you, Dev. Give me one reason I shouldn't kick your ass straight out that window."

No mention of the worst of my sins, and she hadn't realized she'd been felled by a mage's touch, not a charm. Shit. I'd never thought Ruslan would bother to conceal what he sought. Her ignorance would make this twice as hard. I gathered my courage and plunged ahead.

"Because I came here to tell you the truth I couldn't at the convoy."

Her eyes narrowed. "Why now, and not then?"

"I wanted to, then. You've no idea how badly. But the knowledge might've meant your death, and I couldn't risk that."

Cara's knuckles whitened on the knife hilt. "Mother of maidens, do you mean to say those two blood mages who showed up were looking for *you?*" Fury sparked in her blue eyes. "We cursed Pello's name over them, assumed they were after whatever contraband he carried. Most cursed you too, said you must've been involved somehow. I didn't believe it. Now you tell me I was wrong?"

Two blood mages. I swallowed. Damn it, Kiran had told me they cast the biggest spells in pairs. I should've known Ruslan would bring a friend. I eyed the window, longingly. Far easier to dive back out than admit the truth of what I'd done. I ducked my head, and admitted, "They weren't after Pello. But listen, I—"

"Gods all damn it, Dev! *Blood mages!* They took Steffol and Joreal. Touched them on the shoulder, and they followed along meek as kittens. We never saw them again, but Jerik found the spot where the mages must've cast a spell. The rocks were black with blood for a hundred yards, he said. What did you do, to bring that on us?"

I shut my eyes. Steffol I knew; he'd handled wagons for Goranant House for years. Joreal I didn't. The stab of guilt wasn't any less.

"I fucked up. Badly." I sucked down a ragged breath, and then I laid it all out for her, all the way from the moment I'd taken the job.

Cara's expression alternated between stunned and furious as I spoke. "Khalmet's bloodsoaked bony hand," she said, when at last I finished. "You brought a gods-damned blood mage along as your apprentice? All to sneak him past the Alathians so you could sell him out to a second mage who means to start a war? That's not a fuck-up, it's a catastrophe. How many good men are dead now, because you wanted some extra coin?"

"I told you, I didn't know—!" I choked back the rest of my denial. If I let Cara push me into an argument, I'd never keep a cool head. And in the end, she wasn't far wrong. If I'd refused the job, Steffol, Joreal, Harken, and all those killed in Ruslan's avalanche would yet live.

"Nothing can make up for the dead," I said, tightly. "But maybe I can stop more from dying. And Kiran...I wanted him to pay for killing Harken, no matter that he did it to save the convoy. But oh gods, the way Simon looked at him, like..." I struggled to find words to describe the mixture of lust and hunger and unholy delight I'd seen in the mage's face, and failed. "Kiran might be a blood mage, but he doesn't deserve whatever Simon intends."

Cara ran a finger along the blade of her knife, and gave me a sour look. "Funny how you didn't have this little attack of conscience until after you'd been paid."

"Yeah, I should've thought earlier. But better late than never, right? Sethan..." My throat closed and I had to force out the words. "Sethan would never forgive me if I walked away now."

Cara's glare could have pierced granite. "Don't pull that shit with me. Now you care what Sethan would've wanted? You sure as hell didn't when you ditched the convoy. Or took the job in the first place, for that matter."

"I've *always* cared what Sethan wanted," I snapped. "I didn't take the job out of greed. I needed that money for Sethan's sake."

A skeptical scowl darkened Cara's face. "Dead men don't need money."

I braced my back against the wall, as if that might give me strength. I'd known when I'd decided to come that I'd have to tell her everything. I'd kept my vow of silence to Sethan all these years, but surely he'd understand if I broke it now.

"Sethan's dead, but his daughter's not."

"Sethan's *daughter?*" She looked at me like I'd claimed Sethan could jump over the Kanyalin Spire.

I knew why she was so surprised. Sethan had been born and raised in Piadrol, the stronghold of the Dalradian church, down south near the Sulanian border. Dalradians had lots of crazy ideas, but maybe the craziest was their obsession over the purity of bloodlines. Any half-caste kid was considered an offense against their god, and the Dalradian parent damned, all because their priests were so concerned not to pollute the blood of the so-called sacred ancestors. Sethan wasn't so crazy as most Dalradians, and gods knew he'd defied his family to come to Ninavel, but that was one law he'd never meant to break.

Cara's scowl returned, fiercer than ever. "Sethan told me he ran from Piadrol before the priests could betrothe him. If you expect me to believe he lied—"

"No! He wasn't married, just gullible. Sethan was a nice guy, but sometimes he was too nice. He had that soft spot for hard luck cases…"

"Like you," Cara said, darkly.

"Yeah. Well, thirteen years ago he met a girl in Acaltar district, and she played him for all she was worth. Batted her eyes at him, acted all sweet and helpless, got him to fall in love with her, and then sabotaged her fertility charms. Once she got herself with child, the claws really came out. She threatened to send word to the priests down in Piadrol if he didn't pay her a regular share of his earnings."

"Oh, hell." Cara lowered the knife, at last. "Sethan rolled right over for her, didn't he?" She shook her head. "Why didn't he tell anyone?"

"Same reason he rolled over. He didn't want any chance of word getting back to Piadrol. He'd be cast out, exiled for life, and no Dalradian would ever even speak his name. He loved his sisters too much, couldn't bear the thought of never hearing from them again. And later, after Melly was born…she was Tainted, and not lightly. You know how the Dalradians feel about that." One of the teachings Sethan had disagreed with was the Dalradian conviction that Ninavel was the haunt of devils, and the Taint a demon's mark. "If the priests found out Sethan's bastard child was strongly Tainted, they wouldn't have just cast out Sethan. They'd have sent men to kill both Sethan and Melly."

Cara passed a hand over her eyes. "Fine, he was paying this girl money. How long?"

"About three years," I said. "Then the girl got a little too ambitious with some other scheme and chose the wrong mark, or maybe crossed a ganglord. Either way, she ended up dead. So there was Sethan, left with a three-year-old kid he didn't dare acknowledge. And you know Sethan, he never could save a single kenet. That was the year Orvan died, and Sethan had already given away most of that season's pay to Orvan's widow. He didn't have anything left to pay someone to care for Melly in secret."

A hint of curiosity had softened the grim set to Cara's mouth. "What did he do?"

I gave a short laugh. "Something spectacularly stupid. Which is where I come in. Look, that stuff I told you back on my first convoy job, about how my parents died of sun sickness in the desert and Sethan took me in...none of it was true. I never knew my parents. Before I was an outrider, I was a Taint thief."

Cara snorted. "That, I knew."

"Sethan told you?" He'd promised he wouldn't. He'd known how much I hated to talk about it.

Cara gave me a severe look. "No need to sound like that. Sethan never said a word, but he didn't have to. My father was head outrider your first trip out, remember? First time he saw you climb, he said to me you must've had a powerful dose of the Taint as a kid. I asked him how he knew, and he said you climbed like you'd learned without fear. Said if you survived you'd be one hell of a climber, but he figured you'd end up dead before the season was out."

"What? Why would he think that?" Denion had never said anything of the kind to me.

Cara shrugged. "He said those who learn with the Taint often forget it's not there to save them anymore."

"Only if I'd had a lazy handler. The whole point of teaching us to climb was so that we wouldn't waste any effort with the Taint. If he caught us using it to help, we got punished, fast and hard. It doesn't take much of that before you know better."

"Here I just thought you'd gotten lucky," Cara said. "Well, it wasn't hard to guess how a Tainted kid with no apparent family might've survived in Ninavel. You've no cause to blame Sethan."

"Yeah, fine," I muttered, although the knot in my chest eased. "Sethan knew I'd been a Taint thief, and he didn't follow the Dalradian line on that. He was fascinated." At first I'd dodged his questions. Talking about my Tainted days was like yanking my guts out with a hook. But as time went on, the pain had dulled.

"I told him about life as a Tainter, but I wanted so bad to impress him, I only told him the good bits. So when Sethan found out Melly had a good strong dose of the Taint, he got the bright idea to give her to my old handler."

I dug my fingers into a crack between wall boards, uncaring of splinters. Khalmet's hand, but Sethan had been a real idiot sometimes. "It must've seemed perfect to him. He figured she'd be well cared for, and taught to read and write and climb, and he must've thought when she Changed, he'd just go and buy her back from Red Dal. Probably thought he'd take her on as a new outrider apprentice, the way he did with me."

Cara opened her mouth to speak, but I overrode her. "I know, I shouldn't have glamorized it like that. Damn it, if he'd thought to ask me, I could have told him what a dumb idea it was! But no, he ran straight off to Red Dal without thinking twice."

"Maybe I'm stupid too, but I don't get it," Cara said. "Why was it such a bad idea? Like you said, she'd be cared for, and the Dalradians wouldn't find out."

I stared at her, then reminded myself that although she'd grown up streetside in Ninavel, her family was skilled and self supporting and had never been near a ganglord.

"Even for a Tainter, breaking mage wards is a tricky, dangerous business. One mistake, and you're brain-burned or dead. Sure, your handler will be a little disappointed, particularly if your Taint was strong, but he can always find another Tainted kid to replace you. Red Dal's a good handler, and he and his minders train their Tainters well, but even so I'd say less than half even make it to the Change."

Cara's eyes widened. "I had no idea."

"That's not all," I said bitterly. "Sethan didn't think enough about the buy-out at the Change. He just assumed it wouldn't cost much, because he knew mine hadn't. He should've bargained with Red Dal at the first and forced him into a contract specifying the sale price and Sethan as the buyer, but no. He handed her over and assumed everything would work out. There's nothing preventing Red Dal from selling Melly to the highest bidder, and damn it, she takes after Sethan, with that red hair and good looks."

"You think her price will be high," Cara said.

"Hell, yes. The pleasure houses will be panting after her. Before I left, I heard Karonys House was sniffing around."

Cara grimaced. She knew as well as I did how Karonys treated their jennies. "When did you find out about all this?"

"Not until four years ago," I said. "Only hint I had before that was when I started riding as Sethan's apprentice and he made me promise that if something happened to him, I'd—how did he put it?—'take care of some loose ends' for him. He told me there was a letter in a vault in Koliman House I'd need to read. The way he talked about it, I thought it had something to do with his sisters."

Cara pinched the bridge of her nose between her thumb and finger. "And then he died."

I nodded. "When I found him after the rockfall, he begged me…" I coughed, my throat filling with the remembered stink of blood and rock dust. "He didn't…didn't have time to explain it all." He'd choked out a scattered, desperate string of words through the blood pouring from his mouth, one hand fisted in my shirt. "But I vowed on my life I'd take care of Melly. Do whatever his letter asked, and never tell she was his." I'd have promised him anything, at that point. As if by promising I could turn back time and make the rockfall never happen.

"Oh, Dev." Cara's voice sounded rough. "You should've told me. Or Sukia, or Randen…we could've helped you."

I shrugged, not trusting my voice. I'd promised Sethan my silence, and I'd been so sure I could handle it myself, that I had enough time to earn what I needed.

Cara's brows drew together. "But to take this job…why would you need so much coin? I know you've done pretty well over the last few years."

Oh, gods. So much easier to talk about others' stupid mistakes than my own. I turned and faced out the window. The cool night air did nothing to soothe the heat in my face.

"Yeah, well. Sethan's not the only one to make a fool of himself over a woman."

I heard a hiss of indrawn breath. "That black-haired little bitch… Pello was right, then. She played you, all this time?"

"Her name is Jylla," I snapped. "And no, it wasn't 'all this time.'" I couldn't, wouldn't believe that the girl who'd held me tight in Tavian's cellar while I'd shaken with sobs had never cared.

"What did she do?" Cara asked, quietly.

"She set her sights on a mage." My voice sounded strange to my own ears. "You know how it is in Ninavel. Mages live in a whole other realm, beyond even highsiders. Jylla wanted a way in to that world, and she found one."

Found a swaggering asshole of a mage with a penchant for women with the shining black hair and slanted eyes of Korassian descent, and then used me, all unwitting, to deliver the poison that killed his current bedmate. The mage hadn't cared, except to want a new plaything. A role Jylla was happy to take on.

"Thing was, she needed money, and a lot of it. Her mark was used to highsider women."

"You gave your money to her?" Cara's voice rose.

"No!" The windowsill creaked protestingly under my hands. "She managed the business side of things, so she had access to all our accounts at Shasnin House. But that money wasn't enough for her… somehow, she got into the private account I kept for Melly. She took all that, too. Every kenet I owned. She said I didn't need it, I'd make plenty more soon as the season started."

I could remember all too well how she'd stood there in our shared quarters, her things already gone, and told me calmly what she'd done. *You think too small, Dev. You always have. Even so, I'd take you with me if I could. But Beren's the possessive type. He doesn't like to share.*

"Shaikar take that conniving little bitch!" Cara stomped away. I heard the thunk of a knife driven into wood. "Why didn't you stop her?"

I whipped around. "Fuck, Cara, what was I supposed to do? She had the money out of reach long before I realized it. And when I confronted her, she was wearing a scorpion's tail charm, thanks to her new lover." It hadn't stopped either of us from getting violent when words failed. In the end she'd struck me down with the charm. When I'd come to, my bones still burning with liquid fire, I'd smashed everything I could get my hands on, then drank myself back into oblivion. Yeah, no surprise everybody in Acaltar heard the news. Everybody except Cara, who'd been out on the eastbound route.

"The next day, I got a message from Bren saying he had a job for me. I had four years of lost earnings to make up for, and Melly's Change isn't far off. I'd have taken the job for half what he offered."

There was a long silence. I could feel Cara's eyes on me, but I kept mine on the floor. The candle had burned down to a nub while I was talking, and the light flickered and guttered on the wooden boards.

Finally Cara sighed, heavily. "You and Sethan, what a pair," she said.

"What do you mean?"

"I told you that little bitch was no good, and so did Randen and Loril, but you never listened. Just like I bet Sethan didn't listen, back in the day."

My jaw clenched so tight I thought my teeth might shatter. "You didn't know Jylla, not like I did. If she's cold and hard as spelled iron, well, she's got reason. Someone so lightly Tainted as you—Khalmet's hand, you said you hardly even noticed the Change! You haven't the least fucking idea what it's like for a Tainter."

"Oh, come on!" Cara smacked my shoulder. "You Changed same as Jylla, and you didn't turn into a raving asshole." She gave me a considering look. "Most of the time, anyway."

I got a flash of the bone-deep hurt and betrayal on Kiran's face, and flinched. I'd done far worse to him than Jylla had to me. Between the two of us, I figured I was winning the asshole competition. "I know I've fucked up. I'm trying to fix it—if I can get Kiran free of Simon, that'll stop him—but..."

I can't do it on my own, and I need your help. Now I'd come to it, I couldn't get the words out. I'd hurt and endangered Cara so much already. There had to be another way, one where she'd stay safely clear of this mess. I swung a leg back over the window ledge.

Cara grabbed my wrist. "Whoa, whoa. Where do you think you're going?"

"I wanted you to know the truth. Now you do. I said I'd leave, after."

Cara's grip tightened. "You mean to go up against a gods-damned blood mage by yourself? I don't think so. You came to ask for my help, didn't you? I know you too well, Dev. You'd never have told me all this, otherwise. So get back in here, and tell me what I can do."

I shook my head. "I did mean to ask. But, gods, Cara…the last thing I want is anyone else hurt because of my mistakes. What those mages did to Steffol and Joreal…that could've been you."

"I know," Cara said quietly. "But you're not the only one who made a promise to Sethan. He asked me to look out for you, should Khalmet touch him. Try and keep you out of trouble, though all the gods know that's impossible."

Surprise kept me from resisting as she tugged me away from the window. Her mouth quirked. "You know he loved you, right? He told me once he couldn't have been prouder of you than if you were his son. You think he'd try to take care of Melly, and not of you?"

Sethan. My chest ached. "I can take care of myself," I said, around the lump in my throat.

"Yeah, because you've been doing such a terrific job of that." Cara pushed me into a chair. "No more excuses. Tell me your plan, and we'll figure out a way to save Kellan—Kiran—whatever his name is!—without anybody dying."

✳

(Kiran)

"No doubt you've spent the last day constructing an elaborate defense against me." Simon stalked into Kiran's room, the dry amusement in his voice belied by the taut eagerness of his stride.

Kiran didn't waste breath on a reply. He summoned his focus, a simple image of one of the earliest sigils he'd learned. Behind the focus waited a contorted maze of painstakingly assembled imagery that would twist Simon away from the *akhelashva* ritual into endlessly looping chains of false memories.

At Kiran's silence, Simon inclined his head. "Let us see how thoroughly Ruslan trained you." He turned and called, "Iannis!"

The scowling old woman appeared in the doorway, a vial of viscous yellow liquid in one gnarled hand. Morvain loomed behind her.

Kiran's stomach clenched. Drugs...given Dev's comment on Alathian expertise with herbs, he'd suspected Simon might attempt such a tactic. Though Simon couldn't drug Kiran into incoherency if he wished to view Kiran's memories without distortion, a drug that blunted concentration would put Kiran at a severe disadvantage in the mental battle to come.

He aimed a contemptuous look at Simon. "A truly powerful mage wouldn't need the crutch of a drug to defeat a mere apprentice."

Simon lifted a sardonic brow. "Perhaps you confuse me with Ruslan. I am not so blindly arrogant as to refuse a useful tool out of scorn for *nathahlen* methods." His hand flicked in the hatefully familiar gesture.

Kiran's muscles gave way. He shut out anger and frustration, as Morvain hauled him off the floor and dumped him on the bed. For years, Kiran had hidden the memories of his trysts with Alisa from Ruslan, even through mind-shredding pain. He'd hold his focus regardless of what Simon's drug did to him.

Iannis approached the bed. Her black eyes surveyed Kiran with utter indifference, as if he were no more than an animal. Despite her seamed skin and stooped shoulders, her hands moved with practiced efficiency as she broke the vial's seal. She tipped the contents into Kiran's mouth, then held his jaw shut and stroked his throat to force a swallow.

The liquid tasted strongly of cloves, with a thin, sour undertaste far different than the oily bitterness of hennanwort. Iannis gripped Kiran's wrist, her fingers pressing his pulse, her dispassionate eyes studying his.

As long moments passed, a dreamy lassitude overtook Kiran. He seemed to float in a warm, placid pool, like one of the marble baths in Lizaveta's chambers. When Iannis released his wrist and nodded to Simon, her actions felt distant and unimportant as something seen in a scry-vision of the ancient past.

The focus sigil gleaming in his mind took on the weight of a mountain. Far, far easier to let the sigil fade...but Kiran fought off lethargy and held the image, even as cold tendrils of power crawled into his head. Somewhere, Simon was speaking, his voice seeping into Kiran's consciousness like water through fissured stone.

"Think of Ruslan. Think of your master. He raised you, and trained you, and you loved him, did you not? I saw it in your memories as a child. You loved him, and desperately desired his approval. Tell me, Kiran, what changed that love? Show me how it turned to fear and hate…"

No. He clung to the sigil, even though he could no longer remember why it was so important to resist.

Power stung his chest. Simon was tracing Ruslan's mark with a bloodied finger, over and over. "Remember the moment when he gave you this? When he linked you, marked you, bound you? Think of that, Kiran…" Simon's voice murmured on, constantly asking, constantly reminding, as grasping tendrils sought to tear apart Kiran's myriad chains of images.

Kiran clutched the sigil tighter yet. After a timeless interval, the tendrils withdrew. A dull wash of relief rippled through him. His hold on the sigil wavered, but he refused to release it.

A lance of power speared into his mind with the force of a catapulting boulder. The shock dispelled the haze of disconnection enveloping Kiran. He gasped, abruptly aware of the sweat soaking his body, of Simon's fiercely intent face hovering over his own.

And beside Simon, Iannis was contorted in agony, her wrist clamped in Simon's hand. Simon was stealing her life, fashioning her *ikilhia* into a battering ram to smash through Kiran's maze to his true memories beyond.

Simon's blows shook Kiran to the core. Desperately, he held his focus. If he continued to resist, Iannis would die…but surely her life was an acceptable sacrifice, given the stakes? This wasn't like Ruslan's avalanche, where hundreds of innocents would have died if he'd chosen his safety over theirs—or even like Dev on the cliff. This woman was no ally of his. She'd shown no hint of compassion for his plight, and she was old, nearing a natural death…

If you let someone die to protect this memory, of all memories, then you betray everything I believed in. Alisa shimmered into existence beside Kiran's focus sigil, her amber eyes accusing. *Killing for your own gain is wrong—or did you lie, when you told Ruslan that? Are you truly the murderer he desired you to be?*

Iannis's breath was faltering, her face waxen. Power hammered Kiran's mental walls.

I'm not a murderer, Kiran told Alisa. With a silent cry of mingled defiance and regret, he let the sigil blur into nothingness.

Simon's presence burst from the dissolving maze, rifling through Kiran's mind with chill, eager fingers. Memory welled up to drown him.

Kiran stood in darkness, his sight and hearing still cut off by Ruslan's spell. Magic twined around his body, making his nerves prickle and the hairs on his arms stand on end. So much power! He'd never felt anything so strong before.

Hands lifted the fabric off his eyes. Abruptly, his vision cleared, though the world remained silent.

A staggeringly complex set of channels had been inscribed on the workroom floor, hundreds of silver lines twisting over and around each other to spiral inward to the center where he stood. The lines closest to him already burned with a sullen red glow, full of energy. Mikail stood in the channeler's position on the far side of the pattern, his hands extended and his eyes shut. He was completely intent, so still he might have been carved from marble. Kiran couldn't see the pattern's anchor stone, his view blocked by Ruslan in front of him, but he knew the anchor must be massive indeed for a spell requiring so much power.

Ruslan dipped a needle-fine brush into a silver bowl of blood and traced sigils on Kiran's forehead and arms. Kiran didn't twitch, his muscles locked in place by the power coiling around him. Ruslan stepped back a pace, careful to avoid the channel lines, and studied his work. He nodded, satisfied, and stepped in close once more, this time opening the front of Kiran's robe.

He drew a silver dagger, wet it in the blood, and cut a sigil into the skin over Kiran's heart. It hurt, but Kiran kept his gaze steady as Ruslan worked. Ruslan smiled at him approvingly, and lifted the bowl of blood to Kiran's lips.

Kiran drank. Underneath the warm, salty sliminess, magic traced fire down his throat. The power surrounding him flared up higher yet, pressing inward with a force that squeezed a gasp from his lungs.

Ruslan turned and moved aside, revealing the spell's anchor point, an enormous chunk of glassy black onyx. And for an instant, Kiran's mind refused to take in what he saw there.

It was Alisa. His beloved Alisa lying naked on the bloodstained stone, her wrists and ankles bound in silver chains, her tearstreaked face turned toward him. Her eyes were white-rimmed, her face drawn with fear, her lips shaping his name, over and over. As Ruslan crossed out of the maze of channels, Kiran's sense of hearing returned.

"Kiran, help me! Please, Kiran—oh gods, why won't you help—!" The ragged desperation in Alisa's calls stabbed through his ears.

Kiran fought to move, to respond to her, to tell Ruslan there had been some terrible mistake. He'd known, of course he'd known that real magic involved blood and death, but Ruslan had always told him the easiest way was to use men sentenced as criminals by the merchant houses. "Thieves and murderers, they'd die for their crimes regardless. We merely give their deaths a purpose."

The hot copper of Alisa's blood still stained Kiran's mouth, and he couldn't even spit it out.

"I should be angry with you, Kiran," Ruslan said, coming to stand behind the anchor stone. "After all my warnings, still you disobeyed, and not just once, but repeatedly and often." He ignored Alisa, his eyes locked on Kiran's face. "But in the end, your foolishness was a boon. I needed the lives of thirty men for Mikail, but for you, I only need this single one. Love and betrayal will give her blood a hundred times the power of another's." He smiled, beatifically, and raised the silver knife.

Kiran tried to scream, tried harder to call power; but he was bound by the channeled magic around him, helpless to do anything but watch as the knife sliced Alisa's flesh and she shrieked in agony. Ruslan took his time, using the knife expertly. Fear and terror and pain added their fuel to the spell, magic beating in Kiran's head with the force of a sledgehammer. Alisa screamed for a long time, first pleas for Kiran to save her, for him to make it stop. Later, her cries turned wordless as the black stone ran red with her blood and the power built, channels flaring into life.

The horror was so great Kiran's mind buckled under the weight of it.

Darkness danced around the edges of his vision, but he refused to faint. He wouldn't shut his eyes or look away. Alisa deserved a witness.

He watched with burning eyes as her life ran out under Ruslan's knife, and weathered the shock when she finally died and channels blazed with sudden power. I know what you are now, *he thought at Ruslan.* And I will never forget it.

Ruslan raised his head, looking directly into Kiran's eyes. He extended his gore-streaked hands to grip the sharp edges of the anchor stone. Blood from his palms ran into the channels to mix with Alisa's. "With this power, I name you, Kiran ai Ruslanov. I mark and bind you, your soul to mine, forever."

Ruslan shut his eyes in concentration, strain etching deep lines on his face. The channels nearest the anchor stone exploded into searing white. Power raced toward Kiran along the spiraling paths. And beneath, the slow roil of the confluence shifted, realigned, echoing the pattern and infusing it with energy a thousand fold greater than before.

The block on Kiran's voice released as it hit. He screamed as the power slammed into him, ecstasy and agony all at once, ripping him apart and remaking him, sweeping away his attempt to block it as easily as a man flicking away an ant, blasting his consciousness into darkness...

Kiran struggled upright, fighting free of the hands gripping his wrists, and threw up over the side of the bed. He hung there, shuddering and retching, bile searing his throat.

"How melodramatic. I should have known."

Kiran raised his head, glaring at Simon through sweat-soaked tangles of hair.

Simon shook his head. "Honestly, you and Ruslan are more alike than I realized. All this nonsense about love." His contempt shifted into frank appraisal. "Although I see you share his depth of talent along with his weakness. You nearly cost me a good servant."

Iannis lay in a huddled knot at Simon's feet. Her back was to Kiran, but from the quivering of her shoulders, she still breathed. Relief pierced the miasma of lingering horror. At least his surrender hadn't been in vain. But if Simon realized he could force Kiran's compliance by threatening the lives of *nathahlen*, Kiran would lose all hope of opposing him.

"Nearly? She looks at death's threshold, to me." Kiran hoped he'd achieved the right tone of petty, vindictive triumph, despite the unsteadiness of his voice.

"Oh, she'll be useful still, with a little assistance." Simon bent and gripped Iannis's shoulder. His eyes shut, and his lips moved.

Iannis jerked. Gasping, she tottered to her feet. Though her formerly steady hands now trembled and her breath wheezed, her expression remained inscrutable as ever. Kiran wondered if she were in shock.

"There, you see?" Simon smiled at Kiran, gently. "Your resistance, while admirable in strength, has cost me nothing. And now I have what I need, rest assured that soon you'll be mine to command as wholly as this *nathahlen.*" He turned to Iannis, and stabbed a finger at the puddle of vomit on the floor. "Clean that up."

Iannis bobbed her head. As Simon strode for the door, her gaze followed him, her black eyes hard as obsidian.

The moment the door shut, Kiran spoke in a rush. "I'm sorry for what Simon did to you—I yielded to him, to save your life! You know how monstrous he is—will you not help me against him?"

Iannis's stone-faced mask cracked. Her lips drew back from yellowed teeth, her eyes glittering with a hatred so intense it stopped Kiran's breath.

"Help you?" She spat in his face. "A mage-born whelp like you should've been strangled at birth. You're all monsters, every one."

Kiran wiped her spittle from his cheek with a shaking hand. "But…I saved you! And if you help me, I can free you—"

Her mouth curled. "Death is the only freedom from a blood mage's grip. If you speak truth, you've stolen that from me today. I hope he flays your soul to screaming shreds for it." She turned her back on him and stumped out of the room. When she returned with bucket and mop, her face was blank as sand-smoothed stone again. Kiran's continued pleas might have been shouted into a void, for all the attention she paid him as she cleaned.

When the door shut behind her, Kiran sank onto the bed and buried his face in his hands. Flashes of the ritual leaked through his control. Alisa's ragged screams, Ruslan's hot triumph, the taste of blood in his mouth; all overlaid by the bitter hatred in Iannis's eyes.

I should have let Iannis die.

No—surely saving Iannis had been right, regardless of her feelings. Alisa would have been proud of his choice. Kiran tried to picture the brilliance of her smile, the fond warmth in her eyes...but saw only her bloodstreaked face, twisted in agony as Ruslan cut her life away.

He returned to the most basic of centering exercises, taking deep, slow breaths and counting each one. He couldn't change Alisa's fate. Yet if only he could anticipate Simon's plan, he might still change his own.

CHAPTER EIGHTEEN

(Dev)

Once again, I found myself chewing my nails on the roof of the Silver Strike's stables. Only this time, my jangled nerves were for Cara's sake, not my own. The man laughing it up with her in her candlelit room wasn't some lusty trader. It was Pello.

One evening's work was all we'd needed to draw him straight to her. One evening, in which Cara held forth to gossiping traders in the Silver Strike's common room that rumor had it wrong—I was the cause of all the convoy's woes, not Pello. When curious listeners asked for her evidence, she'd shaken her head and muttered darkly that it wasn't good for the health to repeat anything overheard from mages.

The lure of information wasn't something a shadow man could resist. Sure enough, the next day Pello had sent Cara a message asking to meet. She'd played it like I asked, starting off willing but wary at a riverside tavern. She had let him buy her drinks and ply that smooth tongue of his in a series of convincing lies supporting his innocence, while she gradually softened but still refused to speak of Ruslan's visit to the convoy. He'd turned up the charm, asking if he might see her again. Tonight they'd begun with more drinks and talk in the Silver

Strike common room—and now here he was, ripe for Cara to put the first part of our plan into action.

Cara's quick wit and brash demeanor made her a natural at this kind of game, but I still didn't like it. Her main protection was that Pello thought himself the hunter, with no inkling of any hidden motives on her part. A good cover, but I couldn't shake the fear that he'd pick up on something we'd overlooked.

In the bedroom, Cara swaggered over to her pack and withdrew a sealed bottle of *hekavi* spirits. Pello made properly appreciative faces as she cracked the seal and poured out two cups of thick, honey-gold liquid.

I held my breath. Now came the part that knotted my stomach. If Pello detected even the slightest false note in Cara's playacting…

They tapped cups and drank. Pello sipped, while Cara tossed hers back with abandon. She spluttered and broke out into red-faced coughs. Waving off a soliticious Pello, she crossed to the crooked table by the door, shoved the chair aside, and reached for the jug of water beside the empty washbasin. Missed her reach, and knocked the jug over. Water splashed in a gleaming arc to soak the oiled leather of Pello's coat slung over the chair back, and spill onto the muddy-soled boots lying on the floor below.

Perfect. *Get it on both his coat and his boots, if you can,* I'd told her. The jug hadn't contained pure water. I'd spent the last two days working out an updated form of the dye trick I'd used to track Kiran. I'd haunted herbalist shops and experimented with mixtures of plant extracts until I found one that wouldn't stink or stain when applied to leather, yet remained concentrated and distinctive enough for a find-me charm to locate. The mixture wasn't nearly so good a key as blood or hair—based on my experiments, the effect would be too weak outside of a half mile from the target for the charm to work, but that distance was more than enough for safe shadowing. I'd had an herbalist make me a nice big batch, so I'd have enough to key a find-me several times over. I could track Pello now for a solid day, if necessary.

So long as he didn't realize he'd been marked. I squinted at Pello, searching for any sign of wariness or suspicion.

None showed. He only laughed at Cara's apology, shook his head in wry dismissal at her attempt to blot his jacket, and with a flourish offered her a waterskin. She drank, said something, and they both laughed. He moved closer, laid a hand on her arm, murmured in her ear.

Come on, Cara, get rid of him. Gods knew she had plenty of practice in gracefully fending off eager suitors.

Cara raised her hand to his face. Leaned in, and kissed him. I nearly bit through my tongue. What the fuck did she think she was doing? This was no part of our plan.

The kiss deepened, lingered. She stroked a hand through his curls, while his hands slid down her back, pressing her close against him. I resisted the urge to rip off a shingle and hurl it at the window. Gods all damn it, Pello wasn't some gullible trader. Jylla might've fooled a shadow man with a honey trap, but Cara? He'd see right through her if she kept this up. I lifted to a crouch, ready to rush over at the first sign of trouble.

Cara broke the kiss and pulled away. He moved to draw her back, but she put a hand on his chest and spoke, her expression teasing but regretful. Pello traced a finger down her cheek, his brows angled in appeal as he spoke. She replied, firmly. He made a rueful face, and inclined his head. He laced on his boots, collected his dampened coat, and let her usher him out.

Shit. He was too good an actor for me to tell at this distance if she'd roused his suspicion. Though I didn't think it was a good sign he'd agreed to leave so easily. If he'd marked her, his first move would be to pull back to observe from a distance.

Cara locked and warded the door. She snatched up the *hekavi* bottle and downed a healthy mouthful, this time without coughing, then spat in the washbasin. After a glance out the window in my direction, she moved out of my line of sight. I counted out minutes, my teeth clenched. I didn't dare rush straight to her room, in case Pello tried coming back. We'd agreed I'd give the bastard a good hour to clear the area. After that kiss, doubly important to make sure he didn't spot me sneaking in for a visit.

Finally, Cara reappeared and swung open her window. I skulked across the roof and made a full survey of all possible vantage points before I slung myself down and in.

She beamed at me in pleased satisfaction. "Not bad for a first timer, huh?"

I rammed home the latch and jerked the curtains shut. "What the fuck were you playing at with that kiss? He's a shadow man, for Khalmet's sake! They know how to mark a honey trap. He'd have read you didn't mean it."

"Who said I didn't? Spy or no, he's not bad looking. Those bedroom eyes, and that tight ass…" She burst into laughter, as outrage blocked my tongue. "Oh, gods, you should see the look on your face. Relax, all right? I figured one kiss was worth this…" Triumphantly, she held out a hand. Wound around her fingers were a few dark curls of hair. "A little insurance, in case he dumps the jacket."

Clever, yeah, but verging on too clever. I picked the hairs free with a growl. "If he marked what you did, he'll shadow you to learn your game. You're supposed to be switching off shifts with me in that cursed drain hole to watch Simon's house, remember? If he shadows you there, we're fucked."

Cara's eyes widened, but she shook her head. "He didn't notice, I'm sure of it."

"Yet he hardly protested when you shoved him right out the door, after."

"I told him drink had crossed my judgment, but much as I enjoyed the lapse, I had to hold to my rule. No dallying with convoy men, so my head stays clear on jobs."

I nodded, grudgingly. Cara's rule was well known amongst Ninavel drovers and outriders. If Pello asked around, he'd get confirmation. "Got a strip of cloth I can use?"

Cara dug in her pack and handed me a threadbare square of linen covered in old, yellowed salve stains. I rolled the hairs in the linen and tucked the packet away in an inner pocket. "You might think he didn't notice, but we'll have to—"

A rap on the door silenced me. We stared at each other. I mouthed, "Stall them," and rushed to the window. Damn it, not only did the latch squeak like an angry hopmouse, now it'd stuck shut. I'd have to ease it free. I squeezed a fingertip between the metal edges and tugged, keeping one eye on the door.

"Who's there?" Cara called.

Faint and muffled came the very voice I'd feared. "Pello. I apologize for the lateness of the hour—I'd thought to leave a message, but I saw your light…" The doorhandle rattled. A ghostly flicker raced over the lock, so fast and faint most wouldn't notice. Gods all damn it, the lock wouldn't hold against a snap-charm, but the ward should—

The door ward spat a few sparks, then darkened. Shaikar take the Alathians and their half-assed wards! I hammered open the window latch, uncaring of the noise.

The door cracked open. Pello peeked around, still talking. "…was wondering if—" He stopped short, his eyes widening.

Fuck! I might escape if I ran now, but Cara never would. I aborted my reach for the window ledge, and turned to face Pello. Behind my back, I eased a hand toward my belt. My boneshatter charm was powerful enough to trigger the detection spells and bring the Council's mages running. If that was the only way left to protect Cara and stop Simon, I'd do it, no matter the cost for me and Kiran.

Cara strode to the door and yanked it all the way open. "Thank Khalmet," she announced to Pello. "Get in here and help me get rid of this asshole." She turned a vicious glare on me. "Fuck if I'll give you your job back, you sneaking, lying little gutter rat! After what you brought down on the convoy, I'll see you in Shaikar's darkest hell first."

Damn, not bad. I folded my arms and scowled right back. "If you'd just fucking listen! Kellan was a mage, and he cast against me, before we ever left Ninavel! I had no choice but to help him!"

Pello's eyes darted between the two of us. The surprise on his face was now only a mask, but I couldn't tell what thoughts lurked beneath.

Cara stomped toward me. "You think I'll believe one word out of your lying mouth? Go on, crawl back out before I throw you!" She stabbed a finger at the open window. Her pale eyes locked on mine, full of urgency.

I couldn't leave, not without some sign of Pello's intent. She'd stand no chance against him if he decided to strike her down and drag her back to Simon. "The hell I will," I told her. "That bastard Kellan made me abandon you and the convoy. I won't leave until you understand I won't ever do it again."

Cara grimaced in very real frustration. "I said, get out!"

I was so busy concentrating on Pello that her rough shove caught me by surprise. I overbalanced, caught my heel on a loose floorboard, fell. My head cracked into the sharp corner of the window ledge hard enough to send stars bursting over my vision.

An iron-hard grip on my wrist dragged me upright. "Ow," I said, thickly, and reached a hand to my throbbing skull. My fingers came away sticky with blood.

Pello slung my arm over his shoulder and wrapped his own arm tight around my waist. Low at my side, I felt the unmistakable cold prick of a blade. "I'll take him off your hands," he said to Cara.

Cara reached for me, her face white beneath her tan. "You shouldn't trouble—it was me who—"

Pello hauled me toward the door. "Oh, no trouble. I'm most eager to hear Dev's tale. Perhaps you judge him too harshly for actions beyond his control, as Meldon did with me."

Cara started another protest. I struggled to focus my blurred vision, and managed to catch her eye. *Don't,* I willed her, and looked pointedly at the smear of my blood on the window ledge. Blood was the best key for a find-me, and she knew where I'd stashed my charms.

Her eyes narrowed, and she subsided. Thank Khalmet, she hadn't remembered I wore Kiran's magic-blocking amulet, powerful enough to obscure not only me, but Pello's dyed clothing while he stayed close. I didn't want her tracking me. I didn't want her to get anywhere near Pello, or worse, Simon. I stumbled out the door under Pello's guidance, relief easing the pounding hammers in my head. If he brought me to Simon's house, I'd use the boneshatter charm, on myself if necessary. Until then, I'd happily let Pello take me if it meant he left Cara safely behind.

✳

(Kiran)

Kiran started awake with a cry. He pressed the heels of his hands against his eyes. He'd thought he'd grown accustomed to nightmares, but the dreams since Simon's spell were worse than any since the first terrible nights after Alisa's death.

He'd spent hours forcing himself to study his memory of the *akhelashva* ritual. Ruslan hadn't cast any defensive spells during the ritual or otherwise exposed his protections…but the mark-binding spell he'd cast on Kiran had been designed to dismantle all Kiran's innate defenses, in order to anchor the bond.

Kiran's best theory was that Simon meant to use Ruslan's channel pattern from the ritual to deduce the weak points in Kiran's barriers. Simon might intend to take Kiran back into Arkennland, damage his barriers just enough to give Ruslan a foothold, and then strike while Ruslan was focused on subduing the last of Kiran's defenses. Hard to believe that Simon would think distraction a sufficient advantage to overcome Ruslan's protections, but Kiran had come up with no better ideas.

One thing was certain: regardless of his exact intentions, Simon had to leave Alathia. Whatever spells he meant to cast against Ruslan, he wouldn't want interference from the Council's mages, or disruption of his own magic from the powerful border wards. He'd cross the border, and whatever his trap, he surely intended to bring Kiran as the bait.

After so many days without a return visit from Pello, Kiran had to consider the attempt to subvert him a failure; and Iannis remained obdurate. His last hope was to draw the attention of the Alathian mage at the border. A fight with the Alathians might distract Simon for long enough that Kiran might escape. More likely, the Alathians would arrest him along with Simon. But captivity and eventual execution at the Council's hands was a better fate than becoming Simon's mind-burned slave.

Kiran crossed to the door and leaned his ear as close as he dared to the warded wood. No sounds came from outside. He returned to the bed and knelt on the quilt, next to one of the thick carved posts of the frame. Partway down, the carving was inset with flecks of red garnet.

After another glance at the door, Kiran bent and retrieved a wooden splinter from its hiding place between the bed frame and the wall. He'd gouged out the splinter from the underside of the table, using the edge of the silver banding on one arm. The splinter wasn't long, but the wood was hard and it tapered to a blunt point. Not the most ideal of tools, but with enough patient effort, he hoped to work one of the gems free.

Binding power within objects is a skill even the basest of mages may learn, Ruslan had said, long ago when Kiran was first beginning his lessons. *But to bind the power tightly, so it will not react against other magic, and to store it efficiently, so the vessel holds the maximum possible amount without shattering—this requires not only talent, but much practice.*

Kiran and Mikail had spent weeks in Ruslan's practice room attempting to bind magical energies in all types of objects. Ruslan had let them discover for themselves that metals and gemstones could hold far more than other materials, but required delicacy and careful gauging of capacity, lest they shatter.

They'd spent one afternoon deliberately storing power badly and tossing the flawed stones against the warded walls of the practice room. Even the smallest had vanished in violent flares of light as the stored magic reacted against Ruslan's wards. They'd laughed and shouted as they competed to see who could get the brightest flash. Ruslan had reprimanded them both for wasting power and shirking their real practice, but not as harshly as he might have. *A mage should never be afraid to experiment,* Kiran had heard him say to Lizaveta later that evening.

The tiny gemstones in the bed carvings could only hold a correspondingly tiny amount of power, hardly a trickle. Yet even that trickle would be enough to react against the Alathian border wards if Kiran bound it poorly to the stone. Although Simon's charms blocked him from casting magic, they couldn't prevent him from using his blood as a conduit to the stone and passively storing a thread of his own *ikilhia*.

All he need do was keep the gemstone hidden on his person. When

Simon tried to bring him across the border, the Alathian wards would do the rest. The border mage would be sure to notice the magical reaction.

Kiran smiled bitterly as he worked on freeing a thin shard of garnet. After all Ruslan's insistence on working magic with perfect accuracy, who would have thought that shoddy casting might be his salvation?

✳

(Dev)

Pello herded me through the Silver Strike's common room, his knife still pricking its warning under my ribs. This late, the room held only a few traders nursing final beers. None of them glanced up, but the bartender spotted the blood matting my hair and bustled over, his face creased in concern. Pello fended him off with quick assurances of how I'd only slipped and he was taking me straight to a healer.

Gods, I could use one. My vision had cleared, but the vicious throbbing of my head kept my thoughts dangerously sluggish. I clung to my plan: get Pello as far away from Cara as possible, then ignore his blade and spark the boneshatter charm before we reached Simon's house.

I'd expected him to drag me up to the wealthy southwest quarter, but instead he guided me eastward toward the docks. His blade never left my side, and his grip on my arm was clamped over a nerve that'd send me to my knees with a hairsbreadth more pressure. I moved along quiet and obedient as a pack horse, using the time to gather my fragmented wits. The chill damp of the night air soaked through my bloodstained collar and sent painful shivers chasing along my neck. Overhead, a fat moon drifted between ragged-edged clouds. The river fog hadn't yet spread into the streets, but it would soon.

Maybe the boneshatter charm wasn't my only option. I'd never outrun him in this condition, but with fog for cover, I might outclimb him. Cara should've had enough time to clear out of the Silver Strike by now. She'd head for my charm stash in the warehouse attic I'd set up as a bolthole. She'd be safe, there. I'd warded that attic tight as Simon's house.

Pello dragged me into a packing yard some ten streets away from the Silver Strike. I willed the fog to hurry up, as we zigzagged through a maze of alleys between looming stacks of sealed, warded crates. Just as the first ghostly wisps wafted over the stacks, Pello shoved me down a dead-ended alley, then backed to stand blocking the exit. The wicked silver crescent of a nightstar blade glinted in his hand.

"I thought you wanted to talk," I said, my eyes locked on the knife. Had he decided killing me was safest? He might think he had me trapped, but I'd scramper up those crates faster than a whiptail the instant he moved, no matter the pounding ache of my head. Of course, if he could throw that knife as well as he could grapple, I'd be fucked.

"I do," he said. "A private talk, one shadow player to another."

"As you so kindly pointed out at the convoy, I'm no shadow player."

His teeth flashed. "Yet you succeeded not only in slipping your charge past both a blood mage and the Alathians, but held his trust so completely he never saw your betrayal coming. Forgive me for underestimating you."

Digging for some hint of remorse over Kiran, was he? I'd not give him one, no matter how badly his words burned. "The job's over. Bury me in flattery all you like, I've got nothing you can profit over. So how about you leave me the fuck alone?"

Pello didn't move. "Did the boy truly cast a binding on you in Ninavel?"

Remembering my shout at Cara, I opened my mouth to agree, then hesitated. If he and Simon had questioned Kiran, he might know it for a lie. "No," I said, sullenly. "I took the job for the money. But I don't mean to lose my trade over it. Cara'll see I never work as an outrider again, unless I can convince her I had no choice. Thanks a lot for fucking that up, you asshole. Now she'll ward her windows, and I'll not get within twenty feet of her."

"Ah." He sounded disappointed, though I couldn't figure why.

"But you've no need to grovel at her feet. Why work as an outrider, when other aptitudes might earn you so much more?"

"What, you dragged me out here at knifepoint to offer me a gods-damned *job*?" I sneered.

Pello shrugged. "My employer could use a man of your talents. I assure you, the pay far outstrips the pittance you earn scrabbling around in the mountains."

Khalmet's bloodsoaked hand, was he serious? If I pretended to accept his offer, maybe I could get into Simon's house after all... No. A flash of Pello's slack gray face, blood leaking from his mouth, stomped that idea flat. Simon would never allow a stranger inside without the same proof of loyalty he'd demanded from Pello.

"Thanks, but I'd rather scrabble in the mountains. The city's got nothing I want." I risked a brief glance upward. The fog was thickening fast.

"No?" Pello's head cocked. "Not even a certain red-haired Tainter in your old handler's tender care?"

My heart stopped. "How—" I choked off the rest, too late.

Pello's smile was sharp as his blade. "Ninavel holds no secrets I cannot uncover."

Oh, gods. My childhood friend Liana was the only soul in Ninavel who knew of my interest in Melly—but that was one person too many. Pello must've winnowed out my secret before the convoy even left the city, suspecting he might need the leverage. Suliyya grant that was all he'd done. Shadow men had no scruples.

Pello read my fear. "Oh, I've not touched a hair on the child's pretty head." *Not yet,* said the mocking lilt of his voice.

"What do you want?" I spat.

"Serve my employer and the girl is yours, without you owing Red Dal a single kenet," Pello said. "You need not even wait for her Change."

"What, just like that?" I scoffed. "Red Dal won't let a Tainter go so easy." Mother of maidens, I needed time to think. My head still pounded as if attacked by a pick-axe.

Pello turned his free hand palm-up. "My employer is not only wealthy, but wields great influence in Ninavel. He'd find it simple enough to make Red Dal an offer impossible to refuse."

True enough that Red Dal wouldn't refuse a blood mage. Not that I thought Pello's promises were anything but empty. This had to be a trap.

"Let's say I take your employer's offer. What does he ask of me?"

"For now? Dress as a shopkeeper's courier and come to Gilpanis Terrace in the southwest quarter. Knock on the service door of the house with iceflowers carved on the lintels. Once inside, you'll learn more."

Yeah, right. I'd spent long hours staring at those very iceflowers from my cramped drainhole. He meant me to come to Simon's house—and once inside, Simon would pounce on me and tear the truth of my intentions from my head. Now Pello's game made sense. Far easier for him to avoid Alathian attention if I entered Simon's house willingly rather than hauled along at knife-point.

Pello watched me with the keen intensity of a stalking sandcat. "Should you need an extra incentive...you have an account at Bentgate House, I believe? Check the amount, tomorrow. You'll find an increase. A little gift from my employer."

My blood turned to ice. Bentgate was the Alathian banking house where I'd stashed Gerran's money and gems; and an account that could be accessed could be emptied. Pello's message was clear. *Refuse me, and I'll remove all chance of saving her.*

If Pello thought he could fuck me over same as Jylla, he was dead wrong. I glared at him. "You want me to consider this? Then back the fuck off. My head's killing me. The only thing I want right now is a pains-ease charm and a drink."

"Consider, then. Yet after tomorrow's dawn, I warn you, my offer expires. My employer is a generous man, but an impatient one." With a flick of Pello's hand, the nightstar blade disappeared up his sleeve. He backed away and vanished down an alley.

I waited long minutes, then scrambled up a crate stack and surveyed the yard. Nothing showed between the moonlit crates but fat streamers of fog. I dodged and hopped along the stacks, ignoring the spike of pain that stabbed my head with each jarring landing. Gods all damn Pello! His knowledge of Melly was bad enough, but if he'd told Simon...fuck!

I struggled for calm. Simon's magic couldn't harm Melly so long as he remained within Alathia's borders. If our plan succeeded, that's exactly where he and Pello would stay. And as for the money...I'd move it, soon as Bentgate opened for business.

But where? If Pello had found the account at Bentgate, he could find others. Keeping coin and gems outside a banking house was asking for trouble. Kost didn't have Taint thieves, but it had the ordinary kind.

I shoved that worry aside for later. Right now I had to find Cara. Preferably before she did anything stupid, like hunt Pello in hopes of saving me.

No charm could track me while I wore Kiran's amulet, but I didn't doubt Pello was an expert at mundane methods. I circled, backtracked, climbed over roofs and traversed across buildings, until I was sure nobody followed me to our bolthole.

The warehouse I'd chosen was the smallest of three in the yard of an importer specializing in fabric and furs. With winter over, demand for furs had diminished, and the importer had converted the small warehouse into overstock storage. Perfect for me, since it meant visits from workers were rare, and nobody missed the goods I relocated to the attic. The yard was well warded, but as with Gerran's, a good climber could circumvent the protections. I'd blocked off a space amidst the attic rafters and set my own wards to cover every inch of it, keyed to me and Cara. Nobody else could enter. *Except a mage, like Simon*, my fear insisted. If Pello had found Melly and my account, had he found my other secrets as well?

I slithered in the access vent and dropped onto rough-hewn boards, my heart thumping in time with my head. A sudden wash of lanternlight illuminated a crossbow aimed straight between my eyes.

"Dev!" Cara dropped the crossbow and swept me up in a fierce hug. "Thank Khalmet!"

I returned the hug, my throat tight. Mother of maidens, it felt good to hold her, both of us warm and safe and alive.

"Gods, I thought I'd killed you," Cara said into my hair. "First when you fell, and then when you let that bastard drag you off...you rat, you knew I couldn't track you!"

"Yeah," I admitted. "No point in Pello getting both of us."

She drew back and glared at me. "Which is why I told you to get out that window. Next time, don't be so fucking stubborn."

"What, or you'll bash my head in, again?"

She winced. "Sorry. Never thought you'd be so clumsy."

"Thanks a lot," I muttered. I glanced around the attic. Cara had opened the warded box of my charm stash. Supplies lay scattered around her pack on the rough wood of the crate pieces I'd laid over ceiling beams to form a floor. But the bales of fabric I'd hauled up to serve as a makeshift table still stood slightly off kilter, and the furs I used for a bed remained in the exact layered mess I remembered. No guarantee that Pello hadn't paid a visit, but it eased my nerves a touch.

Cara prodded with cautious fingers at the mess on my scalp. "Sit down and tell me what the hell happened while I fix this up."

Obediently, I dropped to the floor beside the pile of furs. "He dragged me off to a packing yard, and—" I hissed in heartfelt relief, as the cool tingle of a pains-ease charm muted the throbbing in my head to a faint whisper. "Oh gods, Cara…he knows about Melly."

Cara froze in the act of wiping my blood-matted hair with a cloth soaked in spirits. "What?"

I recounted the entire conversation, complete with my certainty that Pello meant Melly as the lure to draw me straight into Simon's grasp.

"That sneaking little rat." Cara's hands clenched as if she wished she gripped Pello's throat rather than the fat copper disc of a skin-seal charm. "You think he knows we're trying to free Kiran?"

"If he knew, he wouldn't dance around with threats. We'd be dead, either by Simon's hand, or his." The crawling itch of the sealing charm spread over my scalp, making me shift and grimace. "No…he suspects we're working a scheme, but isn't sure if Simon's our mark. So he pulls out the carrot-and-stick routine with Melly, figuring even I don't fall for the trap, then I'll be so busy moving my accounts I can't interfere with them leaving Kost."

"Pello's deadline—you figure that's when Simon means to make his move?"

I nodded. Cara handed me a tin cup full of dark purple liquid that fizzed and stank like rotting eggs. "Drink this," she said. "I got it from an apothecary on the way here. It's supposed to be good for head injuries."

I took a wary sip. "Gack. Don't the Alathians sell any potions that taste good?" At Cara's severe look, I made a face and downed the lot. "Did you find a longsight charm? If Simon leaves—"

"Don't worry, I got a charm." Cara cast a satisfied look at the crossbow. "Not half so good as Ninavel-made, but it'll do. We're ready for them." She frowned. "If Simon's truly preparing to leave Kost, Pello can't have much spare time. You've got to move your money, sure, but maybe you don't have to worry about hiding it. Why would Pello ferret out money and gems he doesn't even need?"

"With Melly's life at stake, I can't take that chance. I've got to assume he'll try. Just like we've got to assume he means to shadow us. We'll have to trade off Kiran's amulet every time we switch shifts in the drain hole, and have one of us scout first for Pello before the other makes the climb And when we ambush them..." I rubbed a hand over my eyes. "Distraction's still your top priority. But if you get a clear shot at Pello, you take it, understand?"

Cara nodded, her face grim. She worried at the end of her braid. "This mess is my fault, isn't it? He'd not have come back to the room if I hadn't kissed him..."

"If he bothered to access my account at Bentgate, he was suspicious long before. No help for it now. Either we keep on best we can, or cut and run." I met her eyes, straight on. "You want to run, there's no shame in it. This plan was a hell of a risk from the start. With Pello on his guard, it may not work at all."

Her eyes narrowed. "Would you run with me?" When I hesitated, she snorted. "I thought not. You'd go to the Alathians, they'd execute Kiran, and you'd end up charm-bound to slave away in some coal pit when they found out about your smuggling. How would that help Melly, huh?"

"You know about her, now," I said, simply. "The Bentgate account's in my name, but I keyed the vault wards to you as well as me. You can take the money and gems, go back to Ninavel. It should be enough to buy Melly straight out if you sell the gems and put in a bid with Red Dal."

Cara's mouth fell open. "Khalmet's hand, Dev. That's been your backup plan all along, hasn't it? That's why you insisted I'd need to fire the bow from such a distance. To keep me safe, in case you get killed."

"Well, yeah." I'd thought that part was obvious. "Somebody's got to live to help Melly."

"Makes more sense if it's you, doesn't it? Maybe I should go to the Alathians, and you should take the money and run. I haven't done anything illegal."

Oh, the thought was tempting. But the memory of Kiran's desperate, terrified face brought a black wave of guilt welling up. "I can't run. Not while there's still a chance to get Kiran free of both Simon and the Alathians."

"Then we stick to the plan, because I'm not going anywhere." Cara produced a flask, took a swig, and handed it to me. "Here. The Varkevians say that *hekavi* shared between friends brings the touch of Khalmet's good hand."

"You saved the rest of that bottle?" I drank, and shut my eyes in appreciation. It tasted like summer and sunlight.

"Hell, yes. That shit's expensive. Bad enough I had to waste it on Pello." Cara knelt in front of me and traced gentle fingers through my hair. "The swelling's gone down. How's it feel?"

"Much better." Surprisingly so. The fizzy glop had quieted the last whisper of pain, and the *hekavi* kindled mellow warmth in my stomach. I smiled at Cara. "Near good as new, in fact. Thanks for cleaning me up."

"Least I could do, seeing how I was the cause." Her hand stayed on my neck, rubbing tight muscles. I tilted forward to rest my forehead against her shoulder.

"I meant what I said, in your room." The words spilled out of me, released by the lazy circles of her hand. "I won't ever abandon you again, the way I did at the convoy."

She trailed a thumb along my jawline, lifting my face. "I know," she said softly, and kissed me. A slow, tender kiss that sent fire tingling down every nerve, and spread the *hekavi*'s warmth to far lower locations than my stomach. The heat in my blood had me trembling by the time she broke off.

Gods, I wanted nothing more than to taste her again. To unlace her shirt, lay her down, and—I clenched my hands on the silky roll of a marten fur. This was Cara, not Jylla. I couldn't assume she wanted more. I strove to keep my tone light. "What—what was that? Another lapse in judgment?"

"Not this time." Her mouth sought mine. I yielded, gladly, and let my hands slip under her shirt to wander over the smooth, strong muscles of her sides. Far different than Jylla's soft curves, but my desire burned just as hot.

One last shred of reason remained. I nipped Cara's ear, and whispered, "Your rule…"

"Dev…" Her fingers drifted lower, moved in a way that made me gasp. "Shut up."

Reason flamed to ash. I drew her down on the furs, and lost myself in a dance glorious as any I'd done on sunlit stone.

CHAPTER NINETEEN

(Kiran)

The door creaked. Kiran didn't bother to get off the bed. The wards hadn't flared; his visitor would only be sour-faced Iannis, who'd thump down another bland meal on the table and shuffle out without acknowledging his existence.

Pello eased around the door, a bowl of porridge in his hands. Kiran's heart jolted. He leapt up. "You've thought on my offer?"

Pello only fixed Kiran with a cold, grim gaze. "No delays with this meal. Eat, or you'll feel Simon's touch." He thrust the bowl at Kiran. Unlike the usual bland fare Iannis brought, the porridge reeked of cinnamon and nutmeg.

Kiran's heart raced faster yet. Surely the food was drugged, and Simon intended a border crossing. The tiny garnet shoved deep against the seam of his trouser pocket felt large as a millstone. But the lack of mockery in Pello's face, and the hardness of his voice when he'd spoken Simon's name…

"Simon's used the lock-binding on you, hasn't he? I'll tell you how to thwart it, if only you help me."

"I have another proposal." Pello's words were as cold as his eyes.

"Tell me how to break the binding, and I'll not tell Simon about that gemstone hidden in your pocket."

Kiran went rigid. Simon's wards contained no element of scrying; he'd checked. Pello must have spied on him somehow through unmagical means, and either seen him with the stone or noticed the minuscule hole in the bedpost.

"Tell me now, or I summon Simon." Pello put a hand on the door, began to open it.

"Wait!" The gemstone was his last hope. He couldn't let Pello reveal it. "Distance will thwart him—to avoid triggering the Alathian detection spells, Simon must be in sight of you to kill with a lock-binding. And if he crosses the border while you remain behind, the border wards will block the link. If you freed me—"

Pello overrode him. "What if both Simon and I are outside Alathia?"

"Nothing will save you, then. Unless a second mage breaks the binding. I would do that, if you—"

"Enough," Pello snapped. "Eat. Now." He glanced at the door.

Simon must be coming. Reluctantly, Kiran took the porridge.

"If you tell Simon about the stone—or take it from me yourself—I'll tell him you seek to escape his binding." So long as the garnet remained in place, he still had a chance.

Pello made an impatient, disgusted gesture. "I said, eat."

Kiran took a tentative bite. Underneath the cinnamon lurked the rancid oiliness of hennanwort. Kiran nearly spat out the mouthful, but Pello was watching him with narrowed, intent eyes. Refusing to eat would only delay the inevitable. Still, his hand trembled when he took the next spoonful. He'd expected Simon to drug him before the crossing, but it didn't reduce his dread of the disorienting void hennanwort left in place of his inner senses. Only the thought of Simon reactivating the chill taint of his binding allowed him to finish the meal.

Even as he pushed the bowl away, a maddening prickling crept through his mind, his awareness of Simon's wards fading. The sensation wasn't quite as terrifying as it had been in the forest with Dev, perhaps because his magic was already bound, or simply because he knew what to expect.

He focused on the patterns in the rug at his feet in an attempt to keep panic at bay. A difficult task, when every instinct screamed at him to fight the thick, choking numbness that drowned him. But if he remained calm, Simon might not bother to send him unconscious. Though Kiran's hidden gemstone would react to the border wards regardless of his mental state, unconsciousness would remove any hope of escaping during the resulting uproar.

A hand caught his chin and tilted his face up to the light. Simon's face wavered in his sight, glaring yellow halos blurring his features. Kiran hadn't even heard him come in.

Simon leaned in closer, studying Kiran's eyes. The halos crawling over him brightened with satisfaction. "Behave yourself, Kiran, and I won't be forced to take any further steps." His words echoed and danced in the air.

Simon laid his hands over the silver on Kiran's forearms. His gaze grew distant and withdrawn. A sharp stinging pierced Kiran's numbness. Kiran looked down at his arms, which seemed to lie a great distance away. White flames danced over them, fading even as he watched.

Delicate metal filaments retracted until all that remained on Kiran's wrists were two thin, plain bands. Simon lifted his hands away, and the bands opened with a soft click, their magic gone inert. Simon slipped them into a pocket.

"Put him in the carriage."

Hands dragged Kiran to his feet. He tried to walk, but the floor kept jumping away from him. Everything swung sideways, wood-paneled walls jouncing past his head, and then he was in a place where all the air seemed stained with gray. He didn't like it, and started to struggle, but in a small, distant part of his mind, a cold voice said *Wait. Wait.* He relaxed, and let the flickering people put him somewhere dark, where at least the gray was all shut out.

✳

(Dev)

I bolted off the park stairs three terraces below Simon's house, my heart pounding. I'd climbed down from the drain hole so fast I'd nearly ripped the skin from my fingers.

Cara jumped up from the low stone wall bordering the street. Two sturdy gray horses stood tethered to a nearby post, their saddlebags packed as if for a hunting trip.

"We're on?" Cara's face showed the same excited determination I'd seen her display before a difficult climb.

"Yeah." I swung up on my horse. "They left in a carriage not ten minutes gone. Simon doesn't look to have taken any drugs yet—but Kiran's with them, Pello's wearing the gear you marked, and the find-me charm's working."

Cara vaulted into her saddle and patted the bulky outline of the crossbow in her saddlebag. "Soon as they stop, just tell me where you want me." Her fierce grin kindled a confusing mix of warmth and worry in my gut. Gods, it felt good to have her partnering me in this—but at the same time, I wished she'd stayed safely clear.

And since our night together in the attic, every time I looked at her, desire sparked within. Cara had approached bedplay with the same wholehearted, forthright passion she devoted to climbing. A new experience for me after Jylla's mind-twisting games, and one I longed to repeat.

No chance of that, so far. When not on vigil in the drain tunnel, I'd been busy hiding my money in multiple blind accounts in the largest Alathian banking houses. For her part, Cara had sought out Jerik to pump him for mage war stories, in hopes of gaining information on Simon's capabilities that might add to what I'd learned from Kiran. If all went well with our plan, Simon's magic wouldn't be a factor, but I knew better than to count on everything running smooth.

I allowed myself one appreciative glance at Cara's lean, supple form, then locked away the memories of our night on the furs and focused on the find-me. If my years with Jylla had taught me anything, it was how to shut out distractions.

As we worked our way down the terraces toward the riverside

quarter, the streets grew increasingly crowded with carts, carriages, and people. Good cover, but thank Khalmet we hadn't tried to track Simon's carriage by sight. In Ninavel, highsiders and tradesmen alike took pains to embellish their carriages in distinctive ways. Alathians seemed determined to blend into one undistinguished mass. Every carriage we passed was identical to Simon's, painted in unrelieved black with no markings.

When we came to the main riverside road, I stopped my horse, frowning.

"What is it?" Cara drew her horse alongside mine.

"They're going the wrong way." I'd expected them to turn north into the riverside district, heading toward the gate. I'd figured they'd pull into some deserted yard or alley down riverside to hide Simon and Kiran away. Simon would take his hennanwort, and we'd strike.

Instead, the charm signaled they'd turned south. That way lay the city's border, a scant half mile off at the end of the river delta, and beyond, nothing but acres of cinnabar forest. The next border gate was down in Loras, a hundred miles distant.

Cara shrugged. "Maybe they decided the forest's a safer spot to make their final preparations. Less chance of prying eyes, and no city guardsmen to call."

"Yeah, but that'd put them an awfully long ride from the gate. Hennanwort lasts a while, but the herbalist told me the effects are strongest within the first few hours after the dose."

"You think Pello knows we marked him? That he's riding off separately, to draw us away?"

"Maybe, but we have to keep following the charm's lead. We'll never find Simon in time if he's split off from Pello. We ought to know if Pello's still with the carriage once we get outside the city. The guardsman loaded ten trunks of luggage onto the damn thing—it'll leave serious tracks." If we'd lost Kiran, as a last resort I'd send Cara to warn the Alathians a blood mage meant to pass their gate.

"Suliyya grant he didn't mark us." Cara tilted her head back to the sky, and sighed. "At least it's a nice day for a southward ride."

I'd been so intent on the charm I hadn't even noticed, but she was right, the day was beautiful. The last traces of fog had burned off, and we'd passed far enough out of central Kost for the ever present woodsmoke haze to clear, leaving the sky a fresh, pale blue. Below the outlying storage yards, the Elenn River glittered green in the sunlight. Straight ahead, the dark cliffs of the gorge reared skyward, closing back in around the river as it rushed southward toward Loras.

The traffic thinned to almost nothing by the time we reached the Deeplink bridge and crossed off the river delta. A pair of deep wheelmarks showed plain as day in the loamy dirt beyond the bridge. My worry didn't lessen. Had Pello set some kind of trap?

I held us back until the pulse of the find-me charm had almost faded. With so little traffic on the road, we'd be far too easy to spot if we stuck close. Maybe that was Pello's aim. A short diversion down the southward road, to see if anyone followed. Thinking of that, I directed us just off the road into the shadows of the trees. As the gorge closed in, riding parallel to the road got harder, flowering kamma bushes filling in the space between cinnabar pines. The road had become little more than a glorified cart track, striped with roots and dotted with rocks. That carriage of Simon's wasn't meant for rough travel, yet the tracks continued along the dirt. My nerves ratcheted higher.

The charm's warmth stabilized, then increased when we continued. Pello had stopped at last. On the road, the wheel marks took a sudden left turn onto an overgrown side track. Cara turned her horse to follow, but I motioned her back.

"We go on foot from here. Horses make too much noise, and we don't know how close they are." I spoke a whisper, peering warily over the undergrowth. I didn't see any sign of Pello or the carriage, but they couldn't be far. The river was maybe a mile away, and the border less than that. We led the horses into the woods on the other side of the cart track and tethered them behind a screening group of trees.

Cara nocked her crossbow. I put a hand on her arm. "Don't try and shoot Simon, not even if he's taken hennanwort. Even if he can't cast actively, Khalmet only knows what defensive wardings a blood mage wears. This far out from the city, the detection spells are a lot weaker. He won't have to worry so much about the Council."

Cara strapped the bow onto her back, her face tight. "What if it's just Pello?"

"Then we shoot the bastard, straight off," I muttered. Gods, if he'd played me for a fool again…my jaw clenched. No choice but to play this out and see.

We worked our way through the trees in a wide arc, heading in the direction the track had taken. Cara took the lead as the more experienced hunter. Sethan had taught me how to sneak through forest, but I thought hunting a slow, annoying pain in the ass. Much easier to bring my own provisions.

Cara stopped dead and tugged me to her side. Through the kamma bushes, I glimpsed the dark bulk of a carriage. A faint jingling drifted through the air, as of someone adjusting tack. No voices. I nudged Cara and tilted my head toward the cinnabar tree on our left. The fissured red bark was easy to climb, and the stout branches high over our heads were thick with concealing needles. When skulking around on a scout, nothing beats a high perch. People rarely remember to look up.

I eased my way up the tree, testing each hold to make sure the bark wouldn't break off and patter to the ground. Thirty feet up, I found a pair of branches thick enough to hold our weight, with a bristling wall of smaller branches for cover. I motioned for Cara to join me, and cautiously rearranged branches to allow us a view down into the fern-filled clearing where the black carriage stood.

I'd feared to see only Pello, lazing beside an empty carriage with a mocking grin. A surge of relief hit me when I saw both him and the guardsman standing in the clearing. My relief faded when I looked closer. Half of Simon's trunks lay opened on the ground, and a second, saddled mount with bulging panniers stood next to the horse still hitched to the carriage. What were they doing? And where were Simon and Kiran?

"Bring me the warded box."

Cara and I flinched in tandem as Simon's voice rang out, sounding terribly near. He stepped out from behind the carriage, no sign of disorientation or clumsiness showing in his movements. Even as I watched, he brushed a fallen pine needle off his sleeve with a fastidious little flick of his hand. No drugs for him yet, then.

Pello scurried over to the carriage and retrieved a carved wooden chest from beneath the driver's seat. The pattern of the inlaid copper sigils on the box looked awfully similar to my blackshroud ward. Simon must have powerful charms inside. Damn his eyes, what did he intend? And more importantly, why couldn't he hurry up and swallow some hennanwort?

Simon stood still as a statue, facing the forest to the east, his cropped brown hair shining in the early afternoon sun. At last he spoke over his shoulder. "Get the boy, and get ready."

I exchanged a glance with Cara. Get ready for what?

✳

(Kiran)

Kiran let his weight sag in Morvain's bruising grip as the man pulled him from the carriage. His weakness wasn't much of a pretense. During the long muddied interval of time since leaving Simon's house, the drugged fog had gradually lifted from his thoughts, though the smothering numbness remained. But his muscles felt terribly slow to respond and the disorienting visual and aural effects continued unabated. Even now, his surroundings wavered and danced as if seen through a thick heat haze.

He thought he was in a forest clearing ringed by towering pines with cinnamon-colored bark, of the sort he remembered from the forest near Kost. Simon stood a short distance away. One hand was outstretched, his face drawn with concentration. A sigil-marked box lay open at his feet, but Kiran couldn't see what lay inside.

What magic was Simon working? Kiran struggled to sense through the void. Green halos sparked and flickered from the tree branches in front of Simon, in oddly regular patterns. Almost, he could imagine they formed a wall…conviction seized Kiran. There *was* a wall. Simon stood before the border, only steps away from the magic that bounded all of Alathia. The visual distortions from the hennanwort weren't random, as Kiran had assumed—the drug must not be capable of completely severing his perception of magic. Though he could no longer sense it within, he saw traces of it staining the air, affecting the *ikilhia* of everything nearby.

But why was Simon here? The border magic in this spot would be at full strength, unattenuated by an archgate. One errant step too far, and the wards would trigger. The treatises Kiran had read in Ninavel warned that the Council kept a cadre of mages on watch, ready to use the seemingly depthless source that powered their wards to translocate to any disturbance.

Simon dropped his hand, looking satisfied. Metal glinted as he lifted a gem-encrusted silver vambrace large enough to cover a man's entire forearm from the box at his feet. Kiran winced and jerked his gaze away. The charm threw off wavering halos so viciously bright it hurt to look at. Worse, the halos pulsed and writhed in a way that sent waves of nausea heaving through him.

A flickering movement drew Kiran's attention upward. The flowing patterns of the tree-halos closest to Simon had shifted, bending upward and away.

Kiran's stomach sank under the weight of an awful suspicion. Every scholar he'd read had proclaimed the Alathian wards impenetrable. But what if during his long exile Simon had unearthed an artifact like the one that surely powered Alathia's wards? If he had, and found a way to modify it into a charm that would allow him to breach the border undetected…

Cold panic squeezed the breath from Kiran's lungs. He'd assumed Simon would have to pass the border at a gate, where an Alathian mage would be working to sense any illegal magic, no matter how small. Out here in the wild, Kiran's hidden gemstone would react to the magic of the wards, but the tiny discharge of magic would go unnoticed, far too weak to trigger them.

Once in Arkennland, Simon would be free to use the full strength of his magic, and Kiran would be utterly helpless against him.

No. He couldn't let that happen.

The green halos drew Kiran's eye again. One final chance might remain. No matter how far the hennanwort had suppressed his magic, if he himself touched the border, the wards would activate and the Alathians come in force. He just had to get close enough.

The visual distortions from the drug made it difficult to judge distance, but Kiran thought the border lay some hundred feet from his position. Too far, unless he could distract Simon.

The gemstone…his heart skipped a beat. The stone would react against any magic, not only that of the wards. He inched his free hand toward his pocket, taking care to keep his head drooping and his other arm relaxed in Morvain's grasp.

✳

(Dev)

When the guardsman hauled Kiran out of the carriage, I heard Cara inhale sharply. No question that unlike Simon, he was drugged to the hilt. His head lolled and he wavered on his feet like he'd collapse without the guardsman's grip on his arm.

Hold on, I willed him. *We're trying to help.*

Metal flashed in the sunlight, and I shifted my attention to Simon. Silver glittering with gemstones now covered his arm from wrist to elbow. I'd never seen a charm so large.

Pello straightened from his casual slouch against the carriage. He stared at Simon, his brows drawn together. His evident concern pricked at my already strained nerves. Did Pello think Simon was about to work blood magic? Surely not. Even way out here, the detection spells were too strong to allow that. Besides, Kiran had said not even blood magic could break through those border wards.

My gaze snapped back to Kiran. Something about the way he stood…my breath caught. His free arm had tension in the muscles that didn't match the rest of his body, and his hand was moving, so slowly it was almost imperceptible, sliding by degrees into his pocket.

I nudged Cara and pointed at her crossbow.

She cocked her head, her face puzzled. We'd agreed not to act until Simon took hennanwort.

I pointed to my eyes, then to Kiran, and fisted a hand in one of the signs outriders used when the roar of waterfalls or wind drowned out yells. *Ready to move.*

Kiran jerked his hand from his pocket. His fingers flicked, as if throwing something. My knuckles whitened on the cinnabar branch.

The air around Simon burst into yellow flame. A glaring flash whited out my vision.

I blinked away afterimages, fighting to see. Kiran had wrenched his arm free of the startled guardsman and was half-staggering, half-running straight ahead.

Oh, gods! This little clearing must sit right beside the border. Kiran meant to set off the border magic and bring the Alathians down on Simon, hell with the consequences. The flash had blinded everyone for a few key seconds, but I didn't know if it would be enough. Pello was still scrubbing at his eyes, but the guardsman was already racing after Kiran.

Simon's fiery shield vanished. His free hand dropped from his eyes.

"Shoot the guardsman!" I hissed at Cara.

Cara blinked furiously and squinted down the bow, her finger hovering over the release as she fought to track the running man.

Simon slashed a hand in the air. Kiran's legs gave way. Even as he fell, he threw himself forward, one hand extended in a desperate reach.

The guardsman covered the final distance in a furious leap and snatched at Kiran's collar, jerking him backward. Kiran landed in a sprawl at the man's feet, his outflung limbs rigid.

I forced Cara's bow down. Too late, gods all damn it. If she shot now, she'd only get us killed by Simon.

In the clearing, nobody moved. Then Simon let out an explosive breath and spat out a vicious string of words in a language I didn't recognize. He rounded on the guardsman. "Get him away from there," he snapped.

The guardsman dragged Kiran backward toward the carriage. Simon followed, fury mixing with relief on his face.

Cara's face was white. *My fault,* she mouthed, and tapped the bow's sight, then her still watering eyes.

I pressed her wrist and shook my head. No surprise she'd been lagging too far behind the guardsman to shoot, after that flash. *Wait,*

I signed. *Try again.*

Though I wasn't feeling too optimistic a second chance would come. The frantic desperation on Kiran's face as he ran, and that bizarre charm of Simon's...I had a nasty suspicion those damn border wards weren't so impenetrable as everyone thought.

Below, Simon halted in front of Pello. "How did the boy get a gemstone?" His voice was soft and deadly.

Pello turned the color of old parchment. "I don't know. I searched his clothing, as you asked, but if the stone was small...he might have concealed it beneath his tongue, until he was in the carriage. I warned you it was safest to use yeleran in addition to the hennanwort. You were the one who said yeleran would extend the hennanwort's effects for too long."

Simon's hand twitched, and I thought to see Pello fall dead at his feet. But Simon's gaze wandered to the carriage, and his hand relaxed. "We will see," he said, his voice still soft. "Once in Arkennland, Kiran will tell me whose failure this was."

He must still need Pello for something. Though from Simon's tone, Pello's death would come the moment that need ended.

Pello surely knew it, too. His stance radiated tension. My mind raced, chasing new possibilities. Maybe we could use Pello somehow.

Simon knelt at Kiran's side. He said something to Kiran too quiet to hear, and drew a dagger from his belt. He nicked first his palm, then Kiran's, and pressed Kiran's bloody palm against his own.

Kiran's muscles slackened, released from their rigid paralysis. For an instant, I thought that was all Simon meant to do.

And then Kiran screamed. Screamed like he was being burned alive, his body convulsing on the ferns. Sickened, I wanted desperately to cover my ears, but I didn't dare let go of the cinnabar branches. It went on for what felt like forever, and the whole while Simon wore a savage smile, his eyes locked on Kiran's agonized face. At last he sat back, and Kiran's ragged shrieks died away into silence. He collapsed into a limp huddle, his eyes closed.

Simon glanced at the guardsman. "Search him—thoroughly this time!—then bind his wrists and ankles. And you—" he turned to Pello. "Get the carriage ready to leave. Quickly, in case anyone traveling the southward road heard that and comes to investigate."

Hope bloomed. Maybe he still meant to cross at the gate.

Simon stood and extended his arm. The charm flashed and glowed a deep, poisonous green. A matching wash of color rippled outward from a point in the air some ten feet in front of him, until it appeared he stood in front of a shimmering, semi-transparent wall. The guardsman continued to search Kiran without even looking up, but Pello paused in the midst of lashing trunks to the carriage roof, his eyes gone wide.

Awe and dread made my stomach lurch. Mother of maidens, if he could get through the border magic...

Strain tightened Simon's face. Directly in front of him, the airy glimmer of the wall shivered and faded. A hole appeared, spreading outward.

I nearly snapped off a screening branch. Cara gripped my shoulder. She tapped my belt where my boneshatter charm lay, and jerked a thumb at the border.

I shook my head, my jaw clenched, and brought my palms together in the sign for *not enough rope*. No charm I carried would bring the Alathians way out here. We couldn't even set off the wards by trying to walk through them, ordinary as we were. And that blaze of yellow fire around Simon, when Kiran had thrown the supposed gemstone—Simon was protected from attack, all right.

Plan? Cara's eyes burned with urgency.

Thinking. Shaikar take Simon, there had to be something we could do!

The hole in the border had grown large enough for a man to pass. "Take the boy through," Simon ordered the guardsman. His voice sounded rough, and tremors shook his extended arm. I tried to recall every last detail I'd heard from Kiran. Could Simon cast another spell while under so much strain from his charm? Damn it, I didn't know, and the risk of failure was too high.

The guardsman slung Kiran over his shoulder. Kiran's hands and feet were tightly bound with lengths of leather, his body completely slack. No doubt unconsciousness was a mercy. The guardsman edged toward the gap.

"Hurry up," Simon snarled. The guardsman ducked through, with a nervous glance at the pulsing aura at the gap's edge. He dumped Kiran at the base of a cinnabar tree and hurried back.

Simon stabbed a finger at the saddled horse. The guardsman pulled the picket and led the animal up to the gap. The horse snorted, eyes rolling. I prayed for it to balk, but the guardsman spoke in low, soothing tones, and the horse settled.

We'd near run out of time, yet I couldn't figure a plan that'd result in anything but our deaths at Simon's hands.

I put my mouth right against Cara's ear. "We have to wait," I whispered. "Let him go through, then ride back to Kost and tell the Alathians."

Cara twisted to hiss in my own ear, "But if he's in Arkennland, it's too late!"

I whispered, "A blood mage who can walk through their border any time he pleases? The Council will hunt him down, even in Arkennland. And this way they may not arrest Kiran. He's not illegally in Alathia anymore, and he wasn't the one to breach their border."

Cara held my gaze, frowning. She interlaced her fingers in a streetside truthtelling gesture and cocked her head.

I nodded with my best earnest expression. Sure, the Alathians would hunt Simon. But I feared they'd never reach him in time to save Kiran from whatever he'd planned. First they'd demand testimony under truth spell as proof we weren't lying or crazy, then they'd want to investigate, both here and at Simon's house, and then they'd argue over the political implications of setting foot outside their borders… my gut insisted Kiran didn't have that kind of time.

But if I sent Cara to the Alathians, she'd stay safe, and I could trust Melly's fate to her hands. Leaving me free to…what? *There's always a way*, I'd said to Kiran. But going up against a blood mage at the height of his power…how in Khalmet's name would I pull that off?

CHAPTER TWENTY

(Dev)

I stared at the shimmering veil of the border, my mind racing. The gap wasn't large enough for a carriage to pass. Simon must intend for Pello to return to Kost, perhaps bring the remainder of his supplies through the border in the ordinary way. The faint glimmerings of a plan formed. I poked Cara and pointed first at the bow, then at Pello. *Get ready,* I signed.

She braced the bow, her face bleak. Likely she thought I simply meant to kill Pello if Simon left him behind, to remove the threat to Melly.

The guardsman carried Simon's warded box through the gap. Simon gestured for him to stay beyond the border. The edges of the hole wavered and crept inward. Simon grunted with effort, his face twisting, and the hole widened out again.

"Take the carriage back to Kost and through the gate," he said to Pello, harshly.

Pello blinked in apparently innocent confusion. "And after? Where shall I—"

"I will contact you." Simon directed a burning look Pello's way. He sketched a quick sign in the air with his free hand. Pello flinched back as if Simon had struck him. "Speak to the Alathians, and you die."

"I had no intention of it," Pello said, with a dry irony that made me frown. What did Pello intend instead, to save his skin?

Simon moved to the gap, his arm still outstretched. As he stepped through, the charm flared, green sparks showering through the air. I held my breath, but the gap held and the wards didn't trigger. Too bad.

Simon's teeth were bared and his skin shone with sweat when he turned on the gap's far side. He squeezed his eyes shut, and the gap slowly shrunk away to nothing. His charm gave a last green pulse, and all the color vanished, the border fading back into invisibility.

One heavily laden horse, three people, and Simon looked in no condition to speed their travel with a spell. Good.

"Soon as they're gone, I'll climb down," I whispered to Cara. "When I whistle, shoot Pello—but don't kill him."

Cara glanced at me, her brows raised in surprise. I nodded, firmly. She tapped the longsight charm and waggled her hand. I nodded again, to show I understood even a longsight charm might not guarantee that kind of precision. *Try,* I mouthed.

She gave me a look like she thought me brain-burned, but bent to peer through the engraved copper ring of the sighting charm.

On the far side of the border, Simon clambered up on the horse. Kiran sat slumped in front of him, his legs tied to either side of the saddle and Simon's arm tight around his waist to keep him upright. The guardsman stuffed Simon's warded box into a pack, heaved it on his back, and took up the horse's lead. They moved off into the woods, heading east toward the river.

Pello muttered something and raked his hands through his curls. After a moment, he began pacing beside the carriage, his expression dark and inward. Trying to figure a way to survive, no doubt.

I scrambled down the tree, quiet as I could. Edged through the kamma bushes toward the clearing, and paused. By now, Simon should be close enough to the river that the roar of water would mask other noises. Pello was still pacing. Cara should have a good sightline.

I whistled, softly. Pello whirled, a blade dropping into his hand.

Cara's crossbow bolt slammed into his left shoulder. He let out a strangled yelp and toppled backward into the ferns. I rushed forward, kicked his knife away, and planted a knee in his stomach. Gripping the protruding bolt with one hand, I laid my knife against his throat with the other.

"Spark a charm, and you die." I put pressure on the knife. Blood trickled down his throat to join the spreading stain on his shoulder.

He choked and spat, "You blind little fool! *Now,* you choose to act?"

"Yeah, now. When you and I can have a chat without any interference from your gods-damned master."

Pello twisted under me, and I yanked on the bolt. He groaned, his face going gray, and wheezed out, "Simon is no master of mine. I work for the lord of Ninavel, curse you!"

Nice try, but I knew better. "I saw Simon search your mind. You'd be dead now if you worked for Sechaveh. You're nothing but a greedy little rat who wanted a chance at going highside."

"You saw…" He shut his eyes, and gave a pained laugh. "Shaikar take me, no wonder you refused my offer. Yes, Simon searched my mind…but not deeply, his power restricted by fear of the Council's wards. When I gave him what he expected to see, he looked no further."

"You expect me to believe you could fool a blood mage?" He must think me a total idiot.

"It would never work, in Arkennland." He coughed, and groaned again, his copper skin sallow. "Little good it did me. He cast a binding that near crippled my ability to work against him. I'd thought to free the boy, but when Simon found I'd spoken to him, he forbade me any further contact, until the end…I sought to enlist your help, but you were too wary of me."

Gods, but he had a smooth tongue. Almost, I could believe him. Except… "A binding so strong it prevented a shadow man from finding a way to tip off the Alathians? Yeah, right."

Pello grimaced. "My orders…I was to involve the Alathians only as a last resort. Simon Levanian knows much that Sechaveh does not wish in foreign hands." He stopped, panting. Swallowed, and continued. "At the first, we only knew that after years of silent exile, Simon Levanian sought an observer to shadow a young man traveling with a convoy...I was tasked to accept the job, to discover what Simon wanted, and why. By the time I learned the truth, my options were few."

He shut his eyes again. "I hoped you played your own game...I gave you every chance I could to reach the boy. I'd arranged for a diversion down riverside to distract Simon. I thought if I'd misread you, or if you failed—either the boy's gemstone would draw the mage at the gate, or I'd act there before Simon could stop me." He shook his head, and winced. "I didn't...didn't know he could breach the border wards, Shaikar curse him."

I stared at him, my mind whirling. If he told the truth...gods all damn it, I might have saved Kiran days ago.

No. I couldn't afford to trust him. Besides, even if he did work for Sechaveh, that wouldn't help me now.

Cara slid through the bushes, her crossbow aimed at Pello's head. "Did I hear right? This bastard claims to work for Lord Sechaveh?" She sounded as incredulous as I felt.

"It doesn't matter what he claims." I didn't take my eyes from Pello. Despite the blood soaking his jacket and the labored sound of his breath, I'd no doubt he remained deadly as a sand adder. "Cut the reins off the carriage harness, and help me tie him up."

She hurried to the front of the carriage. I said to Pello, "You learned the truth, did you? What does Simon mean to do with Kiran, then?"

"Use him in...some sort of spell, to destroy Ruslan Khaveirin..." Pello's dark eyes were fixed on my face. "Ruslan is...the only mage in Ninavel with power to match Simon's. With Ruslan dead, Simon will make Ninavel his own private charnel house, and...none can stop him." His voice had gone hoarse.

"The Alathians can stop him," Cara called out.

"Within their borders, perhaps, but—"

I tweaked the bolt, and he stopped, gasping. His eyes narrowed; flicked Cara's way, then back to me. I waited, ready to take stronger action, but he held his tongue.

Cara returned, reins in hand. "If Simon's such a threat, why didn't Sechaveh kill him years ago?"

Pello gave another harsh, ragged laugh. "Kill a blood mage... might as well try to snuff out the sun. Even their own kind find it a challenge. A shame...the boy's death would have solved much."

Gods. Of course he'd have killed Kiran if he could, rather than let Simon use him, and never felt a single qualm.

Cara's mouth had set in a thin, hard line. She held the crossbow inches from Pello's head while I bound him against a carriage wheel. Soon as I'd finished, I turned to her.

"If we can provide the Alathians a charm or some other proof of Simon's spellwork, it'll save time and arguing. I want to search his trunks, but I need the supplies in my saddlebag to break their seal wards. Go get our horses—I'll watch Pello."

Cara put a hand on my shoulder. "If we go to the Alathians... what about you? They'll arrest you..."

"That's why you'll give me a head start. Soon as we've checked Simon's trunks, I'll ride for Kost; you wait three hours, then follow. That's enough time for me to collect my gear and get safely into Arkennland. Once past the border gate, I'll ditch the trail and make for Ninavel cross-country. Meanwhile, you march into the nearest guard post, tell the Alathians everything, and soon as they're done with you..." I moved in close and muttered, "Get the money and gems out of my accounts, and ride for Ninavel. Ruslan shouldn't know you're involved—but stick to trailless passes, just in case. When you reach the city, meet me in Acaltar district at the Blackstrike. That's where Red Dal likes to drink."

"Three hours head start..." Her brow creased. "Of course I want you to get clear, but won't that give Simon too much time?"

"Kiran told me the border wards disrupt powerful spells. Simon'll want to get well away before he tries anything against Ruslan, and they won't be moving fast."

"What about him?" She jerked a thumb at Pello, her blue eyes troubled. Her voice lowered to a bare whisper. "I know you meant to kill him, for Melly's safety. But Dev...if he's truly Sechaveh's man, it's not right."

If Pello spoke truth, and I slit his throat…queasiness roiled my gut. Yet my head rang with Jylla's mocking laugh. *Gods, Dev, you're such a soft mark. He's lying—and even if he's not, shadow men are no innocents. Kill him, and have done. He'd do the same, in your place.*

Cara's frown deepened. "Dev. You can't still mean—"

"Let me think on it while you get the horses."

Cara's eyes narrowed, searching my face. I gave her an urgent look. "Hurry, Cara. The sooner we finish here, the sooner you can send the Alathians after Simon. I promise, I won't do anything rash." Not right off, anyway.

Her frown remained, but she jogged off.

"You fear for young Melly," Pello said softly, watching me. His mouth pulled into a rueful, bitter grimace. "A mistake, to offer her as bait. But for my life, I have another offer…"

I laughed, sharply, and took a renewed grip on the bolt. "Why in Shaikar's name would I listen?"

"Because I know how to find Simon—and you don't mean to simply run to Ninavel."

No, I didn't. I'd hoped Pello knew Simon's plans, though I'd expected I'd have to force the information from him during our brief interval of privacy. A bargain was the easier path, and yet…"Simple enough for you to lie, and send me wandering in the forest."

"Simple enough, if I had only words to offer."

My heart sped up. "You have a way to track them?"

Pello nodded, his breath rasping in his throat. "Give me your word that you'll both stay your hand and stop this bleeding…" He twitched his chin toward his sodden jacket. "I'll give you the means to hunt Simon…and my own word, that I'll bring no harm to Melly."

I laughed again. "You'd trust my word?" I sure as hell didn't trust his.

"I learned much of you before leaving Ninavel," Pello said. "Some men break vows easily as wind-weakened twigs…but not you."

Life would certainly be simpler if I broke promises readily as Jylla. My eyes wandered to the trunks, then the carriage. If Pello had hair or blood from Simon hidden away somewhere, maybe I could discover his stash myself.

Pello gave an airless chuckle. "You'll not find it easily—and every moment you waste in searching brings Simon closer to his casting."

True enough, damn him. I chewed my lip. Leaving Pello alive was a risk, no question. But then again, if we left him a prisoner for the Alathians to interrogate…Sechaveh's man or Simon's, either way, the Council would spend long weeks prying information from his head. By the time he returned to Ninavel—if he ever did—Cara should have Melly safely gone from the city.

"Fine," I said. "Hold to your end of the bargain, and I vow on Suliyya's thousand jewels I'll not kill you. When Cara returns, I've a bloodfreeze charm in my pack that'll keep you from bleeding out. Good enough?"

Pello scrutinized my face for a long moment, then nodded. "The saddlebag on the driver's box…inside, there's a wool hat. Cut the stitching on the red patch over the right earflap."

I did as he instructed, taking care to keep him in my field of vision. The hat was the brightly dyed patchwork cap I remembered from his days with the convoy. Inside the red patch's lining, I found a thin, tightly folded slip of linen. Coiled within the linen were several strands of straight brown hair, far longer than Simon's.

My stomach jumped. I rubbed a finger firmly over a hair. When I lifted it away, a faint brown stain marked my skin.

"These are Kiran's." Excitement buzzed in my blood.

Pello grunted an assent. "Took them from him…at Ice Lake."

With these, I could track Kiran directly, and from miles away at that. Gods, I might truly still have a chance to save him.

Pello's dark eyes gleamed, holding mine. "Take me with you. I have charms in Kost that would patch this injury, and even with Simon's binding…I might be of help."

"Fuck, no." I glared at him. "I don't trust you, not even a decet's worth. You've earned your life, but you'll stay right here, where you can't put a knife in my back." I took a spare shirt from his saddlebag, cut it into strips, and bound his wound, leaving the bolt in place. One shred of cloth I dipped into the blood pooling on matted cinnabar needles.

"A little insurance," I told Pello, as I tucked away the reddened cloth. I'd cut the shred in two. One half for me to keep, and the other for Cara to give the Alathians. Even if Pello somehow got free, they'd easily hunt him down with a sample of his blood to key a tracking spell.

"Have I not proven my good faith?" His sharp-chinned face took on an imploring earnestness that near matched Kiran's.

I snorted, snatching up a final cloth strip and a piece of rein. If I left that quick tongue of his free, no doubt he'd convince Cara to untie him before I'd made it half a mile.

"Should you survive…I renew my offer of employment," Pello said. "Sechaveh would be glad to have a man so resourceful and willing to embrace danger."

Khalmet's hand, but he had nerve. I stuffed the cloth in his mouth and bound it tight. Embrace danger. Ha. More like, throw myself on my own funeral pyre. He knew as well as I did that survival against Simon in Arkennland would take a miracle of Khalmet.

✳

(Kiran)

Kiran shifted against the rough rock wall, trying to find a more comfortable position. Chains bound his hands to iron bolts sunk into the stone, one on each side of him. The silvery tendrils of Simon's binding charms once again twisted over his forearms, blocking all his attempts at magic.

He stood against the back wall of a wide-mouthed, shallow cave. The cave floor was unnaturally smooth and level; likely the entire space had been hollowed from the rock by magic. The cave's arched mouth opened onto a gently sloping meadow lined with cinnabar pines. Tiny red flowers dotted lush green grass, and the rippling chuckle of a stream echoed from somewhere beyond the cave's edge.

A beautiful spot, if Kiran could only ignore the dark stains at his feet and the smooth floor, as good a place as any workroom to lay out channels. Simon was now deeply involved in that very task, pacing slowly across the cave to measure, then setting out short lengths of flexible silver links in precise swirls and loops. Once finished, he'd use magic to etch the pattern lines into the stone beneath and coat them with the silver, readying them to channel power.

Kiran watched Simon's every move. Analyzing the channel lines wouldn't tell him everything about the spell, but he'd get an overall sense of what Simon meant to attempt. *The first step in countering any channeled spell is to locate the pattern's weak points, where the energy may be diverted or blocked,* Ruslan said in his memory.

But even though the henannwort's numbness had long since vanished, Kiran's thoughts still felt horribly scattered and slow, his concentration fragile as charm-stretched glass. Not for the first time, he wished he had Mikail's gift for pattern reading. One glance and Mikail could discern a spell's purpose, whereas Kiran had to work through the pattern with careful diligence. *Mikail is a natural channeler,* Ruslan had said. *You, on the other hand, were born to focus. Yet with enough practice, you can approach his skill, and he yours. A mage should be equally prepared for either role.* Kiran had spent endless hours analyzing spells at Ruslan's direction. Yet now when it mattered most, the scrawl of lines and spirals on the cave floor refused to cohere into meaning.

Simon didn't appear to care if Kiran analyzed his spell. Ever since Kiran had woken after his unsuccessful escape attempt, Simon had made sure Kiran never left his sight. *No more surprises,* Simon had snapped at Morvain. Simon had been furious that Pello hadn't crossed the border as planned. Kiran's initial satisfaction over Pello's desertion had faded when Simon brought Kiran to the cave. Whatever supplies Pello had carried were apparently needed for something other than spellcasting. The cave was stocked with crates of metals and gems, and Simon appeared to have more than enough silver to create proper channels.

No surprise Pello had elected to block Simon's binding by remaining in Alathia, after Kiran's failure at the border. Curse it, Kiran should have lied to the man. Insisted the only way he'd live was if Kiran broke the binding. Kiran sighed in frustration.

Simon glanced up from his channel pattern, his brown eyes

sardonic. "You've not identified my spell yet? Ruslan must have sorely neglected your training."

Irritation set Kiran's teeth on edge. "I don't need to read the pattern to know you will fail."

Simon chuckled and stepped over silver to stand before Kiran. "I admit, I begin to understand why Ruslan left your mind untouched. To crush defiance brings a certain pleasure, and the taste of victory is all the sweeter after a struggle."

He gripped Kiran's throat, pressing him against the cave wall. Fingers caressed Ruslan's mark through the thin cotton of Kiran's shirt, then slid downward. Kiran snarled and twisted, unheeding of the rock gouging his back.

Simon laughed and released him. "Ah, but I am a practical man. Only a fool keeps a knife that can turn in his hand. Enjoy what defiance you can, Kiran—you'll have it only a few hours more." He turned back to his pattern.

Kiran fought down nausea. If Simon was in such a talkative mood, perhaps Kiran could learn something of use. "You keep speaking of Ruslan as a fool. How could such a fool force you into exile?"

Simon glanced back. "Foolish as Ruslan is in personal matters, I don't deny he possesses a viper's cunning. Especially when faced with the certainty of a rival's power soon far outstripping his."

"But...you both are master *akheli.*" *Once fully trained, a mage's power remains relatively constant, a function of innate talent, imagination, and strength of will,* Ruslan had said. "How could your magic suddenly grow to overshadow his?"

A cold light sparked in Simon's eyes. "Tell me, Kiran, what do you know of the Well of the World?"

The immense confluence beneath Ninavel...Kiran frowned, and said slowly, "Ninavel's confluence is unique in size. No greater single source of magical energy has ever been identified."

Simon nodded. "Yet even the *akheli* must tiptoe about its edges, barely touching its potential. Imagine if a mage could access the confluence forces directly, without need for cumbersome intermediaries such as these." He waved a dismissive hand at the silver links.

"That's impossible." To touch the confluence energies directly would be like an untalented man plunging into an inferno.

Simon gave him a condescending look. "Yet Tainted children do it every day."

"That's not the same—the Taint only operates on the physical plane," Kiran protested.

"Limited as the ability is, they bend the confluence to their will with hardly a thought."

"You claim you found a way for a mage to do the same?" Kiran made every word a study in skepticism. Simon didn't appear to share Ruslan's hot temper, but he might share Ruslan's eagerness to demonstrate superiority.

"After long years of experiments—yes. I designed a series of spells, cast upon the confluence itself, to bind the energies to my own *ikilhia*..." Naked yearning showed on Simon's face, before his expression hardened. "But after I cast the first spell, Sechaveh—" he spat the name—"interfered. He took exception to the amount of *ikilhia* needed for the spellcasting, complaining I would destroy the productivity of his precious mines."

Kiran swallowed. Sechaveh hadn't blinked an eye when Ruslan killed thirty men for Mikail's *akhelashva* ritual. Hundreds must have died in Simon's casting to draw his attention. And Simon had said that spell was only the first of a series...his nausea increased.

"So Sechaveh told Ruslan what you hoped to accomplish..." Kiran could well believe Ruslan would have hastened to prevent a rival from gaining such advantage. "And you fled to Alathia before Ruslan could cast against you?"

Simon snorted. "Ruslan was the craven one, not I. Sechaveh set his tame mages upon me—and then Ruslan came, claiming sympathy for a fellow *akheli* and saying we had tolerated Sechaveh's shortsighted rules long enough. He cast with me against Sechaveh so I would let him into my counsel—and then the sneaking coward struck down my apprentices rather than face me himself."

"Hardly cowardice, when in one stroke he removed your ability to cast channeled magic." Kiran strove to match Ruslan's arrogance. "I think you the coward, hiding from Ruslan for twenty years."

"Waiting, rather, for the right opportunity," Simon said. "Which you have so kindly provided me." He shook his head. "Still. Twenty years without true magic, my research stagnated without Tainted and formerly Tainted subjects to experiment with...Ruslan will pay for every moment of my wasted time."

Kiran still didn't see how. He stared at the partially completed pattern as Simon bent to set out another series of silver rods. All Simon's talk of the confluence made him wonder...he pressed his back against stone and concentrated.

Beyond the block on his power, a deep, slow pulse of earth energy. The cave must sit over a minor confluence point. Though the confluence beneath Ninavel dwarfed all others, weaker points lay widely scattered throughout western Arkennland. Unlike Ninavel's confluence, the forces here were tame enough to touch directly. Even so, without a partner to channel the energies during his casting, Simon would be restricted to crude, brute force methods. He must intend something more powerful and subtle, against Ruslan...but what?

The pattern section Simon had just finished looked oddly familiar, silver lines coiling in complex tangles toward a wide circle at the center...

Understanding hit Kiran with the force of a magefire strike, the spell exploding into shape in his mind.

"You mean to focus this location's earth-power all through me—through my mark-binding link, at Ruslan."

Simon's face filled with malicious delight. "Very good, Kiran. I see Ruslan's teaching was not completely inadequate."

The pieces fell into place with terrible precision. "That's why you needed the memory! You needed to see the channel pattern he used when he created the link, so you could properly harmonize yours with it!"

"Nothing comes without cost," Simon said softly. "A mark-binding is an excellent means of control, but to be unbreakable, the link must be formed at the deepest level."

"Behind his defenses," Kiran said. "You'll bypass them all. That much power...it'll..."

"Incinerate Ruslan," Simon said, with vicious satisfaction.

Kiran's horror deepened. Simon's casting would serve a double purpose, binding Kiran and destroying his will the moment it obliterated Ruslan. And Simon's spell wouldn't only kill Ruslan. The power would blast through Mikail's mark-binding link, destroying him as well. Unexpectedly, a lump rose in Kiran's throat. He'd never forgive Mikail for his betrayal, but he couldn't hate him, not the way he hated Ruslan.

Worst of all, Mikail's death would only be the prelude to a bloodbath in Ninavel. Icy panic threatened to drown Kiran. He forced it back. One piece was still missing. "This won't work, not with only you to cast. You can't force me to take in the power without both a channel and focus, and no drug will help you."

"Once again, you lack imagination." Simon's smug air intensified as he bent to lay out more silver.

Kiran didn't doubt it, after the muddled mess the drug had left of his head. He studied the pattern with desperate intensity. If his magic was unbound for even a single instant during Simon's casting, he had to be ready to seize the opportunity to disrupt the spell. The alternative was too terrible.

✳

(Dev)

The sun's final rays warmed my back as I lay flat to peer over the edge of a rock outcropping. In the steep-sided valley below, the silver thread of a stream tumbled over short cliffs and wound its way through pine groves and meadows. The find-me charm pulsed with warm urgency on my arm. Kiran was somewhere in this valley. Not hard to guess where, either. In one meadow, a horse grazed. Its color and size matched Simon's mount, and the log wall of a cabin showed through the screening trees at the meadow's edge.

Kiran's amulet dug painfully into my skin, trapped between my chest and the rock. Kiran had implied the amulet would work even when worn by an ordinary guy like me. I sure hoped so. Otherwise, this'd be one short rescue attempt.

Even with the amulet, I didn't dare enter the valley in daylight. At this altitude, the forest was much thinner than down in the Elenn Gorge. Far too easy to get spotted by Simon or his guardsman, and the amulet wouldn't help me then.

I willed the sun to set faster. Suliyya grant Simon hadn't finished his preparations yet! I'd lost precious time in Kost finding and bargaining for the items I needed, and barely made it through the border gate before the deadline I'd given Cara. The whole time, I'd cursed myself for leaving Pello alive, my imagination conjuring up visions of him getting free and finding some new way to fuck me over while he laughed at my gullibility. Yet in the end, I'd passed the gate without incident.

Unbidden, my thoughts turned Cara's way. By now, the Alathians would've questioned her under truth spell and realized she wasn't crazy or pulling some prank. I entertained a brief, happy fantasy of an entire force of Alathian mages rushing into the valley below and taking Simon down without me having to lift a finger.

Yeah, right. No doubt the Alathians would be bound up for days arguing over the political consequences of a raid into Arkennland. Cara'd be stuck giving testimony ten times over. Hell, they might even take her to Tamanath, to speak before the Council.

Just where I wanted her, far distant from Simon's deadly magic. But gods, it'd been hard to leave, knowing I'd likely never see her again. One hug, and a quick, fierce kiss...I'd wanted to hold her longer, but she might've realized the truth of my intent.

At last, the sun slipped below the western hills to leave the valley in shadow. The sky remained pale, only a few bright stars glimmering above, but I judged the forest dark enough for what I had in mind.

When I'd sent Cara to coax mage war stories out of Jerik, I hadn't expected much. Sure enough, most of what he'd said was useless— exciting but uninformative tales like the ones we'd all heard growing up—but one thing had caught my attention.

You always knew when the mages really got to fighting, because it was like fireworks going off. Not the Ninavel kind that make sky-pictures, but those nonmagical ones Sulanians sell, that go off in simple colored flashes and showers of sparks, and bang loud enough to shatter eardrums.

We learned quick that the instant you see that shit, you run, and pray to Khalmet a wall doesn't fall on you, he'd told Cara.

Ninavel fireworks were specially made mage lights, but Sulanians used mixed powders that exploded when exposed to open flame, with different mixtures giving different colors. Alathians loved them, since they held no potentially illegal magic. The Sulanian traders I'd seen on the day I brought Kiran through the gate had carried a crate of fireworks as part of their cargo to sell, and I'd managed to find the Alathian importer who'd bought their wares. I'd had to pay twice what the fireworks were worth, since the old crone had seen I was in such a gods-damned hurry, but a good dozen hand-sized bags of powder and a set of pre-made fuses now sat in my pack. I was hoping that if magic could look like fireworks, the reverse was true as well.

I slithered down a gully between cliffs, heading for the valley floor. Even in the gathering gloom, each pine twig and pebble stood out sharp in my vision, the slightest noises loud in my ears. Fear fell away, leaving only the stark clarity I remembered from countless dangerous climbs and Tainter jobs. My blood sang and I grinned, tight and fierce.

The darkness was deeper amidst the valley pines. I slipped through the forest, placing powder sacks in a widely spaced arc leading toward the cabin. Beside each sack, I laid one of my precious store of Ninavel-made defensive charms, primed and ready; and before I moved on, I lit the twisted cord of the sack's fuse. The Alathian merchant had assured me that once lit, the fuses were both slow burning and difficult to put out.

With the last firework in place, I eased up to the edge of the meadow. Flickering firelight lit the cabin windows, and a sharper, steadier silver glow spilled onto the grass from beyond a bulwark of rock at the meadow's head. The angle was wrong for me to see the source, but no question it was magelight—and far too bright to be cast by something simple as a lightglobe.

I slid off my pack and drew out one last woven cloth sack, smaller than the others, with a fuse cut down to almost nothing. The merchant had said I'd have an hour's grace with the length of fuses she'd cut for the fireworks I'd set in the forest. That time had to be almost up, now.

A great rose-colored flash speared toward the sky, with a violent bang that sent birds squawking from trees. Close on its heels, a startled shout rang out from the cabin. The gray-haired guardsman charged out the door with a long-barreled Sulanian hackbut in his hands.

Simon's dark silhouette appeared against the magelight. The guardsman stopped, hackbut raised, and glanced Simon's way.

Come on, you bastard, I urged Simon silently. *Go investigate.* As the fireworks exploded, the charms I'd laid next to them would spark, in a mimicry of mages fighting. Simon would sense the magic, but if the amulet worked as Kiran said, he'd be unable to sense any people within the valley's confines. Kiran had implied that proximity to a strong source of magic—like whatever threw off all that magelight—could mess with a mage's senses, like a night sentry standing too close to a bonfire; and everything I'd seen of Simon said he was the careful, controlling sort who'd be driven crazy by uncertainty. Surely he'd be tempted to move away from his spellwork, in hopes of figuring out what the hell was going on. He wouldn't be so dumb as to go far, or leave for long—but I meant to seize even the slightest opportunity.

A second Sulanian firework exploded with a deafening bang. Golden sparks shot up over the tops of the trees. Simon raised his hands. A sickly yellow halo of light shimmered over his body.

"Stay here. Shoot anyone you see," Simon snapped at the guardsman. He stalked toward the trees. I held my breath.

Another explosion, this one closer. Simon picked up his pace and disappeared into the forest. The moment his yellow glow faded from sight, I sparked the fuse on the sack in my hand and tossed it straight at the guardsman.

He saw it flying toward him and jumped back, but not far enough. The little firework exploded right in front of him. Small as it was, it popped rather than banged, but the flash was blinding. The guardsman howled as burning powder spattered his clothes and face. He dropped the hackbut and clawed frantically at his eyes.

I raced forward and kicked him hard as I could in the groin. A strangled, high-pitched sound escaped him, and he doubled over. I brought my knee up into his face as he did, and heard the crunch of bone. He crashed to the ground, his face a ruined mess of blood and burns. I kicked him twice more, first in the throat and then the head.

His body jerked limply with the impacts. Yeah, he'd not get up anytime soon.

The find-me's power had faded during the wait for nightfall, but I figured I'd find Kiran at the source of the magelight. I bolted across the meadow to the cliff band, glancing at the woods. No sign of Simon. Five more fireworks remained in the forest. I could only pray they'd keep him busy long enough.

I rounded a boulder and skidded to a stop. Silver-green magelight flooded from a wide-mouthed hollow at the base of the cliff. Brightly glowing lines spiraled inward on the hollow's floor to surround Kiran, spreadeagled on his back in the center, his wrists and ankles bound with silver manacles sunk in the stone. More silver marked his forearms, in the twisted pattern of some type of charm. His shirt had been cut open, exposing his chest and stomach. His chest moved in rapid breaths, but his eyes were closed. I couldn't tell if he was conscious.

"Suliyya, mother of maidens," I breathed. This must be what Kiran had meant by channeled magic. Fear twisted my stomach, but I couldn't afford to delay. I stepped gingerly over the first line. No magefire struck me down. I took a deep breath and kept going.

"Kiran?" My voice came out a little higher pitched than usual.

His eyes flew open, and his jaw dropped.

"You!" The shock on his face turned to fury. If he could have killed with a look, I would've collapsed dead on the stone. He strained against the manacles and spat out, "You work for Simon, too? I should have known."

I yanked a piton hammer and pick from my pack. "For Khalmet's sake, shut up and save the yelling for *after* I've rescued you."

I tapped a manacle with the hammer, and grimaced as the silver flashed blue. They were warded. Well, I'd come prepared.

Kiran had that pole-axed look on his face again. "Rescue?"

I broke the seal on a stoppered glass vial and poured a trickle of dark liquid in a circle about the base of the manacle attachment. The liquid foamed and smoked on the rock, leaving a pitted crack. I jammed my pick into the crack and whacked it with the hammer. The rock split wider, partially freeing the manacle.

"Rock's not as hard as most people think," I told Kiran, and reset the pick on the manacle's other side. Another solid whack, and the manacle came free.

Kiran bent his arm to stare at his wrist, the manacle still locked tight around it. Stunned disbelief glazed his eyes. I hurried to his ankles, throwing a quick glance out at the meadow. All I saw was a dark void. Thanks to all the damn magelight, I'd lost my night vision.

The skin between my shoulder blades crawled as I hacked away at stone. "Can you tell where Simon is?"

"No—he's blocked my magic…" Kiran's breath quickened as I got his right leg free. His stunned look had changed to one of wariness, his dark brows lowered in a distrustful frown.

"Dev…why?"

I wasn't sure if he was asking why I'd come back, or why I'd sold him out in the first place. Unable to meet his gaze, I shrugged and focused on his left ankle. Metal shivered under my hand as I struck repeated blows. Khalmet's hand, this manacle was taking way too long—

"Dev—!" The sheer panic in Kiran's voice jerked me to my feet. His eyes were white-rimmed, focused behind me.

Shit! I tried to run, but an invisible force locked my muscles.

A hand clamped my shoulder. If my throat hadn't been frozen like everything else, I'd likely have embarrassed myself by screaming. I half expected to feel skeletal bones, but the hand was human.

"What foolishness is this?" The hand on my shoulder turned me around. Though Simon's voice held only smooth inquiry, fury lurked in his eyes. Dread washed through me.

Simon took the pick and hammer from my hands and tossed them aside. He studied me, his head cocked to one side, and reached out to catch the chain around my neck. He drew out the amulet, held it up, then let it fall back against my chest.

"Ah," he said. "That explains much."

A scuffling from below drew my eyes downward. Kiran was throwing his weight against the two remaining manacles, his face despairing.

"None of that," Simon said softly, and knelt. His body blocked my view, but when he stood again, Kiran was once more outstretched, his manacles embedded in the rock as if I'd never freed them.

Simon turned his attention back on me. My silent litany of curses faltered at the cold anticipation in his eyes. He flicked his fingers in a twisting gesture. "Did Ruslan send you?"

Gods, I could feel him in my head, an icy pressure forcing words to my tongue. "N-no." I thought fast, and added, "But the Alathians know. About you. And the border. They're coming."

His eyes narrowed, holding mine. Then he laughed. "But not, I think, before I finish here. And afterward, it won't matter. I know them well. They will not cross the mountains." He gripped my arm and drew me away from Kiran, to the edge of the glowing lines.

"I'd thought to use only stored *ikilhia* to control this spell, but fresh blood is always better." He took up an ornate silver knife.

Oh, fuck. I set my jaw and shut my eyes. I'd gambled with my life and lost, but no matter what agonies I endured at Simon's hands, the end result was no different than a fall from a climb, or the rockfall that had killed Sethan. Cara was safe in Alathia, and gods willing, she'd give Melly the life I couldn't. I'd sentenced Steffol and Joreal to this fate; only fair I should join them.

"Simon, wait!" Kiran's voice was ragged but urgent. I squinted one eye open. To my surprise, Simon lowered the knife.

"Would you prefer a better view?" he asked Kiran, mockingly.

"He's strongly Tainted. Or was," Kiran said.

Simon looked back at me, with a thoughtful malice that made my skin crawl. "Was he, now?"

I couldn't see what that had to do with anything. But Simon asked, "Is this true?" His fingers flicked again, the invisible force returning to squeeze an answer from me.

"Yes."

Simon raised his brows. "Very well, I'll not waste a potentially useful subject." He glanced at Kiran. "He'll not be grateful to you. The agony of a mind destroyed piece by piece over long days far outstrips any I'd planned here."

My stomach rolled over. People in Ninavel always said in dire tones that dealing with mages got you killed or worse. Looked like I'd get the chance to find out about the "or worse" part.

CHAPTER TWENTY-ONE

(Kiran)

Kiran twisted to watch as Simon led an unresisting Dev out of the channels. Stacked crates stood against the cave wall, the remains of Simon's spellcasting supplies. Simon pushed Dev down onto a crate.

"Remain here." Simon sketched a quick *voshanoi* sigil in the air, meant to reinforce the bone-binding he'd surely cast the first moment he touched Dev.

Dev's face was blank, but anger glittered deep in his green eyes. Kiran sent a silent apology Dev's way. Anger was better than the terrible look of resignation Dev had worn when Simon raised the knife.

"Your friend was surprisingly clever," Simon said to Kiran, as he took a bulging cloth sack from one of the crates. "But even if he had freed you, believe me, I never would have permitted you to escape. I've waited too long for this."

"Ruslan said the same thing," Kiran said in a low and bitter voice, remembering his first, fraught conversation with Ruslan after the *akhelashva* ritual.

Simon unwrapped a set of dark, faceted crystals. Deep within each crystal, a crimson glow pulsed. Kiran pulled against the manacles. "Those are—"

"*Zhivnoi* crystals, yes." Simon paced around the the pattern, setting crystals at the anchor points. As each crystal touched the pattern, the bright greenish-silver of the lines coiling inward from that point turned to sullen red.

"But...so many..." Seven crystals, and from the size, capable of holding the *ikilhia* of ten or more lives each...he felt sick.

"It took me years to store this much." Simon sounded disgusted. "Kost is nowhere near as enlightened as Ninavel. No slaves, no selling off of condemned criminals...it can be so difficult in Alathia to find people none will miss. Fortunately the authorities expect a certain attrition rate for prospectors and hunters. The mountains are so dangerous, after all."

Kiran shut his eyes, blocking out Simon's poisonous smile. Instead of throwing himself against his physical bonds, he strained at the bonds on his magic. Simon's charms might weaken, this close to so much channeled power.

But the wall still stood about his mind, smooth and unbroken. The sparse tracery of Simon's snare-binding lay underneath. Deeper yet lurked Lizaveta's heart-binding, the result of his blood promise to her, a complex lacework so skillfully interwoven with his own *ikilhia* it was nearly undetectable. Regret flooded him. Why had he ever agreed to her terms? Death would be preferable by far to a twilight existence as Simon's mind-burned slave. And if Simon succeeded against Ruslan, Mikail and scores of innocent *nathahlen* would die in Kiran's place.

Pain stung his bare chest. Kiran swallowed a cry, breathing through clenched teeth as Simon sliced sigils into his skin. All the channel lines glowed red now, power ready and waiting. Fear set his heart hammering. Yet how could Simon cast, without both focus and channeler?

The sigils burning his skin—not just Simon's personal sigil to anchor a new mark-binding, but a twisted spiral of *dobravyi* that would enhance the connection Ruslan had created between Kiran's body and magic. Kiran's panic surged.

Simon didn't need a focus, not if he were to gut Kiran with the knife and simultaneously release the binding on Kiran's power. A mortal wound combined with the *dobravyi* would mean a power draw completely out of Kiran's control, his magic reaching blindly for what his body needed to survive. In response, Simon would channel a veritable cataract of power straight into him, immeasurably greater than needed to repair Kiran's injury, all of it tuned and harmonized to Kiran's link to Ruslan. And the moment Ruslan's death shattered the mark-binding, Simon would burn out Kiran's will and force a new bond.

As Simon's wholly dependent, docile slave, Kiran would slaughter countless innocents and never even know the evil he did.

"Simon." Kiran spoke softly. "Don't do this. Please." His voice was shaking. "Don't do it, not this way. I'll…I'll help you cast against Ruslan. I'll take your mark-bond, willingly." The words were ashes on his tongue.

Simon's knife hand stilled. His dark eyes locked with Kiran's.

Please, Kiran begged, with every spark of *ikilhia* within him. If Simon would only leave his mind intact, then even subject to the soul-crushing constraint of a mark-binding, he might find a way to subvert Simon's plans in Ninavel.

"Oh, you tempt me, Kiran." Simon cupped Kiran's face, his thumb stroking away a drop of blood trickling down Kiran's cheekbone. "But I see you with clearer eyes than Ruslan. I'll have you by my side, but not as you are now. Lesser, it's true, but safer."

He finished cutting the sigil and stood. Hot tears burned Kiran's eyes, matching the sting of Simon's sigils on his skin. He jerked against the manacles, his breath tearing in his chest. There must be a way to stop Simon, to strike back—

Lizaveta's heart-binding, so tightly woven into his *ikilhia*—he couldn't alter her prohibition against self-harm, but if he could warp the shape of her spell just slightly, enhance it *there*, and *there*…the resulting pattern would also deflect harmful energies, enough that it might disrupt the flow of power Simon funneled into him.

Disrupted, the channeled magic would backlash in a cataclysm sure to destroy both him and Simon. He gasped as the heart-binding lanced warning fire through him. Curse Lizaveta! Death wasn't his desire in this, only Simon's defeat.

Lizaveta's binding didn't relent. Kiran twisted, panting. New dismay pierced him as he glimpsed Dev, silent and still on his crate. Success in his plan would mean Dev's death, when uncontrolled power roared through Simon's bone-binding. *I'm sorry*, he thought at Dev. *Iannis was right. Death is the only freedom for us.* Grimly, he fought the burning pressure in his head, struggling to weave a pattern in his own *ikilhia* strong enough to tug Lizaveta's into the proper alignment.

Simon cut sigils into his own palms. He set the knife down and spread his hands, blood dripping into the nearest channels. One by one the channels snapped into life, the sullen red glow brightening into blazing fire.

Hurry, Kiran had to hurry, yet the threads kept slipping from his grasp, fire devouring his focus…

Simon knelt, his eyes shut and sweat standing out on his face. He reached one bloody hand to touch the binding charm on Kiran's left wrist, and raised the knife over Kiran's bare stomach.

Not yet, he wasn't ready, oh please… "Simon, no—!"

The knife came down, and everything turned white.

※

(Dev)

Horror choked me as Simon brought the knife down. The bastard's binding kept me frozen, unable even to close my eyes.

Kiran's panicked shout turned to a ragged, agonized shriek as the silver blade tore through his stomach. All the lines on the floor blazed up so bright it was like staring into the sun. Just when I feared I'd be struck blind, the inferno of light abruptly dimmed. Simon had already pulled the knife out. Kiran's blood was everywhere, black in the eerie light.

A violet flash outlined Kiran's body in a deep, livid glow. Simon threw up an arm, stark surprise on his face.

Kiran screamed again, his voice raw. His body convulsed and arched off the stone so hard I thought he'd rip his limbs off. A great arc of blinding light snapped from his body to Simon's. The lines in the floor flared up again, smaller arcs running from them to Kiran.

On my chest, the amulet burst into white-hot life, searing my skin through my shirt. A yell hung trapped in my throat as pain exploded in my head. The air in my lungs turned thick as molasses, my heart struggling against a tightening vise.

Simon screamed, a sound that filled me with savage joy. The arc between Simon and Kiran grew ever brighter until Simon seemed to be glowing from within, his bones a dark shadow beneath his flesh, his face a rictus of agony. The fire in my head mounted to skull-boiling intensity.

A soundless explosion swatted me backward into darkness.

Something heavy was crushing me. I groaned and struggled to push it away. My hands scraped against rock. Where was I, and why was everything dark?

Memory returned, and I froze. Then slowly, deliberately, moved my hands up to my face. Simon's binding was gone, my body my own to command—but where was Simon? And oh gods, Kiran, with his gut slashed wide open...I stifled the urge to scrabble blindly against rock, and lay still, listening.

No sounds came to my ears other than the distant splashing of the stream. The darkness surrounding me wasn't absolute, and as my eyes adjusted I began to make out shapes.

I was lying on my side, squeezed in a crevice beneath a jumble of rocks and the remains of Simon's crates. Dim light filtered through the splintered wood of a shattered crate at the crevice's end. I wriggled toward the light, praying the rocks would remain stable. Mother of maidens, but I didn't want to die the terrible way Sethan had, my body crushed to a red ruin...

My chest scraped past a crate's edge and I hissed and recoiled. My skin was blistered and raw where Kiran's amulet had rested. No wonder—the damn thing had burned hotter than a live coal, before the cave fell on me. The amulet was cold and dull now, dragging over rock as I crawled. I tied a hasty knot in the chain to raise the amulet above my burn, and tucked it under the collar of my tattered and blackened shirt.

Aside from the burn, I had a host of bruises and a fierce headache, but nothing more. Not like Kiran. With a wound so terrible, was he already dead? Or if he yet lived, was he trapped in wreckage, his life bleeding away?

I struggled onward, ignoring scrapes and punctures from all the gods-damned metal rods and charms mixed with the debris. Most of the charms were strange to me, but I grabbed a few I recognized as useful. If Simon waited out there, I needed every advantage I could get.

Once free, I found myself near the mouth of the cave. Part of the cave ceiling had given way, creating the pile of rocks and splintered wood I'd just escaped from. The rockfall blocked my view of the interior. I edged around it, concern for Kiran warring with my fear of Simon.

But when I peered into the cave, I saw no trace of Simon—only Kiran, sprawled on his back amidst a scorched and darkened scrawl of silver lines. A few unmarred spirals on the cave's far side still glowed like banked coals, enough to illuminate his slack face and shut eyes.

My gaze darted to his stomach—and I sucked in a sharp breath. The great wound Simon had inflicted was completely gone. Blood still blackened the waist of Kiran's pants, and more lay in sticky dark pools beneath his torso. His manacles had vanished, though a few melted, misshapen slugs of silver glimmered on the stone where they'd been, and deep bruises shadowed his wrists and ankles. The silver that had marked his forearms had disappeared as well. A faint dark tracery was all that remained of the marks Simon had cut into his flesh.

He was utterly still, and with that corpse-pale skin of his, he looked dead, but who knew what a mage could survive?

Kill a blood mage…might as well snuff out the sun. I spun in a slow circle, checking again for Simon. No question something had fucked up his spell, but much as I hoped he'd been blasted to vapor, I sure couldn't afford to make assumptions.

A faint sound of footsteps, from the darkness of the meadow. Fuck! I dodged further into the cave. In all this wreckage, there had to be a hiding spot…there! A narrow crevice lurked beneath a boulder wedged over two half-destroyed crates. I threw myself onto my stomach and wriggled backward into the hole.

From the crevice, I could see most of the cave and part of the opening. The steady, measured footsteps grew louder, and I braced for the sight of an angry Simon. But the man who strode out of the darkness was a stranger.

He was tall, and wore a long coat of heavy leather, much longer than the sort outriders wear. He had golden skin and slanted eyes like a Korassian, but his hair was ruddy brown rather than black. The hair was long, Ninavel highsider-style, tied loosely back at the nape of his neck. He moved like a highsider, too, full of that easy arrogance.

Oh, shit. I knew one guy wandering around the Whitefires who'd match a Ninavel highsider's description.

The stranger made straight for Kiran, walking over glowing lines as if they weren't even there. I tensed. If this was Ruslan, Kiran was screwed, and I couldn't do a thing about it.

The stranger knelt and laid a hand on Kiran's forehead, the way a den minder might check one of her kids for fever. He gave a deep sigh, and tight lines around his mouth relaxed. He took his hand away and pulled a thumb-sized crystal from his coat.

The crystal glowed red, and I bit back a curse. Ruslan or no, he was definitely a mage.

He leaned over Kiran, one hand holding the crystal above the blood mage sigil on Kiran's chest, and his other hand hovering over Kiran's forehead. Red light stained Kiran's skin as if he'd been dipped in blood, and the dark bruising on his outflung wrist disappeared.

Kiran twitched and inhaled. The mage withdrew his hands, the red glow of the crystal fading back to darkness. He hid the crystal away in his coat and pulled Kiran half up onto his lap, Kiran's head supported against his chest.

"Open your eyes for me, Kiranushka. My brave son, child of my heart, *ardeshka savoi,* wake for me now…" He spoke softly, his deep voice marked by a far stronger version of the faint accent I'd heard in Kiran's, and stroked Kiran's hair with a gentle hand. Kiran whimpered and turned further into the circle of the man's arms like a child seeking comfort. The man tightened his hold, his expression shifting into a deep and bitter tenderness.

Surely I'd been wrong—this couldn't be Ruslan. But if not, who in Shaikar's hells was he? Something about him was familiar.

Kiran's eyes opened. He gasped and thrust himself away in a convulsive, frantic movement.

"Ruslan! Let me go, let me—" The words were panicky and breathless.

I stared. *This* was Ruslan? The way he'd healed Kiran, held him… it didn't fit at all with my mental image of the master Kiran had tried so hard to escape.

Ruslan released his hold. The tenderness vanished, replaced by a cold amusement uncomfortably reminiscent of Simon.

Kiran scrabbled backward until his back fetched up against the cave wall, his eyes fixed on Ruslan the way a man watches a snake he expects to strike.

"Calm yourself, Kiran. You have nothing to fear from me." Ruslan spoke soothingly, but an irony underlay his words that made me uneasy.

"You lie." Kiran's voice shook.

Ruslan smiled at him. Gooseflesh rose along my arms. The sharp cruelty in that smile outmatched Simon's.

"How could I not be pleased? Simon Levanian, destroyed…I had long desired his death, but he hid behind the Alathian border wards like a child behind his mother's skirt." Ruslan's rich voice dripped contempt. "So I forgive you your foolish rebellion, since it provided me such a wonderful opportunity." His smile softened, gaining a faint echo of that disconcerting tenderness. "You played your part bravely and well."

Kiran's face showed confusion to match my own. He looked around at the scorched and broken lines on the floor, as if seeing them for the first time. His eyes lifted to the pile of rock and crushed wood. He paled, looking sick, and his lips formed my name.

I didn't dare give him any sign I'd survived. Whatever Ruslan's game, I couldn't play against a blood mage. Simon had proved that beyond a doubt.

Kiran's gaze shifted to the drying blood on the stone. He twitched, one hand going first to his stomach, then to the sigil on his chest. Shock harrowed his face.

"The backlash—I should be dead. But Lizaveta's binding, with a pattern so close to what I needed to disrupt Simon's spell—that was deliberate, wasn't it? And when I warped her pattern, a deeper spell triggered that diverted the worst of the backlash away from me through the mark-binding link..." Kiran's voice died away to a whisper. "You...from the beginning, you *planned this?*" He pushed himself to his feet, his eyes wild.

My stomach seized as nagging familiarity resolved into memory. The blood mage I'd seen after leaving Bren's place, his cold amusement when he'd held my gaze—the same man stood before me now. Awful certainty filled me. When Ruslan had seen me that day, he'd known exactly who I was. Shaikar take him, I'd been a blind token from the start. My only comfort was that I wasn't the only one. Pello hadn't known Ruslan's plan, which presumably meant Lord Sechaveh hadn't either.

Ruslan's face was full of arrogant triumph. "It was a difficult task, that heart-binding. Subtle enough to escape detection, yet strong enough to reflect enormous power, and leave you alive...oh, we spent many long nights working on it, Liza and I." A faint, reminiscent smile lifted the corners of his mouth. "Everything else was easy. I merely arranged with the *nathahlen* you contracted with for passage—Bren, I believe his name was?—for word to reach Simon of your intention to go to Alathia, and he did the rest."

Bren and Gerran, working direct for Ruslan...oh gods, that explained so much. I'd thought them crazy for dealing with a mage like Simon, but Ruslan must not have given Bren a choice.

"But...you tried to stop me! The avalanche, and the storms!" Kiran's face was gray.

Ruslan shrugged. "I had my part to play, lest Simon grow suspicious. I also wanted to keep you...motivated." He gave Kiran a gently condescending look. "Do you really think you could have left Ninavel and reached Alathia so easily, had I desired to prevent it?"

Gods all damn it, even after I'd realized Pello hadn't been the threat he seemed, I'd still thought myself so clever for beating Ruslan to the border. Blind token, ha. Total fucking idiot, more like. I'd had not a glimmer of anyone's true intent.

Kiran pointed at the lines on the floor with a shaking hand. "If Simon had detected Lizaveta's binding and broken it—or if I hadn't realized how to enhance her pattern—this spell would have worked. Simon would have destroyed you, and Mikail with you. You wouldn't take such a risk." He sounded like he was trying to convince himself.

A predatory gleam lit Ruslan's eyes. "I counted on Simon believing just that." He laughed. "Poor Simon, always so cautious, so meticulous…he never understood that to win the long game, a man must sometimes gamble everything on a single throw."

Doubtless it didn't disturb him a whit that he'd gambled the lives of everyone in Ninavel along with his own. I didn't think Sechaveh would be so sanguine about the risk of the city falling under Simon's control. If I survived this night, I'd make sure Sechaveh found out the full tale of Ruslan's game.

Ruslan's expression softened again, into fond pride. "As for the chance you'd fail to grasp the heart-binding's possibilities—that was no risk at all. You forget, *akhelysh*, I know your abilities to the last ember. I knew you would not fail me."

Kiran jerked as if struck, his eyes full of new horror.

"Is that why you killed Alisa? To drive me to Simon?" His fists were clenched at his sides, his entire body rigid.

Ruslan's eyes narrowed. "I used her life for your *akhelashva* ritual because it was necessary to show you that disobedience will not be tolerated. It was only afterward, when Lizaveta came to me and told me she feared you would do something foolish if we did not prevent it, that I thought to turn the situation to our advantage."

I flashed on the pain I'd glimpsed in Kiran when Cara had asked him about a lover, and the sick look on his face when he'd talked of the ritual. If Ruslan had tortured his lover to death in front of him, no wonder he'd run.

"Lizaveta came to you…" Kiran's mouth twisted. "I thought she cared. I should have known she'd be just as soulless as you."

"Lizaveta came to me out of love for you," Ruslan said sternly, that condescending look back on his face. He stood and spread his hands. "Kiran, the time for games has ended. Now you will come home."

Khalmet's bloodsoaked hand, he said it with the same casual unconcern as a handler calling his Tainters in from a successful job. Kiran echoed my incredulity.

"Come home, just like that? After what you've done?" His laugh was a terrible sound, grating and broken. "You don't even see what a monster you are."

"Enough of this foolishness." Ruslan took a step forward. "Would you prefer to be the plaything of an *akheli* like Simon?"

Kiran flinched. Ruslan nodded in satisfaction. "Oh yes, I know how Simon treated his so-called apprentices. Pitiful brain-burned creatures…killing them was a mercy. Whereas I raised you, trained you, offered you power and protection, and made you *akheli*, the greatest gift it is possible to give. How, then, am I the monster?"

Gods, he really thought himself reasonable. But then, all the truly sick bastards did. Red Dal, Tavian, Ruslan…the scale might be different, but the type was the same.

Kiran stared at Ruslan, his eyes dark. "I loved Alisa, and you killed her. No, more than killed her—you stole not only her life from her, but her pain, her tears, her blood…" His breathing went ragged, his fists trembling. I winced, thinking of the crushing weight of my fear for Cara when I'd realized Ruslan was a blood mage. She'd survived Ruslan's visit, but if she hadn't, the pain would've torn me raw.

Ruslan made an angry, dismissive noise. "What must I do to make you understand? She was nothing. The *nathahlen* are as far below us as animals."

And this was the man Pello had wanted to save. Ruslan and Simon were two of a kind, far as I could see. How Sechaveh slept at night, I didn't know.

"She wasn't nothing! She was beautiful, and kind, and good, and giving!" Kiran's voice spiraled out of control. "All you do is take, and manipulate, and kill!" His face was anguished. "I'll destroy myself and my magic before I'll live as you do!"

"Don't be ridiculous." Ruslan's voice was cold. "My patience, long though it has been, is now at an end. If you act as a spoiled child, you force me to treat you like one." He drew himself up, his face going intent.

Kiran flinched and put a hand to his temple. My fingers dug futile furrows over stone. Shaikar take Ruslan and his cursed magic! I hated being so fucking helpless.

Kiran's hand dropped. He laughed wildly, his fingers going to the sigil on his chest. "All that backlash...the mark-binding link hasn't restabilized yet. You can't control me..."

Run, I willed him. Khalmet's hand, what was he waiting for?

Ruslan's face darkened. "Do not provoke me." He raised a hand sheathed in red fire.

Kiran raised his own hands. The air before him burst into azure flame, just as a crackling, seething web of light arrowed from Ruslan's hand. Blue and crimson sparks cascaded to the ground, and Kiran staggered backward. He clawed a hand through the air. Dimly glowing lines blazed into furious life, spitting arcs at Ruslan. Ruslan's mouth twisted in a snarl as he blocked them with a shield of his own, sending more sparks sizzling through the air.

Kiran turned and ran, disappearing into the meadow. Ruslan followed. A bright flash threw sharp shadows across the scarred cave floor, and a crashing boom made me flinch. Overhead came the ominous grind of rocks shifting. Dust sifted down in front of my nose.

"Shit," I said in a heartfelt whisper. If they kept at it, the entire rock face would collapse and crush me into jelly. Of course, my other option was to crawl out and get blasted by Ruslan. Just great. Another explosion followed by a louder, crunching noise overhead made my decision for me. I scooted out of the crevice, praying Ruslan was too busy with Kiran to notice me, and that the amulet around my neck still worked.

Cautiously, I poked my head around the rockpile. Kiran and Ruslan stood facing each other in the meadow, just past the crumpled body of Simon's guardsman. Wild coronas of light flared and arced into each other, sparks showering everywhere. Patches of grass were already ablaze. Thank Khalmet it wasn't midsummer, or else the whole meadow would've gone up like a tinderbox. As it was, I thought it high time to be leaving before I got burned to a crisp. I hesitated, looking at the despairing fury on Kiran's face, but there was nothing I could do for him now.

Ruslan's back was to me. If I moved fast, I might make it to the trees unnoticed. I eased forward, ready to run—and a hand gripped my shoulder for the second time that night.

CHAPTER TWENTY-TWO

(Dev)

I whipped around with a choked shout, convinced I'd see Simon. "Quiet!" It wasn't Simon this time, either. My captor was a sandy-haired guy around my own age with a broad, serious face and slanted gray eyes. He held up a hand haloed in green magelight. "If you run, I will stop you." He had the same faint accent as Kiran.

"Oh, for Khalmet's sake," I snarled. "How many of you *are* there, stomping around the Whitefires?"

His head tilted, magefire reflected in his pale eyes. "Just me, my master—and Kiran. You want to help him, don't you? I saw it on your face."

"You must be Mikail." Kiran hadn't said much about him, but at least he hadn't spoken of Mikail with the same dread as he had Ruslan.

Mikail nodded. A bright flash tinted his flat features blue, and his jaw tightened. "Kiran never knows when to quit," he muttered. And then, louder, "He's more like Ruslan than you realize."

My disbelief must've shown, because he huffed a short, ironic laugh. "Did he tell you Ruslan and I were monsters, and he the innocent, helpless victim?"

"I don't have to take his word for it," I said sharply. "Ruslan's doing a great job of proving him right." Why was he talking to me instead of killing me, or binding me with magic the way Simon had?

"And if Kiran weren't equally as obsessive, stubborn, and slow to forgive as Ruslan, none of this would be happening." Mikail sounded weary. He pressed a thick, ornate silver charm-band into my hand. "I found this in Simon's cabin—if you want Kiran's freedom, put it on."

"What does it do? And wait—why would you want Kiran free?" I wasn't about to trust anyone who called Ruslan master.

Mikail gave a one-sided shrug. "Ruslan will push Kiran too far. Look at him." Out in the meadow, Kiran staggered and fell to one knee, bracing his hands on the earth. The writhing spirals of light around him faded, then blazed up with renewed force.

"Ruslan seeks to block Kiran's access to the confluence power here, thinking that will force surrender, but I know my mage-brother. With the mark-binding yet unstable and Lizaveta's heart-binding broken, Kiran will spend his entire life force rather than give in," Mikail said, his voice low and unhappy.

"Then help him! You're a mage!"

"Go against Ruslan, directly?" Mikail eyed me as if I were a slow-witted child. "That, he would not forgive—and I am not Kiran." He gripped my shoulder. "Make no mistake, I think Kiran is being a fool. But I prefer him a live fool to a dead one, so I give the choice to you—help him, or watch him die and then face Ruslan yourself."

Not much of a choice. I stared at the charm in my hand. "What will this thing do?"

Mikail smiled, but it didn't reach his eyes. "Provide a weapon only a *nathahlen* can use."

If I'd ever seen a fool's game, this was it...but I'd been ready to die at Simon's hands on the slim chance I'd save Kiran. This wasn't far different.

Before I could change my mind, I slipped the charm onto a wrist. Mikail laid a hand over it and mumbled something under his breath. The charm flashed green. Prickling heat raced up my arm.

And then—oh, and then—shock stopped my breath, as deep in my mind something unfolded I'd thought I'd lost forever.

The Taint! Stunned, unbelieving exultation near choked me. Could it really be true? My gaze lit on a rock shard lying at Mikail's feet. In an agony of anticipation, I reached out with my mind.

The old familiar twisting sensation sent an ecstatic thrill chasing down my spine. The rock shard sprang into the air and hung there, slowly revolving.

Even as I did it, a deep, vicious cramp stabbed my stomach. I didn't care. Joy bubbled up to fill the dark void I'd carried in my soul since the day I'd Changed. All these years, so dead inside, and now alive again—

A booming explosion shook me free of revelry. I bared my teeth at Mikail. He inclined his head to me, and moved aside.

The rock plummeted to the ground as I shifted my attention to Ruslan. "See how you like this, you arrogant bastard," I growled, and *shoved* at him, hard as I could.

✳

(Kiran)

Sheets of flame crashed upon Kiran, battering his body with raw power while subtle, sneaking tendrils pried at his mind. And all the while, vicious gusts of magic whittled away his connection to the meadow confluence as inexorably as a sandstorm eroding adobe.

Ruslan was so *strong*. How could he attack on so many fronts at once? Every time Kiran tried to stave off the dissolution of his confluence link, his defenses threatened to collapse under Ruslan's other onslaughts. Despair crept through Kiran, whispering of surrender. He fought all the harder, pouring all of his rage and hatred and guilt into his magic, fashioning every scrap of power he possessed into a howling black tornado hurled straight at Ruslan.

The bright blaze of Ruslan's defensive magic shone undimmed under the assault. Kiran groaned, struggling to shore up weakened defenses. His supply of confluence energy dwindled to a mere trickle. Kiran spent his own *ikilhia* instead, abandoning all caution. Sweat dripped into his eyes; his heart raced and then faltered.

Ruslan's attacks doubled in force. Kiran's shield wavered, his inner defenses crumbling. Desperate, he reached deep within himself for more, preparing a counterattack he knew would fail.

Without warning, Ruslan flew sideways as if smacked aside by a giant, invisible hand, and slammed into a cinnabar trunk. His outer shield flickered and failed, right as Kiran's counterstrike hit. A brilliant flash seared the air. Ruslan collapsed.

Confluence energy surged into Kiran unimpeded. The shock sent him sprawling, his shield flaring with overflow. Even as he fell, he snatched at power and cast another raw blast of magic at Ruslan.

Crimson light outlined Ruslan's unconscious body, and Kiran's strike sheeted harmlessly away to dissipate in scattered, guttering fires. Kiran grimaced. Ruslan's barriers had snapped up before the strike reached him, and now his *ikilhia* pulsed in a sullen knot behind protective magic dense and impenetrable as stone. Any further brute force assault would be futile.

Kiran pushed warily to his feet. Ruslan's focus had been shattered by the physical impact with the tree, allowing Kiran's initial counterstrike to reach him before his barriers formed, but what had sent him flying in the first place?

"Hey! Don't just stand there, blast him again!"

Dizzily, Kiran turned to see Dev running toward him. Dirt and blood streaked Dev's skin, his clothes scorched and torn, but his face shone with a fierce, dark glee.

"Dev? But…the backlash, and the rockfall…how…?" Kiran felt caught in some odd, fantastical dream. First the abrupt halt to his fight with Ruslan, and now Dev, alive…he'd been certain Dev was dead, another soul added to the black weight on his conscience.

Dev shrugged, then winced and pressed a hand to his side. "I got beat up pretty good, but it takes more than that to fell an outrider." He cast a sharp glance over his shoulder. Kiran followed his gaze, but saw nothing more than the silent, empty cave. Dev stabbed a finger at Ruslan's silent form, and spoke in a low, urgent voice. "Hurry up and kill him! Unless…he's already dead?" He sounded half-hopeful, half-skeptical.

"No. He's unconscious. But his barriers are up, and they're far too strong for me to breach without a channeled spell."

"Let me have another try, then." Dev's brow furrowed, his breath hissing between his teeth. Above Ruslan, the massive cinnabar tree shook as if lashed by a strong wind—yet Kiran sensed no magic, just as when Ruslan had been knocked aside...a sudden, vivid image of Mero's intent frown as pebbles rattled across the courtyard sprang into his head.

"The Taint! That was you, before—but how? Adults can't—"

Dev thrust an arm at him. A charm band covered in intricate sigils gleamed on his wrist. "Thanks to Simon. Guess that blacksouled viper was good for something after all." He grimaced, his hands fisting. Creaks and pops echoed from the tree. The trunk shuddered, groaned, and toppled toward Ruslan's crumpled body.

"No!" Kiran threw out a hand. A blaze of lightning speared up from burning grass and shattered the trunk to cinders.

Dev rounded on him, eyes burning with startled anger. "What the fuck?"

"You can't kill him that way! Even unconscious, he'll instinctively draw power to heal any injury you inflict—and your *ikilhia* is the easiest source! You'd be the one to die, not him."

Dev's glare turned skeptical. "Smacking him into a tree worked, no problem."

"Only because the surprise broke his focus right as I struck with magic. His shielding spells absorbed the impact with the tree—he's not physically injured." This was only a brief reprieve; already, Ruslan's *ikilhia* grew brighter. Hastily, Kiran drew in further draughts of confluence power to replenish his depleted reserves, readying himself to fight. "He'll wake soon. You need to get out of here, now!"

"Not without you." Dev shoved Kiran toward the forest. "If we can't kill him, then for Khalmet's sake, run!"

Kiran dug in his heels. "Running won't help. He'll find me the moment he wakes—better if I stay and fight while you run—"

Dev yanked his shirt down at the neck, exposing Lizaveta's amulet. "Recognize this?"

"*That's* how you survived when I disrupted Simon's spell!" The amulet, designed to divert magical energies around its wearer like water flowing past a rounded stone…Simon had surely left it on Dev to prevent damage to his "useful subject" from the heightened energies produced by channeled spellcasting. The amulet shouldn't have been enough to save Dev, not against a backlash of that magnitude. But Ruslan must have drawn off enough power through Kiran's mark-binding link to inadvertently save Dev's life as well as Kiran's.

"If you say so." Dev handed the amulet to Kiran. "Just tell me it still works."

Two more gemstones were blackened, and deep scorch marks marred the silver, but if the pattern remained intact…hope rekindled, with painful force. Kiran's heart pounded as he concentrated his inner sight.

"It works." He slipped the amulet on, dizzy with relief.

"Thank Khalmet." Dev pulled him into a stumbling run across the meadow.

About to raise his barriers, Kiran hesitated. The magic of the charm on Dev's wrist was a whisper nearly inaudible beneath the powerful throb of the confluence—but it held an odd, dissonant resonance. Frowning, he narrowed his focus to exclude the earth-energies swamping his senses, though the effort tripped his feet.

Spiky lines of sickly green energy snaked throughout Dev's body in a way he'd never seen. Dev's *ikilhia* burned fever-bright in some places, mottled by dark spots in others.

Dev's grip tightened. "Less daydreaming, more leaving."

"That charm—something's not right," Kiran panted. You should remove it—"

"Take off my one advantage against Ruslan? Hell, no." Dev yanked Kiran onward. "Simon's horse is long gone, after all this excitement. We've gotta go on foot. Thank Khalmet the sky's clear and we've got a good moon." He halted just inside the trees. "Hold on, let me get my pack—we'll need the water and food."

He stretched out a hand. A pack flew out of the darkness straight into his grip. Dev slung it on, winced, spat, then jogged off through moonlit trees.

"Dev, wait…" Kiran tried to catch up, tripping over roots and rocks in the shadows. "If you can use the Taint again—you can fly, right? You should leave me and go—"

Dev shook his head. "It's fading," he said, sounding angry. "The further we go, the less I feel—" he gave a sharp shrug, and hurried on.

Of course—the Taint used confluence energy. Though veins of earth power yet coiled beneath Kiran's feet, they were far weaker than the abundance present in the meadow. Kiran reluctantly rebuilt his barriers, wishing he dared leave them down to monitor Dev's *ikilhia*. Those dark spots worried him.

"If the Taint's fading, then take off the charm," he called.

"Not so long as I feel as single speck's worth," Dev snapped, and picked up his pace.

Kiran scrambled after, a new concern rising. Dev was heading straight back down the valley. Surely that would be the first direction Ruslan searched. "Shouldn't we climb out of the valley? Where are we going?"

"Alathia," Dev said succinctly.

"Through the gate?" Kiran couldn't help the sharp way it came out. He emphatically did not want to take any more hennanwort, or place himself helpless in another's hands.

Dev's teeth showed white in a grin. "I hope not." He untucked his shirt and drew out silver crusted with gemstones. "That Taint charm isn't the only one of Simon's I've got."

Kiran gasped, recognizing the charm Simon had used to cross the border. "Where did you get that?"

"Once a thief, always a thief," Dev said. He coughed, then admitted, "Actually, I stumbled over it. Crawled over it, more like, on my way out of that rockfall. Damn thing has seriously sharp edges." He held it out to Kiran. "Can you use it?"

Kiran touched the charm with a cautious finger. An astonishing amount of power lay within the metal, far more than even a channeled spell could have bound. The spell pattern was strange, covered in tangled, multiple layers as if Simon had laid new pathways overtop of old ones.

The pattern was too complex to fully analyze without long study, but the activation and power pathways were clear. Unlike most charms, this one wouldn't work for an untalented man—from what he could sense, it needed a mage to constantly feed in power—but he didn't have to understand the entire design to use the charm. He'd have to drop his barriers, but if the mark-binding link remained unstable, he might hold Ruslan off long enough to cross the border safely.

"I think so."

Dev gave a gusty sigh of relief and shoved the charm in his pack. "Speaking of Simon's magic…want to tell me what happened back in that cave?"

"It's a little hard to explain." Kiran's breath came short as he clambered over the massive hulk of a fallen cinnabar trunk.

"Skip to the good part," Dev said. "He's truly dead?"

"Yes," Kiran said, with savage satisfaction. His memory of Simon's casting held only fragmented flashes of fire and agony, but he knew well enough what had happened. No channeler could have contained that amount of backlash—Simon had been destroyed utterly, in the same manner he'd intended to destroy Ruslan. Kiran's satisfaction faded, and he shivered. Simon had come terribly close to success.

"Well, thank Khalmet for that." Dev coughed, muffling the sound with his hands. "I guess Sechaveh and everyone else in Ninavel can rest easy."

Surprise slowed Kiran's steps. "You knew what Simon planned to do in Ninavel?"

"Overheard him talking to Pello, in Kost. And later, Pello told me more. Turns out Pello was working for Sechaveh, all along."

"Sechaveh!" Kiran nearly fell face first over a log. "But Pello wouldn't help free me, even though I offered to release him from Simon's binding!"

"He said Simon stopped him—but yeah, I didn't believe him either, until he gave me the hair he snatched off you at Ice Lake. I'd not have tracked you to Simon's cabin without it."

Dev, coming so far and facing Simon alone, all to help him… Kiran was profoundly grateful, but he still didn't understand Dev's motive, after Dev had handed Kiran to Gerran without so much as a warning. "You didn't answer me before, when I asked why."

"If you're asking why I helped sell you to Simon, it's a long story.

The short version is, I needed the money to save someone who's got no hope, otherwise." Dev's voice was tight. "If you're asking why I came back…" He shrugged, awkwardly. "Look, I heard you talking to Ruslan in that cave. You told him you didn't want to be the kind of person he is. Well, back in Kost I decided I don't want to be that kind of person, either."

"Thank you." Kiran said it quietly, but knew from the sudden rigidity of Dev's shoulders that he'd heard.

"Don't thank me yet," Dev said. "We've still gotta cross the border."

The forest thickened, the moonlight fading. Kiran barked his shins on rocks and slipped on pine needles, an uneasy mixture of fear and hope churning in his chest. Ruslan must have awoken by now. He'd waste no time in hunting them, and he'd have all the energy of the meadow's confluence to fuel spells.

Spells…where was Mikail? Surely Ruslan wouldn't have come alone to Simon's valley.

"I can hear the river." Dev's dark form halted at the edge of a moonlit clearing.

Relief scattered Kiran's thoughts. He'd assumed the faint rushing noise was the sound of wind in pines. "How far to the border?"

"Quarter mile." Dev's voice had a brittle quality that brought Kiran's concern flooding back. He hurried forward, hoping to glimpse Dev's face.

Dev strode into the clearing. Halfway across, he stopped and doubled over in a series of harsh, tearing coughs. When he straightened, he ducked out of the moonlight, but not before Kiran saw the blood staining his mouth and chin.

"Dev! You're hurt—why didn't you say?"

Dev spat and wiped blood away. "Wasn't so bad, before. Guess you were right about that charm."

"Take it off!" Kiran grabbed for Dev's wrist.

Dev jerked his arm away. "No! It's still working, I can still feel—"

"Don't be a fool!" Kiran snatched again for the charm. "The Taint won't help you if you collapse before we reach the border!"

Reluctantly, Dev brought his wrist forward. "Fine," he muttered.

"You'll have to do it. I don't know the word to stop the magic."

Kiran laid a hand on the charm. The pattern was horribly complex. "How did you activate it, then?"

Dev shrugged, scowling. "Mikail did it."

"*Mikail* helped you?" Kiran's hand fell from the charm.

"He said he didn't want you to kill yourself fighting Ruslan."

A pang squeezed Kiran's heart, before a wave of bitterness crested. Mikail's help couldn't be trusted. He might not want Kiran to die, but he'd never want Kiran to escape. Kiran grasped the silver band with renewed urgency.

His stomach turned cold and hollow as he grasped the spell's intent. The charm drastically altered the *ikilhia* of the wearer, presumably in a manner that restored a formerly Tainted adult's childhood abilities—but did so by savaging the body's organs. Simon wouldn't have cared if his experiments killed his *nathahlen* subjects.

Curse Simon, where had he hidden the suppression pathway? Kiran sorted frantically through tangled spirals...*there*.

The band dulled and loosened. Kiran yanked the charm over Dev's hand, even as Dev made a grab for it.

"Are you insane?" Kiran held the charm out of reach. "The charm was killing you! You shouldn't even touch it again." More than ever, he regretted his ignorance of healing spells. What if Dev had already sustained fatal damage?

Dev's hands fisted, his eyes fixed on the charm. For an instant Kiran feared Dev would fight him for it. But Dev's shoulders slumped, and he turned away. One hand crept to his stomach. He coughed and spat again, blood dark on the pine needles.

Kiran wanted nothing more than to throw the charm into the forest, but Mikail might be hoping for that—once the charm was away from Kiran's amulet, Ruslan might detect it, even deactivated as it was. And now Kiran was too far from the meadow confluence to mount a successful defense.

"Let me carry your pack," Kiran said. Wordlessly, Dev handed it to him. His lack of protest worried Kiran even more than the blood. "Will you be able to—"

"I'll be fine!" Dev snapped, and started off again, as if to prove it.

Springy-branched bushes choked their path as the rush of the river grew louder. Dev forced his way through with grim determination. Kiran's worry grew deeper yet at the awkwardness of his movements. At last the bushes thinned to reveal a grassy bank. The river beyond ran deep and fast, the other shore more than a hundred feet away, dimly visible through a bank of mist in the sourceless light of approaching dawn.

Dev groaned. "Damn it! Too dangerous to swim, and too far to jump between rocks."

The deep, soundless thrumming of Alathian border magic penetrated Kiran's barriers. The border must lie only a short distance past the far bank. He looked at Dev, whose mouth was a tight line, his body hunched in pain.

"I can get us across," Kiran said quietly.

"How? You can't—" Dev's head tilted. "Oh. You mean with magic. Won't that bring Ruslan down on us, if he's back in action?"

Kiran nodded. "But the mark-binding link shouldn't be fully stable yet, so he can't attack me that way. If we hurry, we have a chance of crossing the border before he can physically arrive. The meadow confluence isn't powerful enough to fuel a translocation spell. There are other ways to speed travel, not quite as fast, but still…" It would be close. But Dev's condition was worsening rapidly—he needed help. Even if Ruslan came, Kiran might hold a gap long enough for Dev to reach safety, at least.

Dev coughed, wetly, and gave a sharp chuckle. "Well, I've been doing nothing but taking chances, lately." Blood showed black on his teeth.

"Do you have a knife?"

Dev fumbled at his belt and produced a fingerlength blade. He watched, frowning, as Kiran sliced a line down one palm. "Do you have to cut yourself every time you work magic?"

"No, but it makes the power draw easier and more efficient if I do." Kiran pulled the amulet off. The magic of his intended spell might be the final blow that broke the amulet's pattern, if he wore it while casting. "The blood makes a sympathetic link between me and the power source."

"Right," Dev said, sounding blank, as Kiran handed him the

amulet. He shook his head. "Here I thought all the finger-pricking to make charms work was annoying. That looks way more painful."

"It's worth it," Kiran said.

Dev gave a small, choked laugh. "Now that part, I understand." A series of coughs racked him, and he bent to brace his hands on his knees.

Kiran pressed his bloody palm to the soil. Even this far from the meadow confluence, enough earth power yet remained for something simple as what he had in mind. But if he was wrong about the stability of the mark-binding link…he forced fear from his mind, and released his barriers.

The forest's *ikilhia* painted the world in a soft glow, beautiful and seductive. And in his mind, a sudden, vicious tug, and a distant echo of furious triumph. Oh yes, Ruslan was awake. But the link remained too unstable to use, though for how much longer, Kiran couldn't say.

Kiran blocked it all out to focus on a simple pattern, one he and Mikail had learned as children. Earth energies shifted, aligning, and the air grew icy around him. The mist over the river condensed into a solid white bridge spanning the distance between the banks.

"Huh." Dev sounded impressed.

Kiran didn't bother to speak. He grabbed Dev's arm and drew him onto the mist bridge, holding his focus tight on the pattern. Halfway across, Dev staggered. Kiran ducked under Dev's arm and helped him stumble the rest of the way to the riverbank.

"Ah, fuck." Dev's legs gave way as they reached solid ground. Kiran let him drop to sit on mossy stones. He released the spell pattern, careful to control the energy spillover. The pull in his mind was increasing by the instant. He slammed up his barriers, and gasped in relief as the pull lessened to a faint itch.

"Want this?" Dev offered him the amulet, but Kiran shook his head.

"Too late," he said. Ruslan already knew their location, and the amulet would only interfere with the magic of Simon's border charm.

Kiran hauled Dev to his feet. Dev groaned and his eyelids fluttered, but he managed to stumble through the undergrowth, leaning heavily on Kiran.

The thrumming of the border magic increased to a level that vibrated Kiran's bones. The amulet flared blue on Dev's chest and spat warning sparks. Cursing, Dev jerked it off and let it fall.

They must be only steps away. Kiran stopped, letting Dev slide to the ground. He yanked off the pack and bound on the silver vambrace of Simon's charm. Now came the real test of his concentration. To pour power into the charm and hold the gap, while Ruslan ripped away his defenses…he snatched at failing confidence. He'd chosen death for Dev in Simon's cave. He'd fight now to his last glimmer of *ikilhia* to give Dev a chance at life.

✳

(Dev)

Pain gnawed my insides and muddied my thoughts, but I held fiercely to consciousness. When Simon had used the border charm, it'd looked like one hell of an effort. No good counting on Kiran being able to drag me, under that much strain. I'd make it on my own even if I had to pull myself through with my teeth.

Kiran shut his eyes, and the charm began to glow. Just like before, a wash of green rippled outward, staining the air and revealing the border magic. A tiny hole appeared. Slowly, much more slowly than with Simon, it spread. I took shallow breaths, trying not to cough. My chest and gut felt full of splintered rock shards.

Kiran's face grew haggard, his jaw muscles tight. The hole still hadn't spread to the ground, and was too small to safely jump through. Khalmet's hand, what if he couldn't make a big enough gap?

"Kiran!" Ruslan burst from the bushes at the river's edge, black anger on his face. Mikail was right behind him.

"You've gotta be fucking *kidding me!*" I yelled. Shaikar curse him, after everything I'd gone through to get Kiran free, how dare he show up when we were nearly safe at last?

Nobody so much as glanced my way. Kiran kept his arm up, not even turning around. The gap edged wider.

"Don't," he said to Ruslan, his voice strained. "You know what will happen if you strike now. The overspill would destroy us all." He enunciated each word as if he had to think hard how to say it.

Ruslan glanced at the shimmering green veil, his expression coldly calculating. He and Mikail both stopped, some ten feet away. Ruslan ignored me completely, but Mikail darted me one swift, unreadable look.

The gap in the wards had finally grown wide enough for a person. I scooted toward it, ignoring the agony shredding my gut.

"Kiran." Ruslan spoke softly now. "Come here." His face had gone stone still, his eyes inward and intent.

I heard Kiran gasp, saw his arm falter. Worse was the look on his face, like a man who fights knowing he's already lost.

"Go through," he said to me, his voice harsh. "Quickly." He took a dragging step backward toward Ruslan. The gap in the wards wavered and began to shrink.

"Fuck this," I said, and shoved myself to my feet. Pain savaged me, my vision darkening. I threw myself at Kiran and crashed my shoulder into his back. He went flying through the gap, and I toppled through right after him.

Ruslan rushed forward, but he was too late. The hole collapsed inward with a violent, sparking flash, missing my feet by inches. Sparks showered off of Kiran's arm, and he cried out in pain.

I had eyes only for Ruslan, who stood just beyond the shimmering veil, incredulous fury twisting his face. I laughed, blood bubbling up in my mouth. "I win, you asshole," I said, and happily surrendered to darkness.

CHAPTER TWENTY-THREE

(Kiran)

Kiran tore off Simon's charm, working frantically to dampen magical energies before they spiraled out of control to catastrophic effect. Forces roiled, crested; submitted to his control, and subsided. He released his focus, his heart still pounding with reaction, and looked up.

Ruslan's hot-eyed gaze stabbed into him. Kiran froze. Ruslan stood scant feet away, so close to the border he was almost touching it.

The mark-binding link remained blessedly still and silent. Ruslan's voice no longer echoed in his mind; his will no longer crushed Kiran's with the pitiless, implacable force of an avalanche. Kiran let out a shaky breath. He stood, slowly.

"This isn't over," Ruslan said coldly. "Don't assume this—" he waved a dismissive hand at the fading veil of color in the air—"will stop me."

"It worked for Simon." Kiran lifted his chin.

Ruslan smiled, dark and terrible. Kiran took an involuntary step backward.

"Simon was nothing to me, compared to you." Ruslan's hazel eyes burned. "You are mine, body and soul, linked, bound, and marked." He sketched the ancient ritual gesture in the air with one long-fingered hand. "*Mine.* Nothing will change that as long as you live, and I promise I will find you, no matter where you hide or how long the search takes me."

Kiran turned his back. Ice choked his stomach and the border wards' protection felt far too thin, but he couldn't let Ruslan see the depth of his fear.

Dev lay huddled on his side, an unhealthy yellow tinge to his skin and blood trickling from his nose and mouth. His *ikilhia* had shrunk to a feeble flicker. Kiran hastily knelt and pressed a hand to Dev's shoulder. He couldn't heal Dev, not without careful study and a channeled spell, but perhaps if he fed in an infusion of *ikilhia* as would help a mage, Dev's condition might stabilize. Kiran sent a trickle of his own *ikilhia* through the contact.

Instead of binding with Dev's, the trickle dissipated.

"I fear the *nathahlen* will escape my vengeance." Ruslan sighed in a mockery of regret. "A pity they die so easily."

Kiran refused to look up. Wild power born of fear and frustration seethed within, perilously close to escaping his control. Dev badly needed a healer's care, but Kiran had no idea of the distance to Kost, or how he might safely convey Dev there.

"Well, hasn't this been *interesting*," a new voice said brightly, making Kiran jump.

A dark-haired man in the blue and gray uniform of an Alathian mage sauntered out of the forest. His round, open face and snubbed nose gave him a cheerful look at odds with his height and his confident walk. Behind him, other uniformed mages appeared, ghosting through the trees to form a loose half circle behind the speaker.

Kiran tensed, rising. Alathians...he quelled the urge to run. He'd never win against so many. Besides, if he offered a peaceful surrender, perhaps they'd agree to help Dev.

"I heard a rumor a blood mage was using a charm to cross our border, but it seemed a little much to swallow...and yet here you are, caught in the act." The Alathian glanced at Simon's charm, then at the telltale *akhelsya* sigil on Kiran's chest, exposed by the shredded remains of his shirt. Despite the man's casual tone, his eyes were sharp.

"This one is mine," Ruslan snarled, pointing at Kiran. "Return him to me, and I promise you, your precious border is safe."

Panic surged through Kiran. He took one stumbling step away, but the Alathian raised a hand, his sigil-marked rings flaring silver in warning.

"Not so fast. You're under arrest by decree of the Alathian Council, for the dual crimes of blood magic and border violation." The Alathian turned to Ruslan, his posture studiously formal. "Any claims on an Arkennlander criminal must be filed with the Alathian ambassador in Ninavel."

"Return him to me, or I will tear down your country stone by stone," Ruslan said, pure venom in his voice. Kiran's heart quailed. Ruslan did not make idle threats.

The Alathian looked unmoved. "Ruslan Khaveirin, isn't it? Oh yes, I've heard of you—best to study snakes before they strike, as the Sulanians like to say. Allow me to introduce myself—Captain Martennan of the Seventh Watch."

His round face hardened to match his eyes. "Perhaps you didn't hear me. I insist you take this matter back to Ninavel. Right now." The casual tone had disappeared, leaving steel in its place. "And take that other with you." He pointed to the silent Mikail.

Ruslan glanced at the air where the border lay, then at the half-circle of mages. His mouth thinned. "I gave you fair warning, Alathian. Remember that." He stalked off eastward.

Kiran swallowed. Ruslan's retreat was purely strategic. He wouldn't engage in a fight when he lacked a major confluence to draw from, while the Alathians had all the immense power of their border wards. But once back in Ninavel, the colossal forces of the Well of the World would be his to use once more in spells subtle as they were powerful.

Mikail lingered, his eyes on Kiran. "You're wrong about him," he said quietly, as if he and Kiran were the only ones present. "He loves you, my brother. Remember that when your temper cools, and come home to us." He strode after Ruslan.

Kiran could only shake his head. The Alathian shifted to face him, ringed hands spread. Kiran drew in a sharp breath, reminded of his hope for Dev. "I'll not fight your arrest, if you'll only get him a healer, please—" he pointed at Dev's limp form.

"We're not barbarians here," Captain Martennan said. "Of course he'll receive healing." He motioned another mage forward, a bird-boned woman with tousled brown hair. "Alyashen, see to him."

She nodded crisply and bent to lay a hand on Dev's forehead. After a moment, she looked up, her eyes dark. "This is damage from blood magic, beyond my skill to heal. He'll need to go to the Sanitorium."

Martennan's expression hardened again as he turned to Kiran. "What do you know of this?"

"It was a charm, not mine, Simon's, Dev only wore it to stop Ruslan and save me..." Kiran stopped, realizing he was babbling. His hands still trembled with reaction, his control dangerously thin after the effort of using the border charm. Taking a deep breath, he continued. "The charm that hurt him is there—" he indicated Dev's pack, half-hidden in the ferns on the far side of the border. "It might help your healers to examine it."

Martennan nodded to another of the silent mages. The man stepped out of the circle and walked straight through the border as if it didn't exist. Only a brief and barely visible flash marked his passage. Kiran stared in amazement.

"Surely you don't imagine we'd design wards we couldn't cross when and where we wanted to." Martennan's casually cheerful tone was back. "Did you think you blood mages were the only ones who can work powerful magic?"

Kiran flushed. He'd assumed exactly that after Ruslan's dismissive attitude toward Alathian magic. Martennan chuckled.

"Very well, people, let's go. Alyashen, you and Kallentor take the injured Arkennlander. Talmaddis and Lenarimanas, contact Captain Sorennas and tell him to double the mages on duty in the Aerie. I don't trust that sly bastard Khaveirin one jot." He looked down at Kiran. "I apologize in advance for this, but you are a blood mage and your magic is unbound."

Kiran fought down an instinctive flare of power. He'd promised not to fight. He stood unresisting as Martennan's hands clamped his shoulders, and a lash of magic burned the world away.

✳

(Dev)

I woke in the slow, muddled way of a recovery from a bad fever, awareness drifting closer, then ebbing out of reach again. When I finally surfaced, the first thing I saw was Cara.

She sat in a wooden chair by an open, sunlit window, one leather-clad leg thrown over the chair's arm. The sun turned her pale hair to molten gold, and lit fire from the metal outrider badge still pinned to her jacket. From the wistful look in her blue eyes, the window surely held a view of the Whitefires.

I savored my own view. I'd hoped, but I hadn't truly thought to see her again. But against all odds, I'd survived not just one, but two angry blood mages. Slow satisfaction warmed my chest. Miracle of Khalmet, indeed.

Cara glanced my way, and her eyes widened. She sprang from the chair, beaming at me. "Dev! You're awake!"

I tried to sit up, and flopped back with a groan. Khalmet's hand, my body felt like tumbling boulders had ground me to powder.

Worse than my weak, aching muscles was the dull emptiness in my head where the Taint had been. Gods, to have it back, only to have it ripped away again…bitterness scalded me. Grimly, I buried it deep. Fuck if I'd fall into sniveling despair like some newly Changed city brat. I'd survived the Change; I could handle this.

Besides, maybe I could get that charm back.

Cara slid a strong arm behind my shoulders and lifted me to a sitting position. "Easy. You've been down a whole week." She stuffed pillows behind my back, one warm hand lingering on my shoulder.

"A week?" The charm had fucked me over, and no mistake. But maybe if I wore it only for brief bursts of time, or if—

I yanked myself free of speculation. Better not to think of it, not until I had a chance at the charm. Instead, I surveyed the room. Polished walls of red-gold cinnabar wood, no decorations, plain but sturdy furniture. No question I was in Alathia. I stiffened and grabbed

Cara's wrist. "Wait, what are you still doing here? We agreed you'd ride for Ninavel!" I'd meant her to take my hard-earned pay and head straight for Red Dal and Melly.

"The Alathians insisted I testify before the Council here in Tamanath," Cara said. "And after...well, if you think I'd leave when you were barely breathing and had one foot in Shaikar's hells, you're crazy."

This was Tamanath, not Kost? Shit.

"The Alathians found us, then." I'd hoped to sneak across the border using Simon's charm and leave the Alathians none the wiser. I should've guessed they'd be watching the border keen as banehawks after I'd sent Cara to them.

"A good thing, too," Cara said severely. "You'd have died if they hadn't. Khalmet's hand, Dev, you nearly died anyway, even with the best healers in Tamanath working on you. They said you used some blood mage charm that chewed your insides to shreds." She glared at me. "What the fuck were you thinking?"

"That I'd prefer a delayed death to an immediate one. Seriously, Cara, that charm's the only reason we survived Ruslan." I had no intention of admitting that while I'd put it on to save Kiran, I'd kept it on for other reasons entirely.

Kiran...oh, hell. "What happened to Kiran? Where is he?" Suliyya grant he'd run before the Alathians came.

But Cara wouldn't meet my gaze, her face suddenly shuttered.

"Cara. Just tell me."

She sighed. "The Alathians arrested him. They saw him use Simon's charm to cross the border. He's charged with both blood magic and border violation."

Gods all damn it, exactly what I'd feared would happen if the Alathians got their hands on him. Both offenses were grounds for execution. Even if Kiran was as hard to kill as Pello had claimed, no doubt the Alathians would find a way in the end.

The skin around Cara's eyes creased with worry. "I asked to see him, but they won't even tell me where he is. Hell, I barely managed to get in here to see you. I did find out they mean to have some kind of Council hearing over Kiran. I think the Council's been waiting for you to wake up—they want you as a witness to the crimes."

I jerked upright, heedless of the protest from abused muscles. "If the Alathians think I'll sign Kiran's execution order for them—after all I just went through to keep him alive!—they can rot in Shaikar's innermost—"

"You won't have a choice. I talked to some of the guards. They said the questioning will be run by mages, and they'll use truth spells." Cara looked unhappy. "They used one on me back in Kost. The way everyone in Ninavel sneers over Alathian magic, I'd thought to find it no stronger than a loosetongue charm—but Dev, that spell was nothing to sneer at. Trust me, you won't be able to hold anything back."

Oh, fuck. No denying Kiran was a blood mage, and that he'd worked blood magic. Harken and the other dead at the convoy...I no longer doubted that Kiran had only meant to save lives, not take them. But the Council wouldn't see it that way. They'd look at him with the same horror and contempt I'd felt back in Bearjaw Cirque's cave, before I met Simon and Ruslan and realized Kiran showed no hint of that casual, arrogant cruelty they so readily displayed.

I'd do my best to make the Council understand, but I'd need a tongue smoother than Varkevian silk to convince a bunch of dour-faced, strict-minded Alathians a blood mage deserved freedom. Wait a minute, smooth tongue...

"What about Pello?"

"No good news there, either. I could've sworn no man could escape the knots we tied, and I took both horses with me when I rode for Kost, but when I brought the Alathians after giving testimony, he was gone. They sent mages to hunt him—the gods know he left enough blood on those ferns to fuel a hundred tracking spells. But if they've found him, I haven't heard about it."

I slumped against the pillows. "I knew I should've killed him."

"You did right." Cara squeezed my shoulder. "You spared his life—surely he'll remember the debt he owes you. Besides, what profit would he find in Melly now?"

"Plenty, if he sells news of my interest in her to Red Dal." I scrubbed a weary hand over my eyes. "Damn it. Just once, I'd like for something to go right."

"You don't think surviving against two separate blood mages counts?" Cara poked me with a stern finger. "If you weren't an invalid, I swear, I'd kick your ass. All that talk of 'I'll not abandon you,' and then you lie to me and run off on a gods-damned suicidal rescue attempt."

Her tone was teasing, but genuine anger heated her eyes. I shrugged uncomfortably. "One of us had to go to the Alathians. Better if that was you, since you've no history of smuggling to distract them. But I didn't think they'd reach Simon in time, so that left me to try and stop him."

She shook her head. "Your logic's not the problem."

"Then what is? The part where I wanted you safe from a blood mage?"

"No, damn you. It's the part where you didn't trust me enough to make my own choice in the matter." She stood and paced to the window with quick, jerky strides. "Damn it, Dev! This is why I had that Shaikar-cursed rule on bedplay. Sex fucks up judgment, every time."

I shoved myself up again. "You think I wanted you safe just because we'd shared a bed? For Khalmet's sake, Cara! You're my *friend*. I'd have done the same for Sethan, in your place."

She studied me, scowling. "And Jylla? If she'd been partnering you in this, would you have lied to her?"

Heat rose to my face. No, I wouldn't have. Because unlike my outrider friends, I could always trust Jylla to be ruthlessly practical. "Jylla never lets her feelings get in the way of a job," I mumbled.

Cara snorted. "Because she doesn't have any, no doubt."

"I didn't say it was a good thing." I picked at the linen sheet rucked around my waist. "If you knew what I intended, even if you didn't try and stop me...I thought it'd cause you pain. I wanted to spare you that."

She settled on the bed. "Trust me, the truth hurts less," she said quietly. "If you'd died..." she rested her forehead against mine, and I heard her breath catch. "I'd have preferred to have said a proper goodbye."

"Me, too," I admitted, and kissed her, slow and sweet.

The door swung open. Cara sprang to her feet. I slouched back, glaring. Trust the Alathians to interrupt *now*.

A skinny, hook-nosed man dressed in a starched brown uniform marched in, carrying a metal rack rattling with glass vials. Behind him, I caught a glimpse of men in the gray and brown of soldiers, bracketing the door.

"I'm pleased to see you've woken at last," the hook-nosed man said. He set the rack down on a side table. I eyed the vials, which contained a veritable rainbow of colored liquids. Did the Alathians mean to drug me before layering me in truth spells?

"Who're you?" I asked warily.

"Third Healer Pevennar." He laid a hand on my forehead, ignoring my involuntary flinch. "Fever's gone, I see. How are you feeling?"

"How do you think I'm feeling?" I snapped. "I'm sore, tired, starving, and under arrest." Cara hadn't said as much, but the guards on the door only confirmed what I'd suspected. Kiran wasn't the only one in trouble with the Council.

Pevennar didn't even blink. "The soreness is to be expected. The charm you used modified your bodily humors in a way that resulted in quite a buildup of harmful toxins. Though the levels have reduced, it'll take some days yet before we fully clear your system." He lifted my eyelid with a thumb and peered at my eye. "I'll have some food brought up, though I warn you, it'll be nice and bland. None of your Arkennlander spices to shock the system."

I produced a bright, false smile. "Wouldn't want to upset the condemned prisoner's stomach."

"That's right," a new voice said. "You know how we mages are. So picky about having clean floors." A dark-haired man in a mage's uniform leaned against the doorframe. His round, smiling face made him look more like a shopkeeper than a mage, and he spoke in a cheerful drawling style notably different than the usual clipped Alathian accent. He straightened and bowed to me from the waist in the Alathian style. "Captain Martennan, Seventh Watch, at your service."

My nerves frayed further, but for once I managed to hold my tongue. Pevennar continued his examination, poking and prodding me with dispassionate efficiency. I gritted my teeth and tried not to swat his hands away.

Martennan bowed to Cara. "How lovely to see you again, Cara. I trust you have no cause for complaint, now?"

Cara's back was straight and her blue eyes cool. "Thank you for allowing me to see him."

Martennan waved a dismissive hand and dropped into the chair by the window. "Dev, I'm sure Cara has made you aware of the situation." His cheerful face remained easy and open, but the calculating intelligence lurking in his eyes raised all my hackles.

"You mean the Council hearing," I said flatly.

"Exactly." He leaned forward in the chair, his expression earnest. "You realize your friend Kiran is in a lot of trouble."

"Isn't he always," I muttered. Pevennar chose that moment to jab me in the arm with a copper needle long as a piton. I yelped and jerked away. "What was that for?"

Pevennar carried his blood-smeared needle over to the rack of vials on the table. "I need to assess the remaining level of toxins in your blood." He slid the needle into an empty vial and plinked in several drops of a dark liquid.

I rubbed my stinging arm. "Khalmet's bony hand. And you people think blood mages are bad."

"You'll have to admit there's a slight difference between Pevennar and a blood mage," said Martennan, with an amused lift of a brow. "In any case, back to your friend. Now that you are awake, the hearing will take place tomorrow. You should be aware that your case will be considered along with his."

"My case?" My stomach sank. If they'd learned how long and how often I'd been smuggling illegal goods across their borders, I was in for near as bad a time as Kiran.

"In the course of our investigation, we learned you were the one to originally bring Kiran into Alathia," Martennan said. "You'll have to explain this to the Council, and they will decide the severity of the offense." He leaned back in the chair, his eyes holding mine. "I suggest caution in your answers. Pevennar told us you remain weak and easily overtaxed."

I knew what Martennan meant. The Alathian spell would force me to tell the truth, but only in answer to the specific question asked, and if I played up my weakness, they might not question me as long. But why bother warning me?

No sign of his thoughts showed. His round face was all smiling benevolence again as he stood and bowed.

"I leave you in Pevennar's capable hands," he announced, and exited.

Cara and I exchanged a look, but didn't speak. Eventually Pevennar finished puttering around with his vials and left, after a parting admonition that I needed to get plenty of rest. I rolled my eyes as the door shut behind him. Rest? Yeah, right. Not when I might spend the rest of my days stuck deep in some mine. Or dead, if the Council was in an unforgiving mood.

"What do you make of that?" I asked Cara.

"Martennan?" She looked thoughtful. "He's pretty relaxed for an Alathian. They'd spent three days stonewalling me about seeing you, and then he showed up and gave me access right away. Maybe he can help you with the Council."

"I don't trust him."

"He hasn't asked you to," Cara pointed out.

"He will. I know his kind. He wants something, I'm sure of it." I'd known men like him in Ninavel. The casual cheer, the friendly smiles…all an act meant to manipulate a useful mark. The minute their game was done, they'd cast you into a viper pit without a backward glance.

"So? If it means he helps you, then good." She leaned in and whispered, "Four guards outside your door, and they keep a mage lurking around, too."

I was in no condition for any daring escape attempts, either. Khalmet's hand, I could barely sit up unaided. Cara was right. If Martennan had some game in mind, I had little choice but to play.

❋

It wasn't Martennan who showed up the next morning to collect me for the hearing, but his first lieutenant, a young mage named Lena. In truth, she'd given her name as an impossibly long mouthful. Alathians in Tamanath held to a bizarre custom of only using formal family names in public, like their first names were some Council secret. She wouldn't tell me her first name, but after listening to me stumble over her full family name a couple times, she shook her head and told me to call her by the short form. Lena wore her dark hair in a tight crown of braids, and her skin was nearly as brown as an Arkennlander's, with an incongruous smattering of dark freckles. She carried herself with a rigid precision that matched my expectations of an Alathian mage, as opposed to Martennan's casual slouch.

Pevennar wanted them to haul me to the hearing in some kind of glorified stretcher, but I insisted on walking, hoping to loosen frighteningly stiff muscles. Lena was surprisingly patient, adjusting her pace to my slow shuffle and making no comment when I stopped to rest, which I did often.

A matched pair of soldiers tromped along with us, to my combined annoyance and amusement. Here I was, barely able to stagger ten steps without stopping, and they treated me like I might singlehandedly overpower Lena and vanish through their border.

If only. I slowed to a crawl once I made it outside, turning my face up to the sun. The warmth did little to ease the queasiness of my stomach. They hadn't let Cara come with me. Lena told me the Council didn't need any further testimony from her. She'd said I'd see Cara again, regardless of the hearing's outcome, but I wasn't sure I believed her.

Not much I could do about it, between her magic and those damn guards.

Behind me, Lena gave a small, polite cough. I sighed and let the soldiers help me into the waiting carriage.

The building I'd just exited was a gray, forbidding bulk. Pevennar had told me it functioned as both a hospital and a teaching facility for Alathian healers. An inscription was carved in stern-looking block letters in the stones above the door.

"What does that say?" I asked Lena, pointing.

"It's a quote from Denarell of Parthus."

Lena must've seen from my face I'd never heard of the guy. "He was the leader of the expedition that founded Alathia. It's in his native language. He was originally from Harsia, over the eastern sea." She looked thoughtful. "The closest translation is probably 'To heal is to add to the world's harmony.'"

As the carriage pulled away, I couldn't keep myself from a small snort. How very Alathian—pompous and flowery all at the same time.

"You don't think much of us, do you?" Lena didn't sound angry, only curious.

I shrugged, watching the city street outside the carriage window. I had to admit that Tamanath was a lot nicer than Kost. The buildings were still mostly squat and wooden, but they were painted in neat shades of white and had beautifully carved balconies full of colorful flowerboxes. The streets were wider, too, and graceful trees and flowering bushes had been planted at intervals along the way. No fog, no woodsmoke, and the rolling hills of central Alathia formed a soft green backdrop under the distant shining peaks of the Whitefires.

Lena was still watching me steadily. "You prefer Lord Sechaveh's credo, that profit and power are all? You'd rather be in Ninavel, where a man like Ruslan Khaveirin can walk the streets with impunity, doing whatever he pleases?"

True enough that I'd cursed Sechaveh's name over that. Yet even so...I looked out the window again. The passers-by wore formal clothing in dull shades of gray and brown, and when they spoke to each other, their faces remained composed and calm. Nobody burst into laughter or gestured emphatically the way they might in similar gatherings in Ninavel. Tamanath had no street performers, no catcalls from vendor stalls. Homesickness twisted deep within me.

"You Alathians try to make everything safe, and tame," I said to Lena. "Some of us prefer things wild." I thought of the stark beauty of the high mountains. Dangerous and unforgiving, yeah, but that was part of their glory.

The carriage pulled to a stop beside another imposing building. No inscriptions marked the gray stone, but an enormous statue of a man with deepset eyes and broad shoulders dominated the courtyard. His face was carved in the serious expression so common to Alathians, his posture commanding. In one hand he held a set of scrolls, and in the other, a complicated looking mechanical device I'd never seen before.

"Let me guess," I said dryly to Lena. "Denarell of Parthus."

She nodded, a hint of a smile ghosting about her mouth. She opened the carriage door, and a lot of saluting and crisp orders followed. I slouched back in my seat. I was in no hurry to enter.

All too soon, they escorted me across the stone courtyard and through a massive set of carved wooden doors. We passed through a series of small chambers filled with Alathian soldiers, and then through another set of carved doors that opened on a broad circular chamber with an impossibly high ceiling. Five levels of galleries rose upward in stacked circles along the wall, full of seated men and women in the blue and gray uniforms of mages.

"Khalmet's hand!" I craned my neck upward. "I didn't know you Alathians had so many mages."

"This is almost all of us," Lena said. "Six of the seven Watches, and all the trainees."

By my guess, more than a hundred people stood up there. The weight of all those Alathian gazes made my skin itch. "But if you've this many mages just in the military—"

"In Alathia, all mages are in the military," Lena said, a faint note of surprise in her voice.

Kiran had said the Council kept mages leashed tight, but I'd not realized that included forced military enlistment. Any poor bastard who dared to want something different got mind-burned, no doubt.

Lena led me across the floor toward a great stone table in the shape of a half-circle, raised just off the floor level. Thirteen men and women sat behind the table, two wearing the blue and gray of mages, three more in the brown and gray of ordinary military, and the rest in red and gray. Some looked stern, others inscrutable.

Lena stopped some twenty feet from the table and bowed with careful precision. "The Arkennlander Devan *na soliin*, present for testimony." Her crisp voice echoed upward through the galleries.

A bald-headed councilor in red and gray inclined his head to her. "Thank you, Watch officer." He glanced at one of the mages. "Councilor Varellian, are you ready to begin?"

Varellian gave a short nod. She was one of the stern-faced ones, her black hair streaked with gray and the olive skin of her brow etched with deep lines. I wondered how old she was. In Ninavel, I'd never seen a mage with gray hair.

A circular pattern of silver and black sigils marked the floor under my feet. Lena positioned me smack in the center. The sigils began to glow, dimly. I started sweating.

"Is your name Devan *na soliin*?" Varellian's brown eyes bored into mine. The mages in the galleries above had gone silent.

"Not really. Just Devan. Or Dev. Only time I use the suffix is when I pass the Kost gate." Gods. This was more subtle than the heavy pressure I'd felt from Simon. Once I opened my mouth, I couldn't stop talking.

"What is your trade?"

"Outrider," I said, shortly. Other answers crowded my tongue. I fought to keep them in. Yet the moment I took a breath, I blurted, "Courier. Smuggler. Former Tainter." I glanced away from Varellian, and spotted Martennan up on the third gallery level, leaning on the rail with his round face set in serious lines.

"Did you illegally transport the blood mage Kiran ai Ruslanov across the border into Kost?"

Oh, fuck, here it was. "Yes." This time I didn't try to stop. "But he doesn't want to be a blood mage. This was the only place he could think of to escape his master. He won't do blood magic here, he'll abide by every one of your stupid rules—"

"Enough," Varellian said, and my mouth snapped shut. She went on, asking questions about Kiran, Simon, and Ruslan, teasing out the entire tale. Every chance I got, I let myself babble on about what bastards Simon and Ruslan were, how terribly they'd treated Kiran, and how desperate he'd been to escape them both.

I gladly told her all about Simon's intent to take down Sechaveh, pointed out a blood mage ruling the Ninavel would've made for a nasty neighbor, and emphasized how hard we'd all tried to stop him. Damn her eyes, Varellian's face stayed hard and cold as an icefield in winter. She seemed most interested in Simon's border charm. She made me recite every detail of both times I'd seen it used, twice over. Her disappointment when I couldn't tell her more was clear.

When she'd squeezed that topic dry, she turned her attention to the subject of Kiran. She asked me question after question about his uses of magic, and the fight I'd seen between Kiran and Ruslan. When I told her how Mikail had given me the Taint charm, her lips pressed into a bloodless line, and several of the others exchanged meaningful looks. No question they didn't like it. Maybe they wished Ruslan had won the fight, so they wouldn't have to concern themselves with Kiran. Anger throbbed in my gut, but I kept it from my voice.

I didn't have to fake exhaustion by the time she finally stopped. My mouth was parched and my legs trembled. Varellian glanced at the other councilors.

"Are there any other questions for the witness?"

A white-haired man in red and gray leaned forward. "Do you believe Kiran ai Ruslanov is a threat to Alathia?"

I snorted. "No." The very thought seemed ludicrous. Kiran only wanted to be safe.

Mikail's voice spoke in my memory: *He's more like Ruslan than you realize.* Once again I saw Kiran standing in the meadow with his face twisted in defiant anger, energy flaring wild all around him, and recalled the naked yearning in his eyes when he'd talked of magic.

Before my traitorous mouth could add anything else, the man spoke again. "What of Ruslan Khaveirin? Is he a threat to this country?"

"Hell, yes." The cheated fury on Ruslan's face when the border snapped shut flashed into my head. "If I were you, I'd watch your backs," I told the Council. And then hastily added, "If you kill Kiran...trust me, he'll stop at nothing to destroy you for it." A truth I was dead certain of, remembering that bizarre tenderness of Ruslan's in the cave. Thanks to Tavian, I could guess Ruslan's mind. Nobody got to hurt Kiran but Ruslan, the sick bastard.

The white-haired guy sat back again, a glimmer of satisfaction in his gray eyes. "I have no further questions."

Another councilor in red and gray stood, this one a spindly, sour-faced man with a shock of auburn hair. He peered down his long nose at me like I was a roach he'd prefer to crush. "This isn't the first time you've broken our laws with blatant disregard for the harm you cause our citizenry. How long have you smuggled deadly magical weaponry into our cities?"

"Weaponry? For Khalmet's sake, I've only brought charms and wards!" I gladly let startled outrage take my tongue before I could blurt out the true answer to his question.

"Tell me the peaceful use for a charm like the one found on you at the time of your arrest, that splinters bone to razor-edged fragments."

I matched his glare. "A man travels in the wild, he needs protection. Charms do the trick easier than crossbows or hackbuts, with a lot less weight to carry."

He smiled unpleasantly. "Protection—a weapon, in other words. But again, I ask: how long?"

I struggled against the insidious pressure within, and lost.

"Four years."

A murmur passed through the galleries above, like wind through pines. The sour-faced man turned to address the other councilors. "Years, he says! I tell you, if we remain lax in our response to lawbreakers, we'll never halt this illegal trade! We must make an example of him to deter others. A public execution by fire at the gate would—"

The original bald-headed councilor rapped a fist on the table. "Enough, Niskenntal," he said, his voice sharp. "Save your rhetoric for our deliberations. Have you any further questions for the witness?"

"I have all I need." Niskenntal sat, not without throwing a final contemptuous glance my way.

Cold sweat soaked my sides. Execution by fire…gods. I opened my mouth to protest, but Varellian spread her fingers and magic closed my throat.

"The testimony is concluded," she said, and nodded to Lena.

Lena drew me away, toward a wooden bench at the outer edge of the floor. I stumbled and nearly fell, my legs leaden weights, but she caught my arm and unobtrusively took some of my weight.

"Bring in the prisoner," the bald-headed councilor said. A deep hush descended over the galleries, mages leaning over the rails. Many of their faces showed the eager, fearful fascination I'd seen once on men crowding around a caged direwolf. My stomach lurched. If they wanted to burn alive a simple courier like me, what might they do to Kiran?

On the far side of the sigil-marked floor, a side door opened. Kiran walked through, surrounded by four mages whose eyes never left him. His head was down, and his shoulders hunched. A length of scaly-looking black cord bound his hands in front of him, and he wore a shapeless gray tunic and pants. He didn't look hurt, thank Khalmet. I tried to catch his eye, but his head stayed bowed as his guards led him to the center of the sigils.

The four mages positioned themselves at the ends of a four-pointed star incised in the floor. They faced Kiran and extended their palms towards each other. The sigils inside the star glowed, much more brightly than for me.

"Kiran ai Ruslanov, you are here to answer to the crimes of blood magic and border violation," Varellian said, her voice stern.

Kiran raised his head, then. "Don't call me that," he said. A hint of anger lurked in his voice, but his pale face looked only weary. "I'm not Ruslan's."

"Do you deny you are his mark-bound apprentice?" Varellian said, coldly.

Kiran's shoulders hunched even higher. He looked down again, shaking his head.

Shaikar take him, wasn't he even going to try and defend himself? I tried to speak, but Varellian's spell still locked my throat. Lena gripped my wrist in warning. I glowered at her, but thought better of trying anything more dramatic.

"We have heard testimony from several witnesses that confirm your guilt in both crimes," Varellian said to Kiran. "Our law demands we now give you the chance to answer for yourself, but you are a blood mage and we cannot trust to a truth spell."

"I will tell you the truth," Kiran said dully.

Varellian shook her head. "The only way we can know for certain is if you willingly allow us within your mind."

Kiran's whole body tensed. The four mages surrounding him stiffened, and the glow of the sigils edged brighter.

I winced in sympathy. The last thing I'd want was for Alathians like Niskenntal to paw around in my head.

"And if I refuse?" Kiran asked.

"Then you will be sentenced to death, without recourse."

Kiran looked around the Council table, a little wildly. "You...you ask for me to submit wholly to you? As Simon wanted?"

I hadn't asked him what he'd endured in Simon's hands. I thought of Simon's sharp, cruel smile, and my skin crawled.

"We are not blood mages, to abuse our power by enslaving others," Varellian said. "We do this only for the purpose of seeking truth."

For the first time, Kiran glanced over at me. One quick, unreadable look, and then he faced Varellian again. "I'll do it."

I wasn't sure whether to be relieved or dismayed. Surely if they read his thoughts they'd see how badly he wanted to reject blood magic. But I feared they'd dismiss that if they saw how much he'd loved it. *Glorious*, he'd said.

Varellian's face didn't change at Kiran's agreement, but Niskenntal's eyes narrowed, while several others looked surprised. A councilor in brown and gray said something to her neighbor in a low voice. Then they stood, and all but the two mages began filing out. Lena tugged me to my feet.

The pressure on my throat vanished as I stood. "What's going on?" I asked Lena.

"Everyone without mage talent must clear the room." Lena pulled me firmly toward the door.

"What about you? You're a mage, right?"

"My ranking is only third level," she said. "They'll use only the strongest of us for this."

Kiran looked awfully small and alone where he stood in the center of the chamber.

"They're not going to hurt him, are they?"

"No," Lena said. But her eyes shifted aside from mine, and I knew she lied.

CHAPTER TWENTY-FOUR

(Kiran)

Kiran's heart jolted as the chamber doors boomed shut. Sweat laced his palms. He had never dropped all his mental defenses before. The Alathians would gain access to his innermost self. They could destroy his will the way Simon had intended, leaving him utterly unable to form a thought on his own, as placidly obedient as a sheep.

But at least they wouldn't use him to channel spells that would bring death to innocents. Mindburning might be as good a punishment as any for the agonies Alisa had endured, and the lives he'd stolen at the convoy.

He braced for a mage to approach him, memories of Simon and his silver knife churning in his head. Instead, Varellian and the other mage councilor stopped just beyond the four mages already surrounding him. Up in the galleries, some twenty mages remained, evenly spaced around the rails.

"Do not speak," Varellian said. "When the ritual begins, drop your barriers."

Kiran glanced around, confused. No channel lines marked the

floor. Without them, surely the Alathians would need blood or physical contact to work the spell?

A low-voiced, droning chant started up in the galleries. It began simply, in unison, but soon voices diverged, following ever more complex tonal patterns. All around Kiran's feet, sigils lit with a soft, ethereal glow far different than the harsh fire of activated channel lines.

Gradually, so gradually that at first he thought he imagined it, power rose to coil around him. The song above continued, wordless but compelling.

Realization dawned. The Alathians were patterning the spell with sound rather than channel lines. Instead of earth power, the Alathians used their own *ikilhia*, each person contributing a small piece harmonized precisely to all the others. The technique was brilliant, yet he couldn't fathom how so many mages could mesh so well and deeply with each other. It had taken him years to learn to join minds properly with only one other at a time.

Magic pressed softly but insistently against Kiran's barriers. He came to himself with a start, fear burying curiosity. Every instinct screamed danger. He gathered his courage and dropped his barriers, one by one.

The Alathians flooded in. They swept through his memories, searching, digging. Flashes overwhelmed him: Ruslan, furious at the border; Dev, blood on his mouth as he grinned; Simon, mocking him as he lay helpless; Pello's sharp, cold eyes as Kiran ate the drugged food; Lizaveta pressing their cut hands together; Mikail, shouting at him as Kiran turned his face to the wall; Alisa, love shining in her eyes, her mouth so sweet and tender on his.

He struggled, drowning, but the Alathians forged on, further back: Ruslan, stroking a hand through Kiran's hair in casual affection as he traced out a pattern; Mikail, grinning at him in excitement when they cast their first seventh-level spell; Lizaveta, cuddling him in her lap. They went all the way back to his first memory, of Ruslan kneeling before him, his hands on Kiran's small shoulders, telling him he was a very lucky boy and would be part of Ruslan's family now.

The Alathians tried to go further still, only to come up against the wall that had long blocked Kiran from any earlier memories. They fought to breach it, pushing until he cried out in pain, but the wall held firm. At last they retreated and he thought the ordeal would be over—until their magic swelled, forcing its way deep within to build a solid, shining cage around the fire of his *ikilhia*.

He fought in earnest then, unable to help himself, tearing at the barrier. But his effort came too late to prevent their casting. The cage shrank in on itself, inexorably crushing his *ikilhia* into an ever-tighter knot. He gasped for air that would not come, waves of fiery agony pulsing through him. His last thought as his resistance failed was of Alisa, straddling the guardwall of the Alton Tower with her arms spread wide to the setting sun, her eyes shut and her voice lifted in a chanted lament as the winter wind tore at her hair.

✳

(Dev)

"What's the gods-damned Council doing now?" I demanded of Lena for the tenth time. Stuck in a locked room with nothing to stare at but gray stone, two ancient wooden chairs, and Lena's solemn face, my nerves buzzed like a swarm of angry stinkwasps.

Lena gave a faint, put-upon sigh. "I told you, the ritual takes time. Our magic is different from what you see in Ninavel. Less showy and more subtle."

"You mean, slow as a hamstrung dune tortoise," I muttered. Simon had only needed minutes with Pello to search his mind. Then again, apparently he hadn't done such a great job. But either the Council was examining every one of Kiran's memories ten times over...or their spellwork held a darker purpose, for all Lena's insistence otherwise.

Damn it, I couldn't even pace to pass the time. After I'd tried that and nearly fallen flat on my face, Lena had pressed me into a chair and ordered me to stay there. Every time I so much as twitched a foot, her dark eyes narrowed in warning.

She stood with her back so straight it pained mine to look at it.

I slouched further in the rickety chair. The harsh zeal in Niskenntal's eyes when he'd talked of burning me to death haunted me.

"You know the Council," I said to Lena. "How many of them think like Niskenntal?"

Lena's brows drew together. "Not all. And Captain Martennan intends to testify that without you sending Cara to us, we'd never have learned of the weakness in our wards that let a blood mage breach them."

Not all—a far cry from the "none" I'd hoped to hear. I fought off images of hungry flames. Martennan's interest signaled I had a chance for leverage, if only I could find it.

"What's Martennan's game in this?"

"What do you mean?"

"He's being awfully helpful to a pair of accused criminals."

"He's a good man." She spoke the words as if she truly meant them.

"Yeah, right." Clever, maybe. But good? Cara had learned from a guard that the seven Watch captains were second only in power and influence to the two mages on the Council. Good men didn't rise so high.

"You truly don't trust anyone, do you?" Pity tinged her voice. My back went nearly as rigid as hers.

"Of course I do," I snapped. "But first, I wait until they've earned it, and second, I always listen to my instincts. Right now, my instincts say Martennan has something to gain from this."

Lena folded her arms. "You're not entirely wrong." She hesitated. "I don't suppose you know much about our politics…"

No, I didn't. Not that I'd admit it. But I'd never cared how the Alathians ran anything other than their border gates. I'd always spent as little time in Alathia as possible, only long enough to deliver goods to Gerran, resupply, and head back out to the Whitefires.

"Captain Martennan and some of the other Watch officers believe the Council is too restrictive on the types of magic we are allowed to perform." She paused again. "He hasn't said so directly, but I believe he hopes these events will force the Council to re-examine their policies."

"He wants to do blood magic?" I said, taken aback.

"Of course not." Distaste darkened Lena's eyes. "But there are other types of spells…he thinks we might advance our own methods, if we didn't automatically reject everything else."

Other types of spells, sure. I figured Martennan wanted the threat of Ruslan as the stick to convince the Council to lift restrictions—no doubt he'd claim he needed more powerful spells for defense—and he wanted Kiran captive rather than executed, so he might pick Kiran's brain for useful knowledge of forbidden magic. Good guy, my ass. But as Cara had so rightly said, I'd take his help now and worry about his motives later, if it meant he saved Kiran's life.

Only problem was, I didn't see why in Shaikar's hells he should save mine.

The door creaked as someone unbarred it on the other side. I leapt to my feet, ignoring Lena's belated grab for my arm.

Martennan herded Kiran through. Kiran looked awful, his blue eyes dark and sweat drying on his skin, but he gave me a wan smile. "Dev. They told me they'd healed you, but I wasn't certain I believed it until I saw you in the Council chamber." His smile faltered, as he peered more closely at me. "You truly are healed?"

"Yeah. Just a little sore and tired." My worry sharpened as Martennan steered him to the second chair. I'd seen that white, set look to Kiran's face before, when he'd endured the pain of his shattered arm. "You look like shit, though. What'd they do to you?"

Kiran sat with obvious relief. He shrugged, his eyes downcast. "The Council bound my magic, that's all. I'll be fine."

A lie, if I'd ever heard one. "Simon bound your magic, but in that cave you didn't look like a man with half his ribs broken."

"I regret to say we haven't a blood mage's finesse with mental bindings. We don't cast such spells often here." Martennan looked down at Kiran, all soft sympathy. "The worst of the pain should fade with time, but I'm afraid a certain level of discomfort will remain as long as the binding is in place."

I opened my mouth, outraged, but Kiran spoke first. "I don't mind." He held my gaze, his own full of conviction. "I'd endure a thousand times worse if it kept me free of Ruslan."

"Let's hope you don't have to," I muttered.

"Believe me, that binding was effort enough." Martennan passed his hands over his face and eyed Kiran with bemused admiration. "It's a shame you weren't born in Alathia. If any of our trainees had half your strength, I'd be a lot less worried about our defenses."

Kiran didn't say anything. I aimed a dark look at Martennen. "What happens now?"

"Now, you wait," Martennan said. "If I know the Council, they'll be up arguing all night, and they'll call in the Watch captains for further discussion before they make a final decision." He put a hand on Kiran's shoulder. "Rest assured, Kiran, now I've seen your memories I'll argue all the more strongly you shouldn't be handed over to Ruslan."

Kiran's head jerked up. "Handed over—? I thought I faced execution, but that—please, you can't—"

My own voice was near loud as his. "You Alathians say you'll kill anyone who helps a blood mage, and yet you'd give Ruslan exactly what he most wants?" Gods, I'd never thought the Council so craven as to simply toss Kiran back to Ruslan.

Martennan spread his hands. "I don't think it a likely outcome. Many on the Council would balk at giving in to a foreign mage's demands. Yet none can deny Ruslan poses a significant threat, and we don't yet understand the flaw in our wards that allowed Simon Levanian to cross our border—"

"I can help you understand," Kiran said in a rush. "Simon created his charm with blood magic. From what I've seen, your methods are completely different—you'll find it a difficult task to unravel his spellwork. But I can do it. Even with my power bound as you have done, I can still read a charm. I'd need time to analyze a pattern so complex—but surely far less time than one of your own mages."

Martennan's eyes gleamed. "An excellent point, Kiran. I'll certainly tell the Council of your offer."

I swallowed sharp words, suddenly sure that Martennan had brought up the specter of Ruslan to provoke exactly this reaction in Kiran. But damn it, Kiran's survival still mattered more than Martennan's methods.

"I do have one condition," Kiran said, with quiet intensity. "Tell the Council I'll only help if they spare Dev's life as well as mine."

I threw Kiran a surprised, grateful glance. For all Martennan's cunning, I wasn't so sure the Council would buy into Kiran's offer—but gods, if it worked...a thread of hope crept through me.

Martennan looked more pleased than ever. "Your loyalty does you credit, Kiran," he said, his voice warm. "And your ordeal today has one happy outcome. Now that your power is bound, we no longer need to hold you in an active sigil circle, though you'll remain under guard by mages of the Watch. I've arranged for you to spend the night in far more comfortable quarters."

He turned to me. "Dev, Pevennar says he's willing to release you from the Sanitorium, as long as you return for a final examination first, and we ensure you keep taking his potions. That means you and your friend Cara can stay with Kiran tonight, if you'd like."

I'd drink a thousand of Pevennar's vile potions if I got to stay with Cara and Kiran instead of in that depressing gray building where anxious healers poked and prodded me every hour.

"How long until we learn the Council's ruling?" I asked Martennan. I didn't intend to count on the Council's forgiveness, but I needed time to think. Even if somehow I got us free of Martennan's mage guards, where could we go? Ruslan lurked beyond the border, and Martennan would hunt us down with ease if we stayed in Alathia.

"The Council will declare their judgment tomorrow at dawn," Martennan said. "Try not to think about it now," he added, gently.

Kiran gave a disbelieving, brittle laugh. I silently agreed with him. This'd be one hell of a long night.

✳

Martennan's comfortable quarters turned out to be a small but lavishly appointed house some five minutes' ride from the Council building. The last time I'd seen a house so highside, I'd been there to steal, not stay. Lena explained the Council had built the house for visiting diplomats. At first I couldn't figure why they'd stashed us in such luxury, criminals that we were. But despite all the talk of Kiran's magic being bound, the guard mages eyed him with the wary tension of men circling a rabid sandcat; and if you looked close in that pretty little house, behind all the silken hangings and ornate oil lamps lurked the most powerful wards I'd yet seen in Alathia. They must think it the safest prison they had on short notice.

Cara had met me at the Sanitorium with one of her crushingly strong hugs. I hadn't protested, only buried my head in her shoulder and breathed in the leather and jahla-soap scent of her skin. I'd told her of the hearing with occasional breaks for cursing whenever Pevennar jabbed me with his gods-damned needles. Cara gladly rode with me and Lena to the guest quarters, and gave Kiran a bone-breaking hug of his own the minute she laid eyes on him. The half-shocked, half-pleased look on his face set us both chuckling, though our laughter faded fast under the cold gaze of his guard mages.

Later, Kiran stuttered out a low-voiced, painful apology to Cara for the dead men at the convoy. She listened gravely, arms folded. What she said in reply was too soft for me to hear, but he squared his shoulders, a little of the strain easing in his face.

They brought us a simple meal of sliced meats and spice bread that none of us more than picked at. Cara did her best to distract with a host of outrageous climbing tales, both her own and some she'd heard from her father. Lena listened with solemn interest, but Kiran was silent, and I couldn't manage even a single grin. My thoughts never strayed far from the mages and the wards. I'd seen no opportunity for escape. I hadn't so much as a single charm, my body felt weak as a soaked reed, and the moment I got within a body length of walls or windows, a mage politely but firmly blocked my path.

It got late, and then very late. Kiran and I sat before a stone fireplace in the opulent main room, staring at flames crackling over pine logs. The fire's warmth eased the deep ache that lingered in my muscles, though it did nothing to thaw the icy knot in my stomach. Cara lay curled on a low couch in the corner, the occasional soft snore escaping her. Lena had left when the guard mages changed shift. The new guards were at least kind enough to sit on the far side of the room, giving us the illusion of privacy.

"Cara talked to me," Kiran said. It was the first time he'd spoken in hours.

I turned to him, glad of the distraction. My head pounded from puzzling over one futile plan after another. "And?"

He sat curled in a tight ball. Red firelight reflected in his eyes and cast shadows beneath his cheekbones. "She told me about Sethan, and his daughter."

I glanced at the two mages sitting silently by the door, and narrowed my eyes at Kiran. Before the hearing, Cara had half-convinced me I ought to explain the whole mess with Melly, play on the Council's sympathies…but my first glimpse of those cold, stern faces had changed my mind. Varellian and her ilk wouldn't soften out of sentiment, and every instinct screamed at me not to give my heart into an enemy's hand. I'd thought to tell the Council of Jylla's betrayal, to explain why I'd taken Bren's job—but in the end, they hadn't even asked my reasons.

Kiran sighed, his own eyes flicking to the mages and back to mine. "I wanted you to know that I understood…and that I know what you did for me. You tried to rescue me from Simon, and you saved me from Ruslan. Twice. You risked your life, and almost died. Even if…if things go badly tomorrow…please know I'm grateful beyond words. And if the Council spares us—" he straightened, his face earnest. "I can never repay you—I owe you too much—but should you ever need my help, you'll have it."

I shrugged, embarassed. "You don't owe me anything. I knew Gerran meant to sell you out, and I said nothing. If I'd warned you, there'd have been no need for any rescues."

"You had no reason to put my welfare ahead of your loyalty to Sethan. Especially after I'd lied to you, and brought death to your friends." Kiran's gaze fell, his arms tightening around his knees.

I winced to hear the echo of my own weaselly rationalizations in his mouth. "Keeping silent wasn't right, and I'm sorry for it."

Kiran gave me a sidelong, surprised look. "But—if you'd warned me, then what of your obligation to Sethan?" His voice lowered to a bare whisper. "At least this way Cara can keep your promise for you, regardless of what happens to us."

All evening, I'd clung desperately to the hope of Cara taking my stash of gems and coin to Ninavel to save Melly. Yet shame still sickened me at the thought of how I'd earned that pay.

"I should've found a better way," I told Kiran. "One that didn't mean fucking you over."

"A better way…I wish I'd found one, as well. A way to escape Ruslan without anyone dying." Kiran dropped his head to his knees. His next words came out muffled and rough. "I regret—so many things. What do you do, when a mistake cannot be undone?"

I stared into the fire, thinking of my blind idiocy in trusting Jylla, and the terrible moment when I'd realized Melly would be the one to suffer for it. At length I said heavily, "You make amends where you can. And if you can't…well. You keep going, and try not to make the same mistake twice."

Kiran was silent for a time. "Does the pain of it ever lessen?"

"Not quickly." The slightest thought of Jylla still cut deep enough to stop my breath. And yet…my gaze settled on Cara's sleeping form. Her steadfast partnership against Simon…the joy we'd shared in our night on the furs…her forthright concern, when I'd woken in Alathia…with those memories shining in my head, Jylla's name no longer triggered the same depth of bitter, impotent fury.

"Sometimes, other people help pain fade," I told Kiran. And prayed to Suliyya the Council would let him live long enough to experience the truth in my words.

✳

Martennan showed up just after dawn. I stood, my stomach churning, as voices echoed in the hall and the two mage guards snapped to attention. Cara scrambled off her couch, her hair fraying from her braid and her face set in tight lines. Kiran woke with a start from his uncomfortable huddle on one of the chairs. He looked as bleary-eyed as I felt. I hadn't slept at all.

Martennan entered, trailed by Lena and another mage, a lanky man with deep laugh lines bracketing his mouth. Dark circles shadowed Martennan's eyes, his greeting smile more weary than cheerful.

"The Council has declared their judgment. I think the result a good one, all things considered," he announced.

"Do you mean they won't give me over to Ruslan?" Kiran asked, cautious hope dawning on his face. I waited, arms folded tight. Martennan's idea of a good result might not match mine.

Martennan's smile brightened. "Correct. Nor execute you, either. They've accepted your offer to help decipher Simon's charms."

Oh, thank Khalmet. I groped for a chair back as a millstone lifted from my shoulders. Cara slid a supportive arm around my waist. Kiran's mouth was open, his blue eyes wide with stunned relief.

Martennan said, "I must confess the victory was hard-won. Several councilors were quite concerned over the part of Dev's tale in which your mage-brother gave him the Taint charm that let you escape. They fear Ruslan may have arranged this entire series of events to entice us to accept you into Alathia, as part of some plot against us."

"If they think Ruslan was faking his hunt of us, they should've seen his face when Kiran made it through the border," I growled. I'd stake every kenet I owned that Kiran in Alathia was no part of Ruslan's plan.

Martennan held up his hands and chuckled. "Oh, I believe you! I was there, after all. Thanks to Kiran allowing us access to his memories, we mages argued the councilors' fear was almost certainly unfounded."

Kiran's quick, sharp glance at Martennan said he'd caught the qualifiers at the end of that sentence, same as I had.

Martennan's round face turned serious. "The Council agreed to forego execution, Kiran, but it's not all sweets and roses. They don't trust you, not one bit. You'll be kept under constant guard, and you're expected to work with our arcanists to analyze not only Simon's border charm, but others we found when we searched his house."

"I can do that." Kiran wore the look of a man who fears to wake from a dream.

Cara's arm tightened around my waist. "What about Dev?"

"Dev…the Council agreed to spare your life, as Kiran requested." But Martennan wasn't smiling, and the lanky mage behind him now stood like a man braced for a fight. Lena's eyes were fixed on the floor, her face clean of all expression.

"But," I said. My relief vanished, leaving a cold hole in my chest.

"I'd hoped the Council might be persuaded to merely fine you for your crimes, given your efforts to stop Simon Levanian…but I'm sorry to report the Council feels a fine isn't enough. In addition to confiscating your accounts at Haroman, Baltai, and Serover houses in Kost, they've sentenced you to ten years' forced labor in the Cheltman mines."

"What?" Kiran and Cara spoke in shocked chorus. I stood frozen, a black pit yawning within. Haroman, Baltai, and Serover were the houses I'd split my pay between when I moved it out of Bentgate. I'd been trying to hide the coin and gems from Pello, not the gods-damned Council, and I'd assumed Cara would take everything straight back to Ninavel.

Khalmet's hand, better if they'd killed me. Even if I escaped the mines, I'd never earn back that coin before Melly changed. To fail now, after I'd thought Melly's safety assured at last…despair threatened to swallow me.

"You can't do this!" Kiran darted an agonized glance at me. "Dev risked everything to stop Simon—and this is how you repay him for it?"

Cara's face was near as pale as Kiran's, her fists clenched like she meant to throw herself at Martennan, hell with his magic. She knew as well as I what this meant for Melly. I shifted, pressed her wrist. Violence did no good against mages, but during my sleepless night I'd thought up one more token to play. I locked eyes with Martennan.

"What if I were to help you stop the smuggling trade? You might've arrested Gerran already, but that won't stop his partner in Ninavel. But I know how Bren thinks, and I'll bet you every kenet the Council took that I can mark his couriers far better than any of your mages." I'd never be safe again in Ninavel once Bren found out I'd betrayed him so thoroughly, but I'd gain time to find another solution for Melly.

Martennan shook his head, regretfully. "I suggested as much to the Council, but they prefer to deal with the problem in their own way. Yet…" He turned to Kiran. "Kiran, several councilors told me if you showed us wholehearted assistance by deciphering Simon Levanian's spellwork before the turn of the year—the Council might agree to hear a plea on Dev's behalf."

I barked out a sharp, bitter laugh. Oh, I should've seen this coming, after Kiran had tied us so neatly together. "So, I'm both bait and hostage. Congratulate the Council for me, Martennan—that's a move worthy of a Ninavel ganglord."

The gentle sympathy on Martennan's face made me wish I still had my boneshatter charm. "The Council must be cautious when it comes to Alathia's safety," he said. "But I truly believe your situation can change, once immediate fears fade."

Kiran said, "I'd have given the Council my best effort anyway, out of gratitude for a life free from Ruslan. If there's anything else I might do to help Dev, you have but to ask."

I rounded on him. "Khalmet's bloodsoaked hand! Can't you see the Council won't ever let me go, so long as you roll over like that? They'll only make you empty promises, and ask for more, and more—"

"I give you my word as Watch captain that the Council keeps its promises," Martennan's casual air had disappeared, his shoulders squared and his voice full of authority. "When the time comes to approach the Council, Kiran, I'll help you seek Dev's release."

Gratitude brightened Kiran's eyes. I ground my teeth. I didn't buy Martennan's helpful act, not for an instant. He'd probably been the one to suggest the hostage idea to the Council in the first place.

I started to say as much, but Cara jabbed my side. "Leave it," she hissed in my ear, and faced Martennan. "When does Dev's sentence begin?"

Martennan sighed. "Now, I'm afraid." Behind him, the lanky mage drew out a thin gold torc. I tensed. The Council might forbid their citizens from deadly charms, but they didn't balk at using them on criminals. I'd heard tell of the snapthroat charms worn by men sentenced to forced labor. Once around my throat, the cursed thing would tighten to cut off my breath with a twitch of an overseer's finger. And given my status as the Council's leverage against Kiran, I didn't doubt I'd be watched closer than one of Sechaveh's famed cobalt diamonds.

Martennan beckoned the mage with the snapthroat charm. "Talmaddis will convey Dev to the mines. Cara, I'll escort you through the border at a spot of your choosing—it need not be at a border gate, if you fear Ruslan's attention—and we'll be happy to provide whatever supplies you require for mountain travel."

"Wait!" Cara shoved in front of me, glaring at the advancing Talmaddis. "Let me say goodbye to him first, can't you?"

"The Council ordered Dev collared without delay, but after, I'll gladly permit him a short span for farewells," Martennan said. "Though I fear we cannot give you privacy."

A short span. Better than none, but oh, gods…I breathed deep, seeking the calm clarity I used for climbs. Melly…there had to be some way left to save her. If I swallowed my distrust of Martennan, and begged him for help—no, damn it, I'd only give him another carrot to dangle.

Cara grudgingly gave way for Talmaddis. I refused to flinch from the cold sting of the torc as he locked it shut around my neck. He muttered a string of singsong gibberish, and tapped the torc. The metal warmed and contracted tight enough to wring a choked gasp from me.

"Hey!" Fury sparked in Cara's eyes. "Leave him be, you—"

"My apologies." Talmaddis flicked a ringed finger and the torc loosened again. "I had to test the spell." He backed to stand beside Martennan. Not far enough away, for my taste. My fingers itched to claw at the torc, as if that would get it off.

Kiran approached, pale as chalk. "Dev…" He swallowed, and spoke low but firm. "I know you think I'm a fool to believe the Council will hold to any bargains. Maybe I am. But I meant what I said last night. After what you've risked, and lost, all to help me—I swear to you, I'll find a way to gain your freedom."

An ember of warmth lessened the chill of the torc against my skin. Despite everything, despite the cost, I couldn't regret the choice to save him. And his mention of bargains had inspired one final glimmer of an idea for Melly.

"Don't think I'm not grateful that you'll try," I said. "Just…don't make any moves without thinking them through first. And watch who you trust, all right? Not all vipers show their fangs as readily as Ruslan." I gripped his shoulder and held his gaze. "You're not like him, you know. A man like you, I'm glad to call friend."

Kiran's eyes widened. A fleeting, shy smile touched his mouth, a hint of color returning to his face. "You were right, last night," he said quietly. "Sometimes people do help." He backed away, with a glance at Cara.

She threw her arms around me. "I won't wait on the Council to free you," she whispered.

Nerves set my heart racing. My plan for Melly depended on Cara—but mother of maidens, if she refused to listen…I kissed her hair, then her ear, and whispered, "No. Go to Ninavel. Find Pello and offer him the truth of Ruslan's game, in exchange for Melly's freedom." A thin hope, but the only one I had.

I felt her hesitation in her muscles. "Please, Cara. You've got to try—I can't bear this, else."

Her grip tightened, but she moved her head in a minuscule nod. Relief dizzied me. I relaxed into her hold and murmured, "Gods, I'll miss you. After Jylla—after all I've done—I hadn't thought to find someone I could trust without fear."

She drew back and took my face in her hands. "You're a better man than you realize, Dev. Sethan was right to put his faith in you. Whatever comes of this, never doubt he'd be proud of you. Suliyya knows I am."

My eyes grew hot. I traced the line of her cheek, my throat too tight for speech.

In answer, she kissed me. An ardent, fiery kiss that for a blessed interval swept all thought away. I lost myself in the sweet taste of her, the warmth of her lean body pressed against mine.

Martennan cleared his throat. Reluctantly, Cara released me.

"A proper goodbye this time, at least," I told her.

"That wasn't goodbye." Her blue eyes held a fierce promise. Behind her, Kiran inclined his head to me, solemn and resolute.

The sight of their determination steadied my feet as Talmaddis drew me away. *No matter how difficult the climb, a summit's never beyond reach so long as a man has partners he can depend on,* Sethan had once said. I meant to prove him right.

✳

ACKNOWLEDGEMENTS

Thanks to Jeanne Atwell, Michelle Leisy, and Dustin Putnam for convincing me to try NaNoWriMo with them in 2007. Without them, *The Whitefire Crossing* would have remained an idea floating around in my head and never made it to the page. And special thanks to Jeanne, who not only beta-read countless drafts of the novel, but patiently listened to all my freakouts and kept me sane (more or less!) throughout the journey to publication. I hope every writer has a friend so steadfastly supportive.

Of course getting words down on the page is only a start; then you have to make the story good. Heartfelt thanks to Susan Smith, who invited me to join her critique group at the Rocky Mountain Fiction Writers conference in 2008 and has been a wonderful friend ever since, and to Carol Berg, Curt Craddock, Catherine Montrose, Brian Tobias, Laurey Patten, and the late but not forgotten Glenn Lewis Gilette. Their insightful, expert critique helped me take *The Whitefire Crossing* from a raw mess of words to a fully realized novel, and I'm grateful beyond the telling for the support and advice they have so generously provided.

Thanks also to Jim Atwell, Catherine Boone, Tim Leisy, Minda Suchan, Matt Hilliard, and especially Chris Boone for beta-reading early drafts; to Teresa Frohock, who provided a fresh set of eyes on my first few chapters when I needed it most; and to Jason Hollinger, for his mad web skills, his eager enthusiasm to read more of the story, and for first introducing me to the joy of the mountains in our Caltech days.

I don't know what I'd do without my amazing agent, Becca Stumpf, who believed in me from our first meeting (even though *Whitefire* was far from ready!), and who has guided me through the wilds of publishing with patience and unflagging enthusiasm. And I'm indebted to my editor, Jeremy Lassen, for loving *The Whitefire Crossing* enough to buy it, and for helping me take the book to new heights. Thanks also to Ross Lockhart, Amy Popovich, Rebecca Silvers, Liz Upson, and the rest of the Night Shade crew for their hard work on the book; and to David Palumbo for his beautiful cover art.

Last but not least, my deepest thanks and love to my husband Robert. It's not an easy thing to be the spouse of a writer, especially while parenting a severely colicky baby. Thanks for hanging in there, and may we share many more mountain adventures together.

Night Shade Books Is an Independent Publisher of Quality Science-Fiction, Fantasy and Horror

WWW.NIGHTSHADEBOOKS.COM

$14.99

ISBN 978-1-59780-289-5

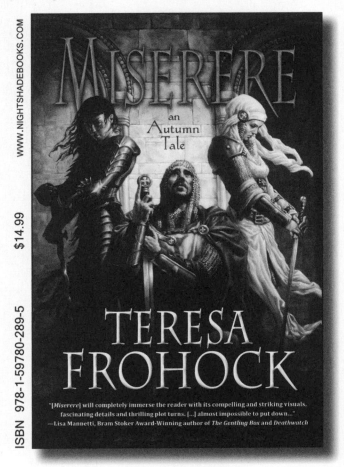

"[*Miserere*] will completely immerse the reader with its compelling and striking visuals, fascinating details and thrilling plot turns. [...] almost impossible to put down..."
—Lisa Mannetti, Bram Stoker Award-Winning author of *The Gentling Box* and *Deathwatch*

Exiled exorcist Lucian Negru deserted his lover in Hell in exchange for saving his sister Catarina's soul, but Catarina doesn't want salvation. She wants Lucian to help her fulfill her dark covenant with the Fallen Angels by using his power to open the Hell Gates. Catarina intends to lead the Fallen's hordes out of Hell and into the parallel dimension of Woerld, Heaven's frontline of defense between Earth and Hell.

When Lucian refuses to help his sister, she imprisons and cripples him, but Lucian learns that Rachael, the lover he betrayed and abandoned in Hell, is dying from a demonic possession. Determined to rescue Rachael from the demon he unleashed on her soul, Lucian flees his sister, but Catarina's wrath isn't so easy to escape.

In the end, she will force him once more to choose between losing Rachael or opening the Hell Gates so the Fallen's hordes may overrun Earth, their last obstacle before reaching Heaven's Gates.

Night Shade Books Is an Independent Publisher of Quality Science-Fiction, Fantasy and Horror

WWW.NIGHTSHADEBOOKS.COM

$14.99

ISBN 978-1-59780-216-1

"One of the more graceful wordsmiths currently writing fantasy."
— *Fantasy & Science Fiction*

The CLOUD ROADS

MARTHA WELLS

The new novel from the author of *The Death of the Necromancer*

Moon has spent his life hiding what he is--a shape-shifter able to transform himself into a winged creature of flight. An orphan with only vague memories of his own kind, Moon tries to fit in among the tribes of his river valley, with mixed success. Just as Moon is once again discovered and cast out by his adopted tribe, he discovers a shape-shifter like himself. . . someone who seems to know exactly what he is, who promises that Moon will be welcomed into his community.

What this stranger doesn't tell Moon is that his presence will tip the balance of power. . .that his extraordinary lineage is crucial to the colony's survival. . . and that his people face extinction at the hands of the dreaded Fell.

Moon must overcome a lifetime of conditioning in order to save and himself. . . and his newfound kin.

Night Shade Books Is an Independent Publisher of Quality Science-Fiction, Fantasy and Horror

www.nightshadebooks.com

$14.99

ISBN 978-1-59780-218-5

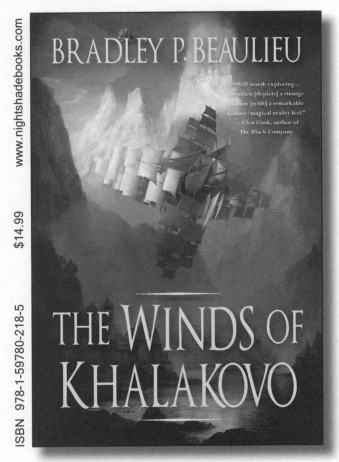

BRADLEY P. BEAULIEU

"Well worth exploring...
Beaulieu [depicts] a strange
culture [with] a remarkable
Fantasy/magical reality feel."
—Glen Cook, author of
The Black Company

THE WINDS OF
KHALAKOVO

Among inhospitable and unforgiving seas stands Khalakovo, a mountainous archipelago of seven islands, its prominent eyrie stretching a thousand feet into the sky. Serviced by windships bearing goods and dignitaries, Khalakovo's eyrie stands at the crossroads of world trade. But all is not well in Khalakovo. Conflict has erupted between the ruling Landed, the indigenous Aramahn, and the fanatical Maharraht, and a wasting disease has grown rampant over the past decade. Now, Khalakovo is to play host to the Nine Dukes, a meeting which will weigh heavily upon Khalakovo's future.

When an elemental spirit attacks an incoming windship, murdering the Grand Duke and his retinue, Prince Nikandr, heir to the scepter of Khalakovo, is tasked with finding the child prodigy believed to be behind the summoning. However, Nikandr discovers that the boy is an autistic savant who may hold the key to lifting the blight that has been sweeping the islands. Can the Dukes, thirsty for revenge, be held at bay? Can Khalakovo be saved? The elusive answer drifts upon the Winds of Khalakovo...

Night Shade Books Is an Independent Publisher of Quality Science-Fiction, Fantasy and Horror

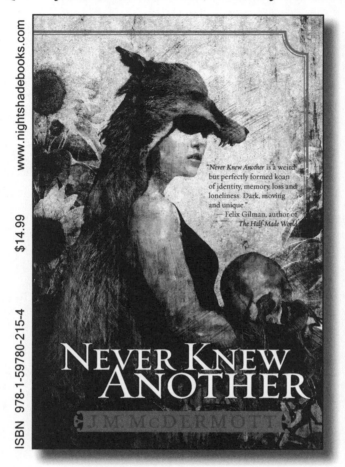

www.nightshadebooks.com

$14.99

ISBN 978-1-59780-215-4

"*Never Knew Another* is a weird but perfectly formed koan of identity, memory, loss and loneliness. Dark, moving and unique."
— Felix Gilman, author of *The Half-Made World*

NEVER KNEW ANOTHER

J. M. McDERMOTT

J. M. McDermott delivers the stunning new fantasy novel, *Never Knew Another* -- a sweeping fantasy novel that revels in the small details of life.

Fugitive Rachel Nolander is a newcomer the city of Dogsland, where the rich throw parties and the poor just do whatever they can to scrape by. Supported by her brother Djoss, she hides out in their squalid apartment, living in fear that someday, someone will find out that she is the child of a demon. Corporal Jona Lord Joni is a demon's child too, but instead of living in fear, he keeps his secret and goes about his life as a cocky, self-assured man of the law. Never Knew Another is the story of how these two outcasts meet.

Never Knew Another is the first book in the Dogsland Trilogy.

Night Shade Books Is an Independent Publisher of Quality Science-Fiction, Fantasy and Horror

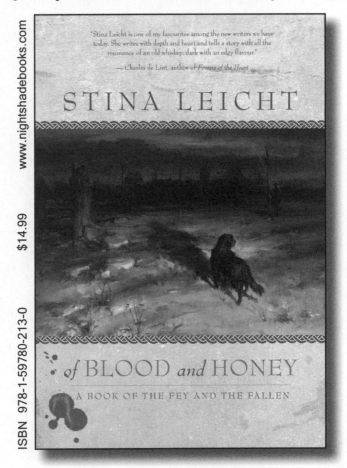

"Stina Leicht is one of my favourites among the new writers we have today. She writes with depth and heart and tells a story with all the resonance of an old whiskey: dark with an edgy flavour."
— Charles de Lint, author of *Forests of the Heart*

STINA LEICHT

of BLOOD *and* HONEY

A BOOK OF THE FEY AND THE FALLEN

Fallen angels and the fey clash against the backdrop of Irish/British conflicts of the 1970s in this stunning debut novel by Stina Leicht.

Liam never knew who his father was. The town of Derry had always assumed that he was the bastard of a protestant—His mother never spoke of him, and Liam assumed he was dead.

But when the war between the fallen, and the fey began to heat up, Liam and his family are pulled into a conflict that they didn't know existed. A centuries old conflict between supernatural forces seems to mirror the political divisions in 1970s era Ireland, and Liam is thrown headlong into both conflicts.

Only the direct intervention of Liam's real father, and a secret catholic order dedicated to fighting "The Fallen" can save Liam... from the mundane and su-pernatural forces around him, and from the darkness that lurks within him.

Night Shade Books Is an Independent Publisher of Quality Science-Fiction, Fantasy and Horror

Nyx had already been to hell. One prayer more or less wouldn't make any difference...

On a ravaged, contaminated world, a centuries-old holy war rages, fought by a bloody mix of mercenaries, magicians, and conscripted soldiers. Though the origins of the war are shady and complex, there's one thing everybody agrees on—

There's not a chance in hell of ending it.

Nyx is a former government assassin who makes a living cutting off heads for cash. But when a dubious deal between her government and an alien gene pirate goes bad, Nyx's ugly past makes her the top pick for a covert recovery. The head they want her to bring home could end the war—but at what price?

The world is about to find out.

ABOUT THE AUTHOR

Courtney Schafer was born in Georgia, raised in Virginia, and spent her childhood dreaming of adventures in the jagged mountains and sweeping deserts of her favorite fantasy novels. She escaped the East Coast by attending Caltech for college, where she obtained a B.S. in electrical engineering, and also learned how to rock climb, backpack, ski, scuba dive, and stack her massive book collection so it wouldn't crush anyone in an earthquake. After college she moved to the climber's paradise of Boulder, Colorado, and somehow managed to get a masters degree in electrical engineering from the University of Colorado in between racking up ski days and peak climbs.

She now works in the aerospace industry and is married to an Australian scientist who shares her love for speculative fiction and mountain climbing. She's had to slow down a little on the adrenaline sports since the birth of her son, but only until he's old enough to join in. She writes every spare moment she's not working or adventuring with her family.